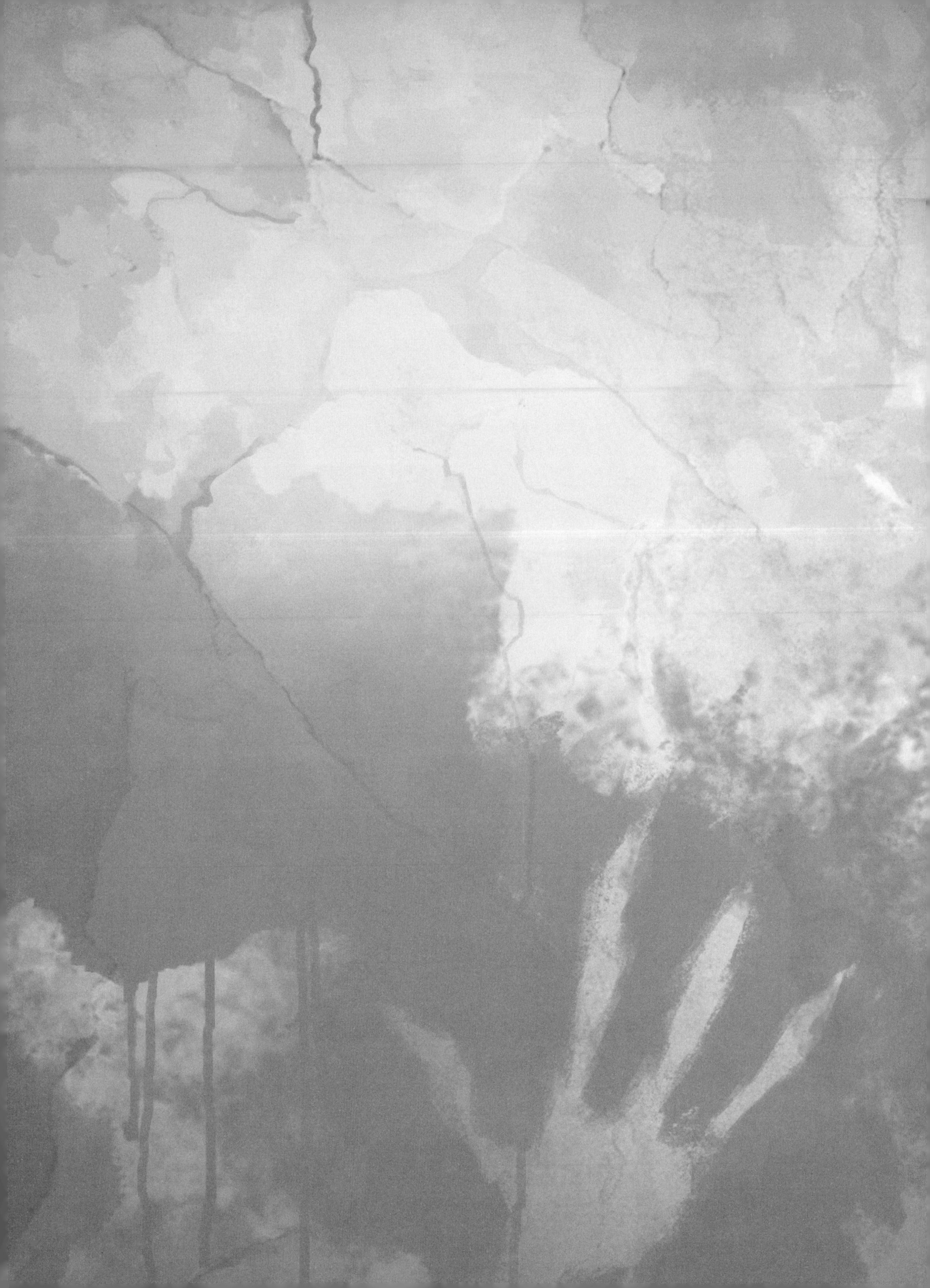

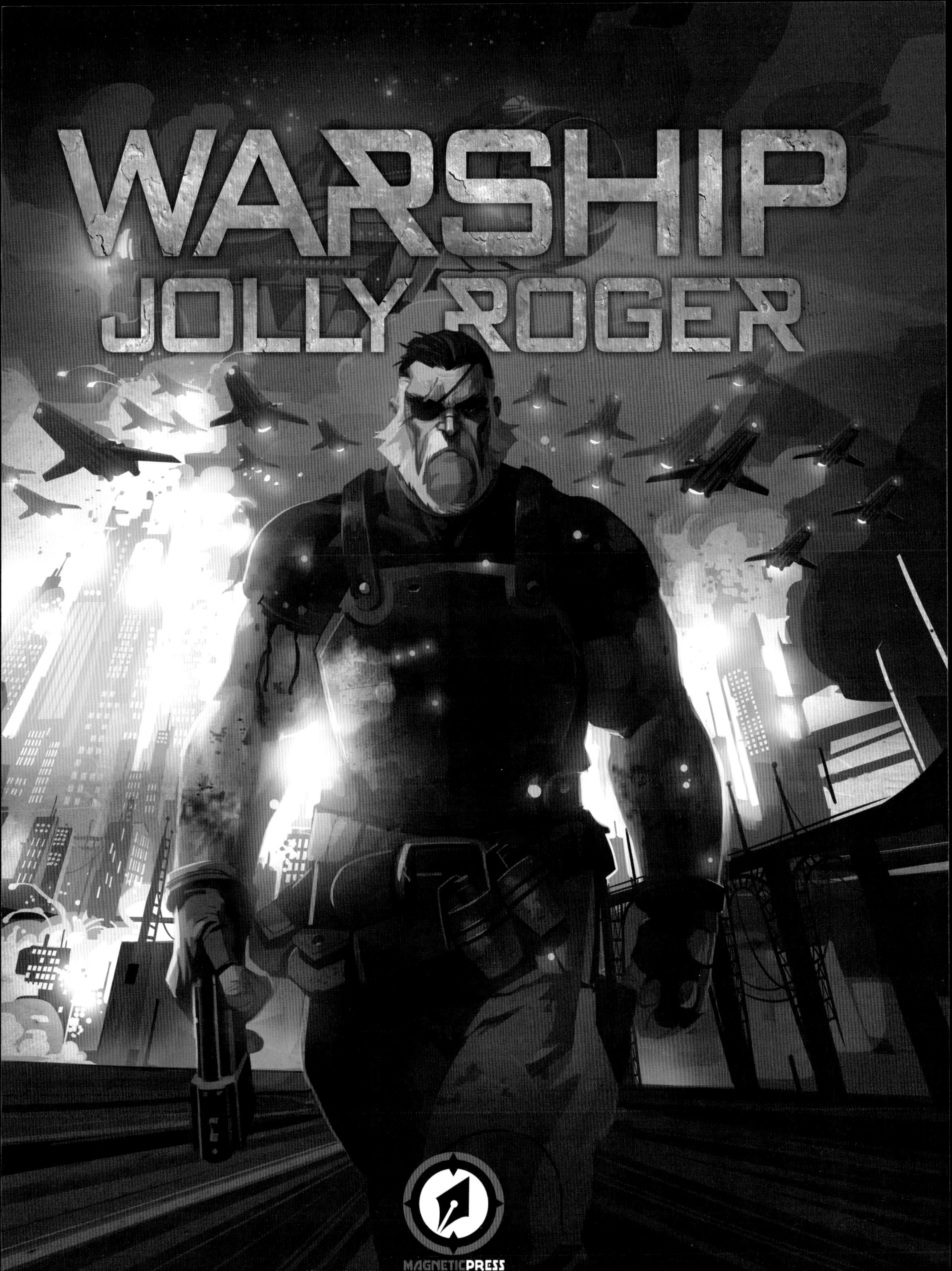
WARSHIP
JOLLY ROGER
MAGNETICPRESS

WARSHIP
JOLLY ROGER

BOOK ONE

WRITTEN BY
SYLVAIN RUNBERG

ILLUSTRATED BY
MIQUEL MONTLLÓ

TRANSLATED BY
MIKE KENNEDY

LETTERING AND DESIGN BY
NEUROBELLUM PRODUCTIONS

MAGNETIC PRESS

MIKE KENNEDY, *President/Publisher*

WES HARRIS, *Vice President*

DAVID DISSANAYAKE, *PR & Marketing*

4910 N. WINTHROP AVE #3S

CHICAGO, IL   60640

WWW.MAGNETIC-PRESS.COM

WARSHIP JOLLY ROGER, BOOK ONE

JULY 2016. FIRST PRINTING

ISBN: 978-1-942367-23-9

FIRST PUBLISHED AS

WARSHIP JOLLY ROGER 1 - SANS RETOUR © DARGAUD BENELUX (DARGAUD-LOMBARD S.A.) 2014, BY RUNBERG (SYLVAIN), MONTLLÓ (MIKI),

WARSHIP JOLLY ROGER 2 - DÉFLAGRATIONS © DARGAUD BENELUX (DARGAUD-LOMBARD S.A.) 2015, BY RUNBERG (SYLVAIN), MONTLLÓ (MIKI),

WWW.DARGAUD.COM   ALL RIGHTS RESERVED

To my parents, my brothers, my family.

To my friends Uri, Jevi, Helena, Yuri, Aleix, Conrad, and so many others, for the million hours we spent drawing together, waiting to be published.

To my friend Javi for letting me stay at his place, and for his help.

To Lu, for being there since the beginning and living it with me.

To Sylvain, because working with him has been a pleasure and a great education.

To Santi Navarro, wherever you are.

To Christel, for giving me the opportunity.

To Igor and Mara, for the friendship and shelter.

To Sergi, Mariona and Uri for the time spent together, past, present, and future.

To Mike Kennedy and Magnetic Press, for their trust in my work.

To everyone who ever supported me. And to those who didn't, they made it more interesting.

To Laura, I love you.

Miki

Thanks to Miki and all the crew from Magnetic Press for their commitment

This album is dedicated to Mr. Lemmy Kilmister.

Sylvain

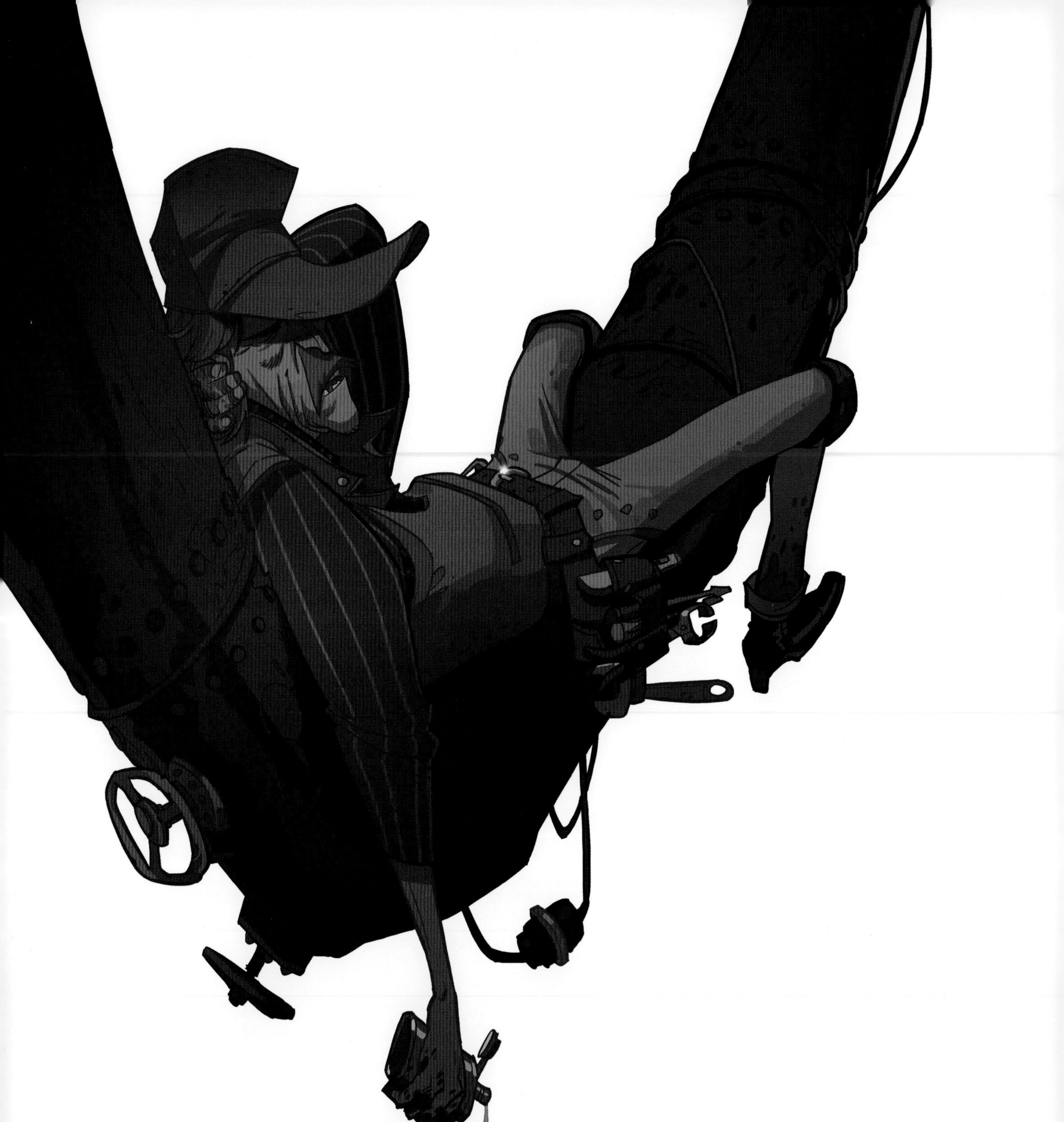

Chapter One :
No Turning Back

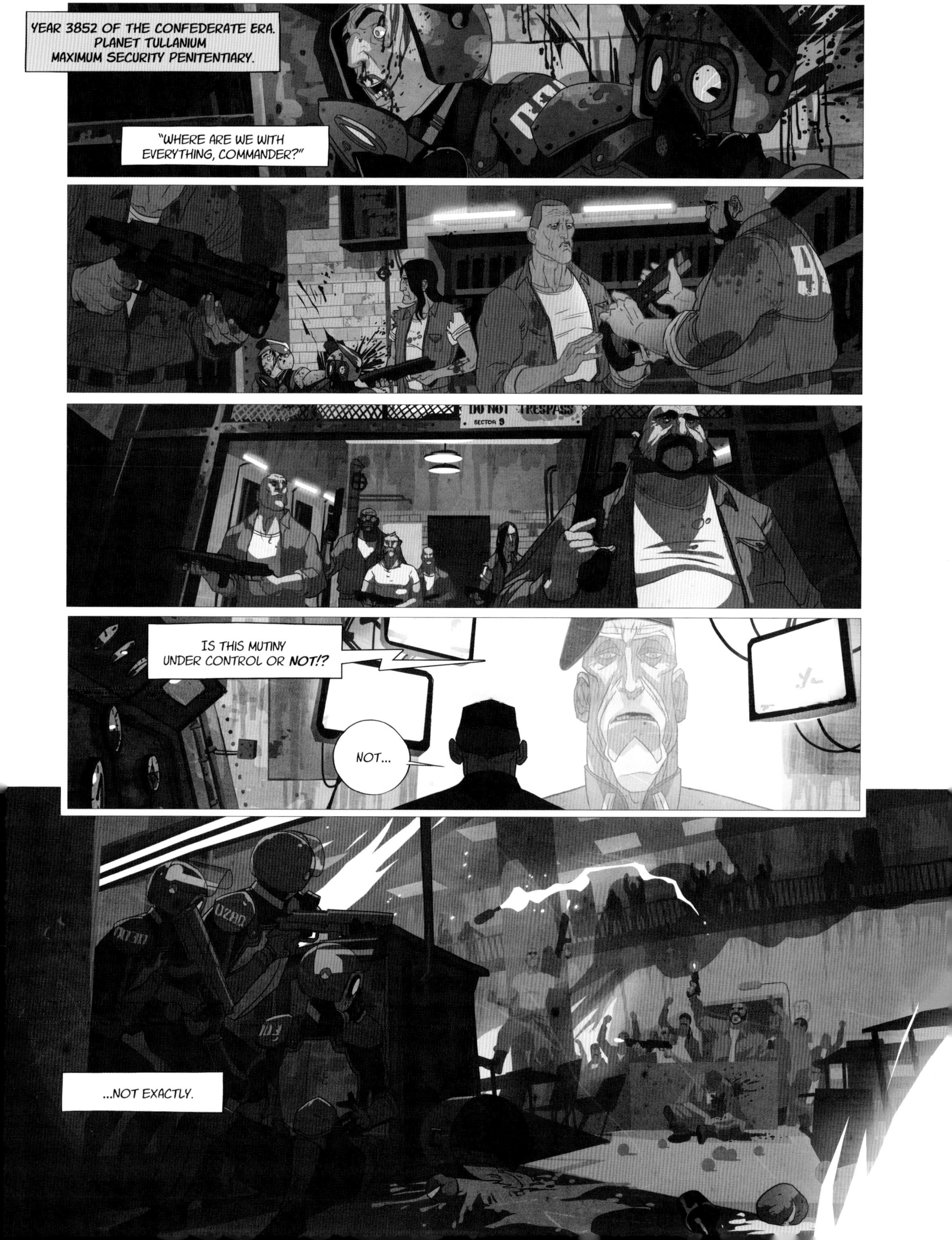

YEAR 3852 OF THE CONFEDERATE ERA.
PLANET TULLANIUM
MAXIMUM SECURITY PENITENTIARY.
"WHERE ARE WE WITH EVERYTHING, COMMANDER?"
DO NOT TRESPASS
SECTOR 9
IS THIS MUTINY UNDER CONTROL OR NOT!?
NOT...
...NOT EXACTLY.

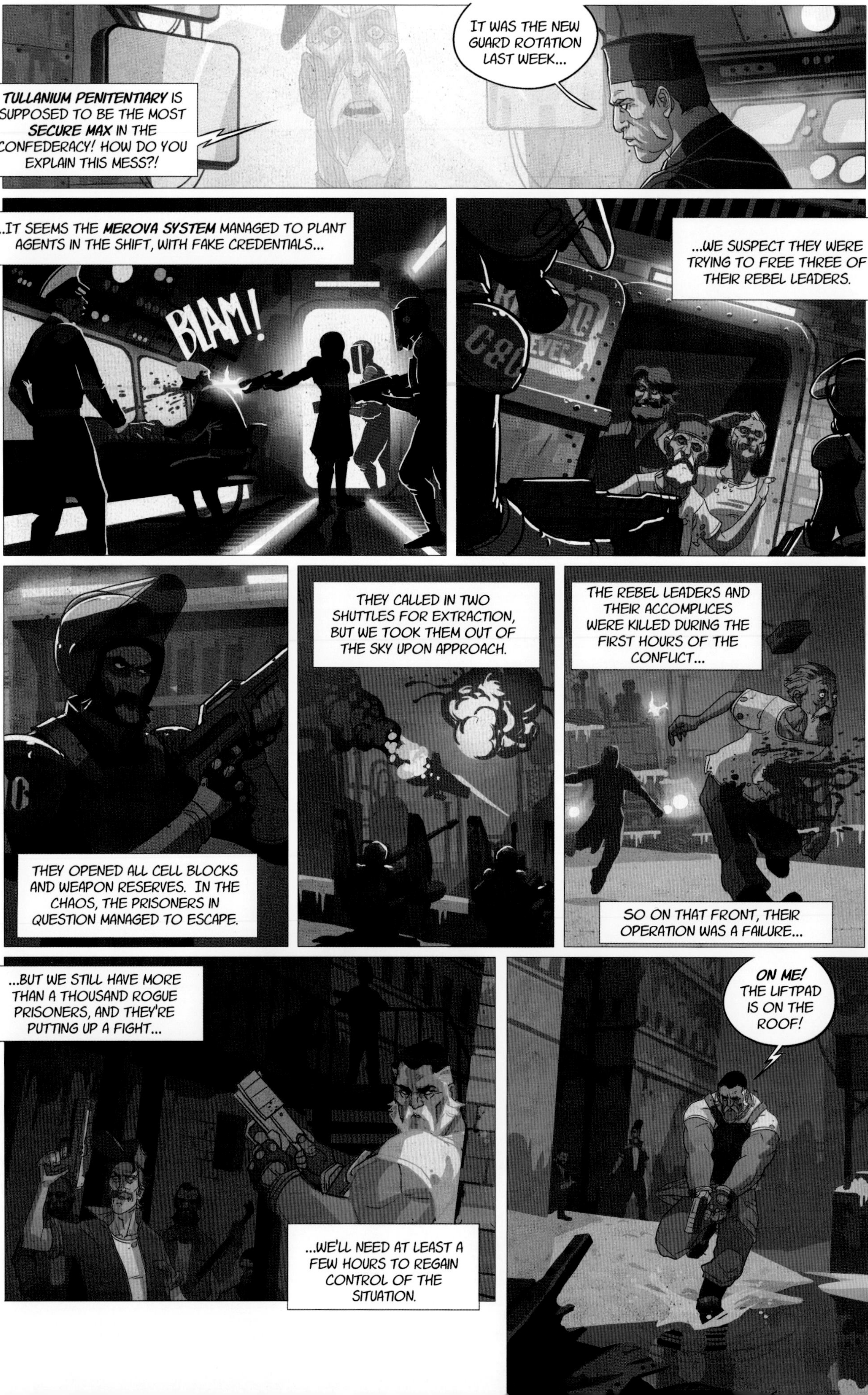
TULLANIUM PENITENTIARY IS SUPPOSED TO BE THE MOST SECURE MAX IN THE CONFEDERACY! HOW DO YOU EXPLAIN THIS MESS?!
IT WAS THE NEW GUARD ROTATION LAST WEEK...
...IT SEEMS THE MEROVA SYSTEM MANAGED TO PLANT AGENTS IN THE SHIFT, WITH FAKE CREDENTIALS...
BLAM!
...WE SUSPECT THEY WERE TRYING TO FREE THREE OF THEIR REBEL LEADERS.
C80
THEY OPENED ALL CELL BLOCKS AND WEAPON RESERVES. IN THE CHAOS, THE PRISONERS IN QUESTION MANAGED TO ESCAPE.
THEY CALLED IN TWO SHUTTLES FOR EXTRACTION, BUT WE TOOK THEM OUT OF THE SKY UPON APPROACH.
THE REBEL LEADERS AND THEIR ACCOMPLICES WERE KILLED DURING THE FIRST HOURS OF THE CONFLICT...
SO ON THAT FRONT, THEIR OPERATION WAS A FAILURE...
...BUT WE STILL HAVE MORE THAN A THOUSAND ROGUE PRISONERS, AND THEY'RE PUTTING UP A FIGHT...
...WE'LL NEED AT LEAST A FEW HOURS TO REGAIN CONTROL OF THE SITUATION.
ON ME! THE LIFTPAD IS ON THE ROOF!

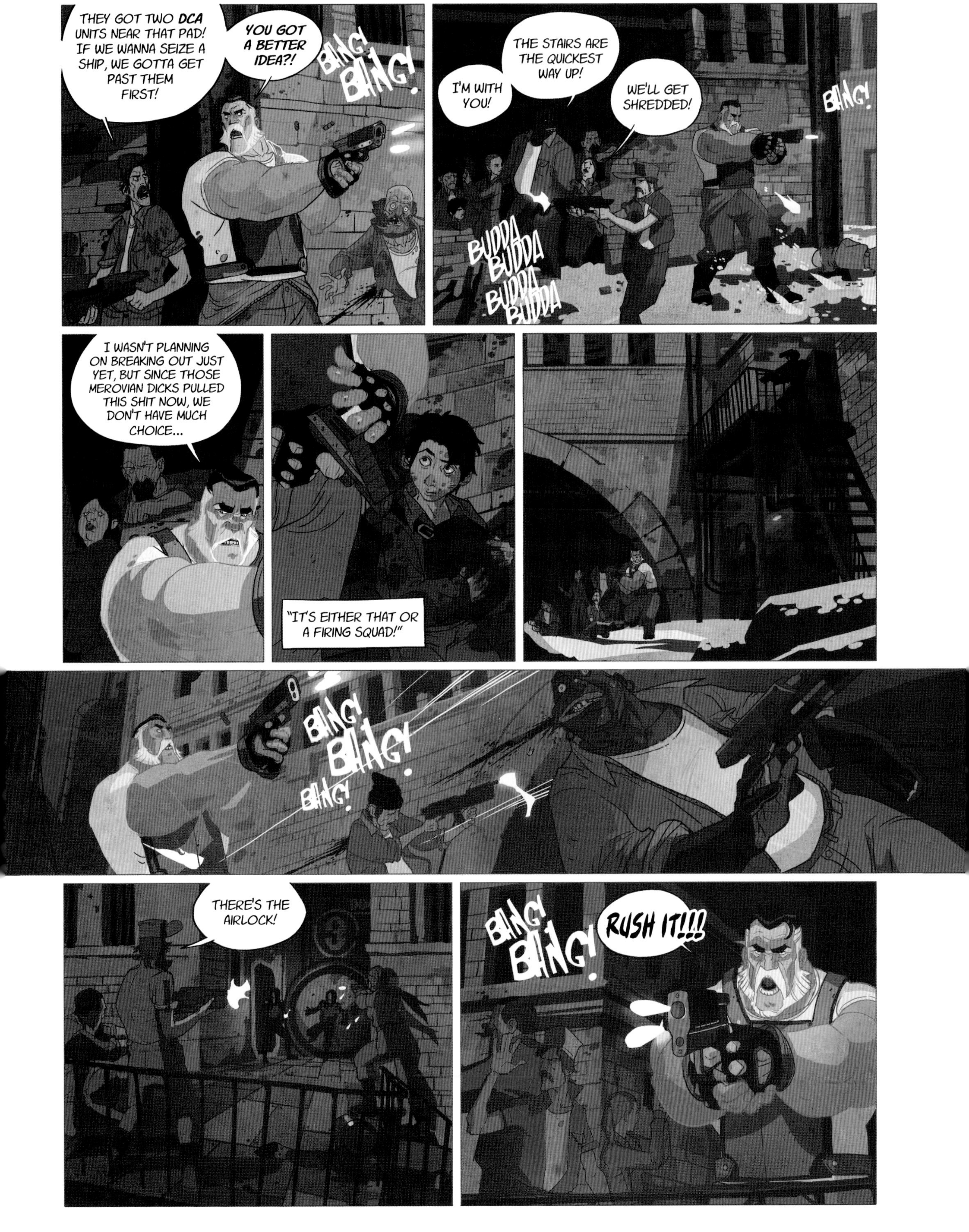
THEY GOT TWO DCA UNITS NEAR THAT PAD! IF WE WANNA SEIZE A SHIP, WE GOTTA GET PAST THEM FIRST!
YOU GOT A BETTER IDEA?!
BANG! BANG!
I'M WITH YOU!
THE STAIRS ARE THE QUICKEST WAY UP!
WE'LL GET SHREDDED!
BANG!
BUDDA BUDDA BUDDA BUDDA
I WASN'T PLANNING ON BREAKING OUT JUST YET, BUT SINCE THOSE MEROVIAN DICKS PULLED THIS SHIT NOW, WE DON'T HAVE MUCH CHOICE...
"IT'S EITHER THAT OR A FIRING SQUAD!"
BANG! BANG! BANG!
THERE'S THE AIRLOCK!
BANG! BANG!
RUSH IT!!!!

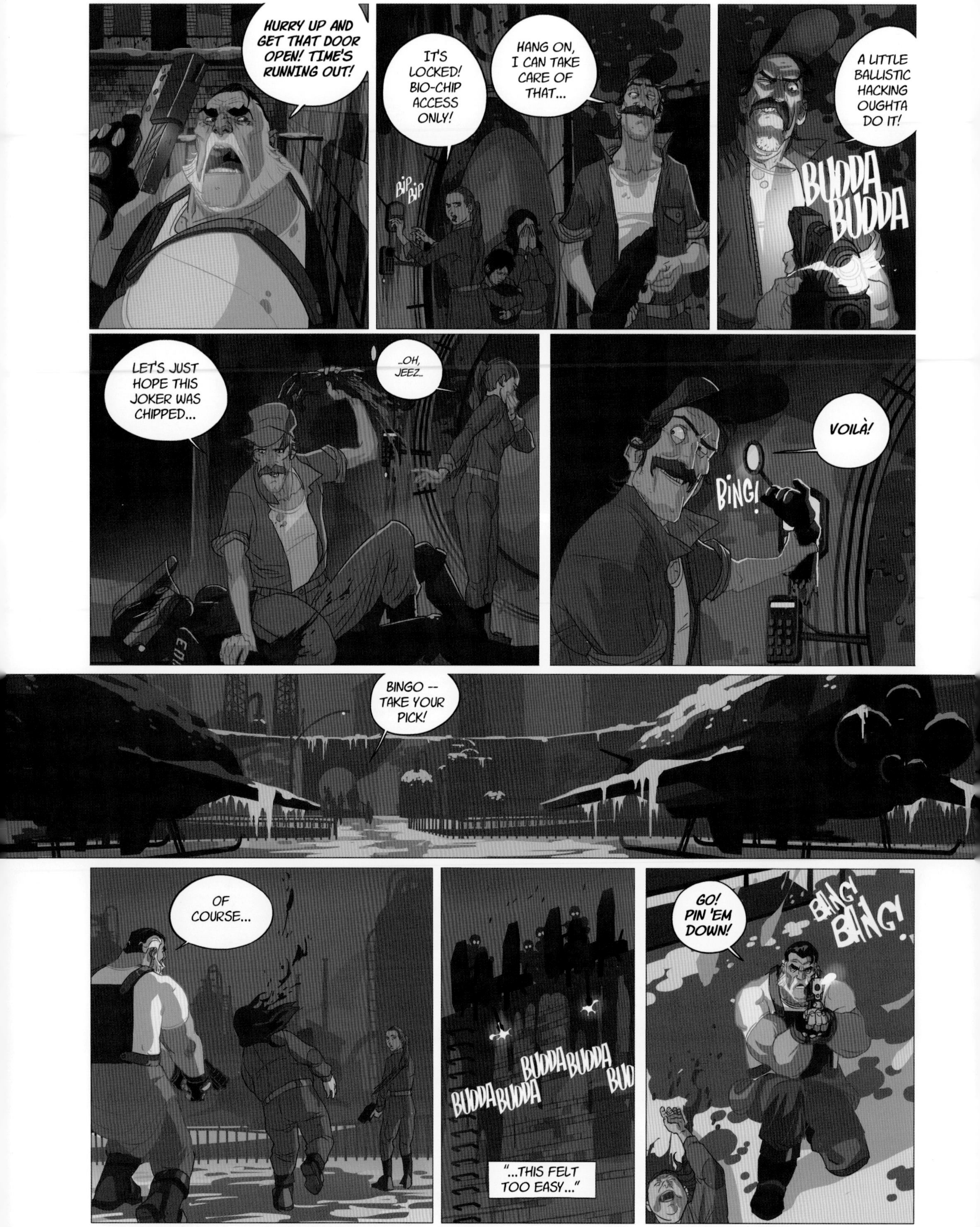
HURRY UP AND GET THAT DOOR OPEN! TIME'S RUNNING OUT!
IT'S LOCKED! BIO-CHIP ACCESS ONLY!
BIP BIP
HANG ON, I CAN TAKE CARE OF THAT...
A LITTLE BALLISTIC HACKING OUGHTA DO IT!
BUDDA BUDDA
LET'S JUST HOPE THIS JOKER WAS CHIPPED...
...OH, JEEZ...
VOILÀ!
BING!
BINGO -- TAKE YOUR PICK!
OF COURSE...
BUDDA BUDDA BUDDA BUDDA BUD
"...THIS FELT TOO EASY..."
GO! PIN 'EM DOWN!
BANG! BANG!

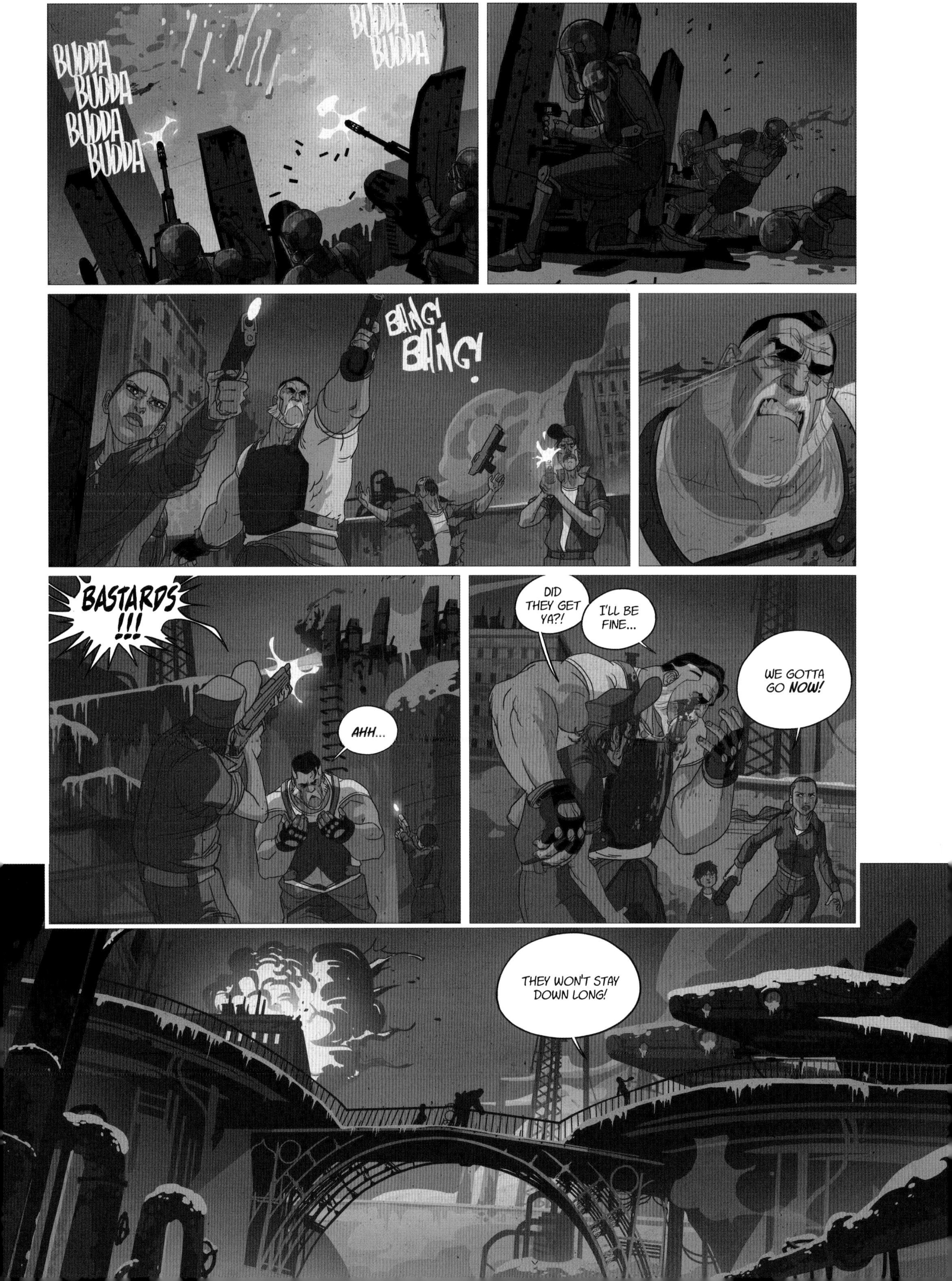
BUDDA BUDDA BUDDA BUDDA
BUDDA BUDDA
BANG! BANG!
BASTARDS !!!
AHH...
DID THEY GET YA?!
I'LL BE FINE...
WE GOTTA GO NOW!
THEY WON'T STAY DOWN LONG!

I READ THE SPEECH YOU PREPARED, REBECCA...

CONFEDERATE YEAR 3852. PRESIDENTIAL CRUISER.

...IT'S PRETTY GOOD.

THANK YOU, *MR. PRESIDENT.*

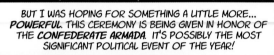

BUT I WAS HOPING FOR SOMETHING A LITTLE MORE... *POWERFUL.* THIS CEREMONY IS BEING GIVEN IN HONOR OF THE *CONFEDERATE ARMADA.* IT'S POSSIBLY THE MOST SIGNIFICANT POLITICAL EVENT OF THE YEAR!

AND I JUST DON'T FEEL THAT... *UNIFYING ENERGY* IN YOUR TEXT.

IT DOES MENTION OUR SOLDIERS' COURAGE TO DEAL WITH THOSE REBEL SYSTEMS SET ON DESTROYING OUR STELLAR FEDERATION, BUT...

...WELL, WILL YOU BE A DEAR AND REWRITE IT FOR ME BY THIS AFTERNOON? THE SEPARATISTS ARE RISING UP ALL AROUND OUR GALAXY, AND YOUR SPEECH JUST LACKS... *HOPE.*

WE NEED TO CONVEY OUR CONFIDENCE IN THIS EFFORT!

I'LL GET RIGHT ON IT.

DOCTOR VULLI! THESE INJECTIONS SEEM MORE PAINFUL THAN USUAL.

I'M SORRY, SIR! THE TISSUE ABSORBS THE WRINKLE SERUM SO QUICKLY...

...BUT IT DOESN'T LAST VERY LONG...

?!

PRESIDENT VEXTON?

I HAVE BAD NEWS FROM *TULLANIUM.*

10

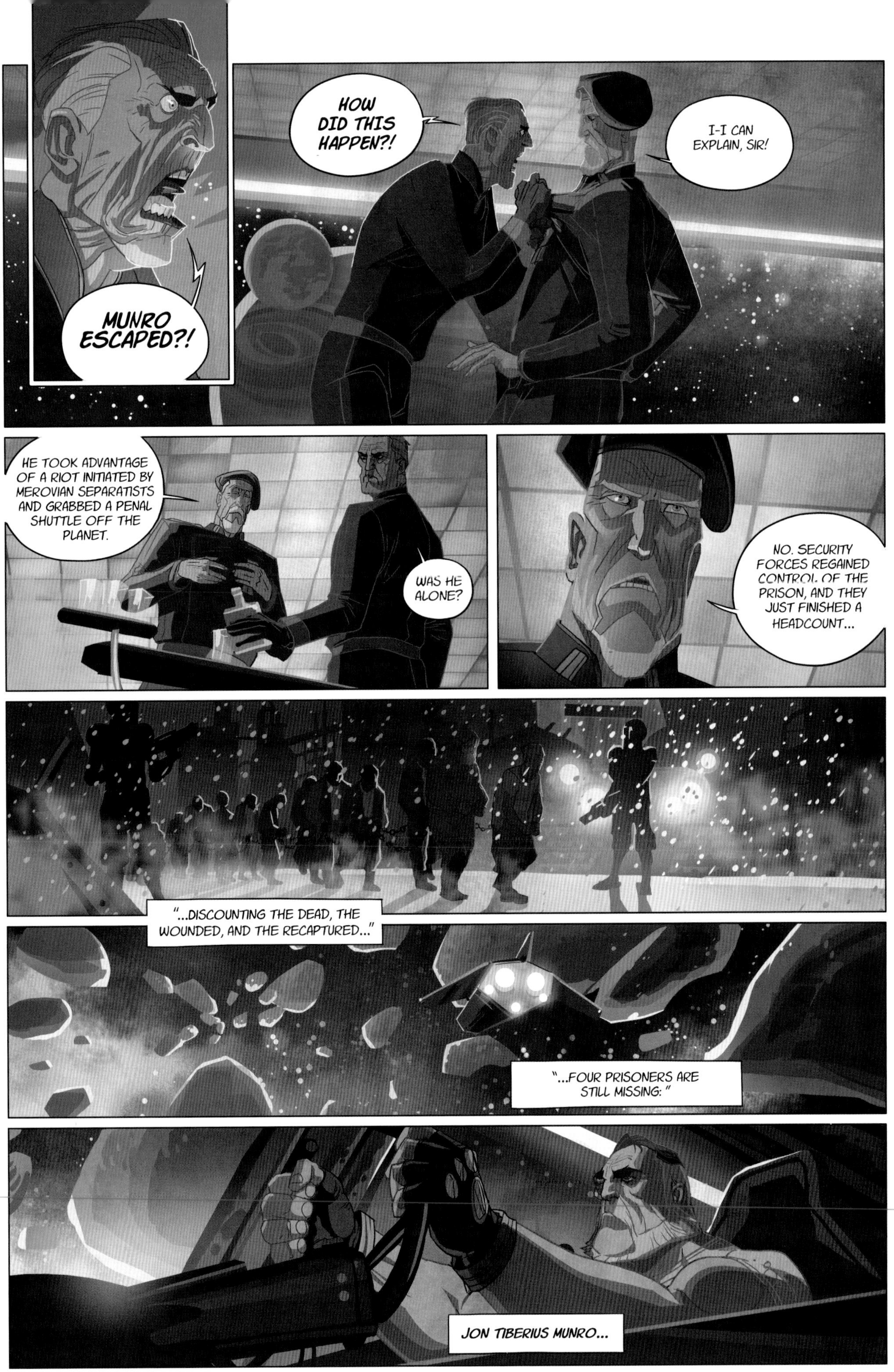
MUNRO ESCAPED?!
HOW DID THIS HAPPEN?!
I-I CAN EXPLAIN, SIR!
HE TOOK ADVANTAGE OF A RIOT INITIATED BY MEROVIAN SEPARATISTS AND GRABBED A PENAL SHUTTLE OFF THE PLANET.
WAS HE ALONE?
NO. SECURITY FORCES REGAINED CONTROL OF THE PRISON, AND THEY JUST FINISHED A HEADCOUNT...
"...DISCOUNTING THE DEAD, THE WOUNDED, AND THE RECAPTURED..."
"...FOUR PRISONERS ARE STILL MISSING:"
JON TIBERIUS MUNRO...

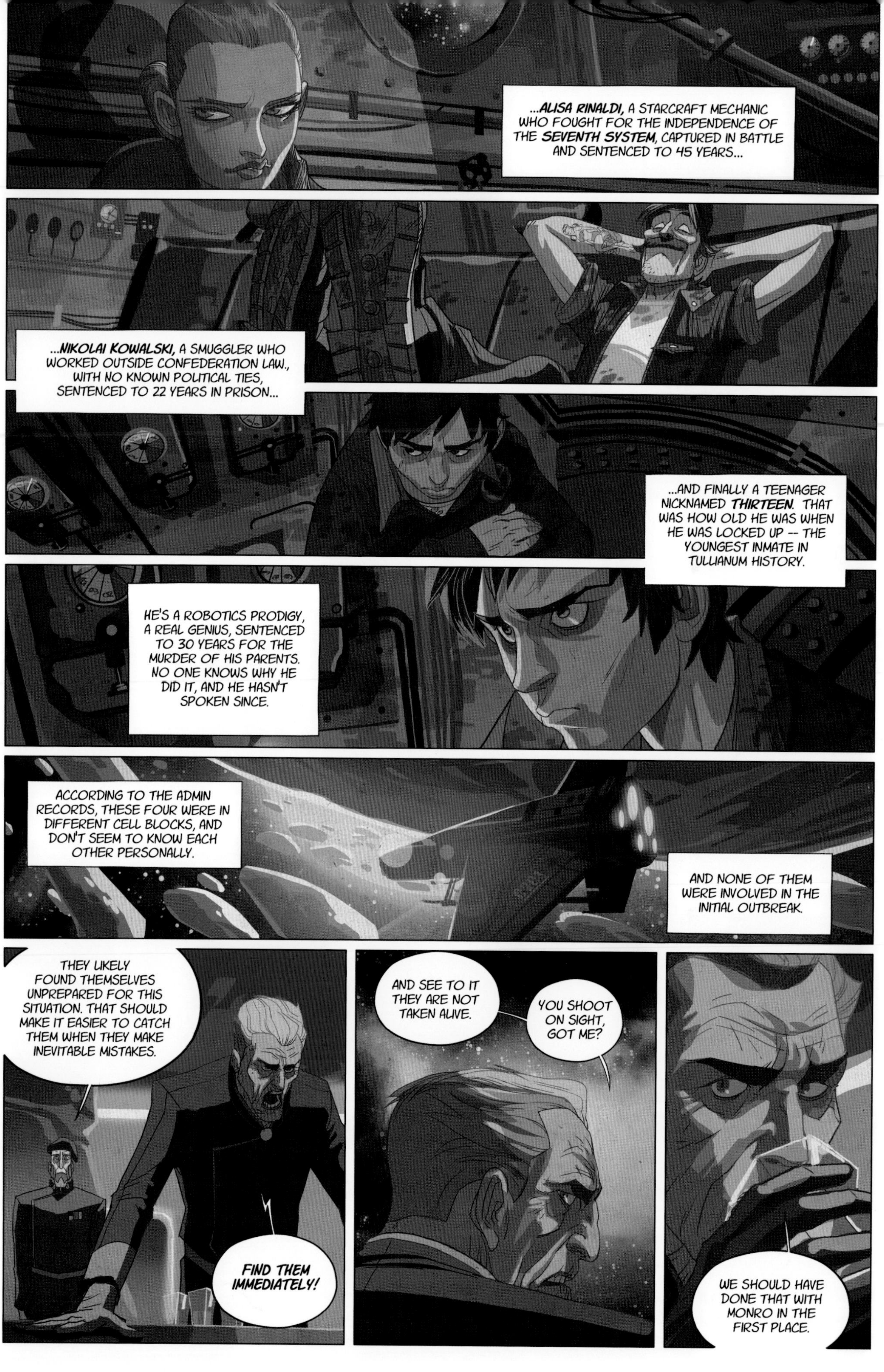

...ALISA RINALDI, A STARCRAFT MECHANIC WHO FOUGHT FOR THE INDEPENDENCE OF THE SEVENTH SYSTEM, CAPTURED IN BATTLE AND SENTENCED TO 45 YEARS...
...NIKOLAI KOWALSKI, A SMUGGLER WHO WORKED OUTSIDE CONFEDERATION LAW., WITH NO KNOWN POLITICAL TIES, SENTENCED TO 22 YEARS IN PRISON...
...AND FINALLY A TEENAGER NICKNAMED THIRTEEN. THAT WAS HOW OLD HE WAS WHEN HE WAS LOCKED UP -- THE YOUNGEST INMATE IN TULLIANUM HISTORY.
HE'S A ROBOTICS PRODIGY, A REAL GENIUS, SENTENCED TO 30 YEARS FOR THE MURDER OF HIS PARENTS. NO ONE KNOWS WHY HE DID IT, AND HE HASN'T SPOKEN SINCE.
ACCORDING TO THE ADMIN RECORDS, THESE FOUR WERE IN DIFFERENT CELL BLOCKS, AND DON'T SEEM TO KNOW EACH OTHER PERSONALLY.
AND NONE OF THEM WERE INVOLVED IN THE INITIAL OUTBREAK.
THEY LIKELY FOUND THEMSELVES UNPREPARED FOR THIS SITUATION. THAT SHOULD MAKE IT EASIER TO CATCH THEM WHEN THEY MAKE INEVITABLE MISTAKES.
FIND THEM IMMEDIATELY!
AND SEE TO IT THEY ARE NOT TAKEN ALIVE.
YOU SHOOT ON SIGHT, GOT ME?
WE SHOULD HAVE DONE THAT WITH MONRO IN THE FIRST PLACE.

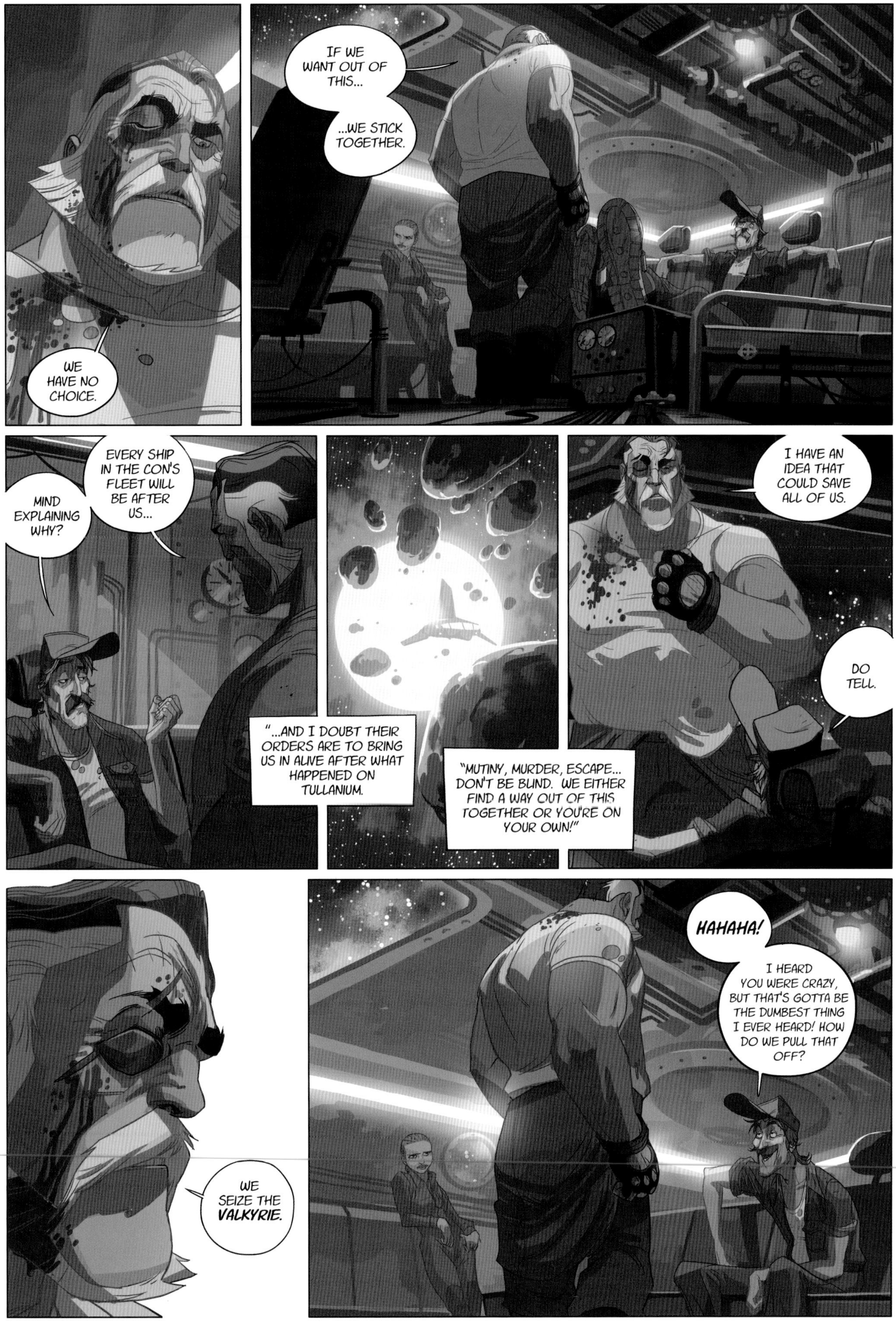
WE HAVE NO CHOICE.
IF WE WANT OUT OF THIS...
...WE STICK TOGETHER.
MIND EXPLAINING WHY?
EVERY SHIP IN THE CON'S FLEET WILL BE AFTER US...
"...AND I DOUBT THEIR ORDERS ARE TO BRING US IN ALIVE AFTER WHAT HAPPENED ON TULLANIUM.
"MUTINY, MURDER, ESCAPE... DON'T BE BLIND. WE EITHER FIND A WAY OUT OF THIS TOGETHER OR YOU'RE ON YOUR OWN!"
I HAVE AN IDEA THAT COULD SAVE ALL OF US.
DO TELL.
WE SEIZE THE VALKYRIE.
HAHAHA!
I HEARD YOU WERE CRAZY, BUT THAT'S GOTTA BE THE DUMBEST THING I EVER HEARD! HOW DO WE PULL THAT OFF?

THAT SHIP WAS UNDER MY COMMAND BEFORE THOSE DOGS THREW ME IN JAIL...

RIGHT NOW, IT'S IN ORBIT AROUND IO FOR THE ARMADA MEMORIAL CEREMONY.

I KNOW THE SECURITY PROTOCOLS FOR THAT KIND OF EVENT, AND THAT'S THE LAST PLACE THEY'D EXPECT TO SEE US.

WE'LL HAVE THE ELEMENT OF SURPRISE, AND THE SHIP WILL BE PRACTICALLY EMPTY, WITH THE CREW ATTENDING THE CEREMONY. WE CAN TAKE IT.

WITH LUCK, I ADMIT.

BUT WITH THAT VESSEL IN OUR POSSESSION, WE CAN GET FAR ENOUGH AWAY TO DECIDE OUR NEXT MOVE.

HMMM... SO HOW EXACTLY DO WE TAKE IT?

THEY'D HAVE CALLED IN A BUNCH OF PRIVATE MERC COMPANIES TO FILL IN SECURITY DURING THE CEREMONY, SINCE THE CREWS THEMSELVES WILL ALL BE ATTENDING.

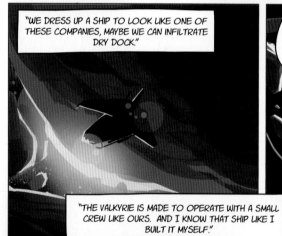

"WE DRESS UP A SHIP TO LOOK LIKE ONE OF THESE COMPANIES, MAYBE WE CAN INFILTRATE DRY DOCK."

"THE VALKYRIE IS MADE TO OPERATE WITH A SMALL CREW LIKE OURS. AND I KNOW THAT SHIP LIKE I BUILT IT MYSELF."

SOUNDS LIKE SUICIDE, BUT...

COUNT ME OUT!

ESCAPING TOGETHER WAS ONE THING, BUT WE PART WAYS AT THE NEXT VIABLE PLANET!

NO WAY I'M TEAMING UP WITH THE BIGGEST WAR CRIMINAL IN THE GALAXY!

SAY THAT AGAIN AND YOU CAN DIE RIGHT HERE!

LET GO OF ME OR I'LL --

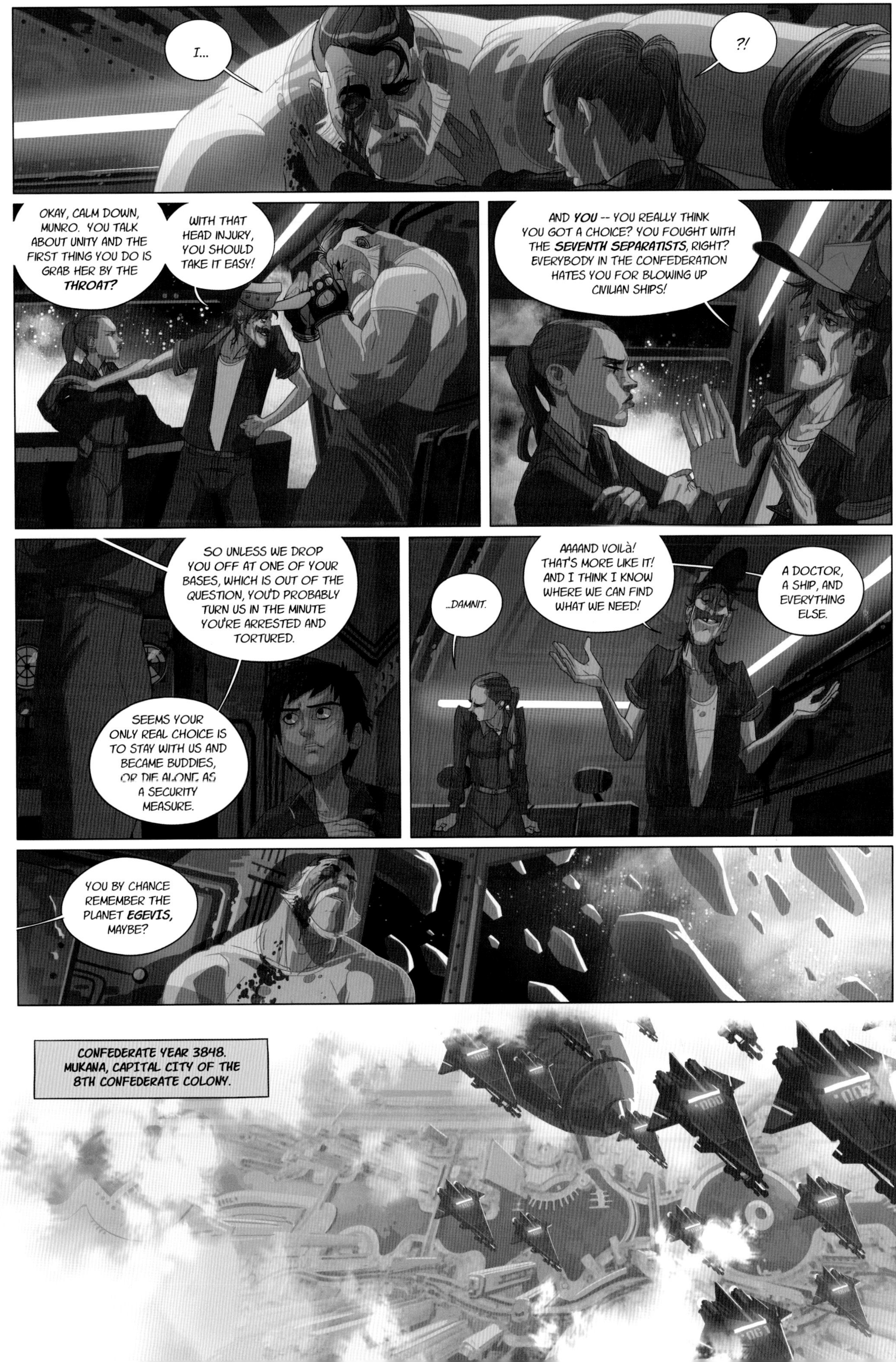
I...
?!
OKAY, CALM DOWN, MUNRO. YOU TALK ABOUT UNITY AND THE FIRST THING YOU DO IS GRAB HER BY THE THROAT?
WITH THAT HEAD INJURY, YOU SHOULD TAKE IT EASY!
AND YOU -- YOU REALLY THINK YOU GOT A CHOICE? YOU FOUGHT WITH THE SEVENTH SEPARATISTS, RIGHT? EVERYBODY IN THE CONFEDERATION HATES YOU FOR BLOWING UP CIVILIAN SHIPS!
SO UNLESS WE DROP YOU OFF AT ONE OF YOUR BASES, WHICH IS OUT OF THE QUESTION, YOU'D PROBABLY TURN US IN THE MINUTE YOU'RE ARRESTED AND TORTURED.
SEEMS YOUR ONLY REAL CHOICE IS TO STAY WITH US AND BECAME BUDDIES, OR DIE ALONE AS A SECURITY MEASURE.
...DAMNIT.
AAAAND VOILà! THAT'S MORE LIKE IT! AND I THINK I KNOW WHERE WE CAN FIND WHAT WE NEED!
A DOCTOR, A SHIP, AND EVERYTHING ELSE.
YOU BY CHANCE REMEMBER THE PLANET EGEVIS, MAYBE?
CONFEDERATE YEAR 3848. MUKANA, CAPITAL CITY OF THE 8TH CONFEDERATE COLONY.

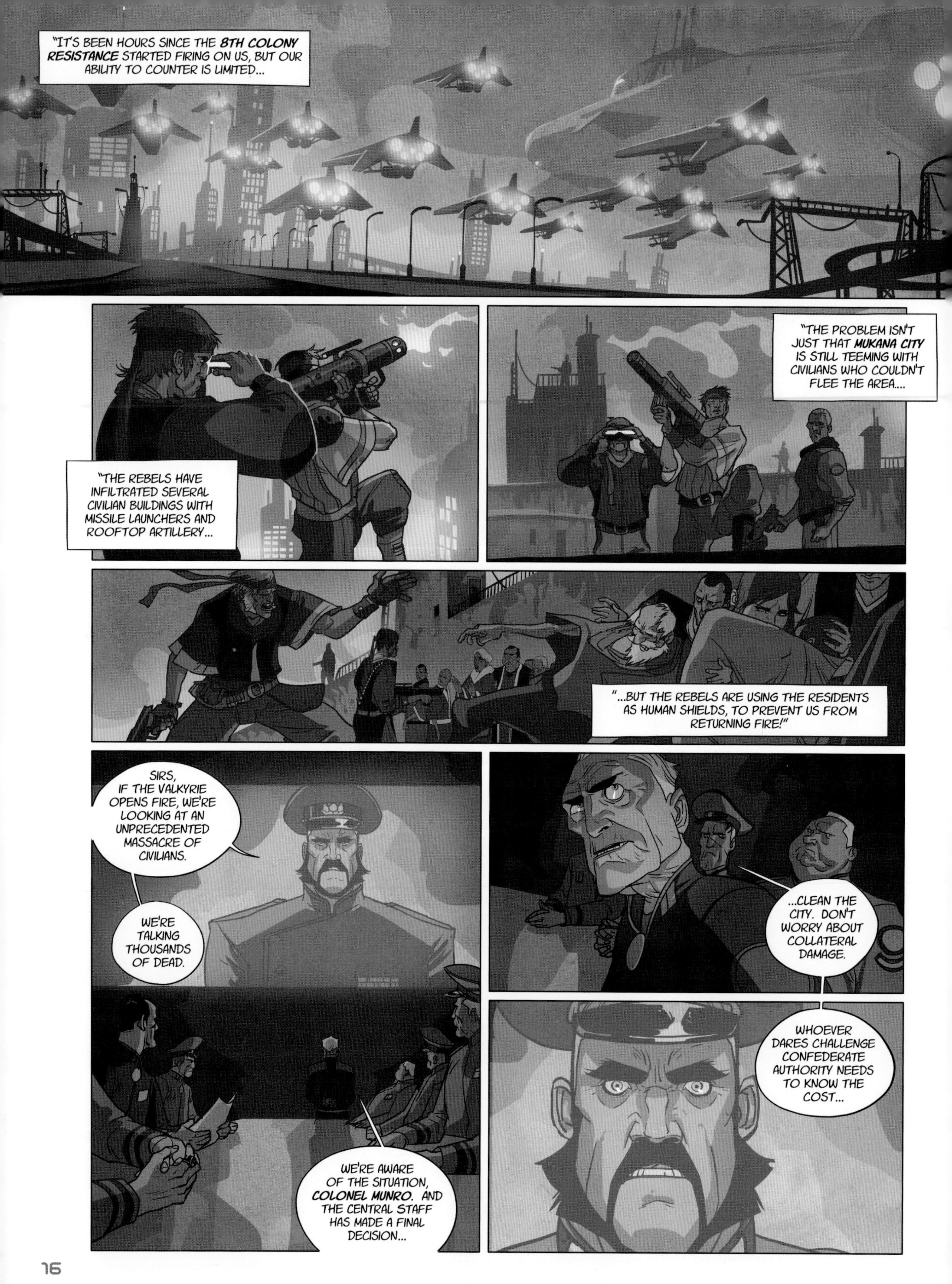
"IT'S BEEN HOURS SINCE THE 8TH COLONY RESISTANCE STARTED FIRING ON US, BUT OUR ABILITY TO COUNTER IS LIMITED...
"THE REBELS HAVE INFILTRATED SEVERAL CIVILIAN BUILDINGS WITH MISSILE LAUNCHERS AND ROOFTOP ARTILLERY...
"THE PROBLEM ISN'T JUST THAT MUKANA CITY IS STILL TEEMING WITH CIVILIANS WHO COULDN'T FLEE THE AREA....
"...BUT THE REBELS ARE USING THE RESIDENTS AS HUMAN SHIELDS, TO PREVENT US FROM RETURNING FIRE!"
SIRS, IF THE VALKYRIE OPENS FIRE, WE'RE LOOKING AT AN UNPRECEDENTED MASSACRE OF CIVILIANS.
WE'RE TALKING THOUSANDS OF DEAD.
WE'RE AWARE OF THE SITUATION, COLONEL MUNRO. AND THE CENTRAL STAFF HAS MADE A FINAL DECISION...
...CLEAN THE CITY. DON'T WORRY ABOUT COLLATERAL DAMAGE.
WHOEVER DARES CHALLENGE CONFEDERATE AUTHORITY NEEDS TO KNOW THE COST...

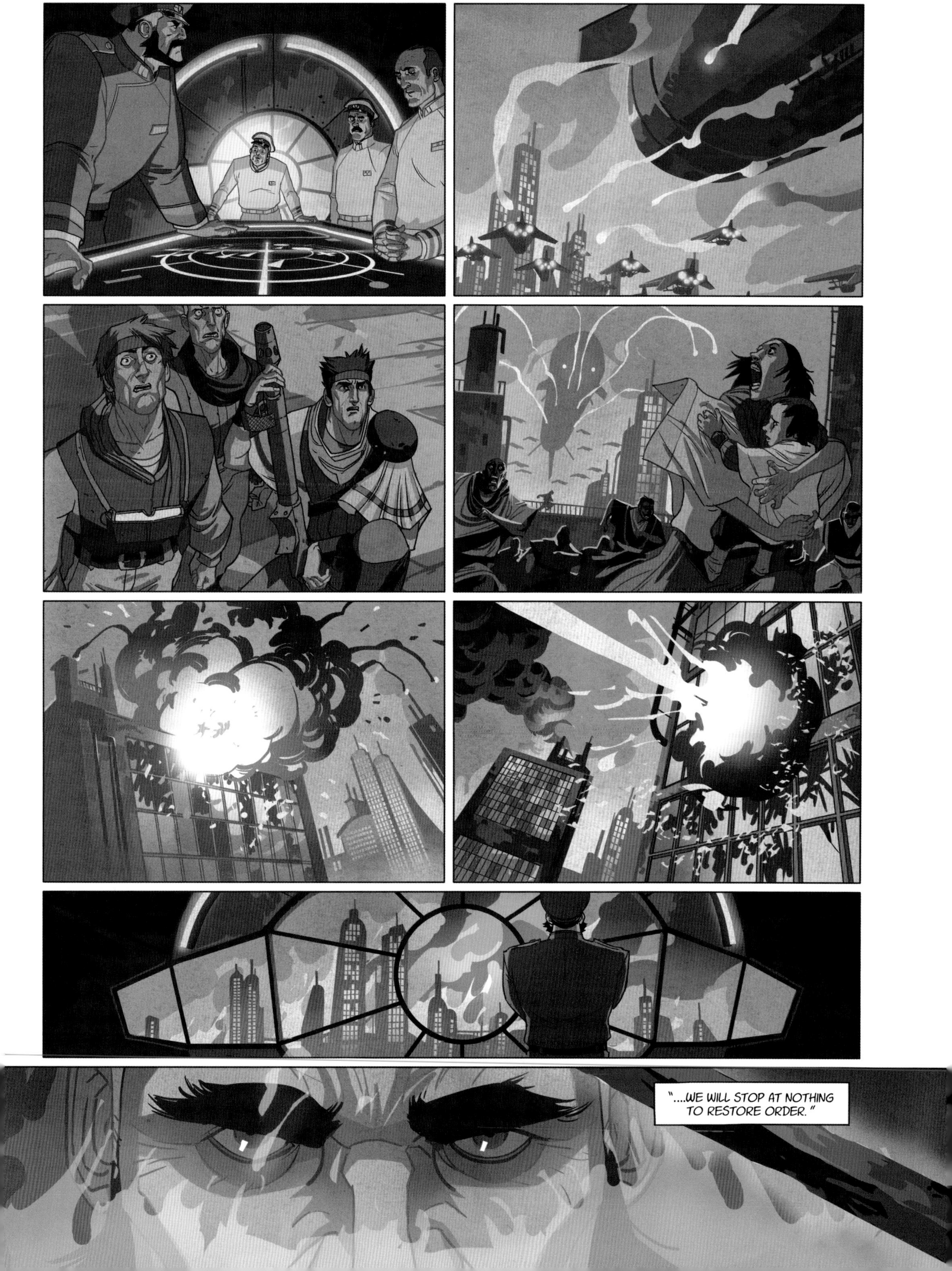
"....WE WILL STOP AT NOTHING TO RESTORE ORDER."

CONFEDERATE YEAR 3852.
PLANET EGEVIS.

"NIKOLAI KOWALSKI...!?

"...BACK IN *TASOS CITY*!?
WHAT HAPPENED?

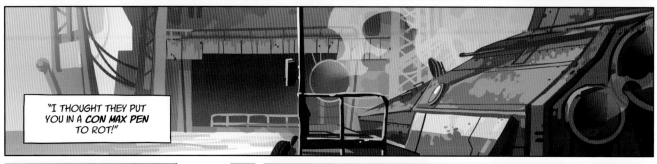

"I THOUGHT THEY PUT
YOU IN A *CON MAX PEN*
TO ROT!"

BUT
YOU'RE ALIVE,
SO WHO'S
COMPLAINING?

GOOD
TO SEE YOU
AGAIN,
SCRUGGS.

THINK YOU
CAN HELP
US?

GOT
MONEY?

LOOKIN' AT THE
CARNIVAL OF FUGITIVES
YOU'RE WITH, INCLUDING A
GALACTIC CELEBRITY, THE
CON'S GONNA HAVE THEIR
TEETH OUT!

I'LL PAY
YOUR
PRICE...

...DON'T
YOU WORRY
ABOUT THAT,
PAL.

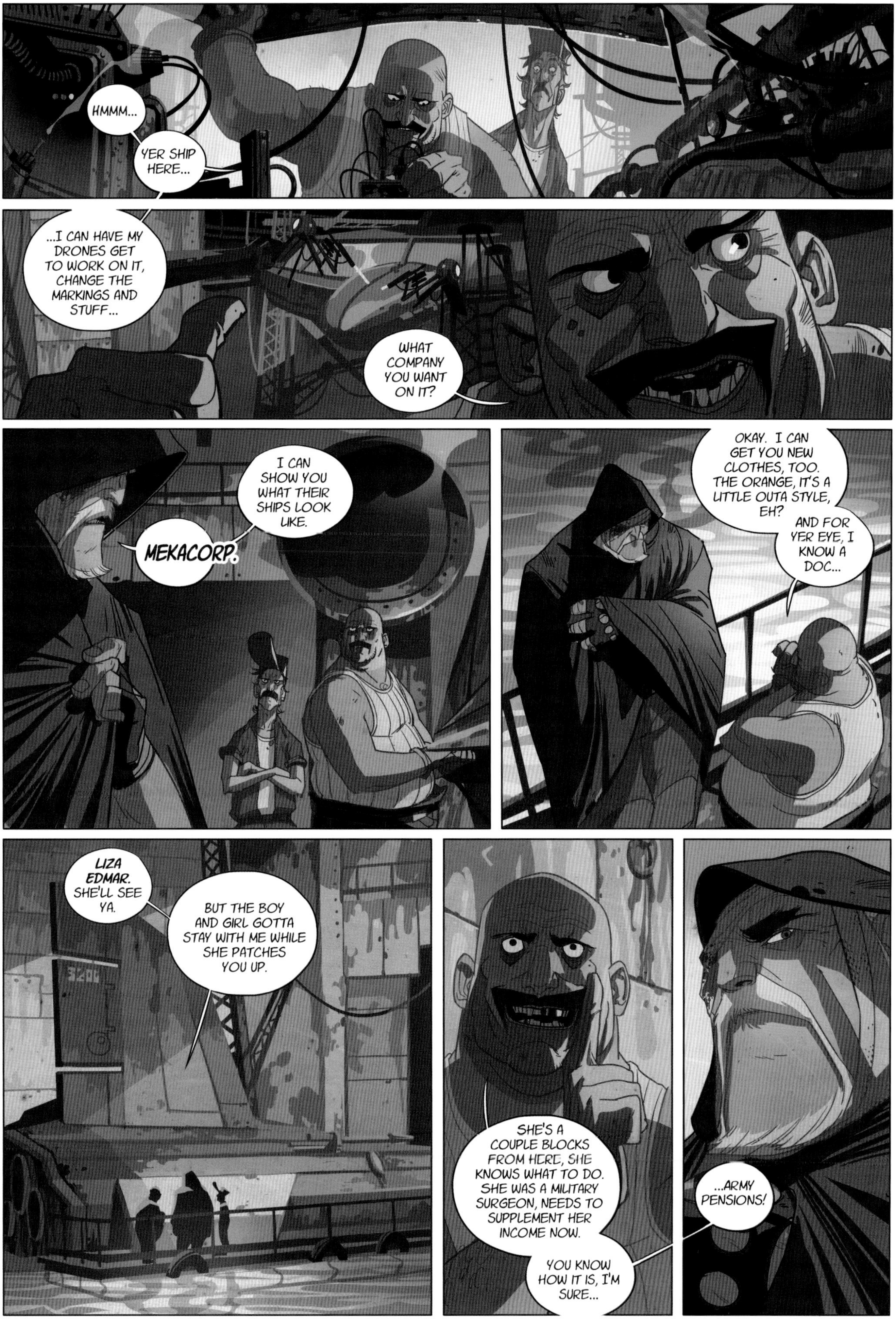

HMMM...
YER SHIP HERE...
...I CAN HAVE MY DRONES GET TO WORK ON IT, CHANGE THE MARKINGS AND STUFF...
WHAT COMPANY YOU WANT ON IT?
MEKACORP.
I CAN SHOW YOU WHAT THEIR SHIPS LOOK LIKE.
OKAY. I CAN GET YOU NEW CLOTHES, TOO. THE ORANGE, IT'S A LITTLE OUTA STYLE, EH?
AND FOR YER EYE, I KNOW A DOC...
LIZA EDMAR. SHE'LL SEE YA.
BUT THE BOY AND GIRL GOTTA STAY WITH ME WHILE SHE PATCHES YOU UP.
SHE'S A COUPLE BLOCKS FROM HERE, SHE KNOWS WHAT TO DO. SHE WAS A MILITARY SURGEON, NEEDS TO SUPPLEMENT HER INCOME NOW.
YOU KNOW HOW IT IS, I'M SURE...
...ARMY PENSIONS!

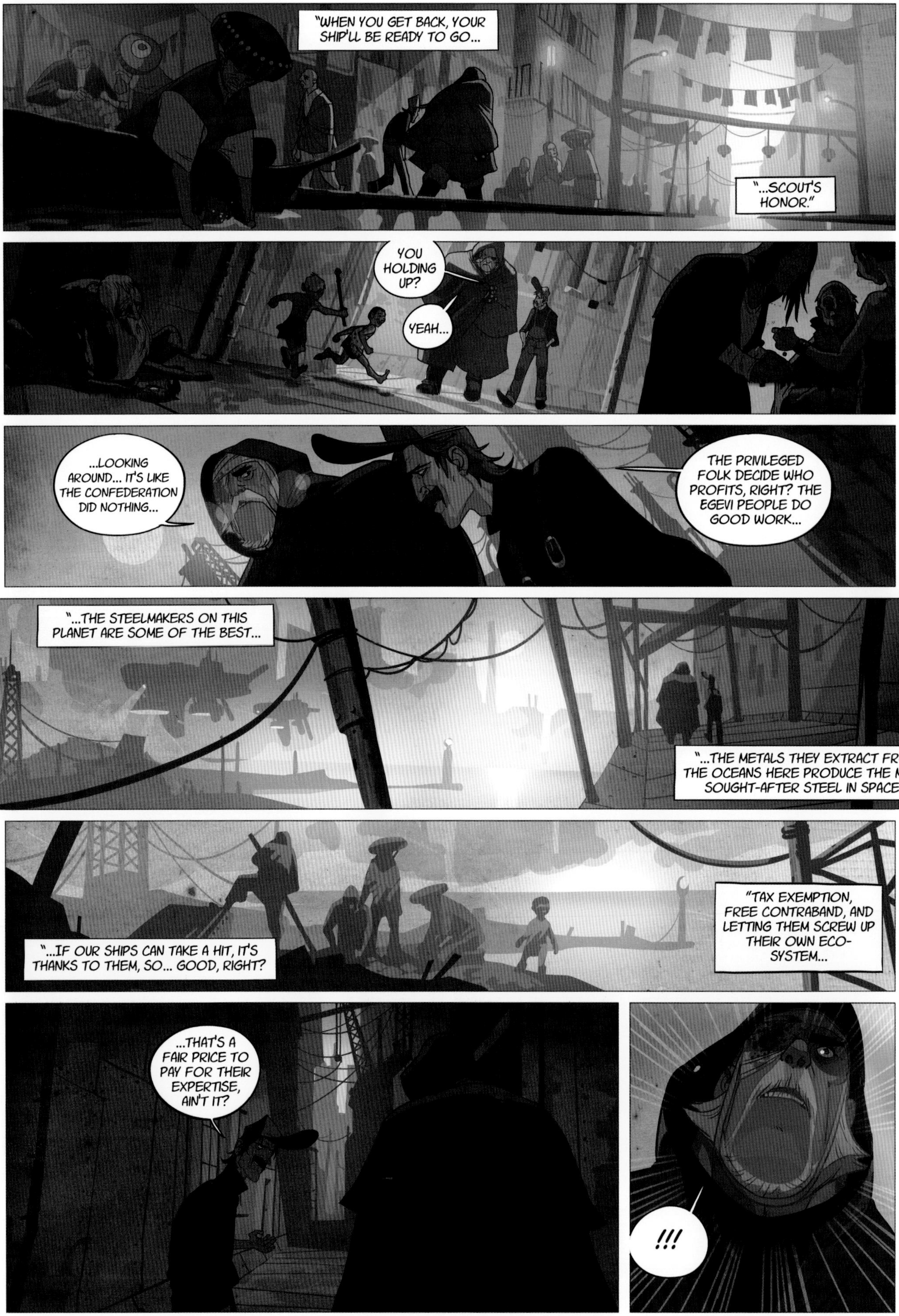
"WHEN YOU GET BACK, YOUR SHIP'LL BE READY TO GO...
"...SCOUT'S HONOR."
YOU HOLDING UP?
YEAH...
...LOOKING AROUND... IT'S LIKE THE CONFEDERATION DID NOTHING...
THE PRIVILEGED FOLK DECIDE WHO PROFITS, RIGHT? THE EGEVI PEOPLE DO GOOD WORK...
"...THE STEELMAKERS ON THIS PLANET ARE SOME OF THE BEST...
"...THE METALS THEY EXTRACT FROM THE OCEANS HERE PRODUCE THE MOST SOUGHT-AFTER STEEL IN SPACE...
"...IF OUR SHIPS CAN TAKE A HIT, IT'S THANKS TO THEM, SO... GOOD, RIGHT?
"TAX EXEMPTION, FREE CONTRABAND, AND LETTING THEM SCREW UP THEIR OWN ECO-SYSTEM...
...THAT'S A FAIR PRICE TO PAY FOR THEIR EXPERTISE, AIN'T IT?
!!!

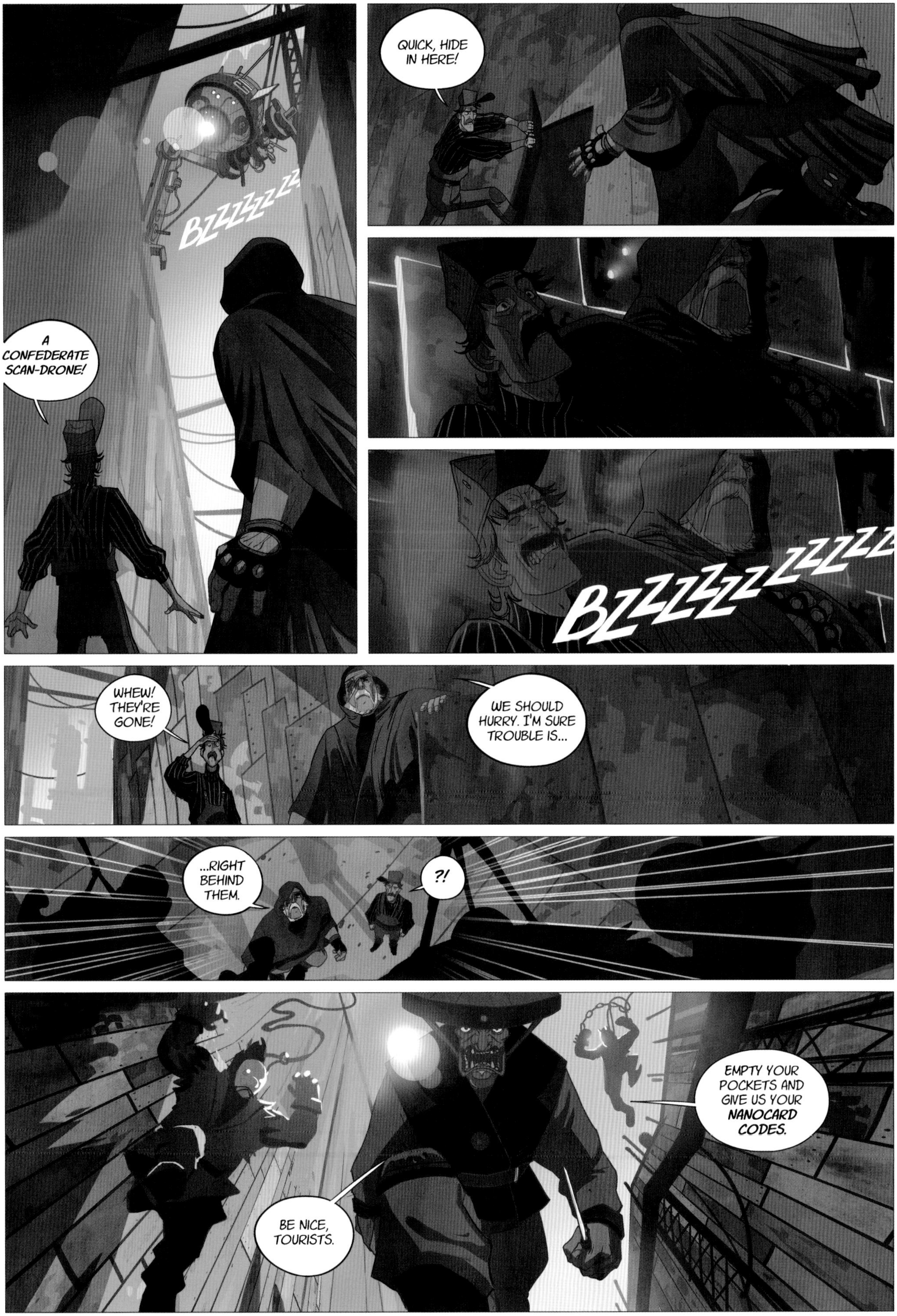
BZZZZZZZ
A CONFEDERATE SCAN-DRONE!
QUICK, HIDE IN HERE!
BZZZZZZZZZZZZ
WHEW! THEY'RE GONE!
WE SHOULD HURRY. I'M SURE TROUBLE IS...
...RIGHT BEHIND THEM.
?!
BE NICE, TOURISTS.
EMPTY YOUR POCKETS AND GIVE US YOUR **NANOCARD CODES.**

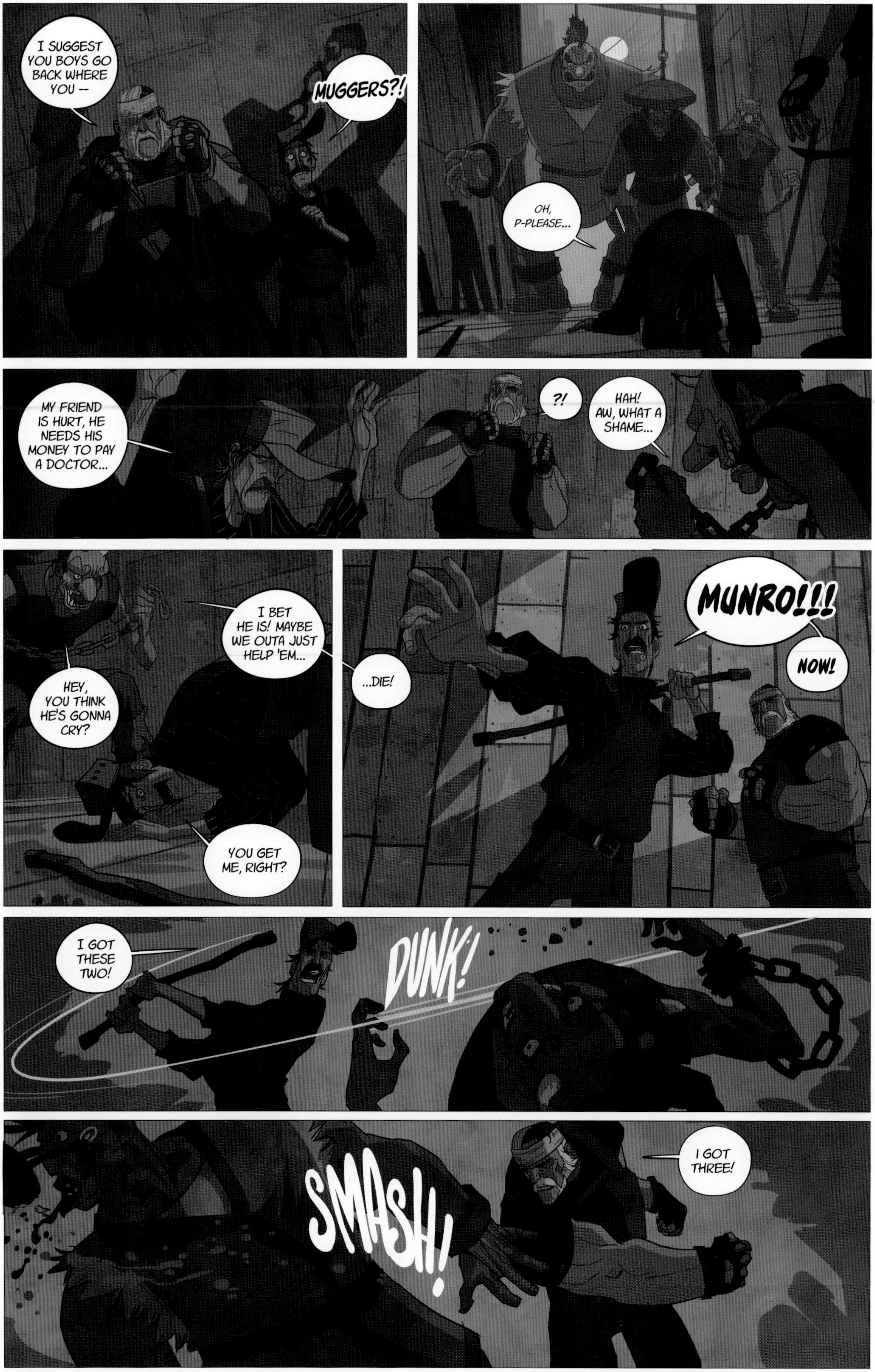
I SUGGEST YOU BOYS GO BACK WHERE YOU --
MUGGERS?!
OH, P-PLEASE...
MY FRIEND IS HURT, HE NEEDS HIS MONEY TO PAY A DOCTOR...
?!
HAH! AW, WHAT A SHAME...
I BET HE IS! MAYBE WE OUTA JUST HELP 'EM...
...DIE!
HEY, YOU THINK HE'S GONNA CRY?
YOU GET ME, RIGHT?
MUNRO!!!
NOW!
I GOT THESE TWO!
DUNK!
SMASH!
I GOT THREE!

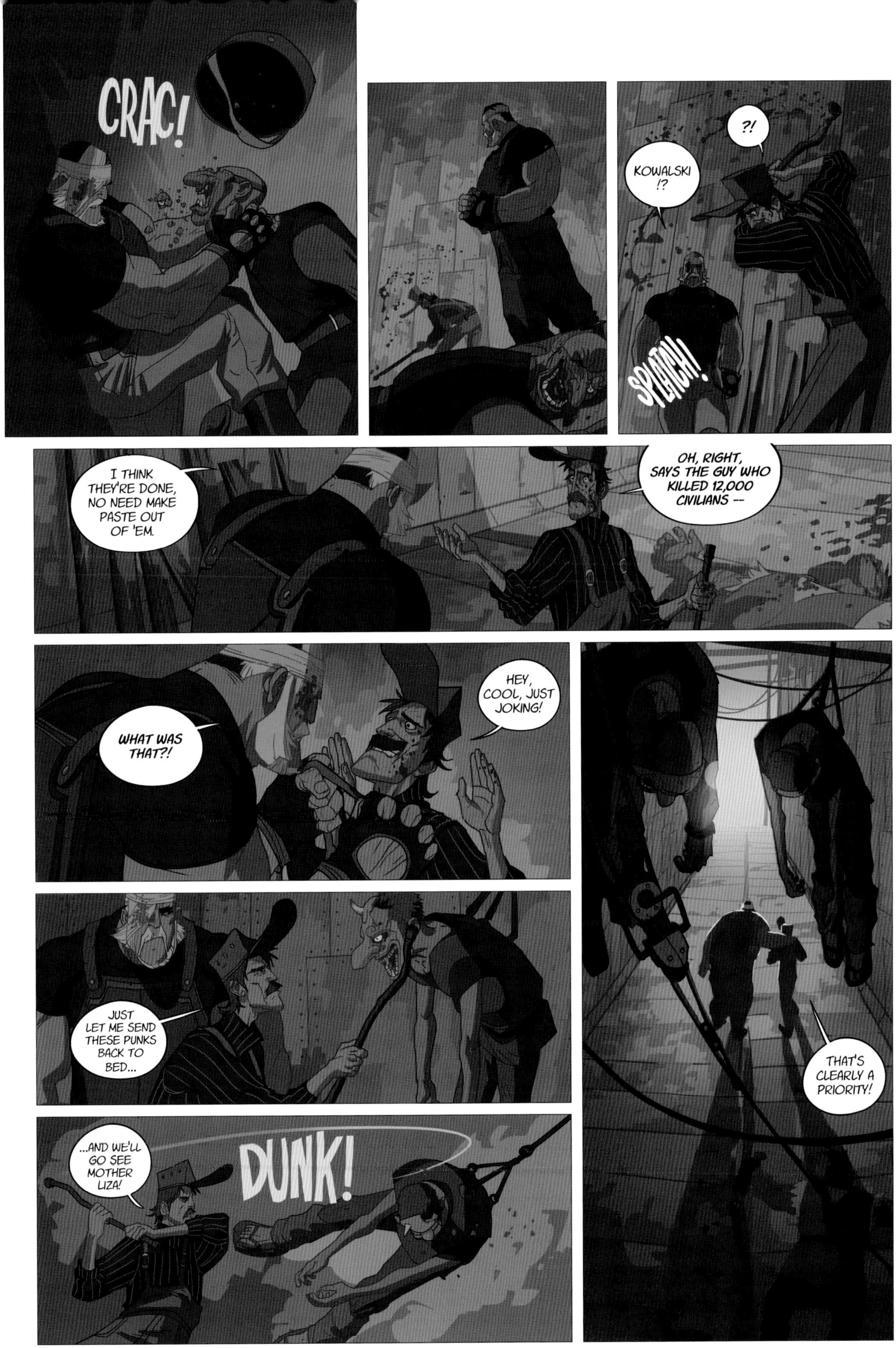
CRAC!
KOWALSKI !?
?!
SPLATCH!
I THINK THEY'RE DONE, NO NEED MAKE PASTE OUT OF 'EM.
OH, RIGHT, SAYS THE GUY WHO KILLED 12,000 CIVILIANS --
WHAT WAS THAT?!
HEY, COOL, JUST JOKING!
JUST LET ME SEND THESE PUNKS BACK TO BED...
...AND WE'LL GO SEE MOTHER LIZA!
DUNK!
THAT'S CLEARLY A PRIORITY!

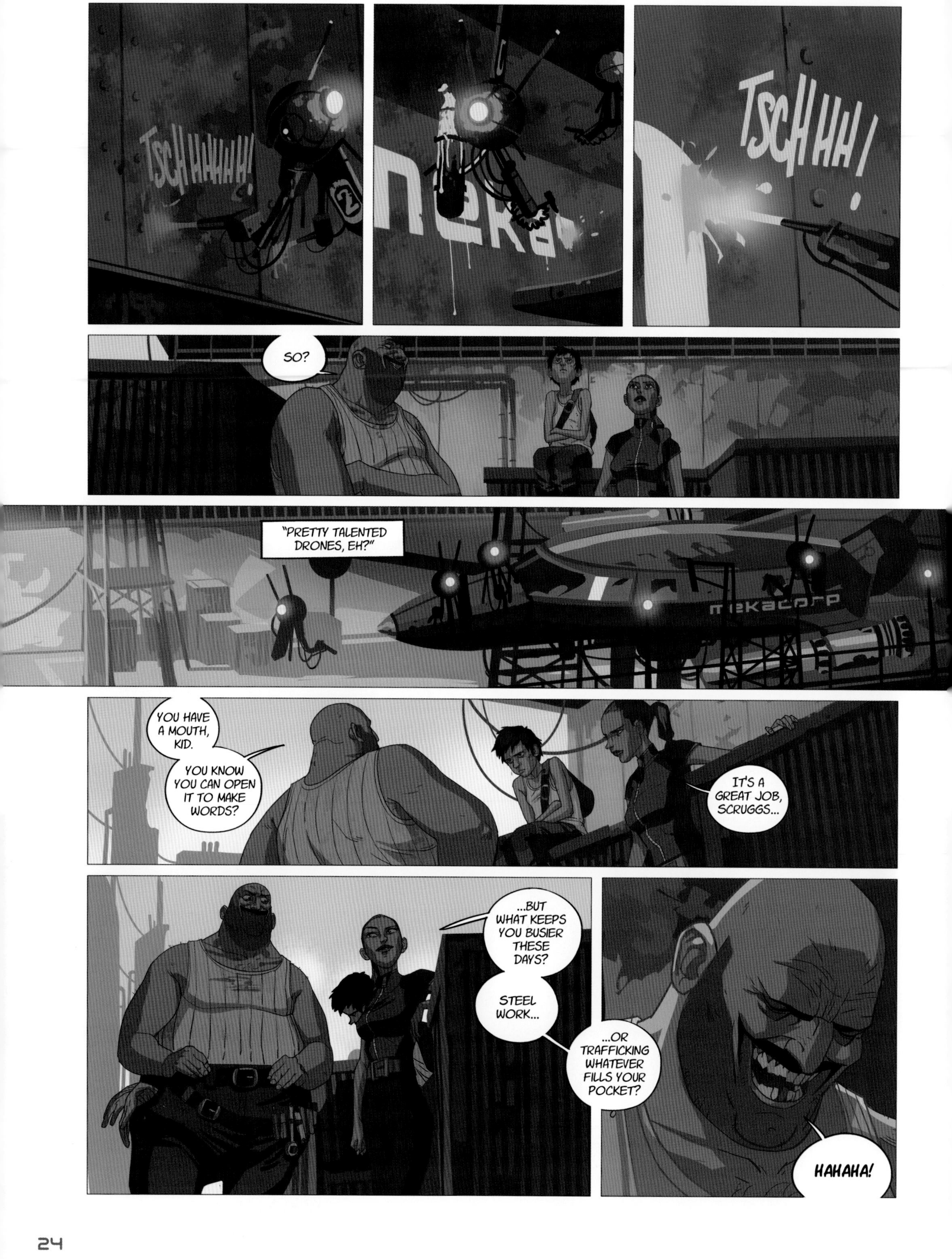
TSCHHHHHH!
TSCHHHH!
SO?
"PRETTY TALENTED DRONES, EH?"
mekacorp
YOU HAVE A MOUTH, KID.
YOU KNOW YOU CAN OPEN IT TO MAKE WORDS?
IT'S A GREAT JOB, SCRUGGS...
...BUT WHAT KEEPS YOU BUSIER THESE DAYS?
STEEL WORK...
...OR TRAFFICKING WHATEVER FILLS YOUR POCKET?
HAHAHA!

WHATEVER PUTS A LITTLE HONEY IN THE SAUCE...

IT'S ALL HERE ON EGEVIS, Y'KNOW?

I SEE YOU SIGN YOUR WORK...

...A REAL ARTIST, HUH?

YEAH.

BUT ART DOESN'T ALWAYS PUT FOOD ON THE TABLE...

...NOT LIKE A 500,000 MARK REWARD FOR FOUR FUGITIVES FROM *PRESIDENT VEXTON*...

...YOU CAN'T ARGUE THE VALUE OF THAT...

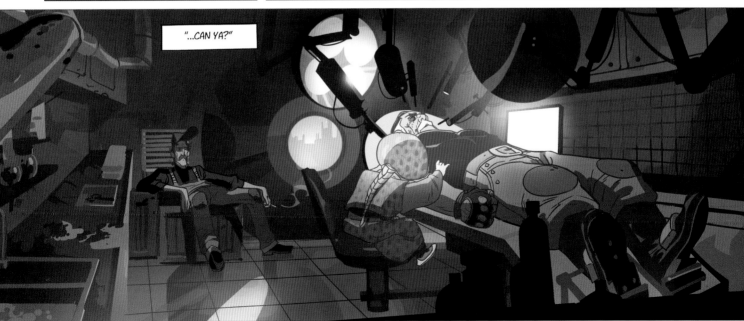

"...CAN YA?"

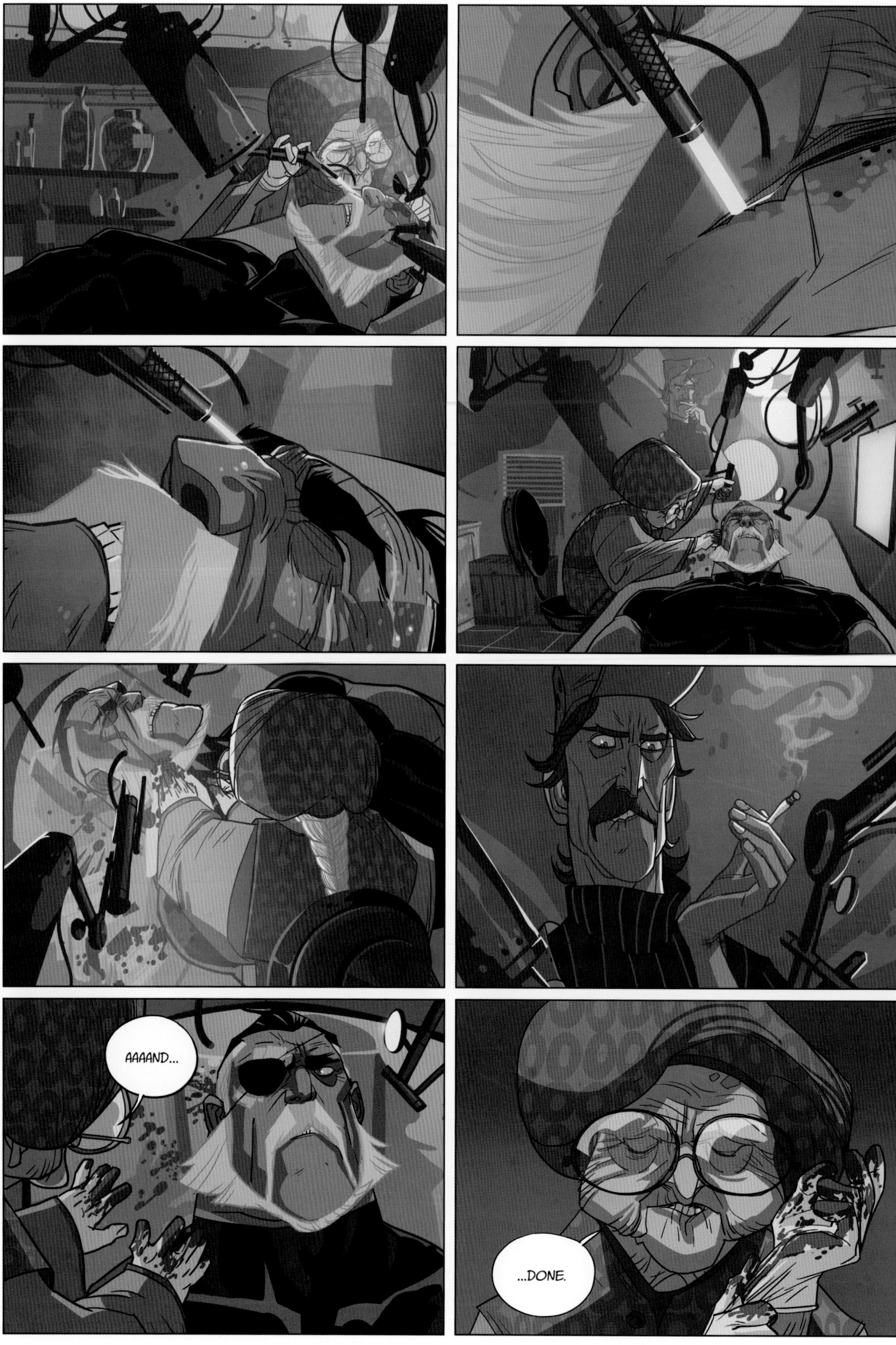
AAAAND...
...DONE.

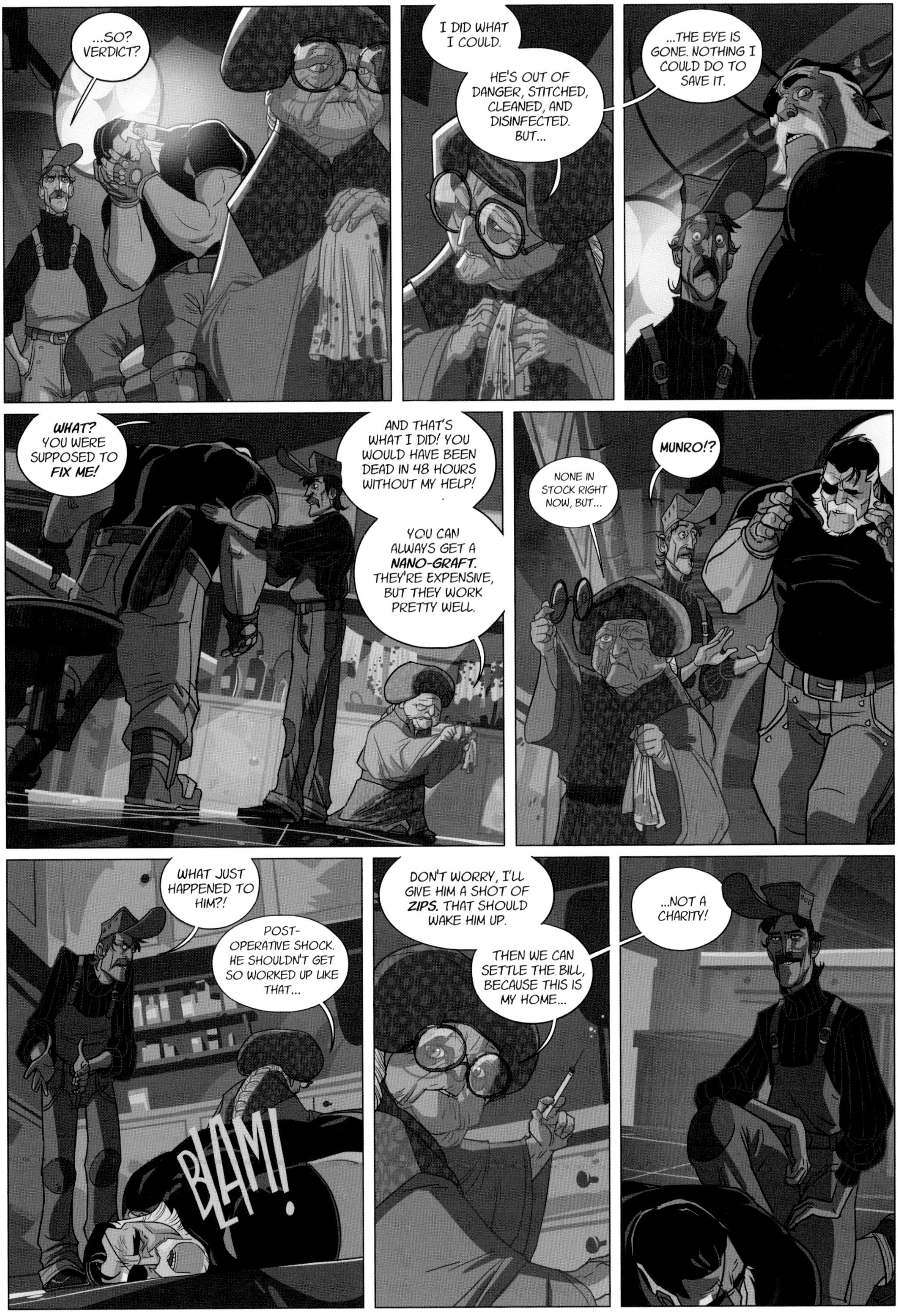
...SO? VERDICT?
I DID WHAT I COULD.
HE'S OUT OF DANGER, STITCHED, CLEANED, AND DISINFECTED. BUT...
...THE EYE IS GONE. NOTHING I COULD DO TO SAVE IT.
WHAT? YOU WERE SUPPOSED TO FIX ME!
AND THAT'S WHAT I DID! YOU WOULD HAVE BEEN DEAD IN 48 HOURS WITHOUT MY HELP!
YOU CAN ALWAYS GET A NANO-GRAFT. THEY'RE EXPENSIVE, BUT THEY WORK PRETTY WELL.
NONE IN STOCK RIGHT NOW, BUT...
MUNRO!?
WHAT JUST HAPPENED TO HIM?!
POST-OPERATIVE SHOCK. HE SHOULDN'T GET SO WORKED UP LIKE THAT...
BLAM!
DON'T WORRY, I'LL GIVE HIM A SHOT OF ZIPS. THAT SHOULD WAKE HIM UP.
THEN WE CAN SETTLE THE BILL, BECAUSE THIS IS MY HOME...
...NOT A CHARITY!

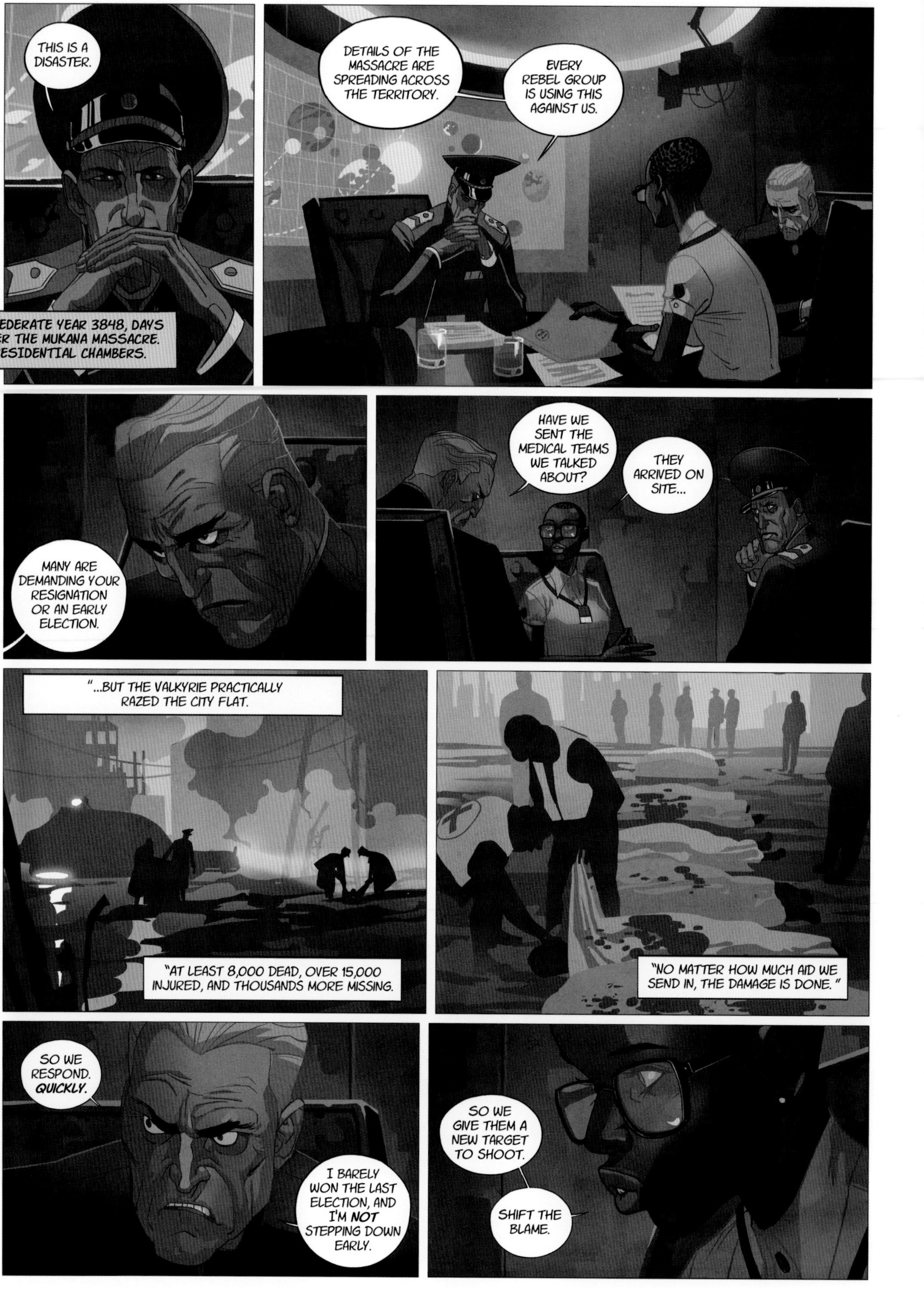

THIS IS A DISASTER.
CONFEDERATE YEAR 3848, DAYS AFTER THE MUKANA MASSACRE. PRESIDENTIAL CHAMBERS.
DETAILS OF THE MASSACRE ARE SPREADING ACROSS THE TERRITORY.
EVERY REBEL GROUP IS USING THIS AGAINST US.
MANY ARE DEMANDING YOUR RESIGNATION OR AN EARLY ELECTION.
HAVE WE SENT THE MEDICAL TEAMS WE TALKED ABOUT?
THEY ARRIVED ON SITE...
"...BUT THE VALKYRIE PRACTICALLY RAZED THE CITY FLAT.
"AT LEAST 8,000 DEAD, OVER 15,000 INJURED, AND THOUSANDS MORE MISSING.
"NO MATTER HOW MUCH AID WE SEND IN, THE DAMAGE IS DONE."
SO WE RESPOND. QUICKLY.
I BARELY WON THE LAST ELECTION, AND I'M NOT STEPPING DOWN EARLY.
SO WE GIVE THEM A NEW TARGET TO SHOOT.
SHIFT THE BLAME.

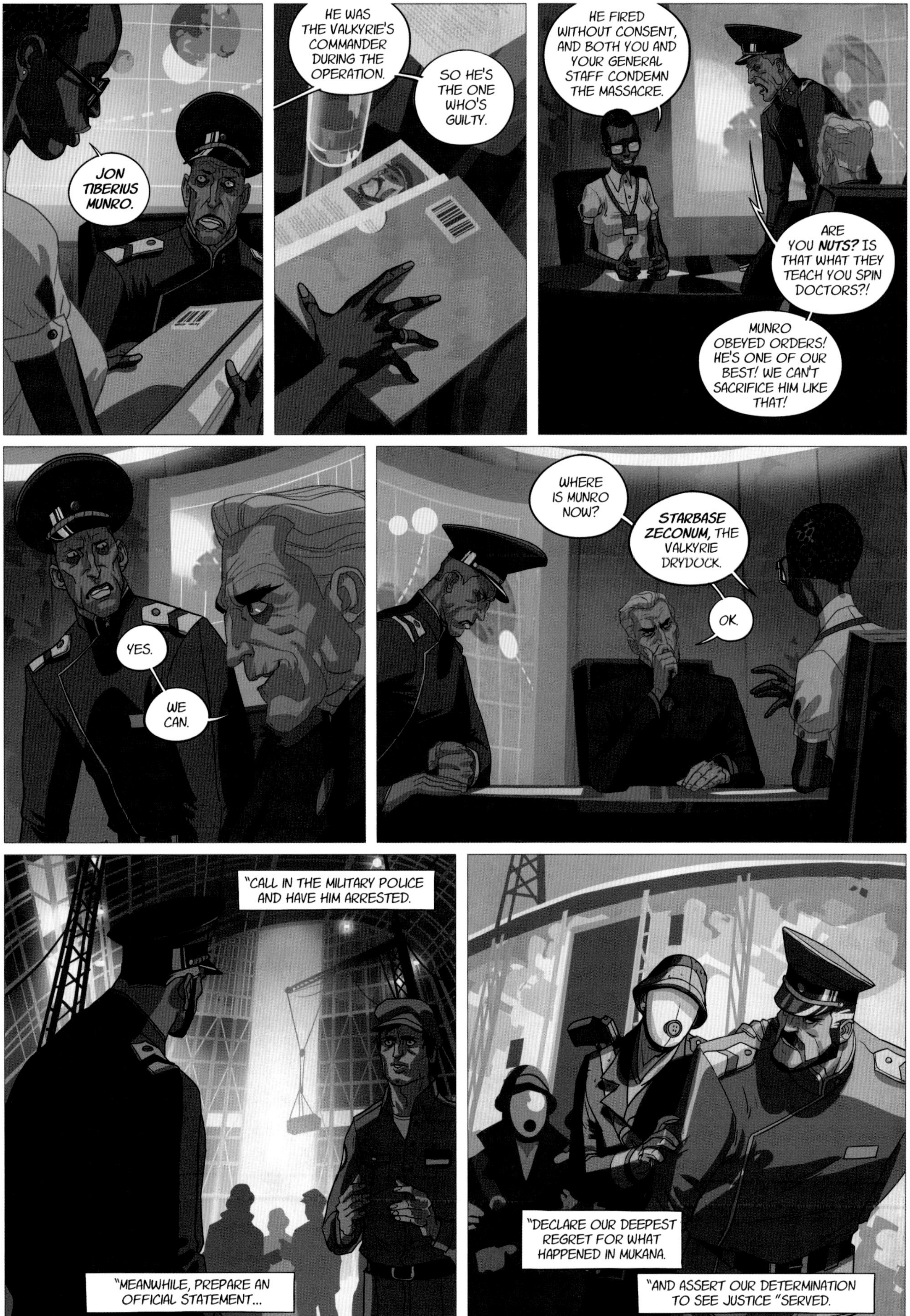
JON TIBERIUS MUNRO.
HE WAS THE VALKYRIE'S COMMANDER DURING THE OPERATION.
SO HE'S THE ONE WHO'S GUILTY.
HE FIRED WITHOUT CONSENT, AND BOTH YOU AND YOUR GENERAL STAFF CONDEMN THE MASSACRE.
ARE YOU NUTS? IS THAT WHAT THEY TEACH YOU SPIN DOCTORS?!
MUNRO OBEYED ORDERS! HE'S ONE OF OUR BEST! WE CAN'T SACRIFICE HIM LIKE THAT!
YES.
WE CAN.
WHERE IS MUNRO NOW?
STARBASE ZECONUM, THE VALKYRIE DRYDOCK.
OK.
"CALL IN THE MILITARY POLICE AND HAVE HIM ARRESTED.
"MEANWHILE, PREPARE AN OFFICIAL STATEMENT...
"DECLARE OUR DEEPEST REGRET FOR WHAT HAPPENED IN MUKANA.
"AND ASSERT OUR DETERMINATION TO SEE JUSTICE "SERVED.

CONFEDERATE YEAR 3852.
PLANET EGEVIS.

MAGGOT!

WAS THIS KOWALKSI'S PLAN?

NOT THIS TIME, DOLL.

FOR ONCE, THAT BASTARD GETS ZIP!

THIS WAS ALL MY IDEA.

WEEN YOU INTO SMALLER GROUPS....

...EASIER TO NAB.

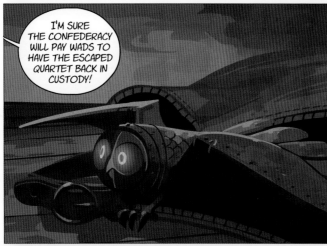

I'M SURE THE CONFEDERACY WILL PAY WADS TO HAVE THE ESCAPED QUARTET BACK IN CUSTODY!

?!!!

?!!!

SKRIIIIIIIII!!

30

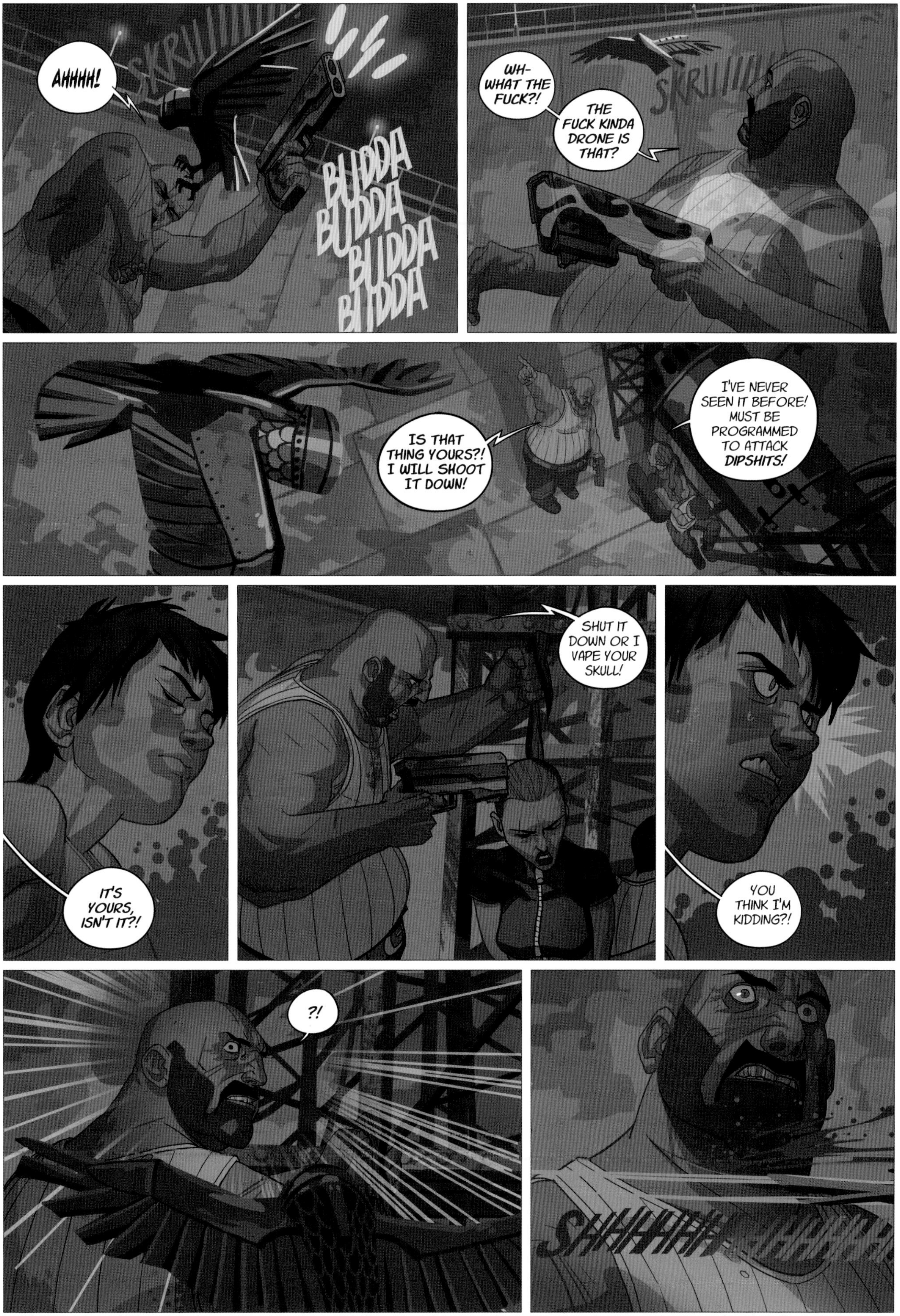
AHHHH!
SKRIIIIIII
BUDDA BUDDA BUDDA BUDDA
SKRIIIII
WH- WHAT THE FUCK?!
THE FUCK KINDA DRONE IS THAT?
IS THAT THING YOURS?! I WILL SHOOT IT DOWN!
I'VE NEVER SEEN IT BEFORE! MUST BE PROGRAMMED TO ATTACK DIPSHITS!
IT'S YOURS, ISN'T IT?!
SHUT IT DOWN OR I VAPE YOUR SKULL!
YOU THINK I'M KIDDING?!
?!

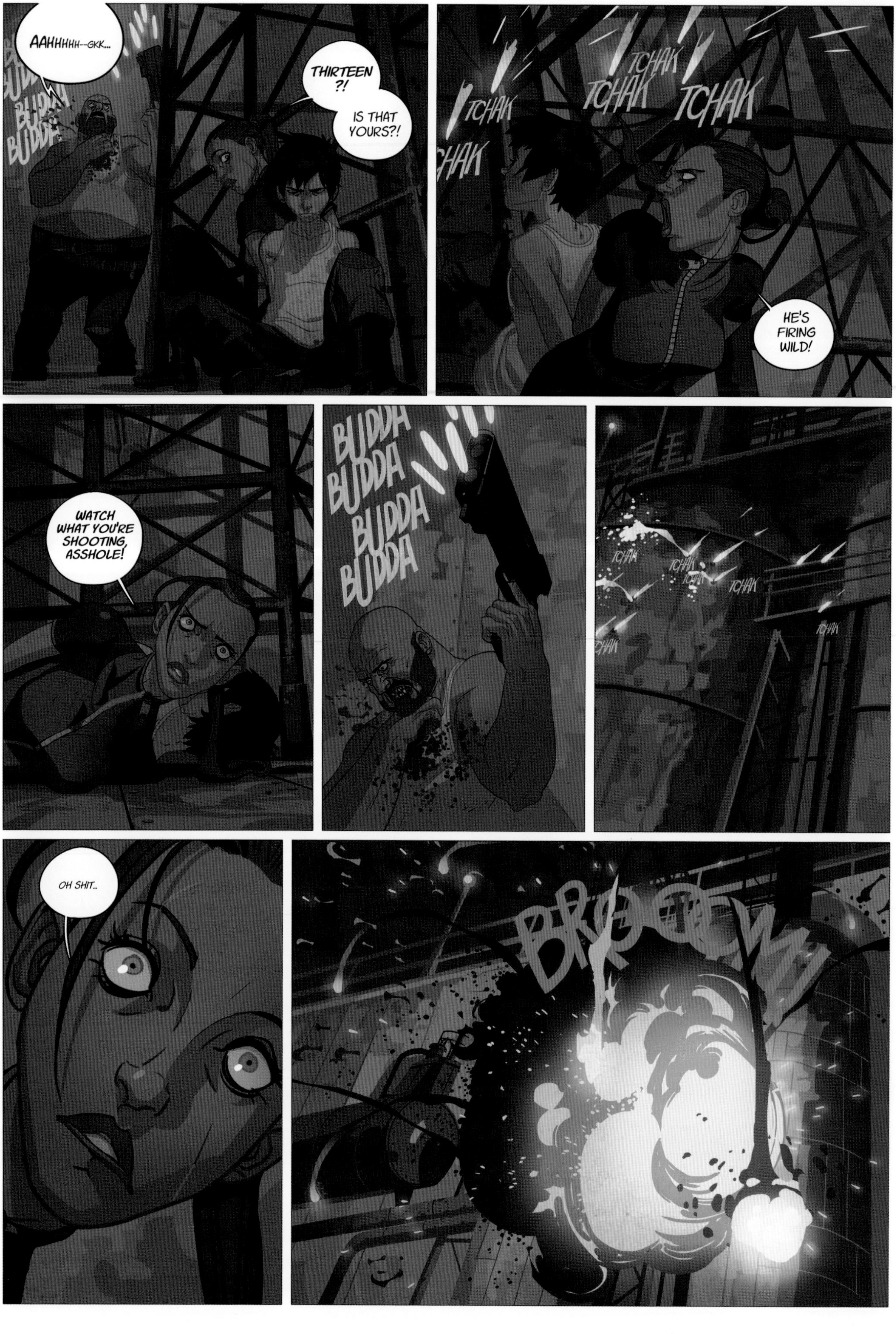
AAHHHHH--GKK...
BUDDA BUDDA BUDDA
THIRTEEN ?!
IS THAT YOURS?!
TCHAK TCHAK TCHAK TCHAK
TCHAK
HE'S FIRING WILD!
WATCH WHAT YOU'RE SHOOTING, ASSHOLE!
BUDDA BUDDA BUDDA BUDDA
TCHAK TCHAK TCHAK TCHAK TCHAK TCHAK
OH SHIT...
BROOOM!

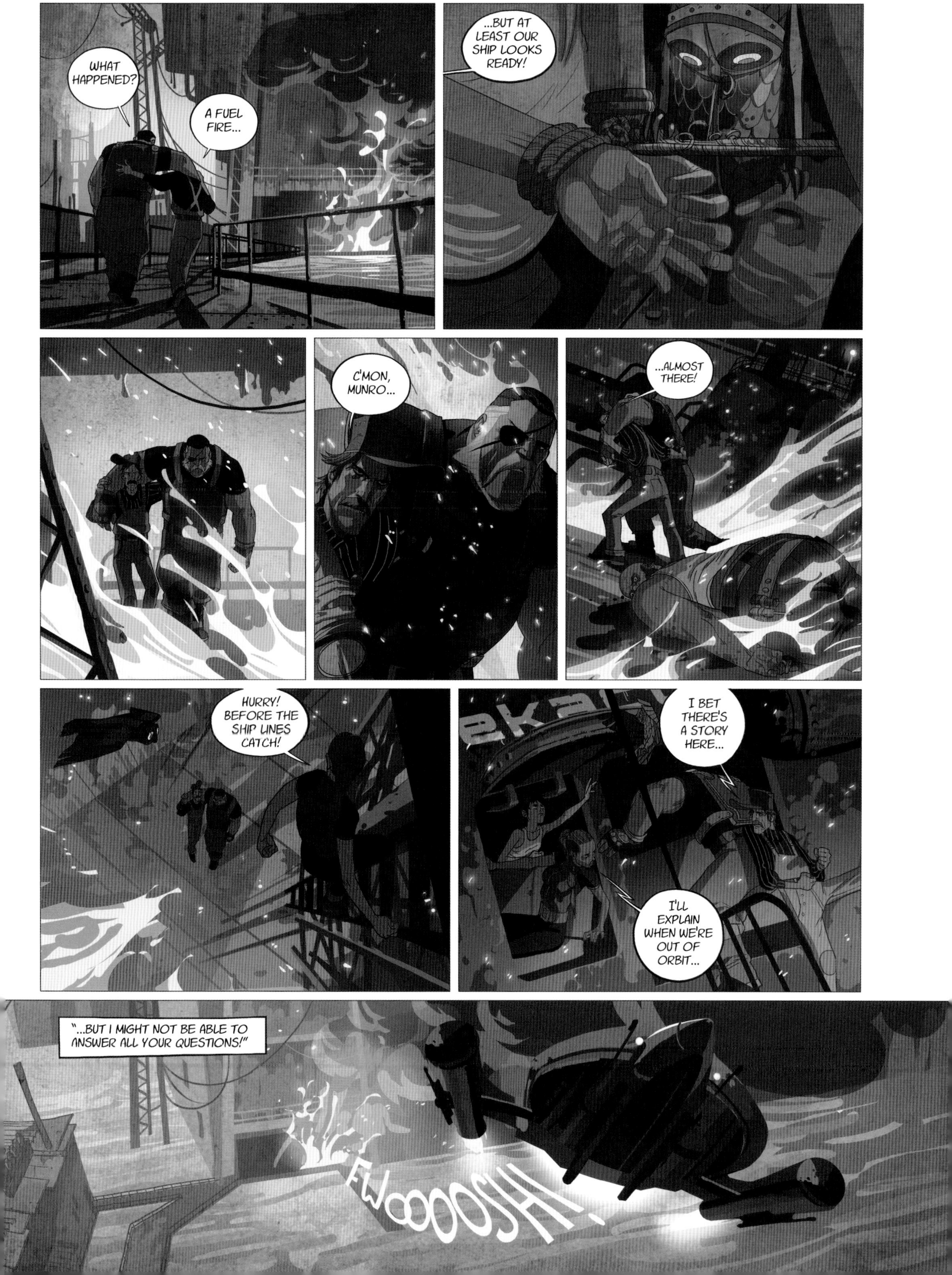
WHAT HAPPENED?
A FUEL FIRE...
...BUT AT LEAST OUR SHIP LOOKS READY!
C'MON, MUNRO...
...ALMOST THERE!
HURRY! BEFORE THE SHIP LINES CATCH!
I BET THERE'S A STORY HERE...
I'LL EXPLAIN WHEN WE'RE OUT OF ORBIT...
"...BUT I MIGHT NOT BE ABLE TO ANSWER ALL YOUR QUESTIONS!"
FWOOOOSH!

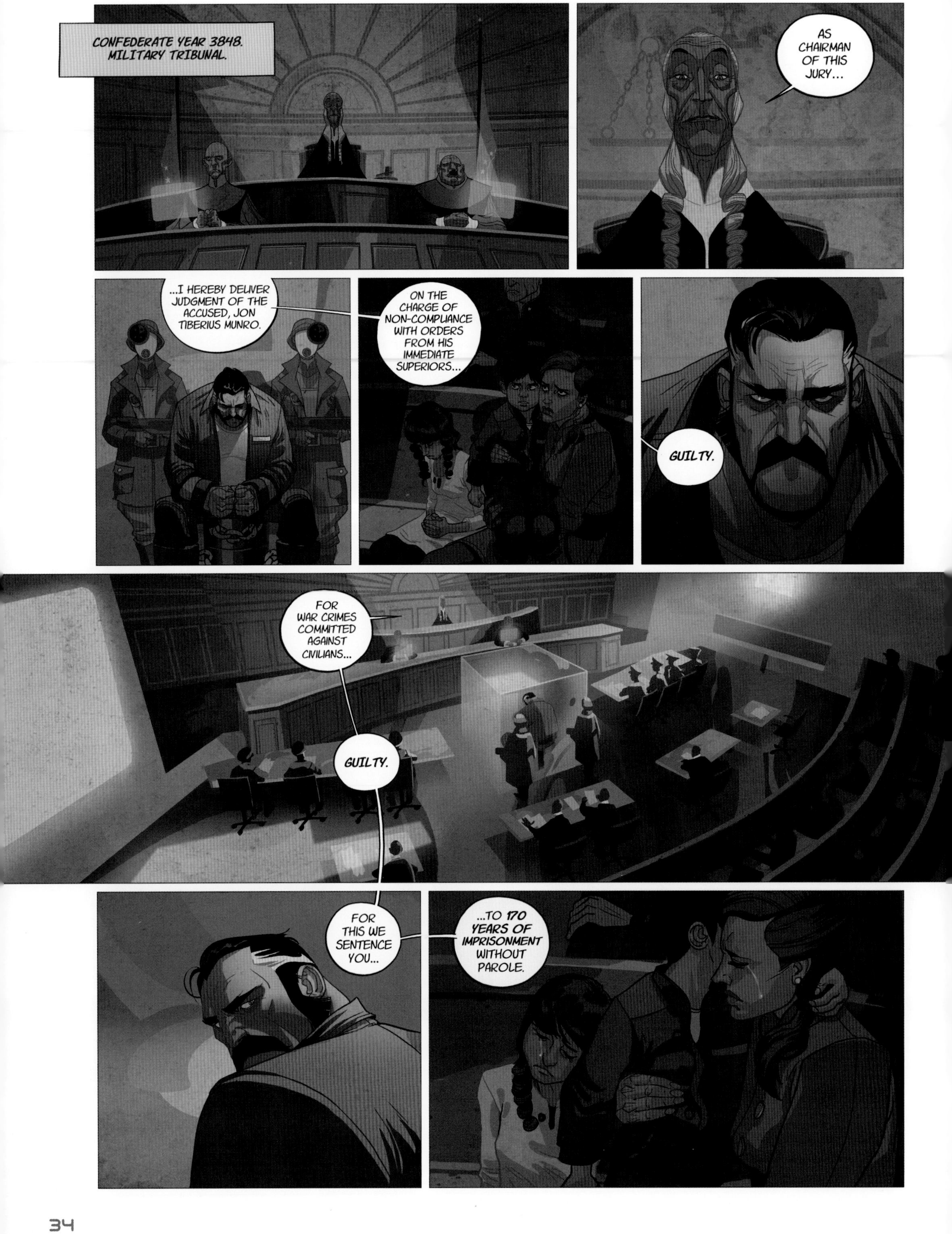
CONFEDERATE YEAR 3848. MILITARY TRIBUNAL.
AS CHAIRMAN OF THIS JURY...
...I HEREBY DELIVER JUDGMENT OF THE ACCUSED, JON TIBERIUS MUNRO.
ON THE CHARGE OF NON-COMPLIANCE WITH ORDERS FROM HIS IMMEDIATE SUPERIORS...
GUILTY.
FOR WAR CRIMES COMMITTED AGAINST CIVILIANS...
GUILTY.
FOR THIS WE SENTENCE YOU...
...TO 170 YEARS OF IMPRISONMENT WITHOUT PAROLE.

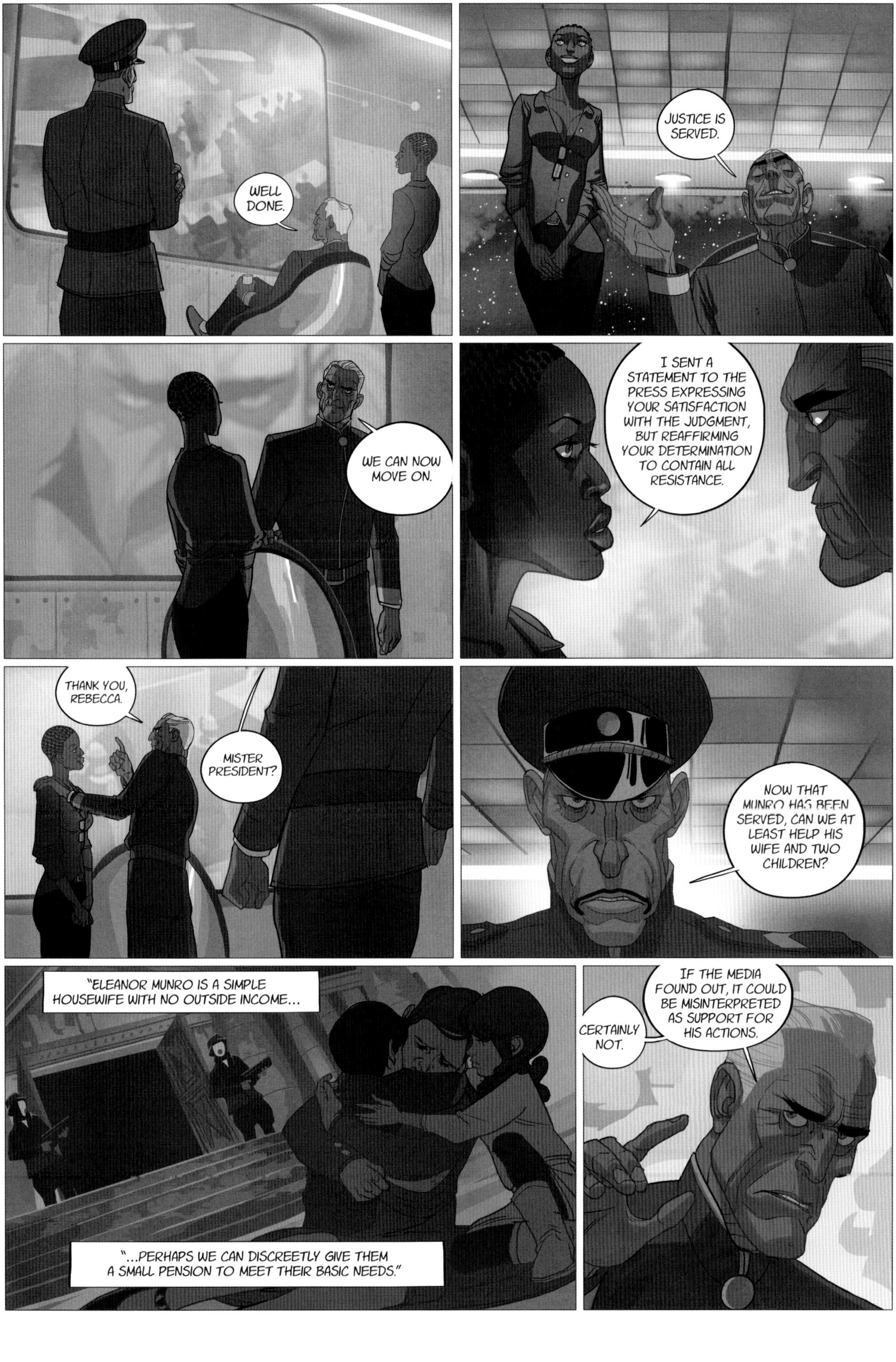
WELL DONE.
JUSTICE IS SERVED.
WE CAN NOW MOVE ON.
I SENT A STATEMENT TO THE PRESS EXPRESSING YOUR SATISFACTION WITH THE JUDGMENT, BUT REAFFIRMING YOUR DETERMINATION TO CONTAIN ALL RESISTANCE.
THANK YOU, REBECCA.
MISTER PRESIDENT?
NOW THAT MUNRO HAS BEEN SERVED, CAN WE AT LEAST HELP HIS WIFE AND TWO CHILDREN?
"ELEANOR MUNRO IS A SIMPLE HOUSEWIFE WITH NO OUTSIDE INCOME...
"...PERHAPS WE CAN DISCREETLY GIVE THEM A SMALL PENSION TO MEET THEIR BASIC NEEDS."
CERTAINLY NOT.
IF THE MEDIA FOUND OUT, IT COULD BE MISINTERPRETED AS SUPPORT FOR HIS ACTIONS.

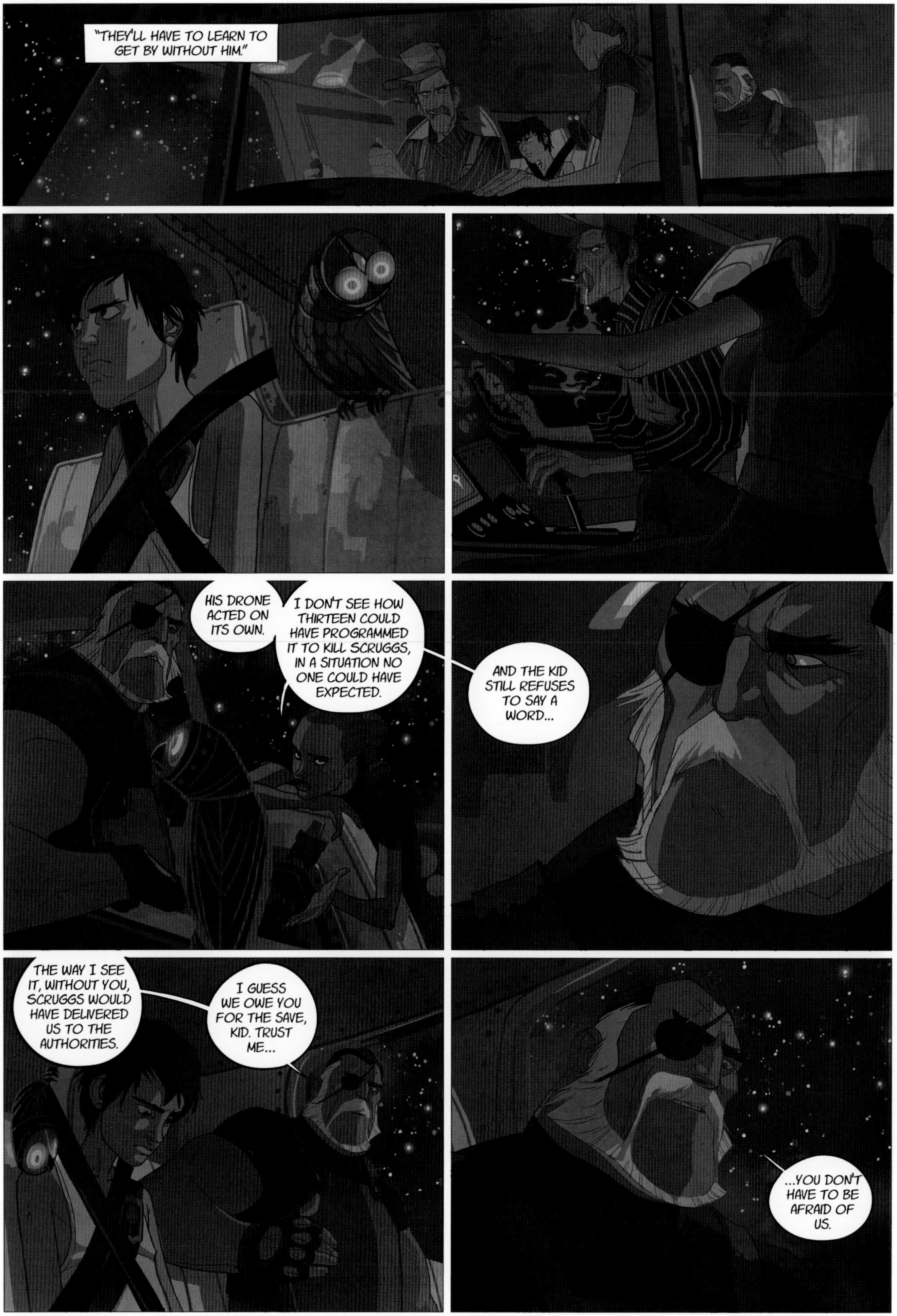
"THEY'LL HAVE TO LEARN TO GET BY WITHOUT HIM."
HIS DRONE ACTED ON ITS OWN.
I DON'T SEE HOW THIRTEEN COULD HAVE PROGRAMMED IT TO KILL SCRUGGS, IN A SITUATION NO ONE COULD HAVE EXPECTED.
AND THE KID STILL REFUSES TO SAY A WORD...
THE WAY I SEE IT, WITHOUT YOU, SCRUGGS WOULD HAVE DELIVERED US TO THE AUTHORITIES.
I GUESS WE OWE YOU FOR THE SAVE, KID. TRUST ME...
...YOU DON'T HAVE TO BE AFRAID OF US.

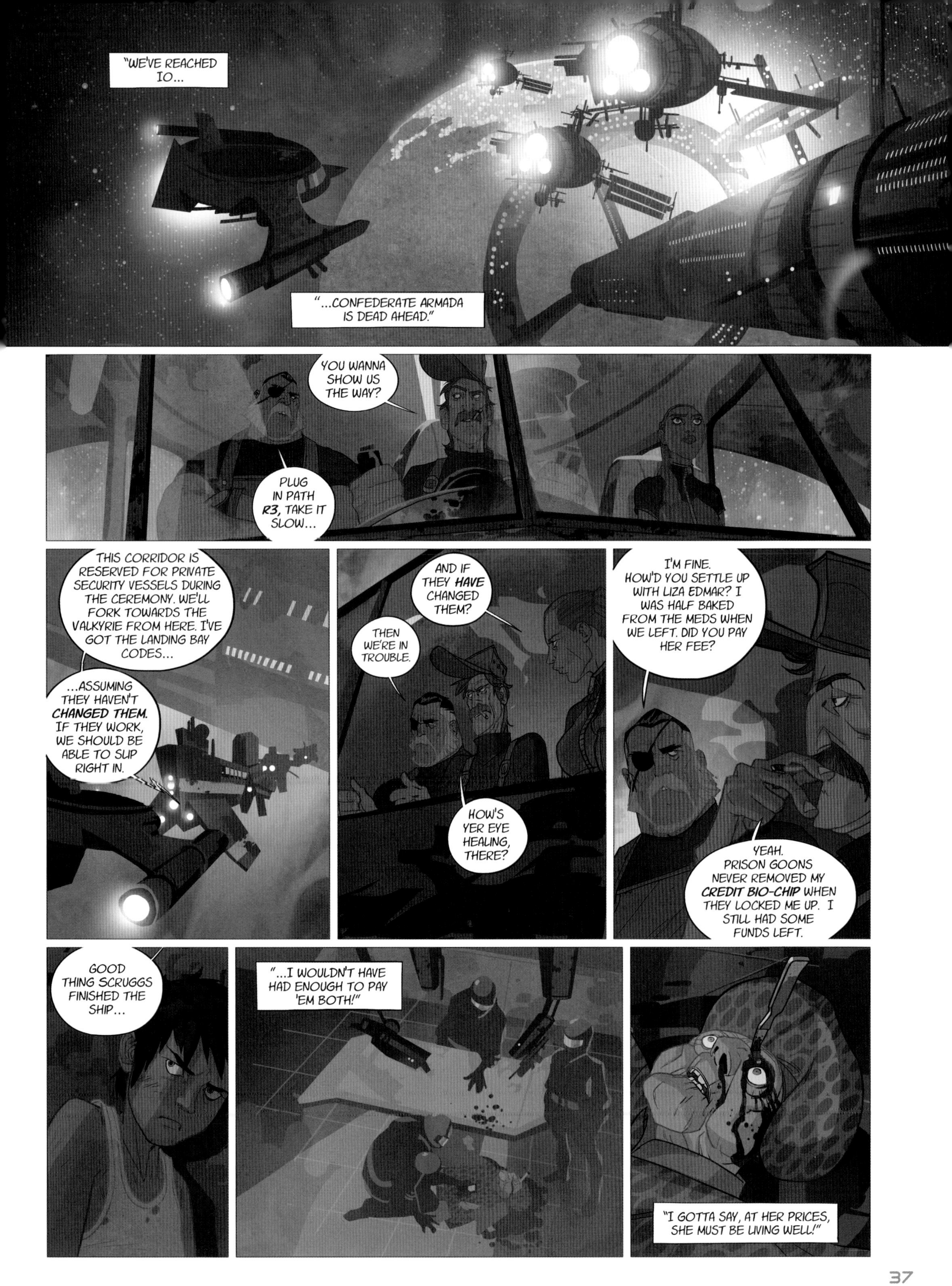

"WE'VE REACHED IO...
"...CONFEDERATE ARMADA IS DEAD AHEAD."
YOU WANNA SHOW US THE WAY?
PLUG IN PATH **R3,** TAKE IT SLOW...
THIS CORRIDOR IS RESERVED FOR PRIVATE SECURITY VESSELS DURING THE CEREMONY. WE'LL FORK TOWARDS THE VALKYRIE FROM HERE. I'VE GOT THE LANDING BAY CODES...
...ASSUMING THEY HAVEN'T **CHANGED THEM.** IF THEY WORK, WE SHOULD BE ABLE TO SLIP RIGHT IN.
AND IF THEY **HAVE** CHANGED THEM?
THEN WE'RE IN TROUBLE.
HOW'S YER EYE HEALING, THERE?
I'M FINE. HOW'D YOU SETTLE UP WITH LIZA EDMAR? I WAS HALF BAKED FROM THE MEDS WHEN WE LEFT. DID YOU PAY HER FEE?
YEAH. PRISON GOONS NEVER REMOVED MY **CREDIT BIO-CHIP** WHEN THEY LOCKED ME UP. I STILL HAD SOME FUNDS LEFT.
GOOD THING SCRUGGS FINISHED THE SHIP...
"...I WOULDN'T HAVE HAD ENOUGH TO PAY 'EM BOTH!"
"I GOTTA SAY, AT HER PRICES, SHE MUST BE LIVING WELL!"

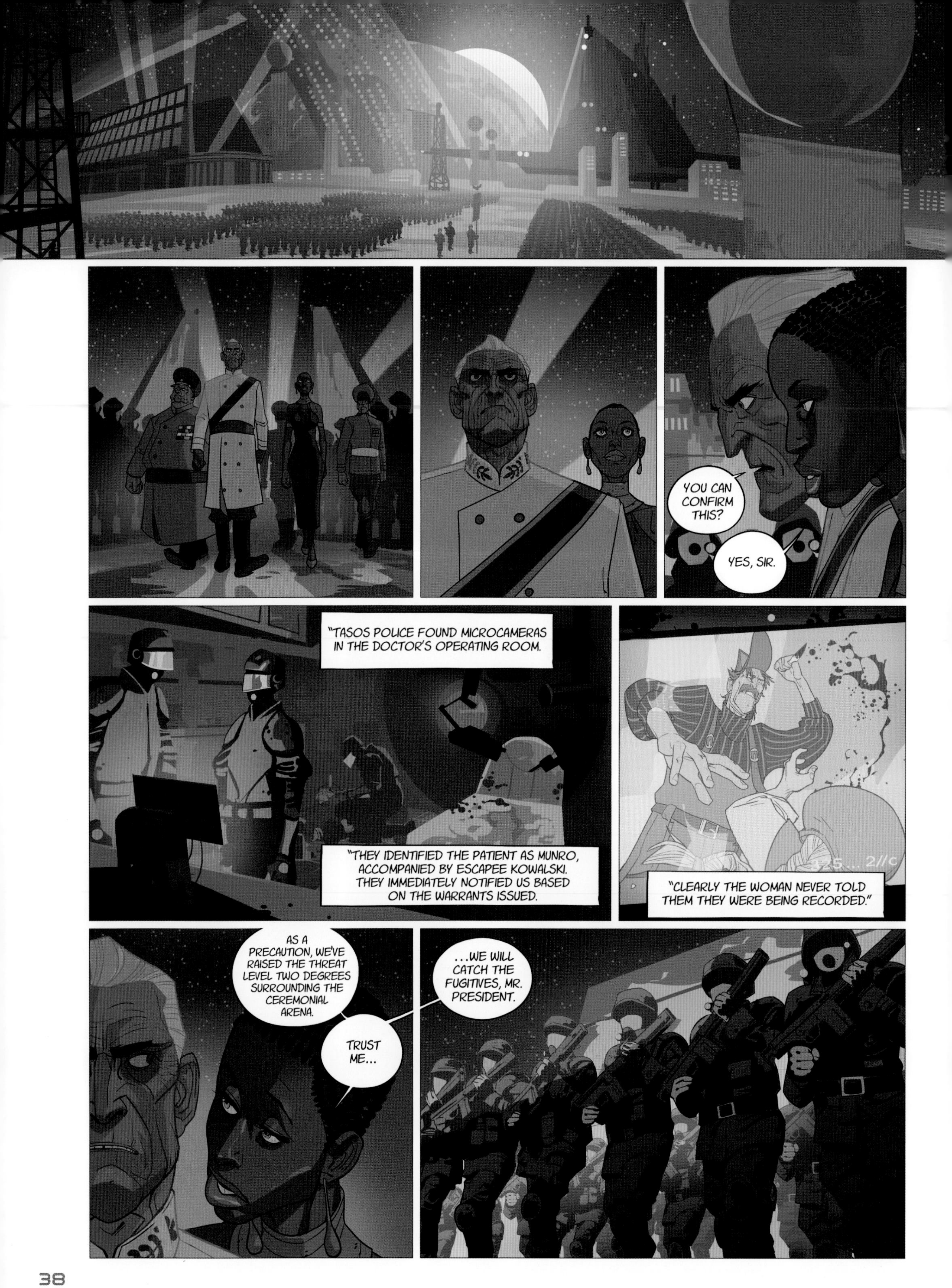
YOU CAN CONFIRM THIS?
YES, SIR.
"TASOS POLICE FOUND MICROCAMERAS IN THE DOCTOR'S OPERATING ROOM.
"THEY IDENTIFIED THE PATIENT AS MUNRO, ACCOMPANIED BY ESCAPEE KOWALSKI. THEY IMMEDIATELY NOTIFIED US BASED ON THE WARRANTS ISSUED.
"CLEARLY THE WOMAN NEVER TOLD THEM THEY WERE BEING RECORDED."
AS A PRECAUTION, WE'VE RAISED THE THREAT LEVEL TWO DEGREES SURROUNDING THE CEREMONIAL ARENA.
TRUST ME...
...WE WILL CATCH THE FUGITIVES, MR. PRESIDENT.

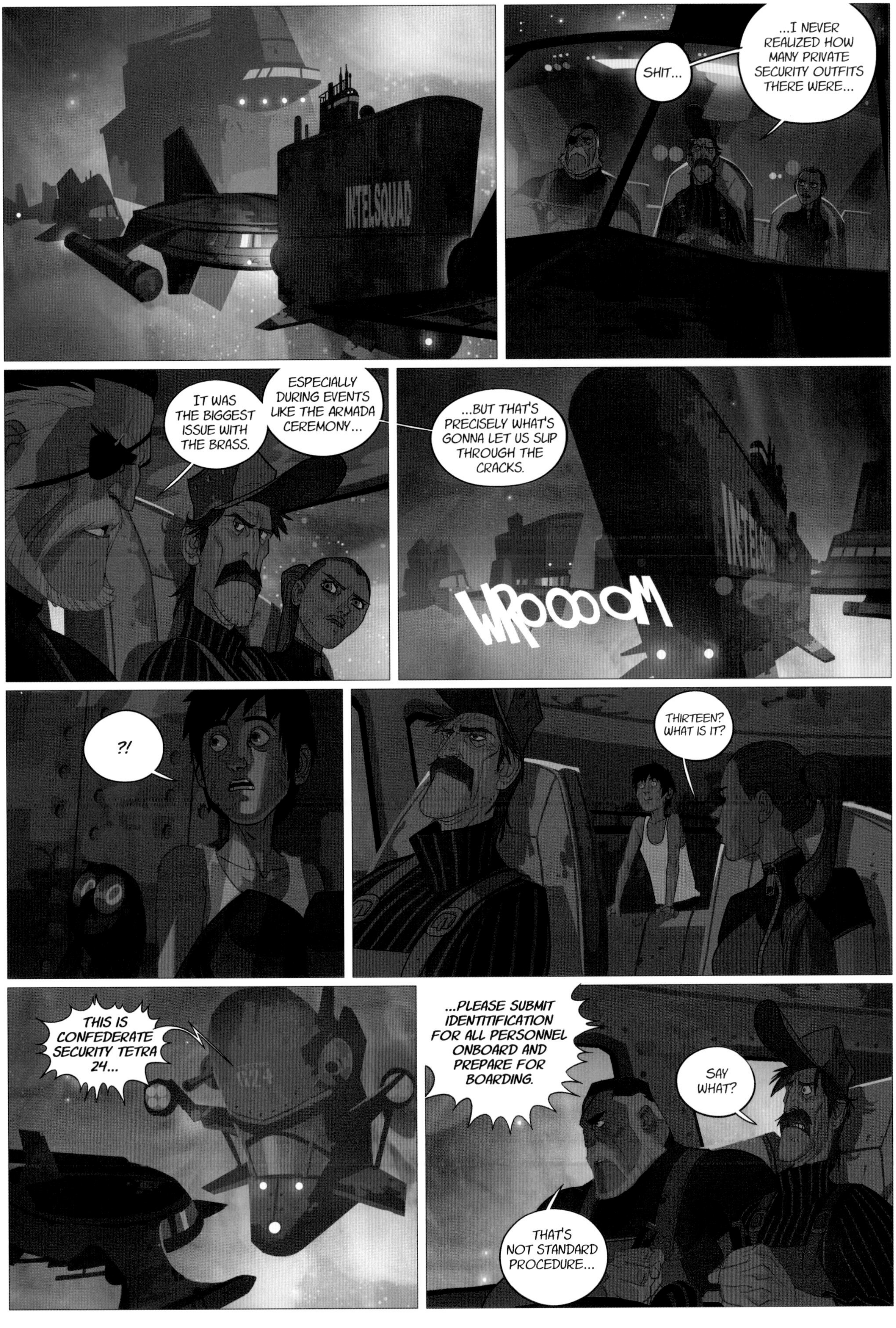
INTELSQUAD
SHIT...
...I NEVER REALIZED HOW MANY PRIVATE SECURITY OUTFITS THERE WERE...
IT WAS THE BIGGEST ISSUE WITH THE BRASS.
ESPECIALLY DURING EVENTS LIKE THE ARMADA CEREMONY...
...BUT THAT'S PRECISELY WHAT'S GONNA LET US SLIP THROUGH THE CRACKS.
WRPOOOM
?!
THIRTEEN? WHAT IS IT?
THIS IS CONFEDERATE SECURITY TETRA 24...
...PLEASE SUBMIT IDENTITIFICATION FOR ALL PERSONNEL ONBOARD AND PREPARE FOR BOARDING.
SAY WHAT?
THAT'S NOT STANDARD PROCEDURE...

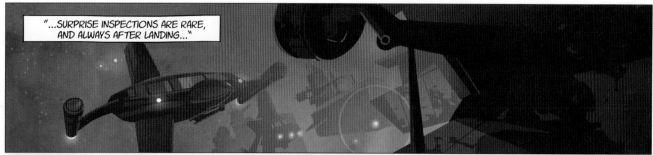

"...SURPRISE INSPECTIONS ARE RARE, AND ALWAYS AFTER LANDING..."

...NEVER IN FLIGHT.

FINAL NOTICE: POWER DOWN AND TRANSMIT CREW MANIFESTO OF ALL PERSONNEL ONBOARD!

KOWALSKI, PASS ME THE MANUAL CONTROLS.

EVERYONE BUCKLE UP.

?!

YOU TOO, THIRTEEN!

MUNRO!? WHAT ARE YOU GONNA DO?

THEY RAISED THE THREAT LEVEL. THAT THROWS OUR PLAN OUT THE WINDOW.

WE'LL HAVE TO GRAB THE ONLY REAL BARGAINING CHIP FOR THE VALKYRIE...

...PRESIDENT VEXTON.

MUNROOOO!?

FWOSSSSH!

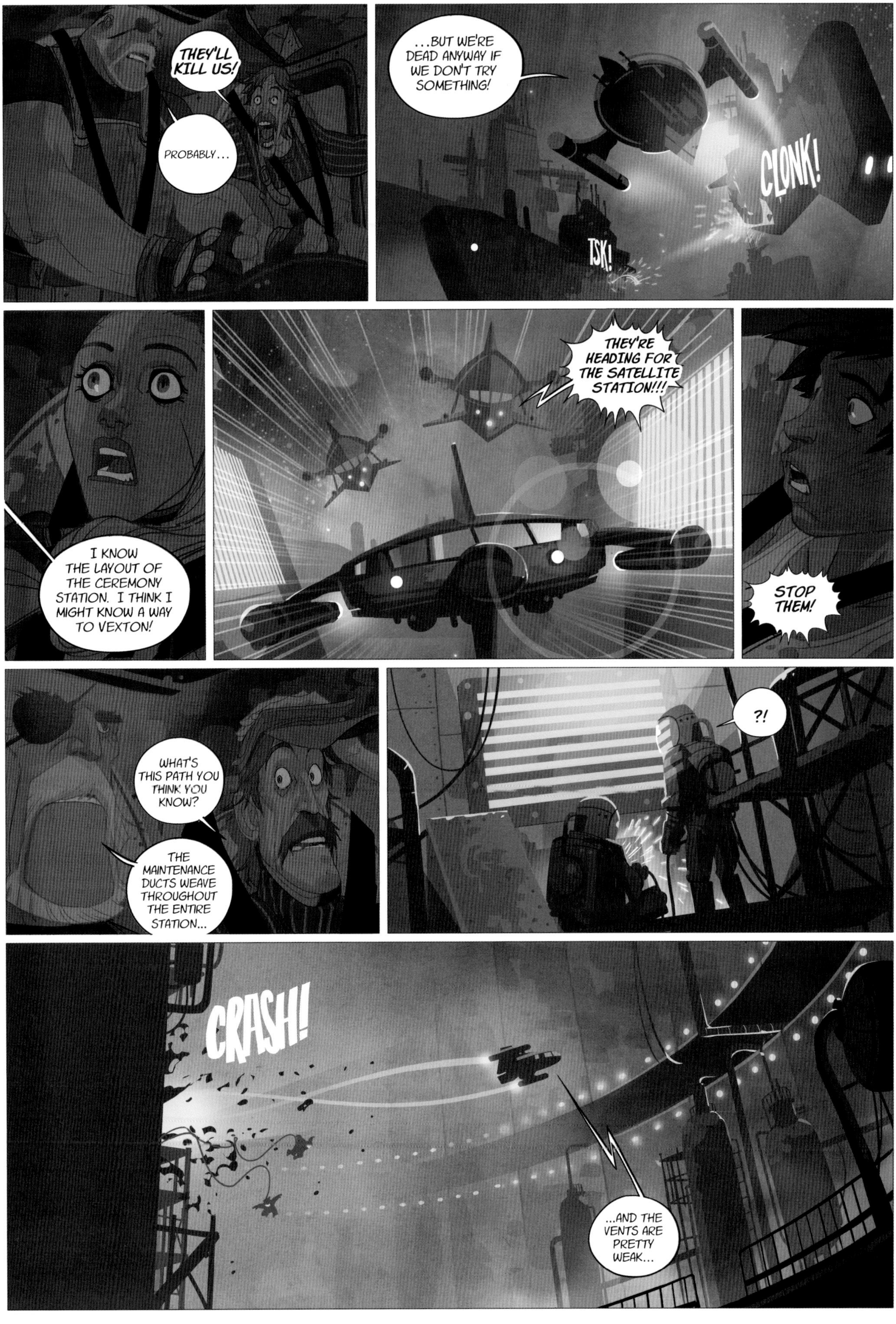
THEY'LL KILL US!
PROBABLY...
...BUT WE'RE DEAD ANYWAY IF WE DON'T TRY SOMETHING!
CLONK!
TSK!
I KNOW THE LAYOUT OF THE CEREMONY STATION. I THINK I MIGHT KNOW A WAY TO VEXTON!
THEY'RE HEADING FOR THE SATELLITE STATION!!!
STOP THEM!
WHAT'S THIS PATH YOU THINK YOU KNOW?
THE MAINTENANCE DUCTS WEAVE THROUGHOUT THE ENTIRE STATION...
?!
CRASH!
...AND THE VENTS ARE PRETTY WEAK...

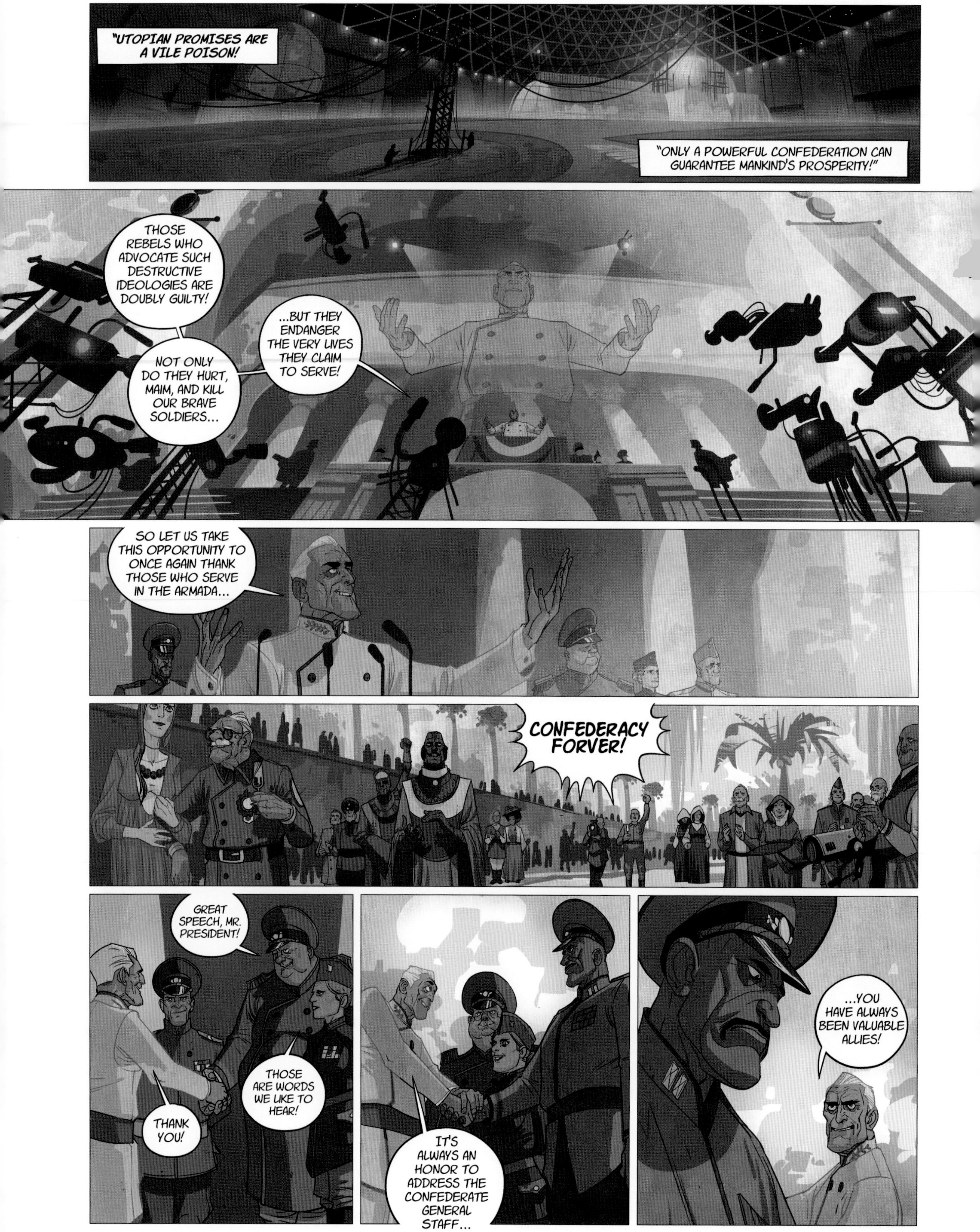
"UTOPIAN PROMISES ARE A VILE POISON!
"ONLY A POWERFUL CONFEDERATION CAN GUARANTEE MANKIND'S PROSPERITY!"
THOSE REBELS WHO ADVOCATE SUCH DESTRUCTIVE IDEOLOGIES ARE DOUBLY GUILTY!
NOT ONLY DO THEY HURT, MAIM, AND KILL OUR BRAVE SOLDIERS...
...BUT THEY ENDANGER THE VERY LIVES THEY CLAIM TO SERVE!
SO LET US TAKE THIS OPPORTUNITY TO ONCE AGAIN THANK THOSE WHO SERVE IN THE ARMADA...
CONFEDERACY FORVER!
GREAT SPEECH, MR. PRESIDENT!
THOSE ARE WORDS WE LIKE TO HEAR!
THANK YOU!
IT'S ALWAYS AN HONOR TO ADDRESS THE CONFEDERATE GENERAL STAFF...
...YOU HAVE ALWAYS BEEN VALUABLE ALLIES!

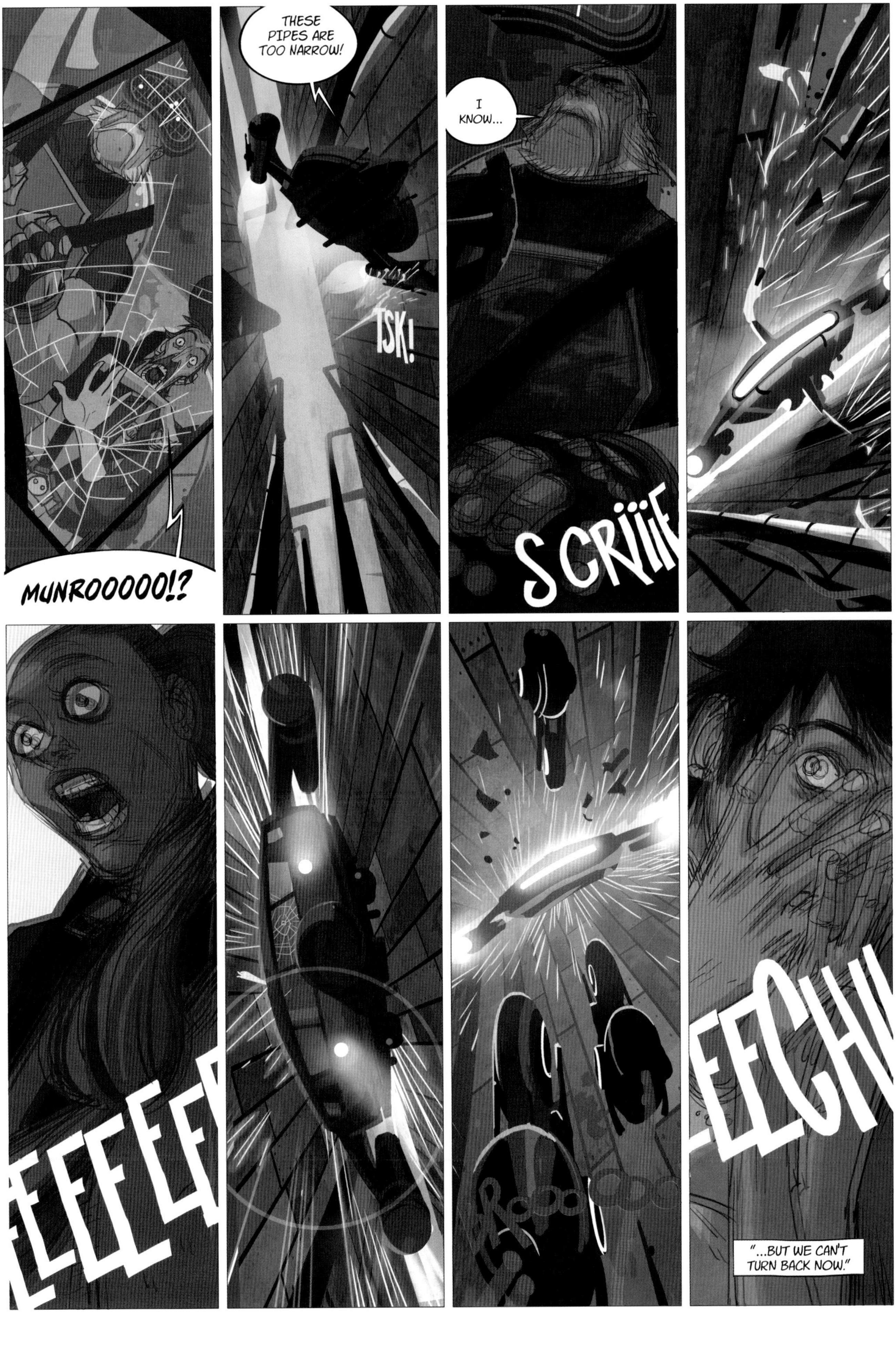

MUNROOOOO!?
THESE PIPES ARE TOO NARROW!
TSK!
I KNOW...
SCRÏÏIE
EEEEEE
EECHH
"...BUT WE CAN'T TURN BACK NOW."

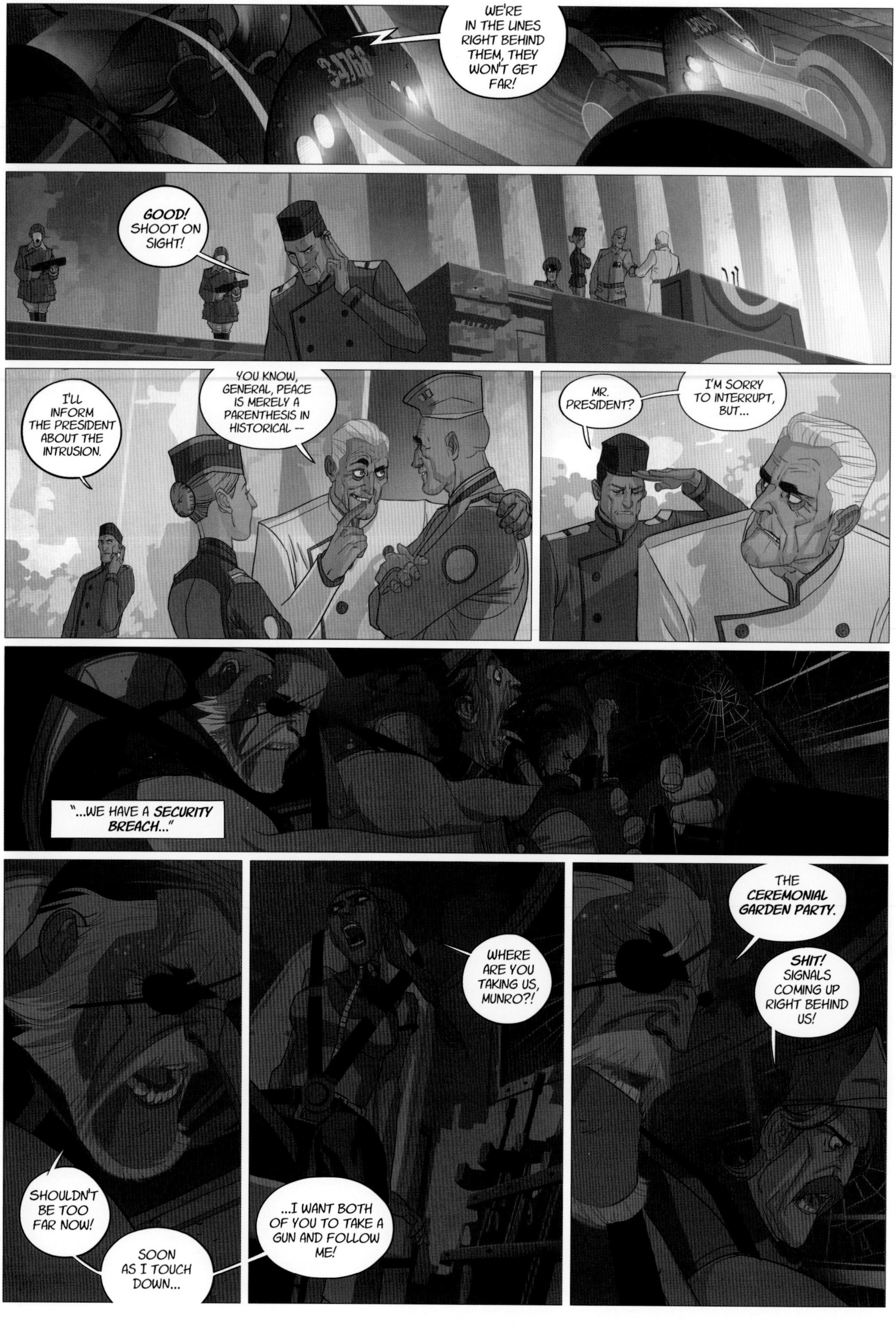
WE'RE IN THE LINES RIGHT BEHIND THEM, THEY WON'T GET FAR!
GOOD! SHOOT ON SIGHT!
I'LL INFORM THE PRESIDENT ABOUT THE INTRUSION.
YOU KNOW, GENERAL, PEACE IS MERELY A PARENTHESIS IN HISTORICAL --
MR. PRESIDENT?
I'M SORRY TO INTERRUPT, BUT...
"...WE HAVE A SECURITY BREACH..."
SHOULDN'T BE TOO FAR NOW!
SOON AS I TOUCH DOWN...
...I WANT BOTH OF YOU TO TAKE A GUN AND FOLLOW ME!
WHERE ARE YOU TAKING US, MUNRO?!
THE CEREMONIAL GARDEN PARTY.
SHIT! SIGNALS COMING UP RIGHT BEHIND US!

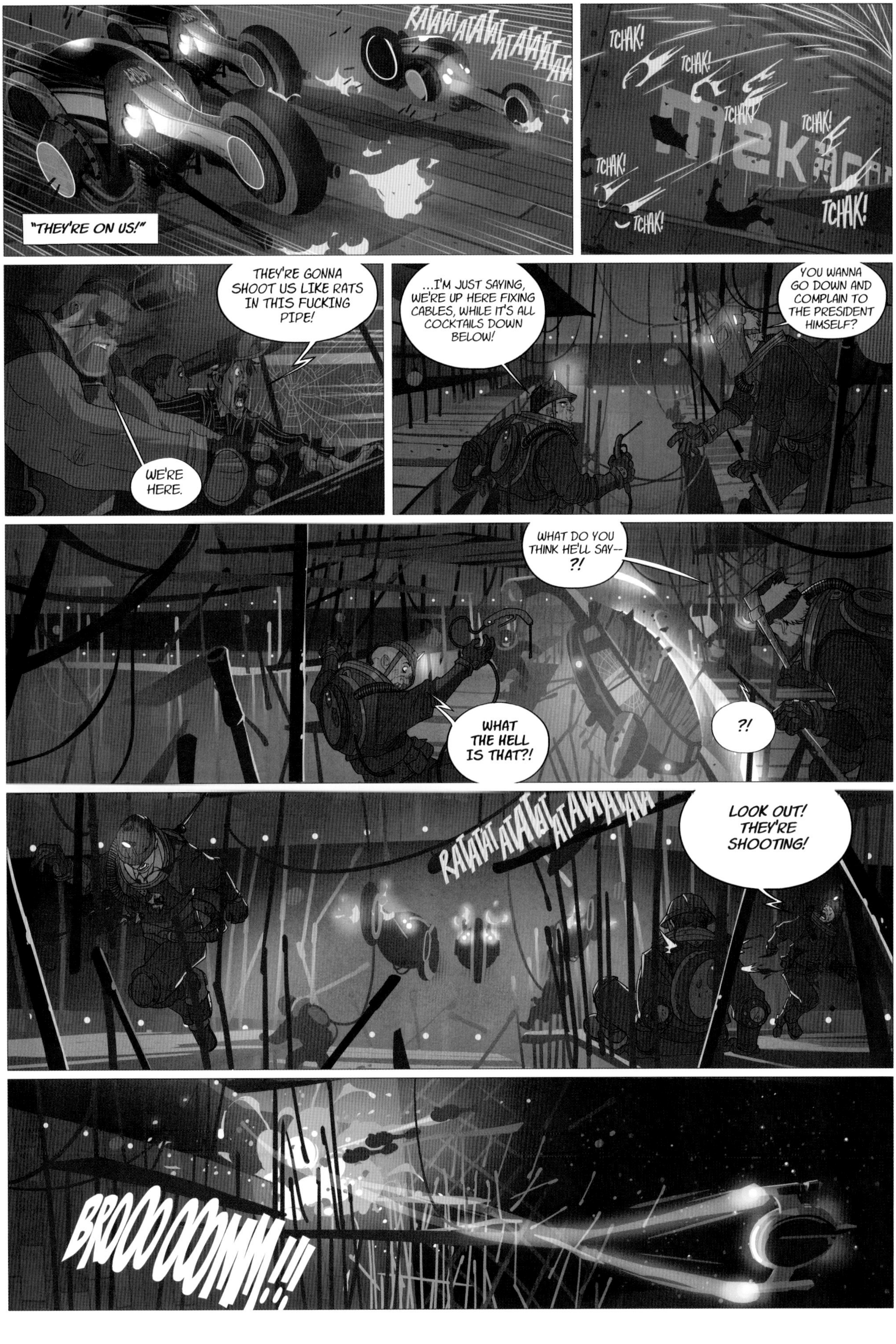

RATATATATATATATATATATATA
"THEY'RE ON US!"
TCHAK!
TCHAK!
TCHAK!
TCHAK!
TCHAK!
TCHAK!
TCHAK!
THEY'RE GONNA SHOOT US LIKE RATS IN THIS FUCKING PIPE!
WE'RE HERE.
...I'M JUST SAYING, WE'RE UP HERE FIXING CABLES, WHILE IT'S ALL COCKTAILS DOWN BELOW!
YOU WANNA GO DOWN AND COMPLAIN TO THE PRESIDENT HIMSELF?
WHAT DO YOU THINK HE'LL SAY-- ?!
WHAT THE HELL IS THAT?!
?!
RATATATATATATATATATATATA
LOOK OUT! THEY'RE SHOOTING!
BROOOOOOMM!!!

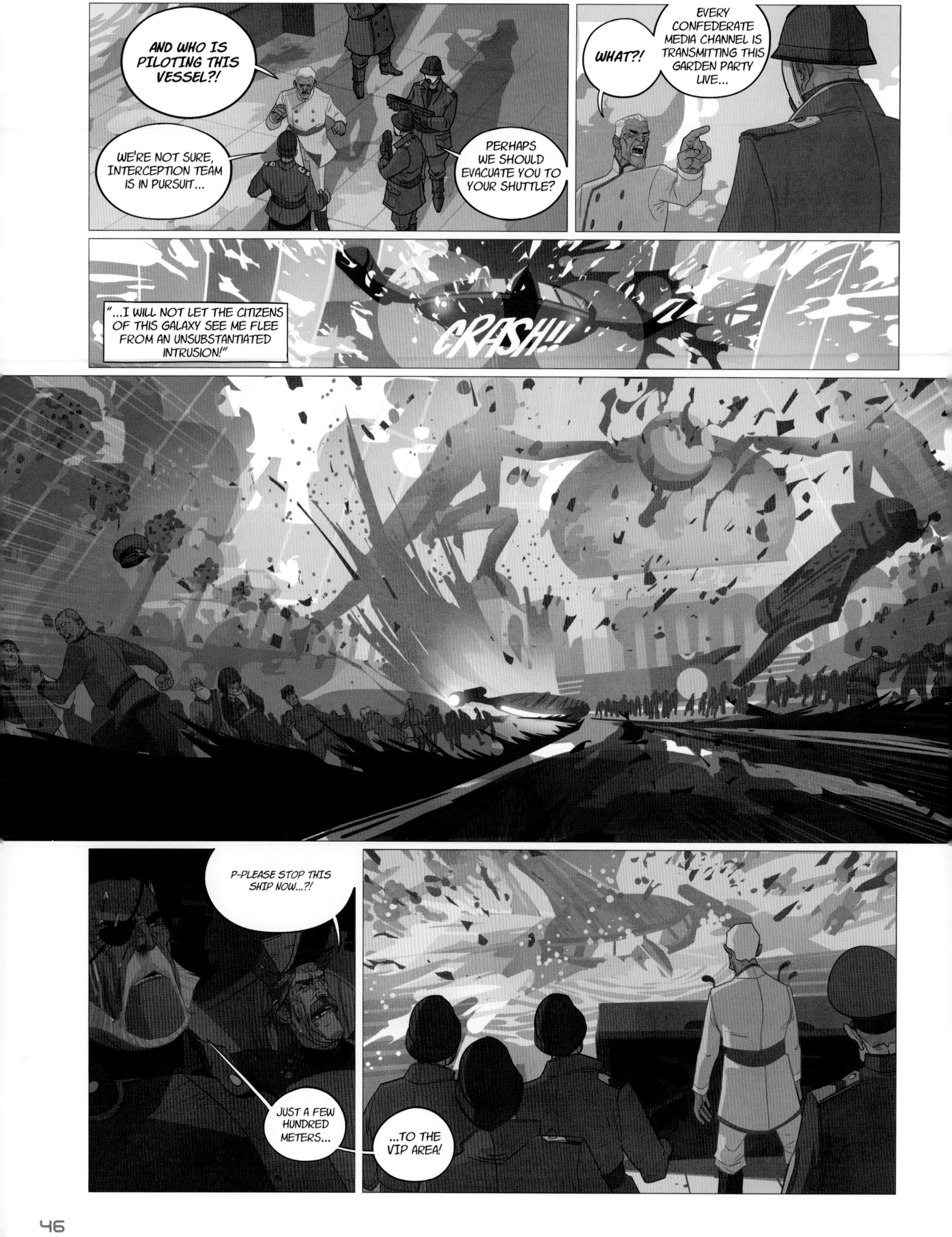
AND WHO IS PILOTING THIS VESSEL?!
WE'RE NOT SURE, INTERCEPTION TEAM IS IN PURSUIT...
PERHAPS WE SHOULD EVACUATE YOU TO YOUR SHUTTLE?
EVERY CONFEDERATE MEDIA CHANNEL IS TRANSMITTING THIS GARDEN PARTY LIVE...
WHAT?!
"...I WILL NOT LET THE CITIZENS OF THIS GALAXY SEE ME FLEE FROM AN UNSUBSTANTIATED INTRUSION!"
CRASH!!
P-PLEASE STOP THIS SHIP NOW...?!
JUST A FEW HUNDRED METERS...
...TO THE VIP AREA!

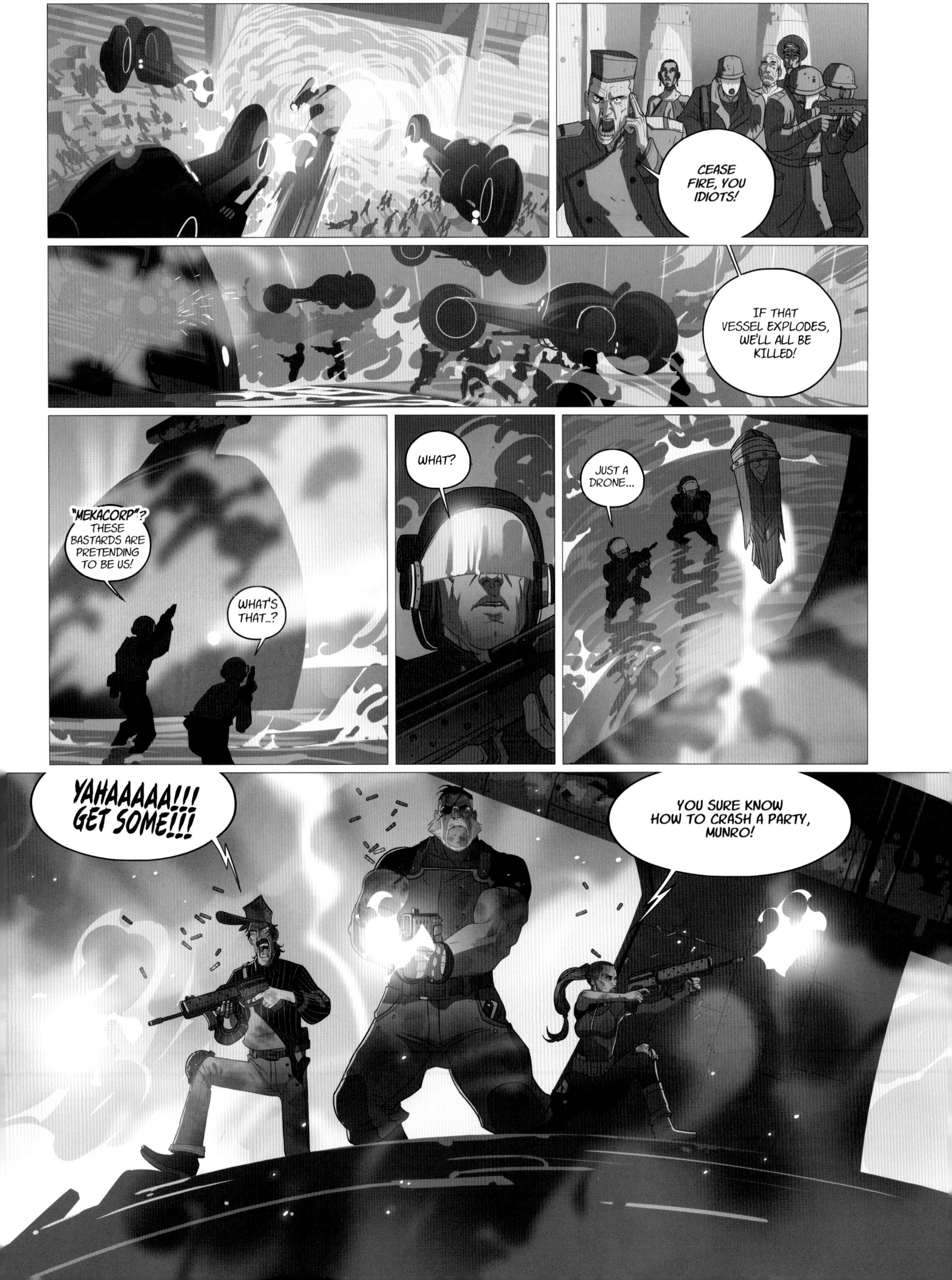
CEASE FIRE, YOU IDIOTS!
IF THAT VESSEL EXPLODES, WE'LL ALL BE KILLED!
"MEKACORP"? THESE BASTARDS ARE PRETENDING TO BE US!
WHAT'S THAT...?
WHAT?
JUST A DRONE...
YAHAAAAA!!! GET SOME!!!
YOU SURE KNOW HOW TO CRASH A PARTY, MUNRO!

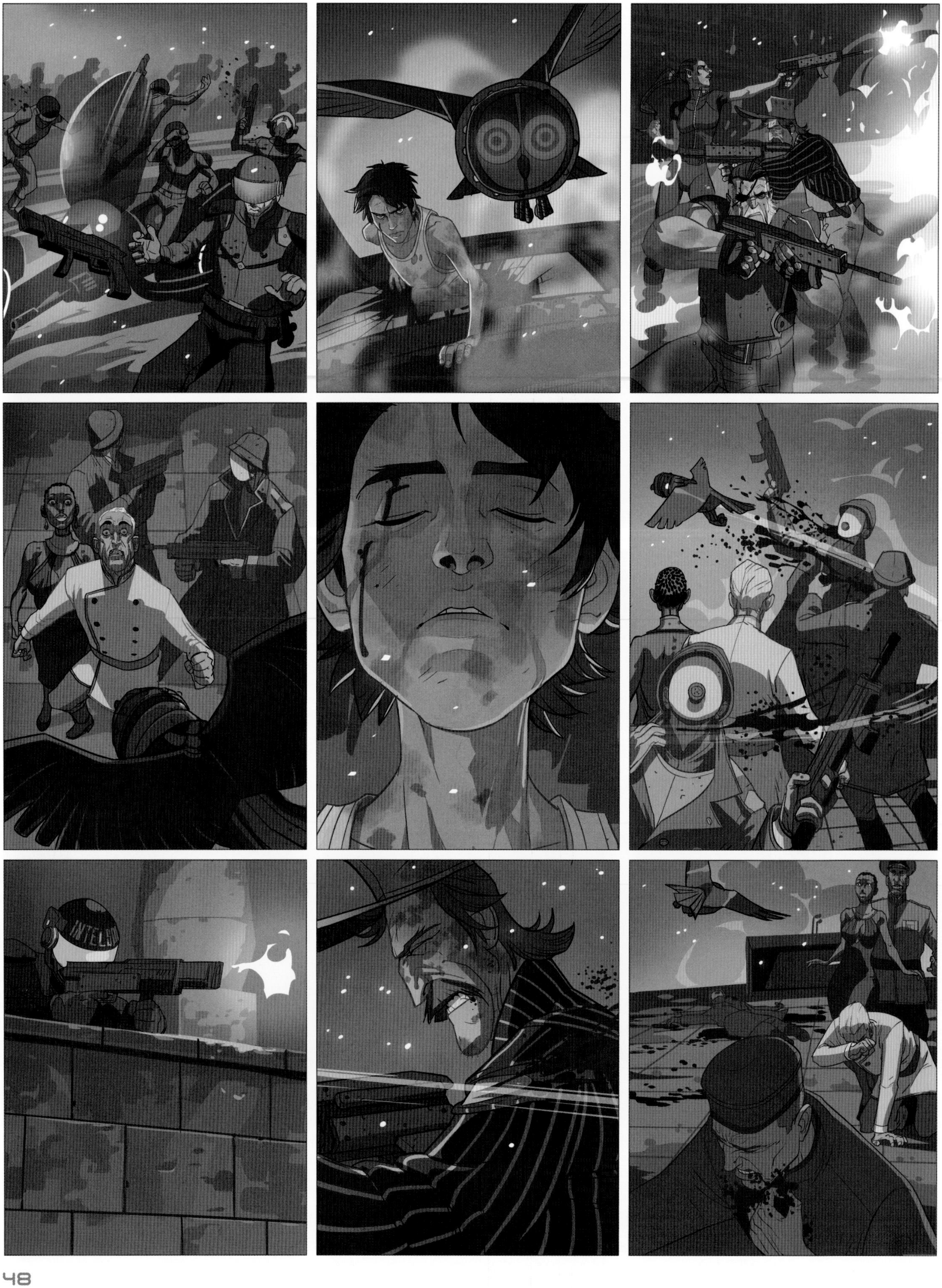

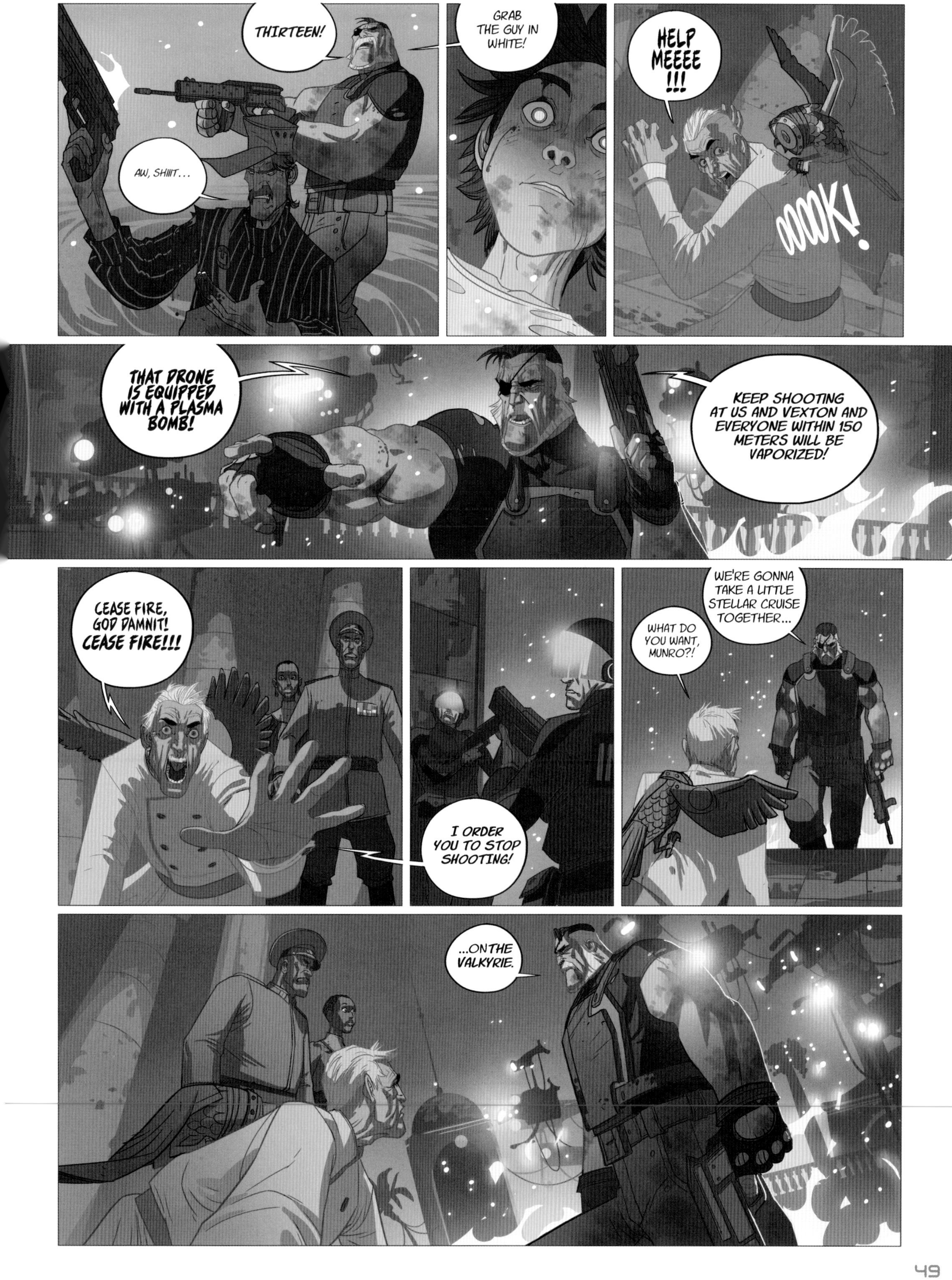
THIRTEEN!
AW, SHIIIT...
GRAB THE GUY IN WHITE!
HELP MEEEE !!!
OOOOK!
THAT DRONE IS EQUIPPED WITH A PLASMA BOMB!
KEEP SHOOTING AT US AND VEXTON AND EVERYONE WITHIN 150 METERS WILL BE VAPORIZED!
CEASE FIRE, GOD DAMNIT! CEASE FIRE!!!
I ORDER YOU TO STOP SHOOTING!
WHAT DO YOU WANT, MUNRO?!
WE'RE GONNA TAKE A LITTLE STELLAR CRUISE TOGETHER...
...ON THE VALKYRIE.

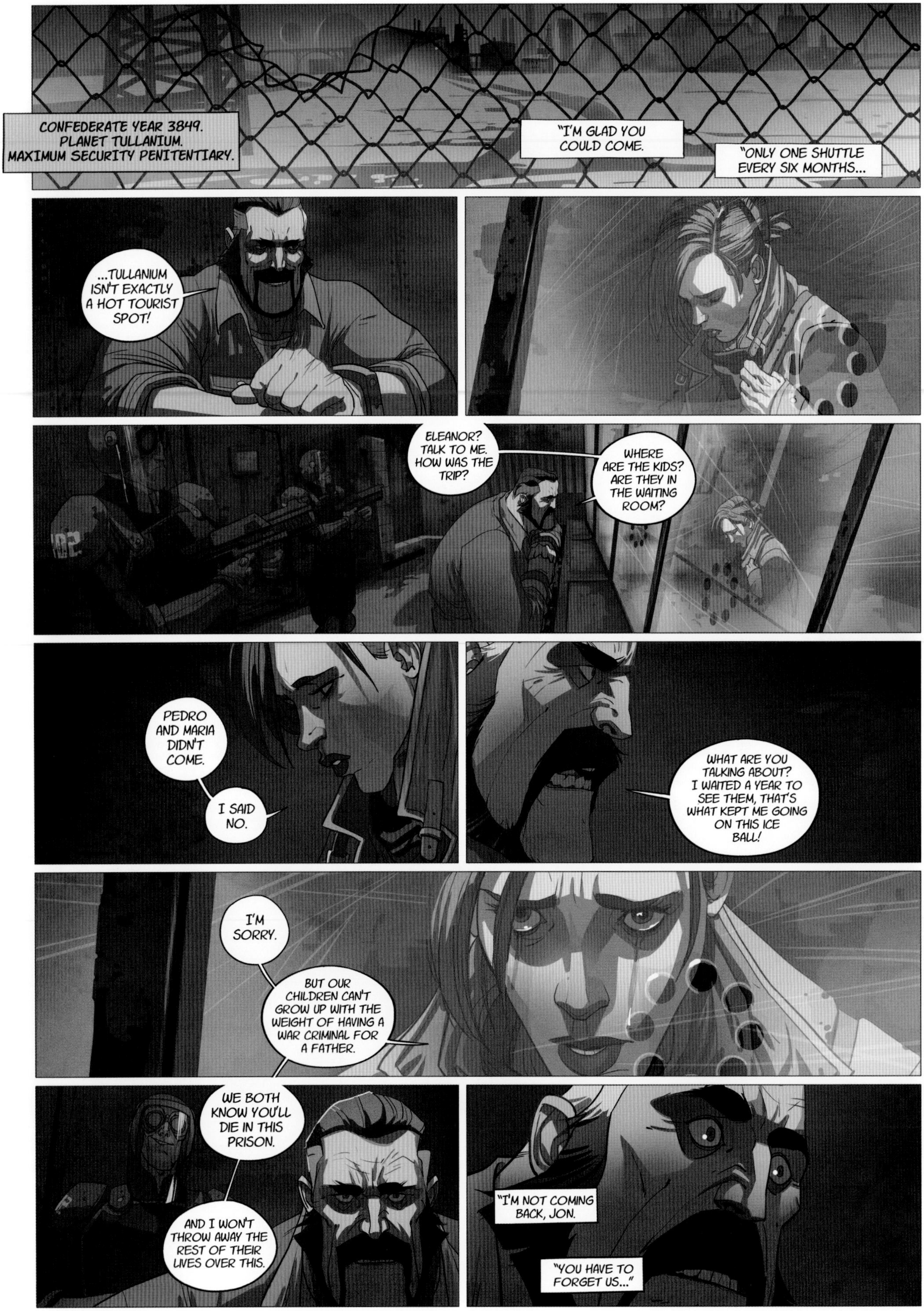

CONFEDERATE YEAR 3849.
PLANET TULLANIUM.
MAXIMUM SECURITY PENITENTIARY.
"I'M GLAD YOU COULD COME.
"ONLY ONE SHUTTLE EVERY SIX MONTHS...
...TULLANIUM ISN'T EXACTLY A HOT TOURIST SPOT!
ELEANOR? TALK TO ME. HOW WAS THE TRIP?
WHERE ARE THE KIDS? ARE THEY IN THE WAITING ROOM?
PEDRO AND MARIA DIDN'T COME.
I SAID NO.
WHAT ARE YOU TALKING ABOUT? I WAITED A YEAR TO SEE THEM, THAT'S WHAT KEPT ME GOING ON THIS ICE BALL!
I'M SORRY.
BUT OUR CHILDREN CAN'T GROW UP WITH THE WEIGHT OF HAVING A WAR CRIMINAL FOR A FATHER.
WE BOTH KNOW YOU'LL DIE IN THIS PRISON.
AND I WON'T THROW AWAY THE REST OF THEIR LIVES OVER THIS.
"I'M NOT COMING BACK, JON.
"YOU HAVE TO FORGET US..."

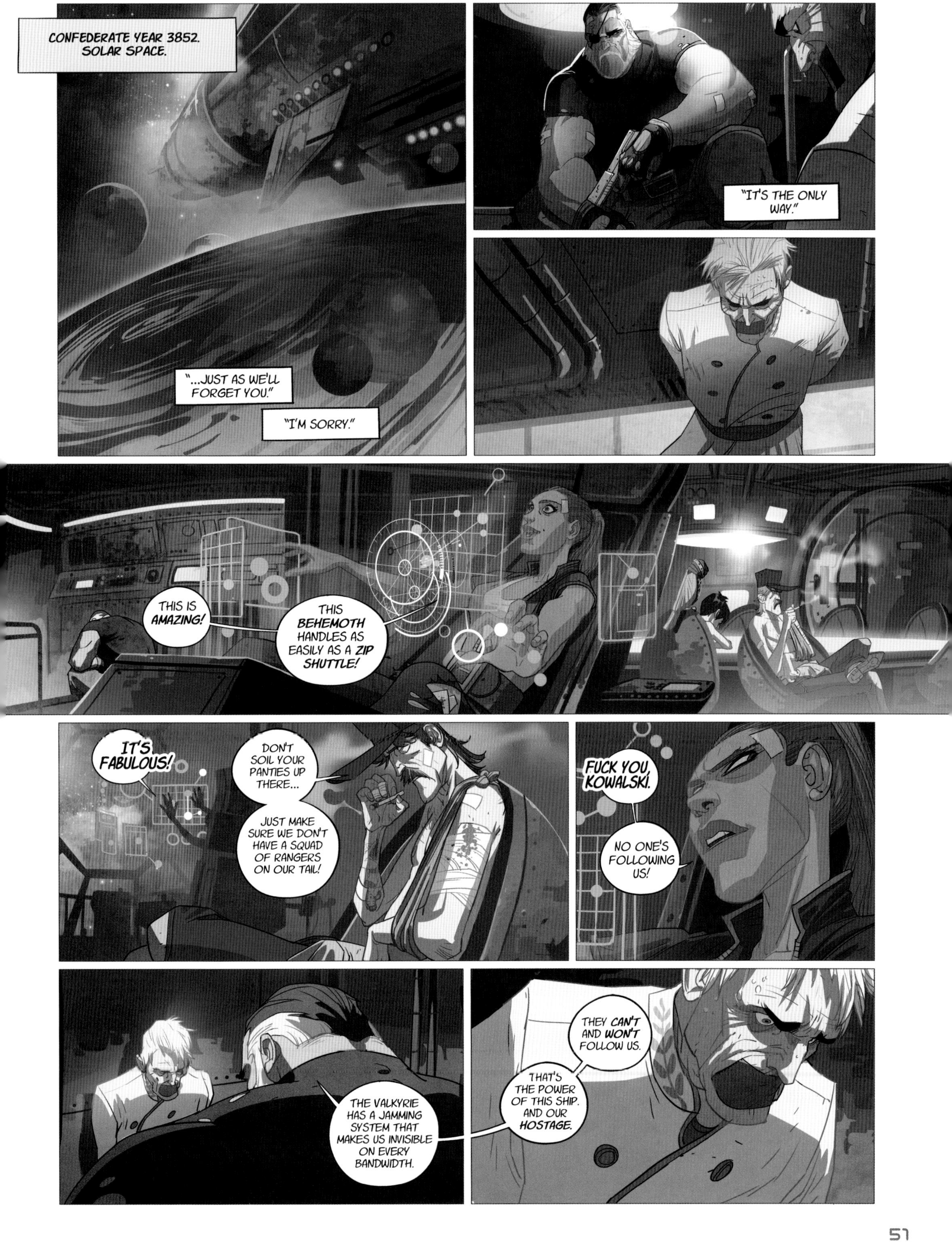
CONFEDERATE YEAR 3852.
SOLAR SPACE.
"...JUST AS WE'LL FORGET YOU."
"I'M SORRY."
"IT'S THE ONLY WAY."
THIS IS AMAZING!
THIS BEHEMOTH HANDLES AS EASILY AS A ZIP SHUTTLE!
IT'S FABULOUS!
DON'T SOIL YOUR PANTIES UP THERE...
JUST MAKE SURE WE DON'T HAVE A SQUAD OF RANGERS ON OUR TAIL!
FUCK YOU, KOWALSKI.
NO ONE'S FOLLOWING US!
THE VALKYRIE HAS A JAMMING SYSTEM THAT MAKES US INVISIBLE ON EVERY BANDWIDTH.
THEY CAN'T AND WON'T FOLLOW US.
THAT'S THE POWER OF THIS SHIP. AND OUR HOSTAGE.

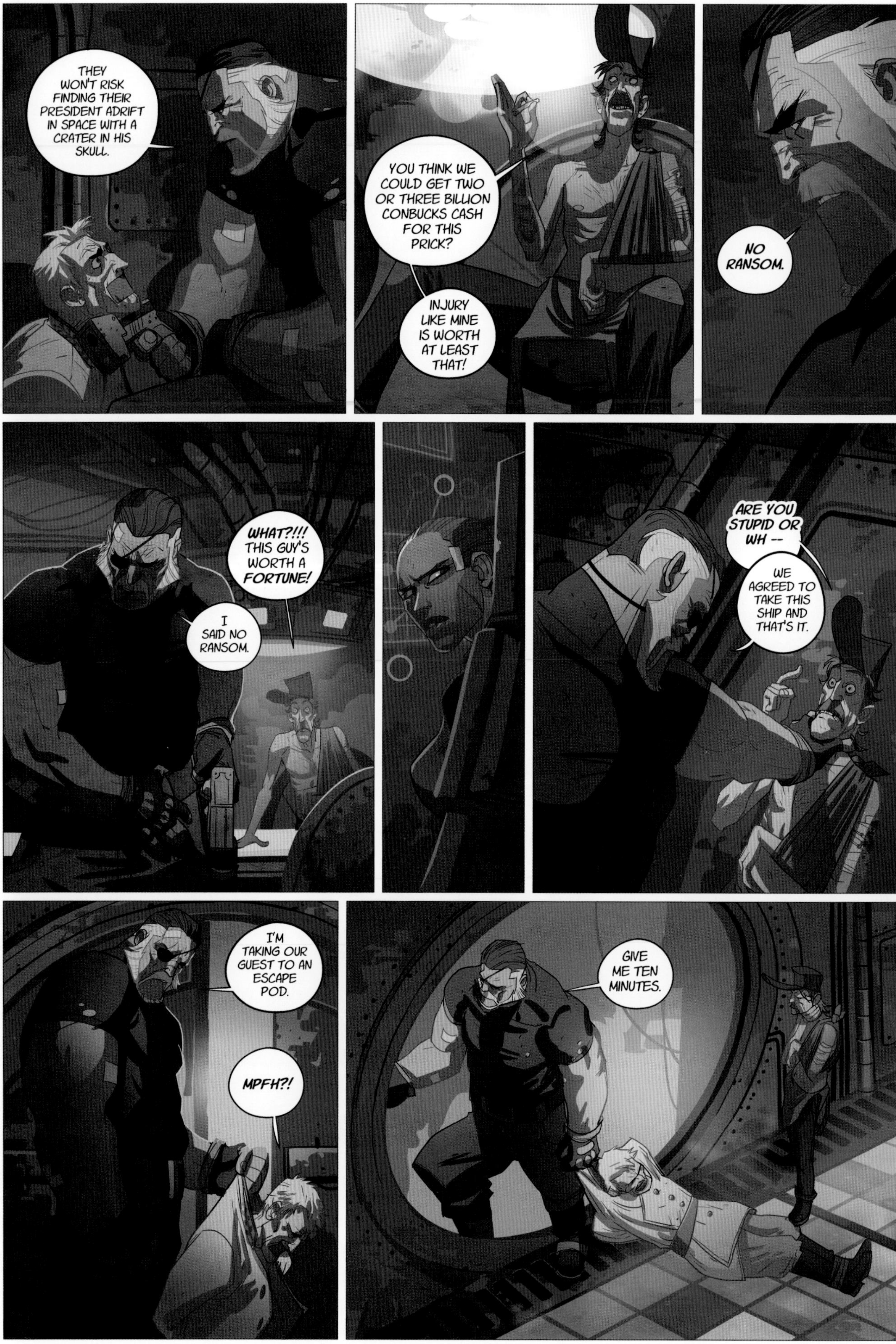
THEY WON'T RISK FINDING THEIR PRESIDENT ADRIFT IN SPACE WITH A CRATER IN HIS SKULL.
YOU THINK WE COULD GET TWO OR THREE BILLION CONBUCKS CASH FOR THIS PRICK?
INJURY LIKE MINE IS WORTH AT LEAST THAT!
NO RANSOM.
WHAT?!!! THIS GUY'S WORTH A FORTUNE!
I SAID NO RANSOM.
ARE YOU STUPID OR WH --
WE AGREED TO TAKE THIS SHIP AND THAT'S IT.
I'M TAKING OUR GUEST TO AN ESCAPE POD.
MPFH?!
GIVE ME TEN MINUTES.

WHY?

WHY LET ME GO, MUNRO?

TO BECOME YOUR WORST NIGHTMARE.

"YOU WILL REGRET SURVIVING THIS...

FWOOOOOOOOSH!

"...BECAUSE I PROMISE YOU, VEXTON...

"...FOR YOU..."

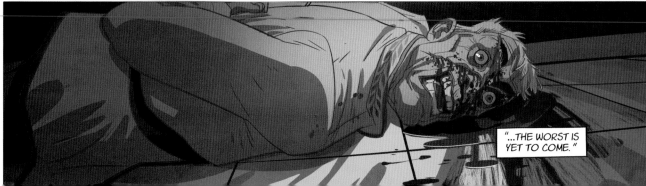

"...THE WORST IS YET TO COME."

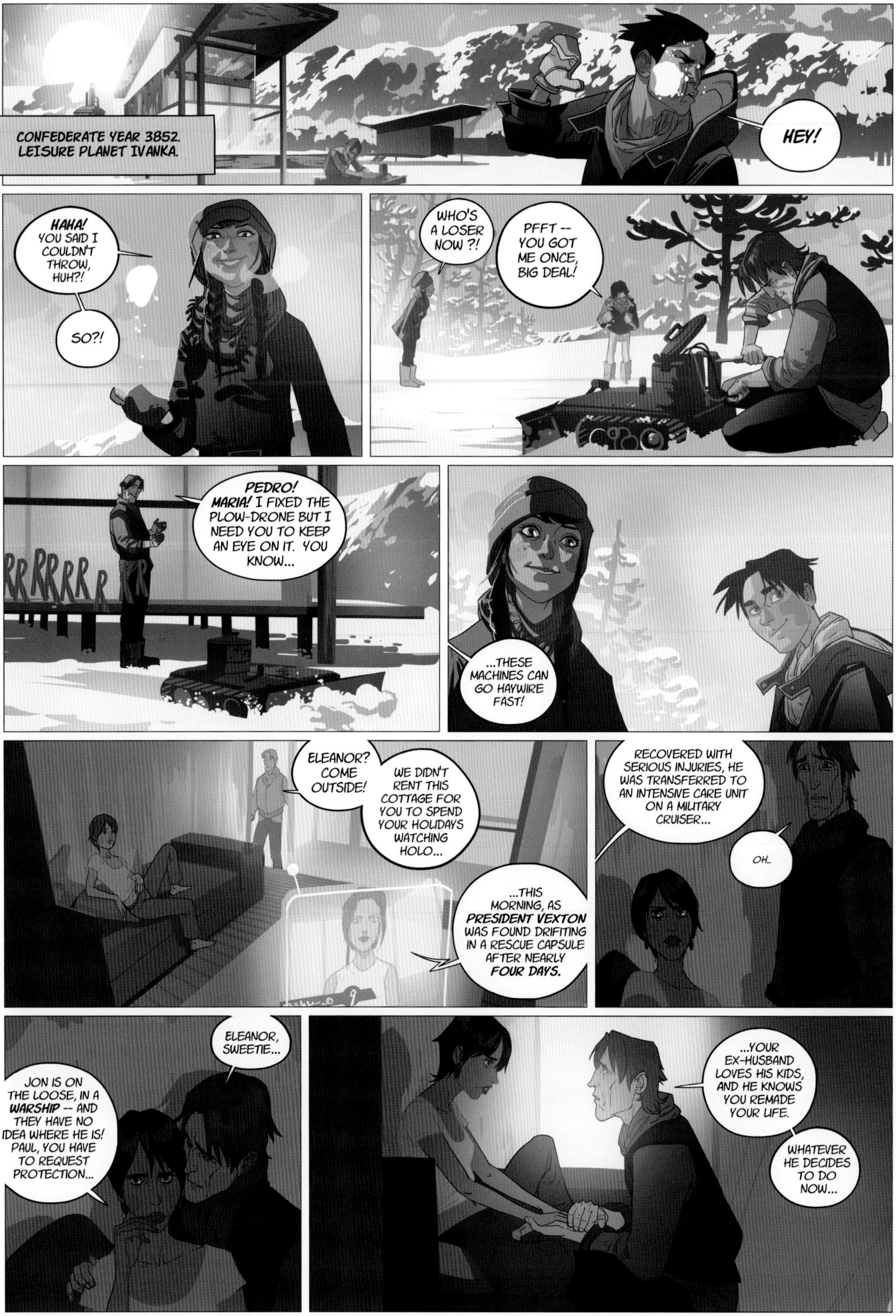
CONFEDERATE YEAR 3852.
LEISURE PLANET IVANKA.
HEY!
HAHA! YOU SAID I COULDN'T THROW, HUH?!
SO?!
WHO'S A LOSER NOW ?!
PFFT -- YOU GOT ME ONCE, BIG DEAL!
PEDRO! MARIA! I FIXED THE PLOW-DRONE BUT I NEED YOU TO KEEP AN EYE ON IT. YOU KNOW...
RRRRRRR
...THESE MACHINES CAN GO HAYWIRE FAST!
ELEANOR? COME OUTSIDE!
WE DIDN'T RENT THIS COTTAGE FOR YOU TO SPEND YOUR HOLIDAYS WATCHING HOLO...
...THIS MORNING, AS PRESIDENT VEXTON WAS FOUND DRIFITING IN A RESCUE CAPSULE AFTER NEARLY FOUR DAYS.
RECOVERED WITH SERIOUS INJURIES, HE WAS TRANSFERRED TO AN INTENSIVE CARE UNIT ON A MILITARY CRUISER...
OH...
ELEANOR, SWEETIE...
JON IS ON THE LOOSE, IN A WARSHIP -- AND THEY HAVE NO IDEA WHERE HE IS! PAUL, YOU HAVE TO REQUEST PROTECTION...
...YOUR EX-HUSBAND LOVES HIS KIDS, AND HE KNOWS YOU REMADE YOUR LIFE.
WHATEVER HE DECIDES TO DO NOW...

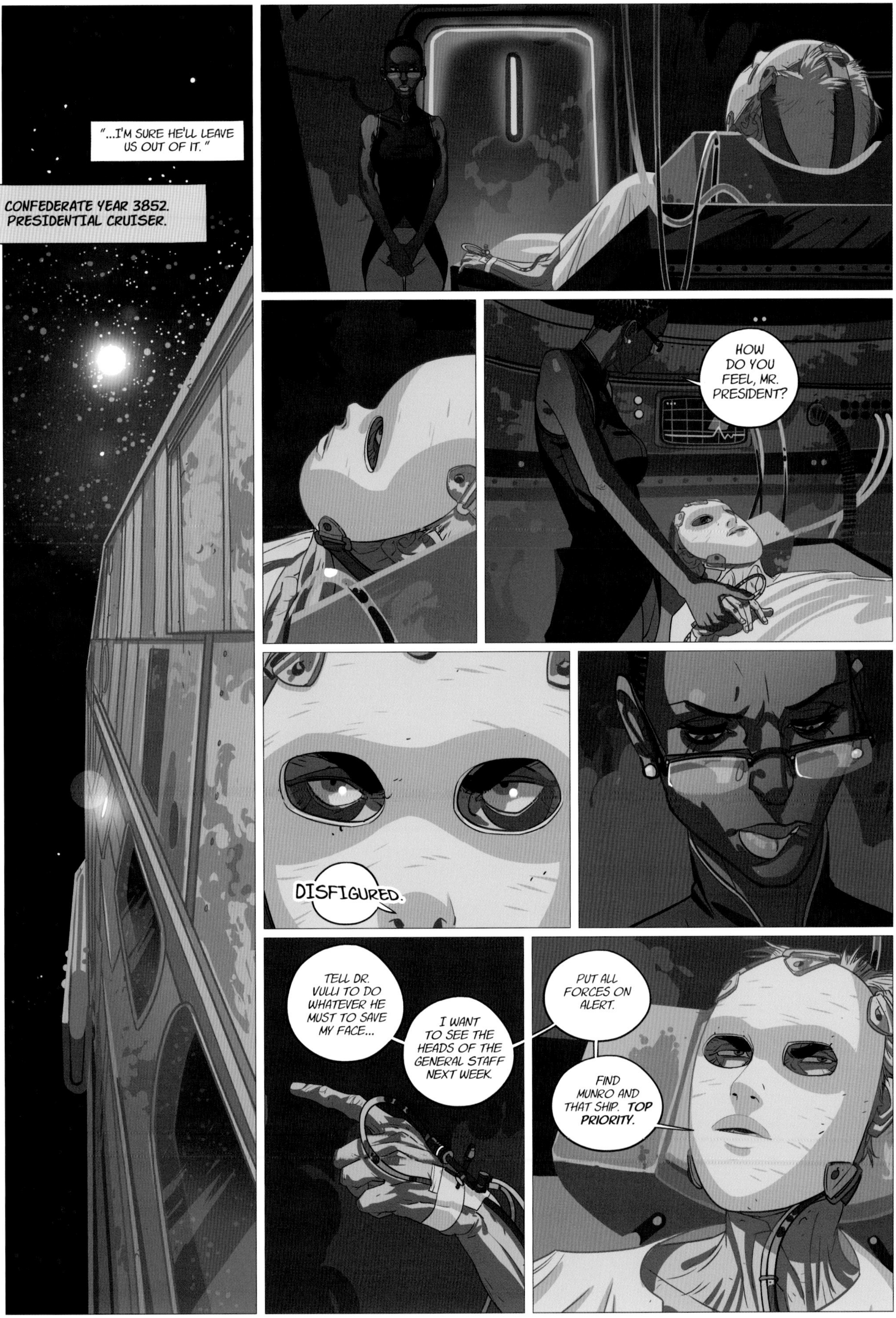
"...I'M SURE HE'LL LEAVE US OUT OF IT."
CONFEDERATE YEAR 3852. PRESIDENTIAL CRUISER.
HOW DO YOU FEEL, MR. PRESIDENT?
DISFIGURED.
TELL DR. VULLI TO DO WHATEVER HE MUST TO SAVE MY FACE...
I WANT TO SEE THE HEADS OF THE GENERAL STAFF NEXT WEEK.
PUT ALL FORCES ON ALERT.
FIND MUNRO AND THAT SHIP. **TOP PRIORITY.**

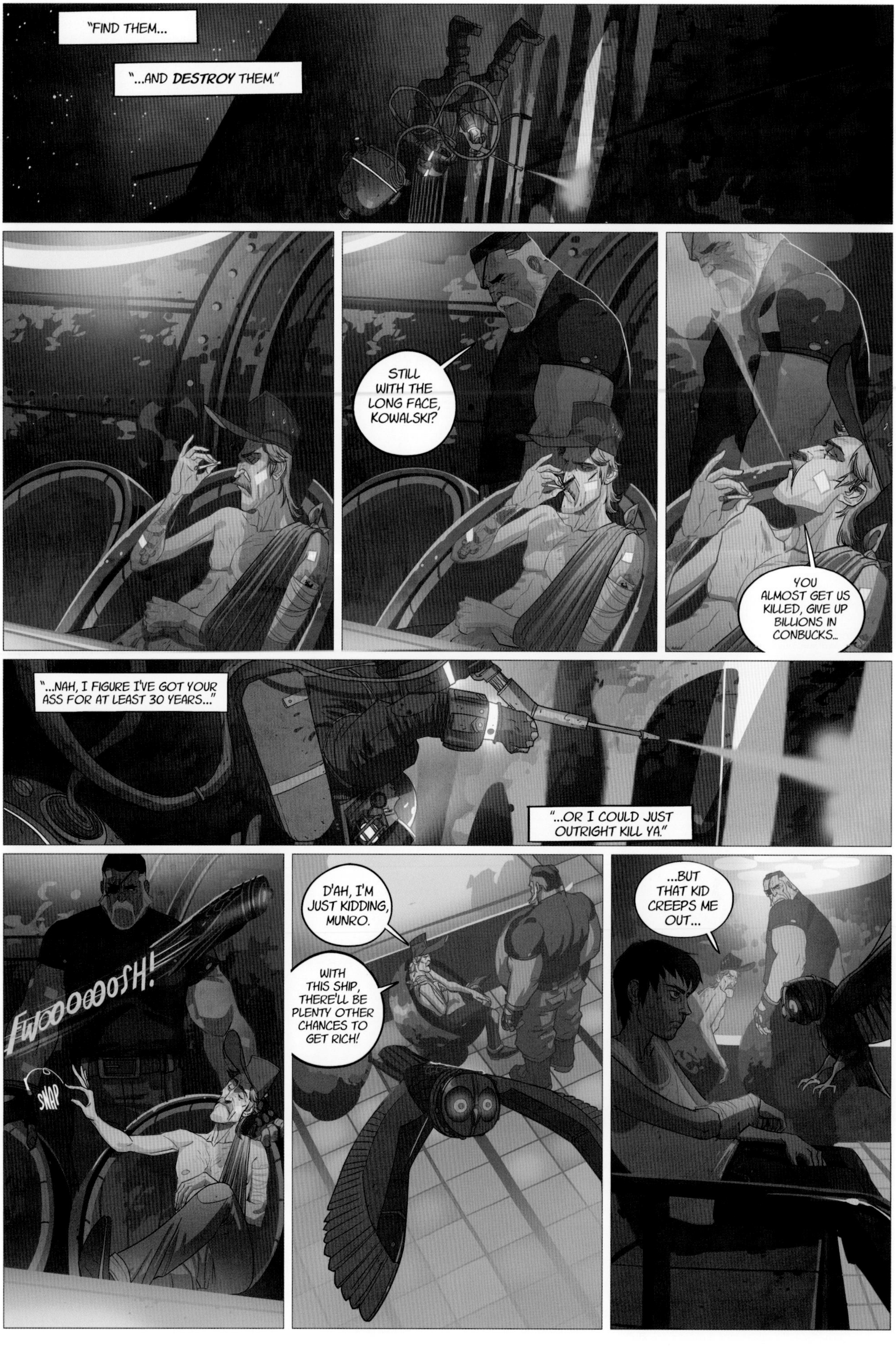
"FIND THEM...
"...AND DESTROY THEM."
STILL WITH THE LONG FACE, KOWALSKI?
YOU ALMOST GET US KILLED, GIVE UP BILLIONS IN CONBUCKS...
"...NAH, I FIGURE I'VE GOT YOUR ASS FOR AT LEAST 30 YEARS..."
"...OR I COULD JUST OUTRIGHT KILL YA."
FWOOOOOOSH!
SNAP
D'AH, I'M JUST KIDDING, MUNRO.
WITH THIS SHIP, THERE'LL BE PLENTY OTHER CHANCES TO GET RICH!
...BUT THAT KID CREEPS ME OUT...

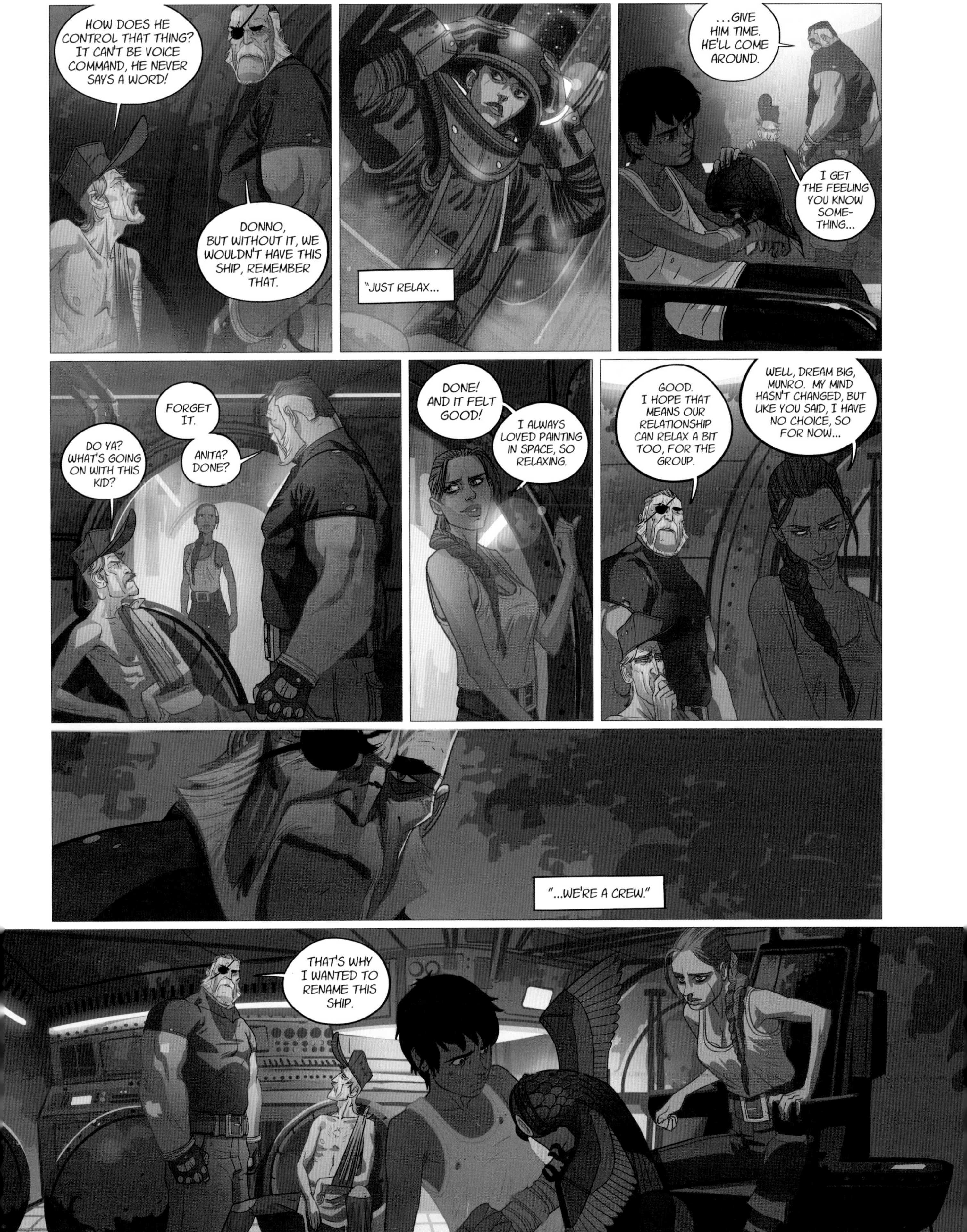
HOW DOES HE CONTROL THAT THING? IT CAN'T BE VOICE COMMAND, HE NEVER SAYS A WORD!
DONNO, BUT WITHOUT IT, WE WOULDN'T HAVE THIS SHIP, REMEMBER THAT.
"JUST RELAX...
...GIVE HIM TIME. HE'LL COME AROUND.
I GET THE FEELING YOU KNOW SOME-THING...
DO YA? WHAT'S GOING ON WITH THIS KID?
FORGET IT.
ANITA? DONE?
DONE! AND IT FELT GOOD!
I ALWAYS LOVED PAINTING IN SPACE, SO RELAXING.
GOOD. I HOPE THAT MEANS OUR RELATIONSHIP CAN RELAX A BIT TOO, FOR THE GROUP.
WELL, DREAM BIG, MUNRO. MY MIND HASN'T CHANGED, BUT LIKE YOU SAID, I HAVE NO CHOICE, SO FOR NOW...
"...WE'RE A CREW."
THAT'S WHY I WANTED TO RENAME THIS SHIP.

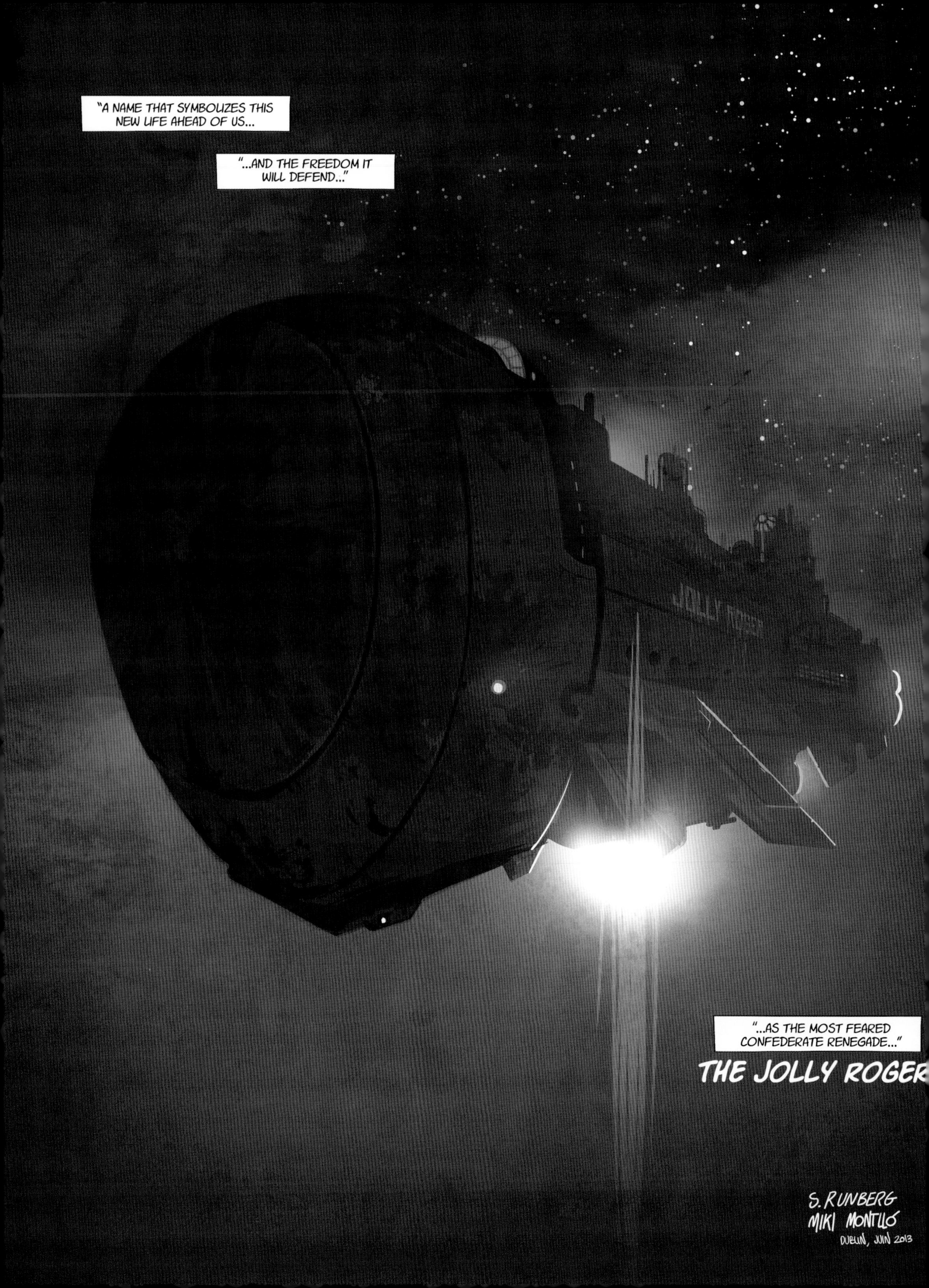
"A NAME THAT SYMBOLIZES THIS NEW LIFE AHEAD OF US...
"...AND THE FREEDOM IT WILL DEFEND..."
JOLLY ROGER
"...AS THE MOST FEARED CONFEDERATE RENEGADE..."
THE JOLLY ROGER
S. RUNBERG
MIKI MONTLLÓ
DUBLIN, JUIN 2013

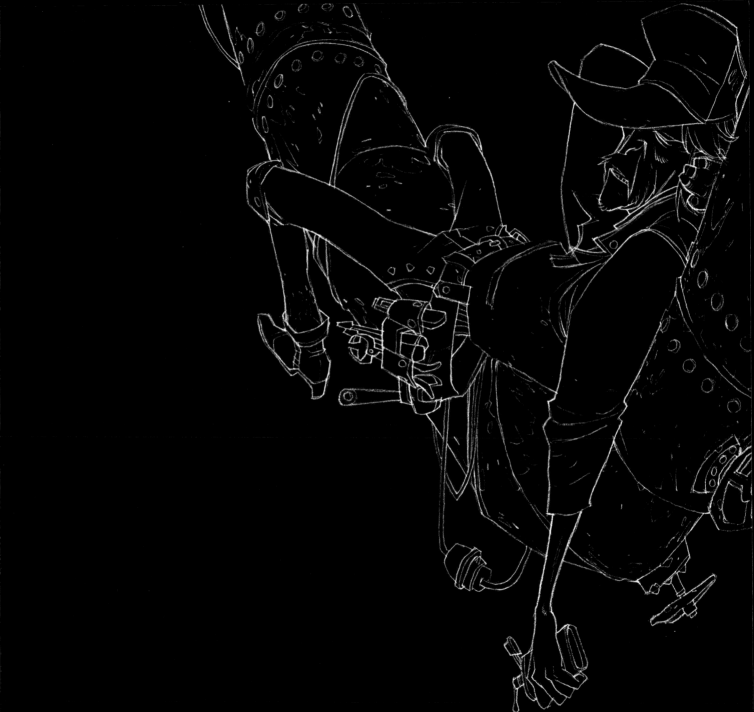

CHAPTER TWO :
DETONATIONS

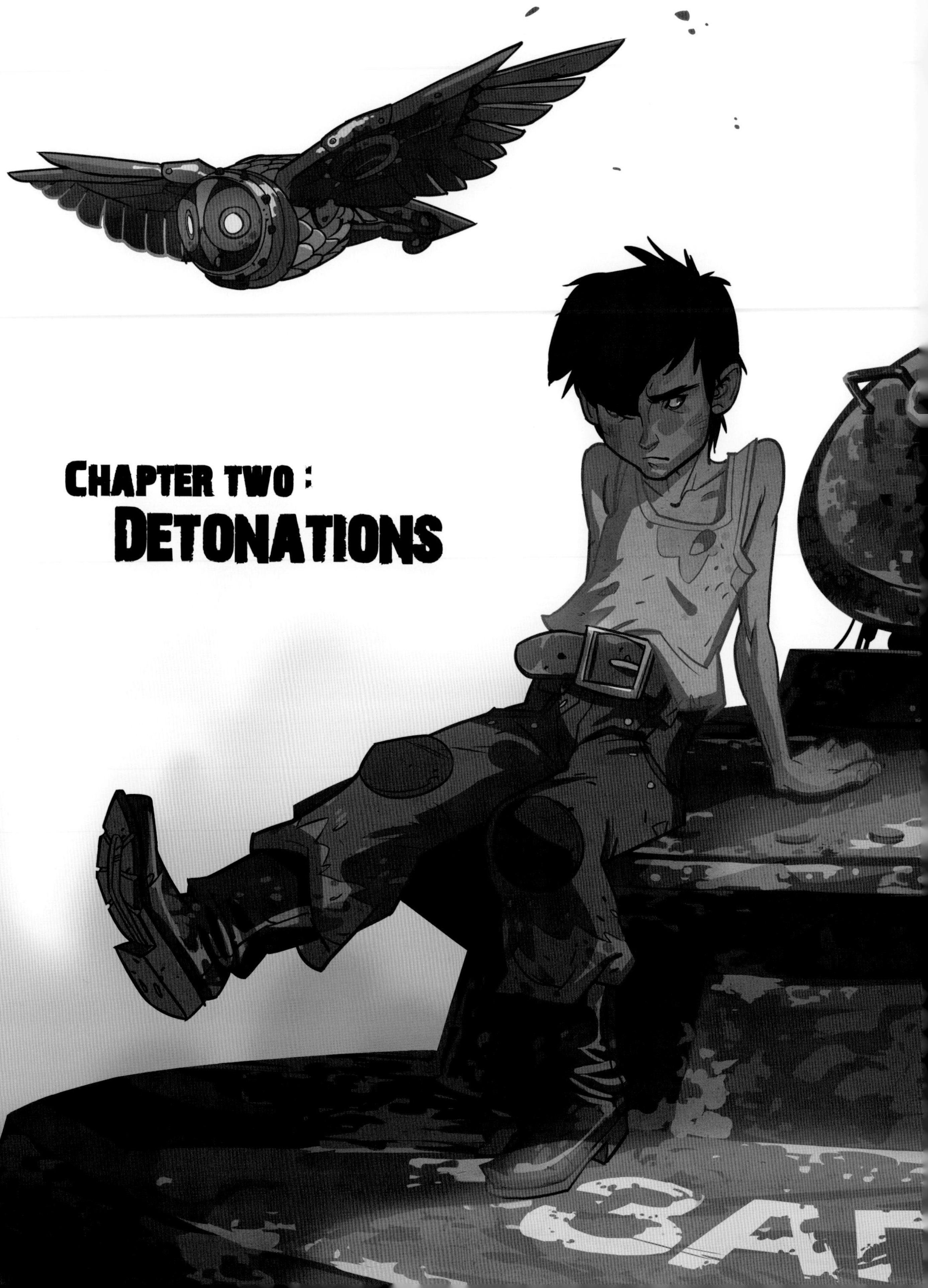

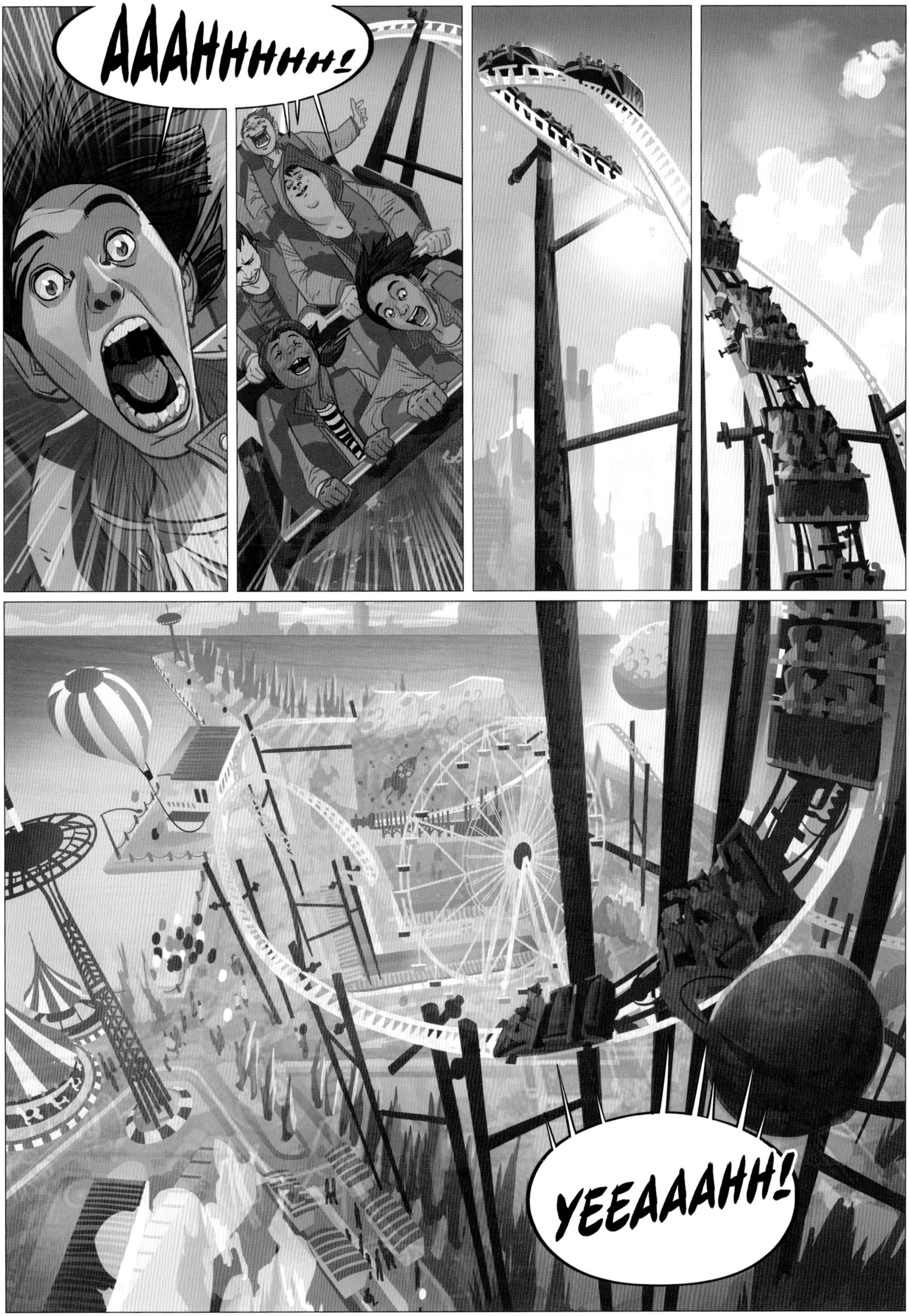
AAAHHHHH!
YEEAAAHH!

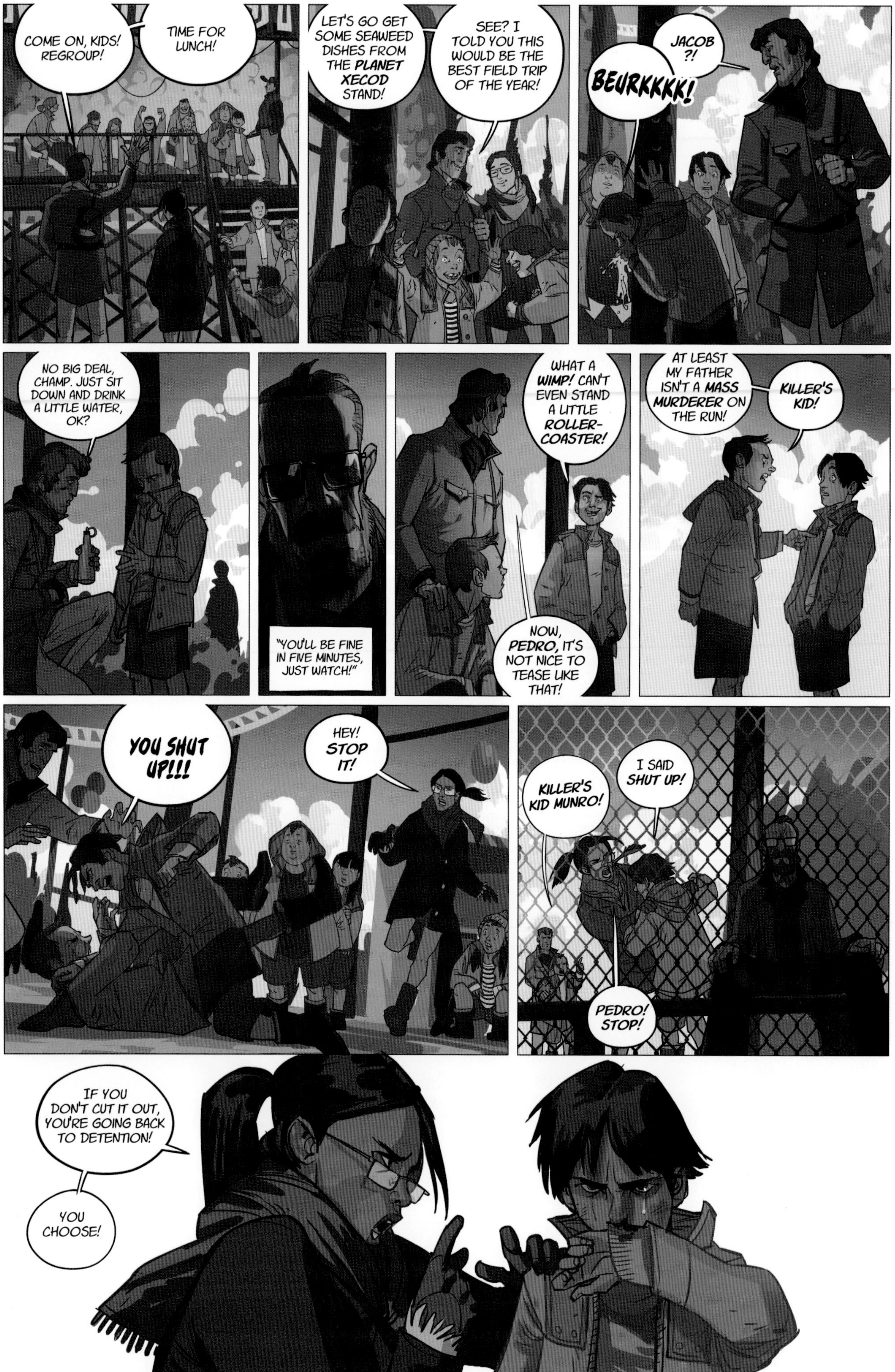
COME ON, KIDS! REGROUP!
TIME FOR LUNCH!
LET'S GO GET SOME SEAWEED DISHES FROM THE PLANET XECOD STAND!
SEE? I TOLD YOU THIS WOULD BE THE BEST FIELD TRIP OF THE YEAR!
JACOB ?!
BEURKKKK!
NO BIG DEAL, CHAMP. JUST SIT DOWN AND DRINK A LITTLE WATER, OK?
"YOU'LL BE FINE IN FIVE MINUTES, JUST WATCH!"
WHAT A WIMP! CAN'T EVEN STAND A LITTLE ROLLER-COASTER!
NOW, PEDRO, IT'S NOT NICE TO TEASE LIKE THAT!
AT LEAST MY FATHER ISN'T A MASS MURDERER ON THE RUN!
KILLER'S KID!
YOU SHUT UP!!!
HEY! STOP IT!
KILLER'S KID MUNRO!
I SAID SHUT UP!
PEDRO! STOP!
IF YOU DON'T CUT IT OUT, YOU'RE GOING BACK TO DETENTION!
YOU CHOOSE!

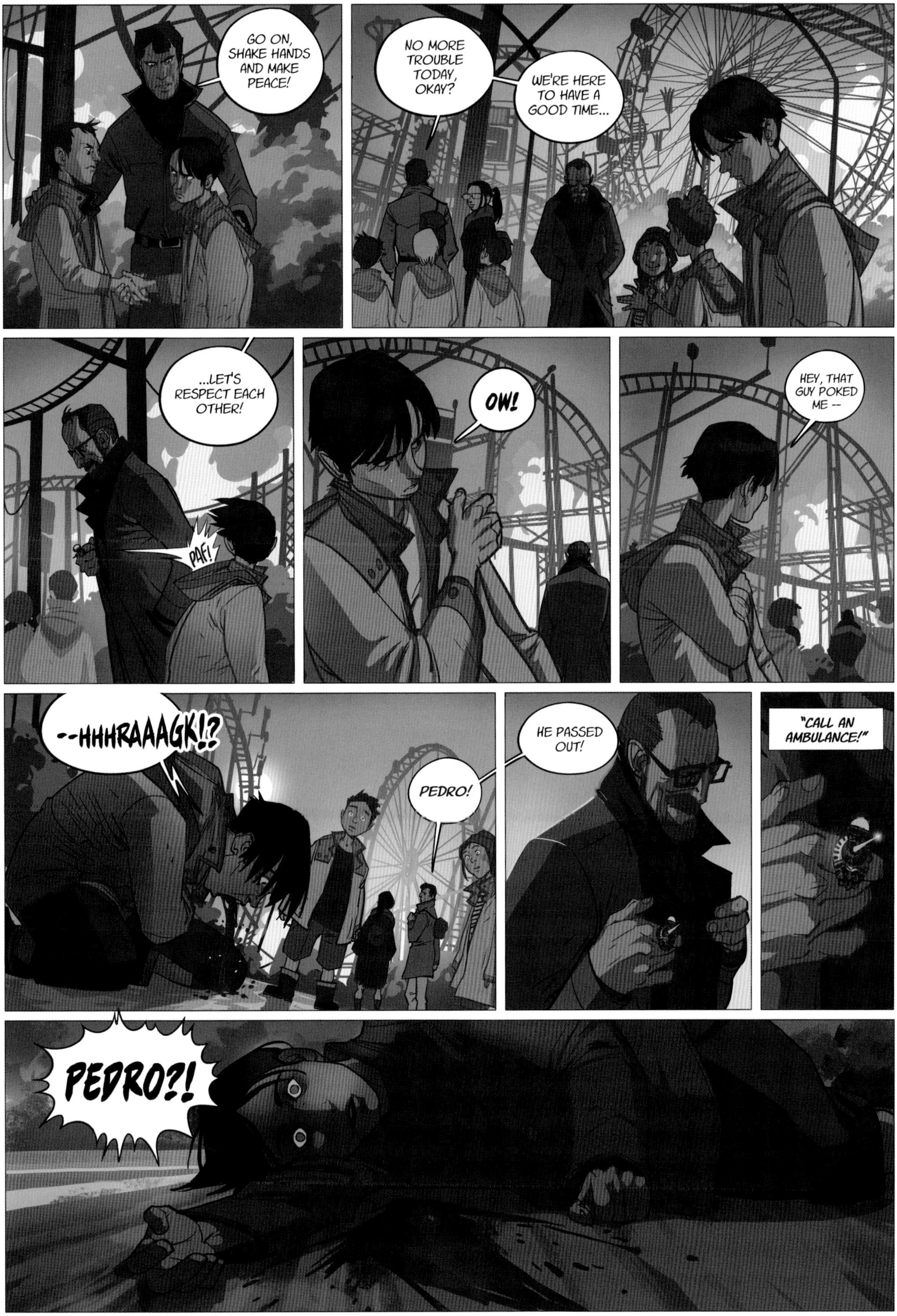
GO ON, SHAKE HANDS AND MAKE PEACE!
NO MORE TROUBLE TODAY, OKAY?
WE'RE HERE TO HAVE A GOOD TIME...
...LET'S RESPECT EACH OTHER!
PAF!
OW!
HEY, THAT GUY POKED ME --
--HHHRAAAGK!?
PEDRO!
HE PASSED OUT!
"CALL AN AMBULANCE!"
PEDRO?!

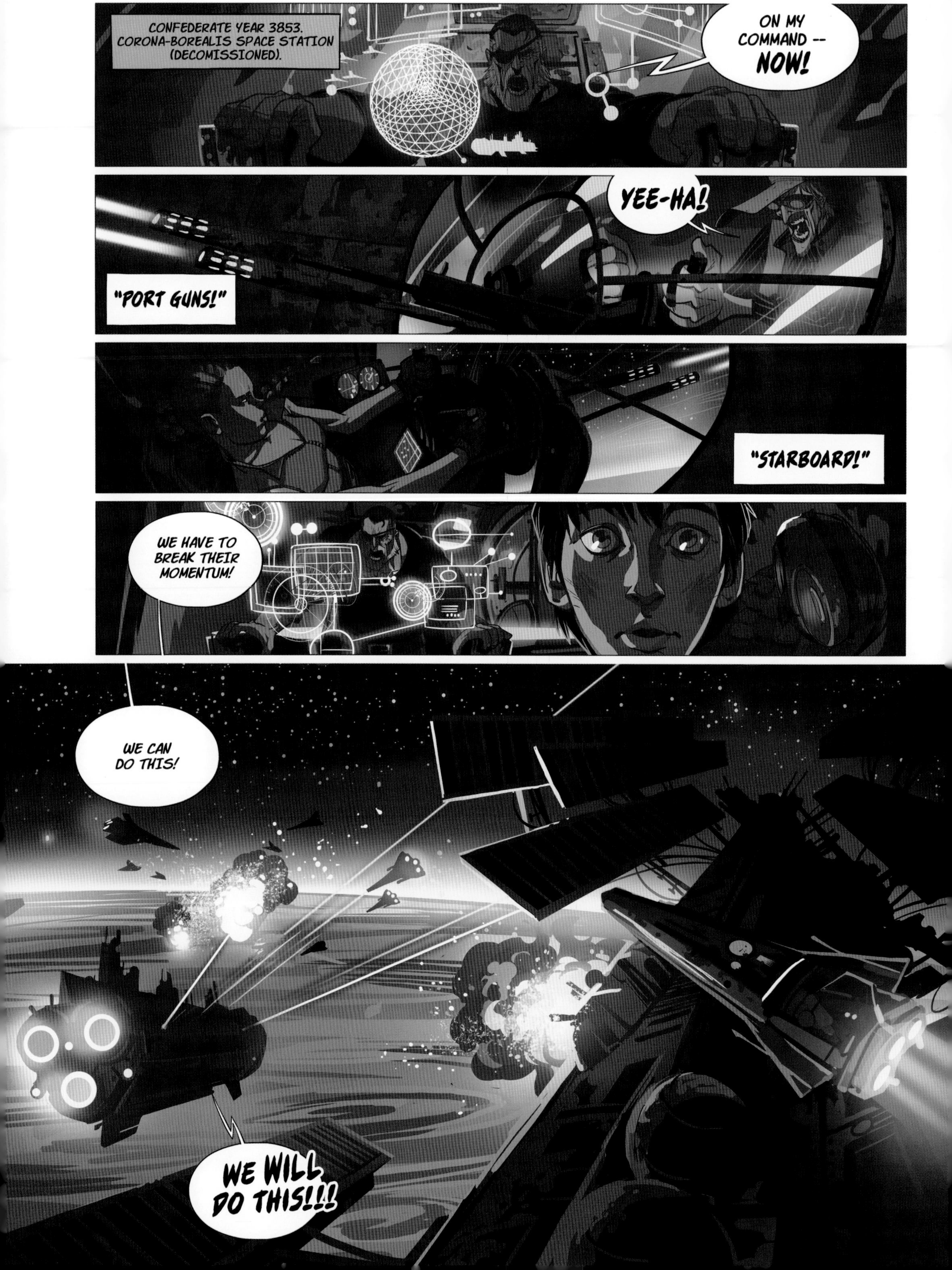
CONFEDERATE YEAR 3853. CORONA-BOREALIS SPACE STATION (DECOMISSIONED).
ON MY COMMAND -- NOW!
YEE-HA!
"PORT GUNS!"
"STARBOARD!"
WE HAVE TO BREAK THEIR MOMENTUM!
WE CAN DO THIS!
WE WILL DO THIS!!!

HEY, MUNRO?!

GREAT IDEA CHECKING OUT THIS OLD ABANDONED POWER STATION!

"NOW WE KNOW THE BEST WAY TO SCARE UP A CONFEDERATE PATROL!"

BOON!!

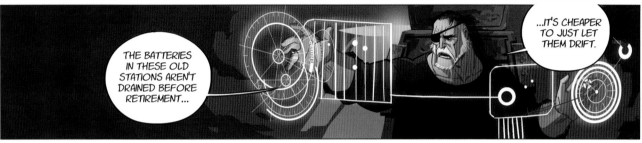

THE BATTERIES IN THESE OLD STATIONS AREN'T DRAINED BEFORE RETIREMENT...

...IT'S CHEAPER TO JUST LET THEM DRIFT.

"IT SHOULD HAVE BEEN A SIMPLE PLAN!"

THE FACT THAT THERE WAS A PATROL IN THE AREA AT THE SAME TIME IS JUST BAD LUCK!

"BESIDES, KOWALSKI --

TSCHH!

WRAHHAA!

"...FUCK YOU!"

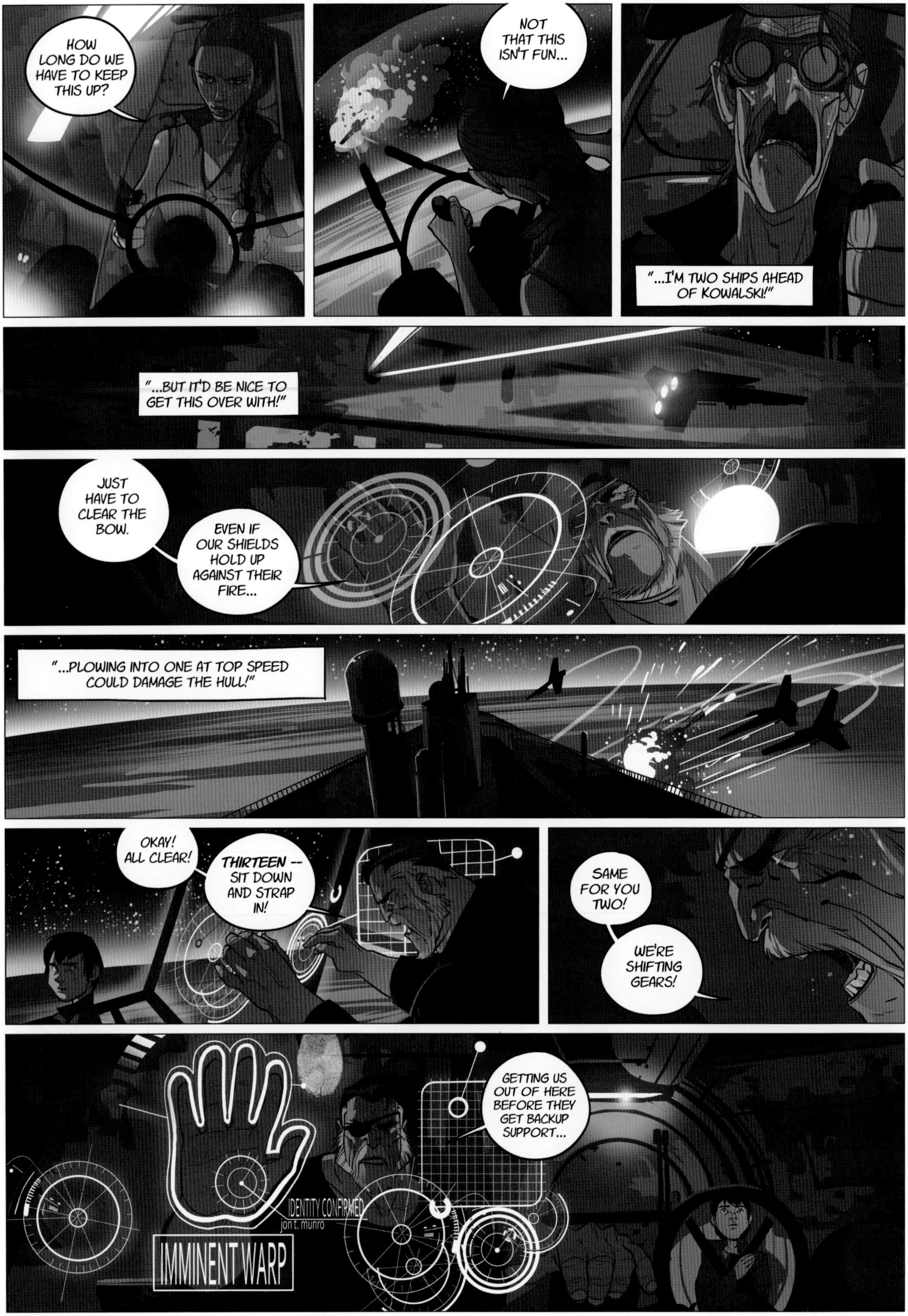
HOW LONG DO WE HAVE TO KEEP THIS UP?
NOT THAT THIS ISN'T FUN...
"...I'M TWO SHIPS AHEAD OF KOWALSKI!"
"...BUT IT'D BE NICE TO GET THIS OVER WITH!"
JUST HAVE TO CLEAR THE BOW.
EVEN IF OUR SHIELDS HOLD UP AGAINST THEIR FIRE...
"...PLOWING INTO ONE AT TOP SPEED COULD DAMAGE THE HULL!"
OKAY! ALL CLEAR!
THIRTEEN -- SIT DOWN AND STRAP IN!
SAME FOR YOU TWO!
WE'RE SHIFTING GEARS!
GETTING US OUT OF HERE BEFORE THEY GET BACKUP SUPPORT...
IDENTITY CONFIRMED
jon t. munro
IMMINENT WARP

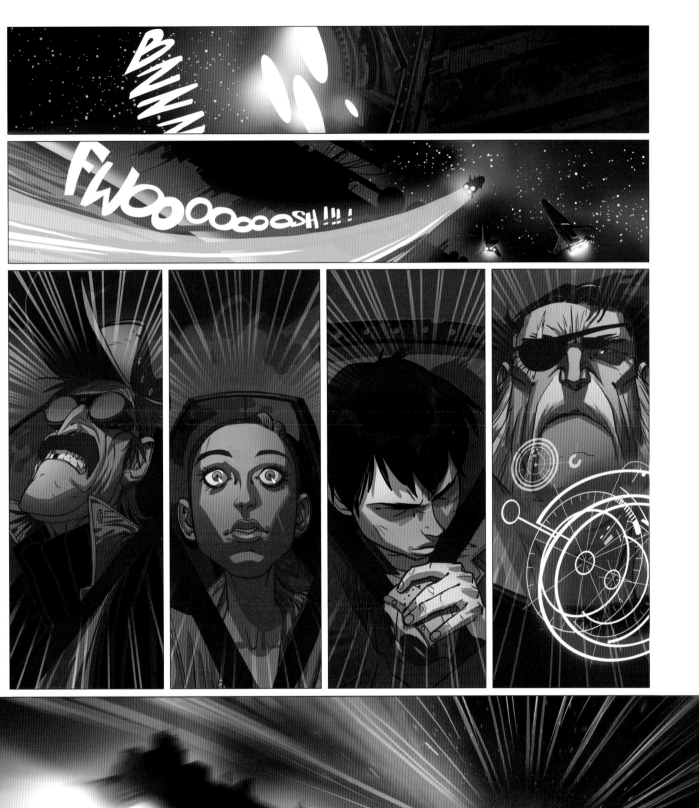

GADAMNIT!
IF WE HAD KEPT
VEXTON WITH US --

...NOT ONLY WOULD WE BE *RICH AS SHIT*...

...BUT WE WOULDN'T HAVE THE ENTIRE CONFEDERATE ARMADA ON OUR ASS!

INSTEAD, WE'RE ON THE RUN LIKE RABBITS, JUST WAITING FOR THEM TO CATCH US IN THE CABBAGE PATCH!

WE ELUDED THEM ONCE, WE'LL DO IT AGAIN. THAT'S WHAT THIS SHIP IS GOOD AT.

TELL ME, KOWALSKI, THIS NERVOUS BREAK-DOWN...

...IT WOULDN'T BE BECAUSE *ALISA* HANDLES ARTILLERY BETTER THAN YOU, WOULD IT?

WHAT? DID I TOUCH A NERVE?

BAH.

THE FACT REMAINS THAT THE JOLLY ROGER STILL HAS A SUPPLY PROBLEM.

THAT'S PROBABLY HER ONLY WEAKNESS...

"...SHE NEEDS JUICE...

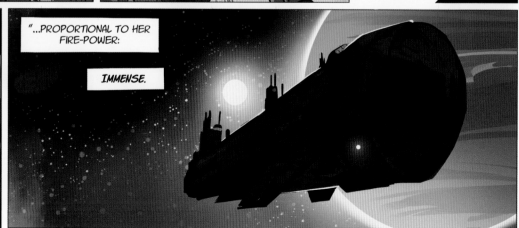

"...PROPORTIONAL TO HER FIRE-POWER:

IMMENSE.

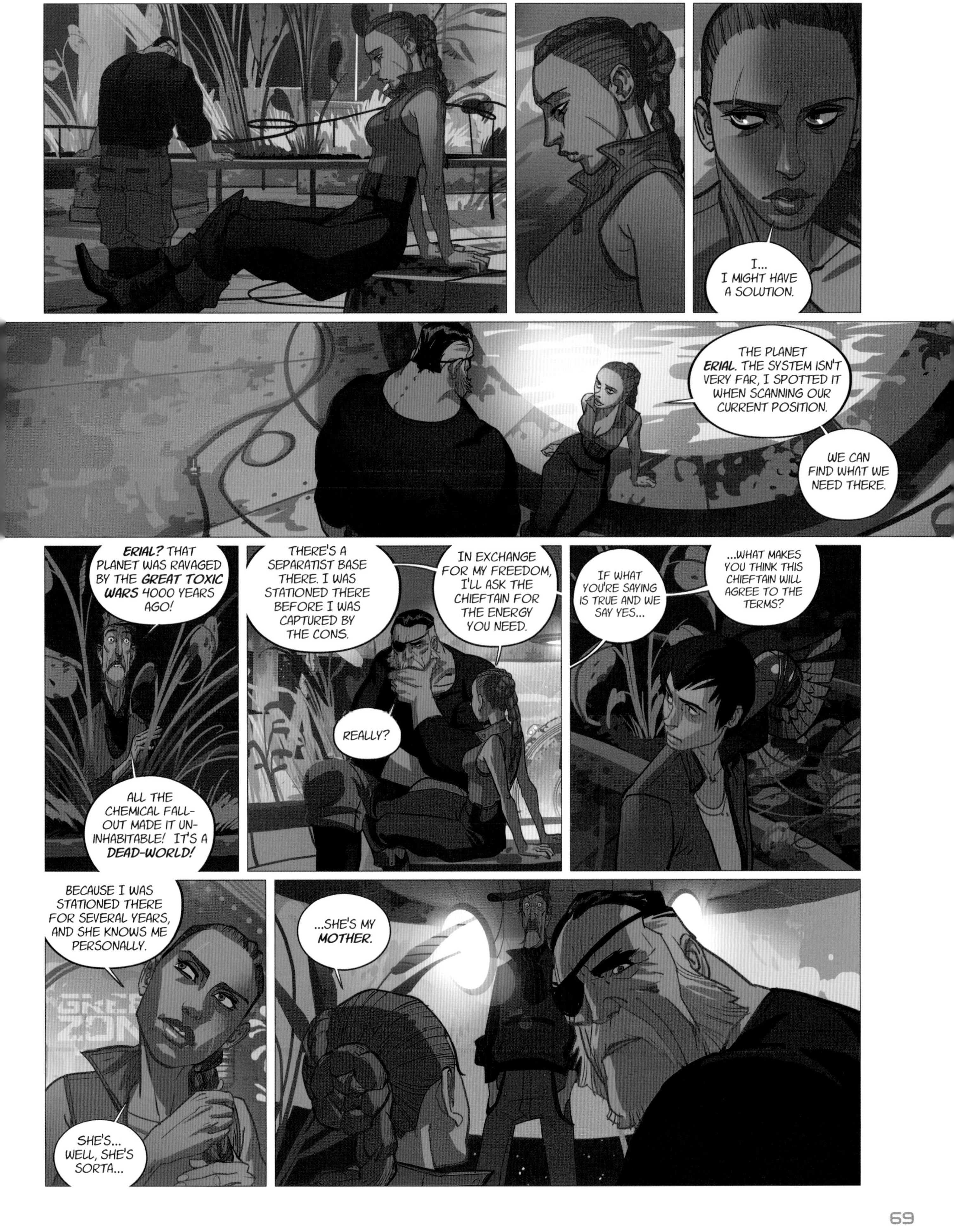
I... I MIGHT HAVE A SOLUTION.
THE PLANET ERIAL. THE SYSTEM ISN'T VERY FAR, I SPOTTED IT WHEN SCANNING OUR CURRENT POSITION.
WE CAN FIND WHAT WE NEED THERE.
ERIAL? THAT PLANET WAS RAVAGED BY THE GREAT TOXIC WARS 4000 YEARS AGO!
ALL THE CHEMICAL FALL-OUT MADE IT UN-INHABITABLE! IT'S A DEAD-WORLD!
THERE'S A SEPARATIST BASE THERE. I WAS STATIONED THERE BEFORE I WAS CAPTURED BY THE CONS.
IN EXCHANGE FOR MY FREEDOM, I'LL ASK THE CHIEFTAIN FOR THE ENERGY YOU NEED.
REALLY?
IF WHAT YOU'RE SAYING IS TRUE AND WE SAY YES...
...WHAT MAKES YOU THINK THIS CHIEFTAIN WILL AGREE TO THE TERMS?
BECAUSE I WAS STATIONED THERE FOR SEVERAL YEARS, AND SHE KNOWS ME PERSONALLY.
SHE'S... WELL, SHE'S SORTA...
...SHE'S MY MOTHER.

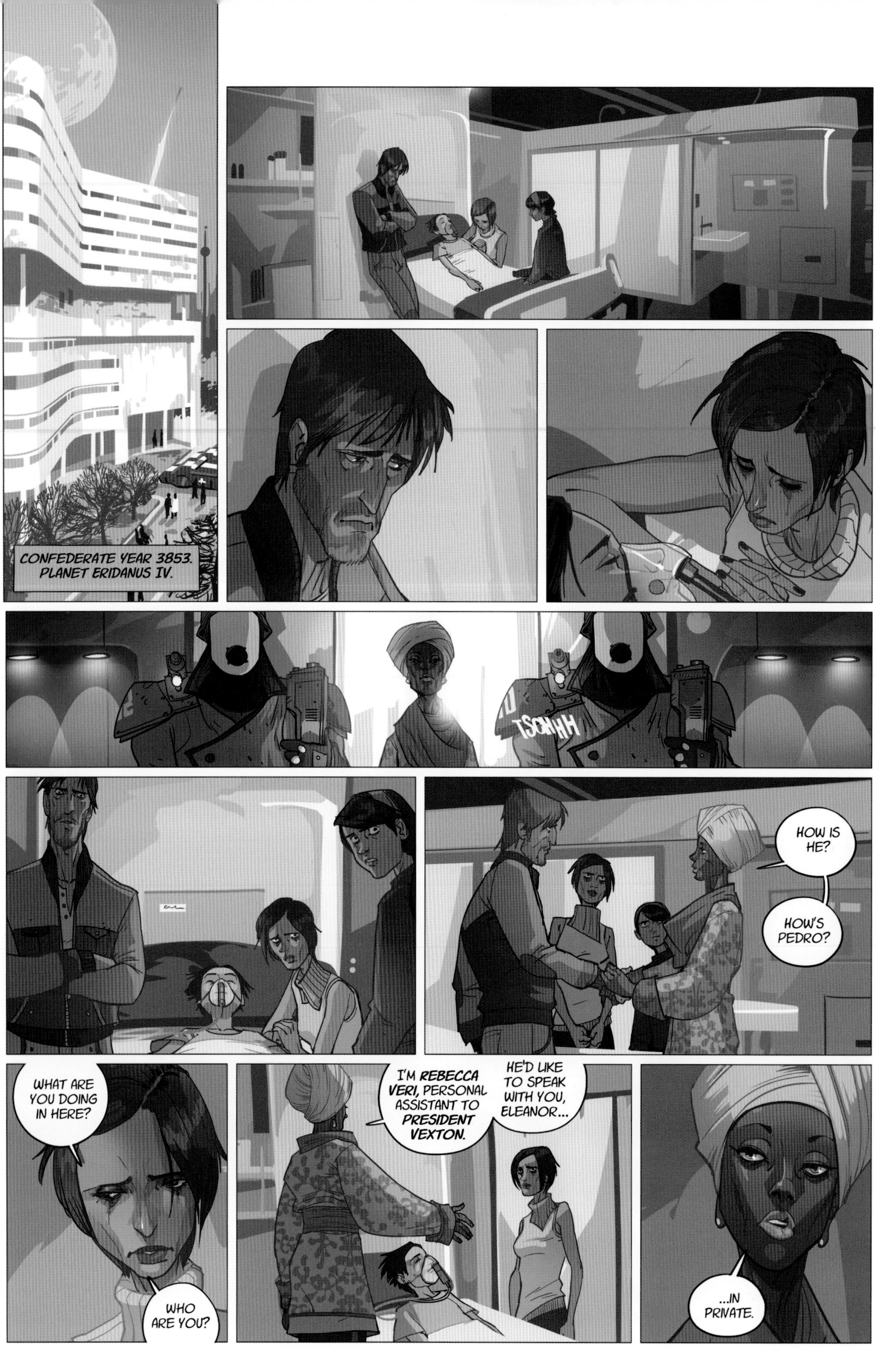

CONFEDERATE YEAR 3853. PLANET ERIDANUS IV.
HOW IS HE?
HOW'S PEDRO?
WHAT ARE YOU DOING IN HERE?
WHO ARE YOU?
I'M REBECCA VERI, PERSONAL ASSISTANT TO PRESIDENT VEXTON.
HE'D LIKE TO SPEAK WITH YOU, ELEANOR...
...IN PRIVATE.

"THE DOCTORS DON'T KNOW WHAT IT IS.

"IT MAY BE A VIRUS, BUT TESTS HAVE BEEN INCONCLUSIVE.

"THE ONLY THING WE KNOW IS HE'S GETTING WORSE...

"...HE MAY ONLY HAVE A FEW DAYS LEFT IF WE DON'T FIND A TREATMENT...

...BUT WHAT I DON'T UNDERSTAND, MR. VEXTON...

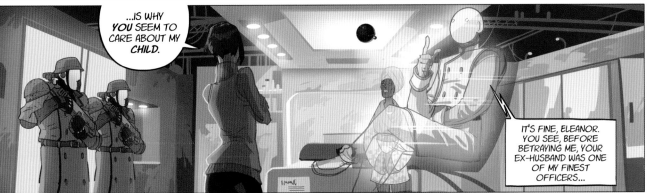

...IS WHY YOU SEEM TO CARE ABOUT MY CHILD.

IT'S FINE, ELEANOR. YOU SEE, BEFORE BETRAYING ME, YOUR EX-HUSBAND WAS ONE OF MY FINEST OFFICERS...

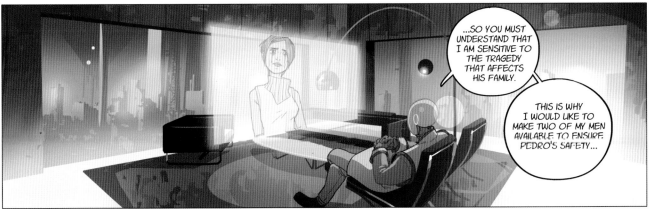

...SO YOU MUST UNDERSTAND THAT I AM SENSITIVE TO THE TRAGEDY THAT AFFECTS HIS FAMILY.

THIS IS WHY I WOULD LIKE TO MAKE TWO OF MY MEN AVAILABLE TO ENSURE PEDRO'S SAFETY...

"ONE CAN NEVER BE TOO CAREFUL.

"AND I COULD POSSIBLY ASK MY PERSONAL PHYSICIAN IF HE COULD LOOK AT YOUR SON. HE'S THE BEST IN THE CONFEDERATION."

WHAT DO YOU MEAN BY... POSSIBLY?

"WELL, LET'S JUST SAY THAT IS A SERVICE WE COULD PROVIDE...

"... JUST AS IT COULD BE VALUABLE FOR YOU TO RECORD A CALL WHICH COULD THEN BE POSTED ON THE NETWORKS...

"... A CALL WHEREIN YOU ASK YOUR EX-HUSBAND TO SURRENDER, TURNING OVER THE SHIP HE STOLE, SO THAT HE MIGHT COME TO HIS DYING SON'S BEDSIDE.

"WERE HE TO ACCEPT...

"...I'M SURE PEDRO COULD BE SAVED."

71

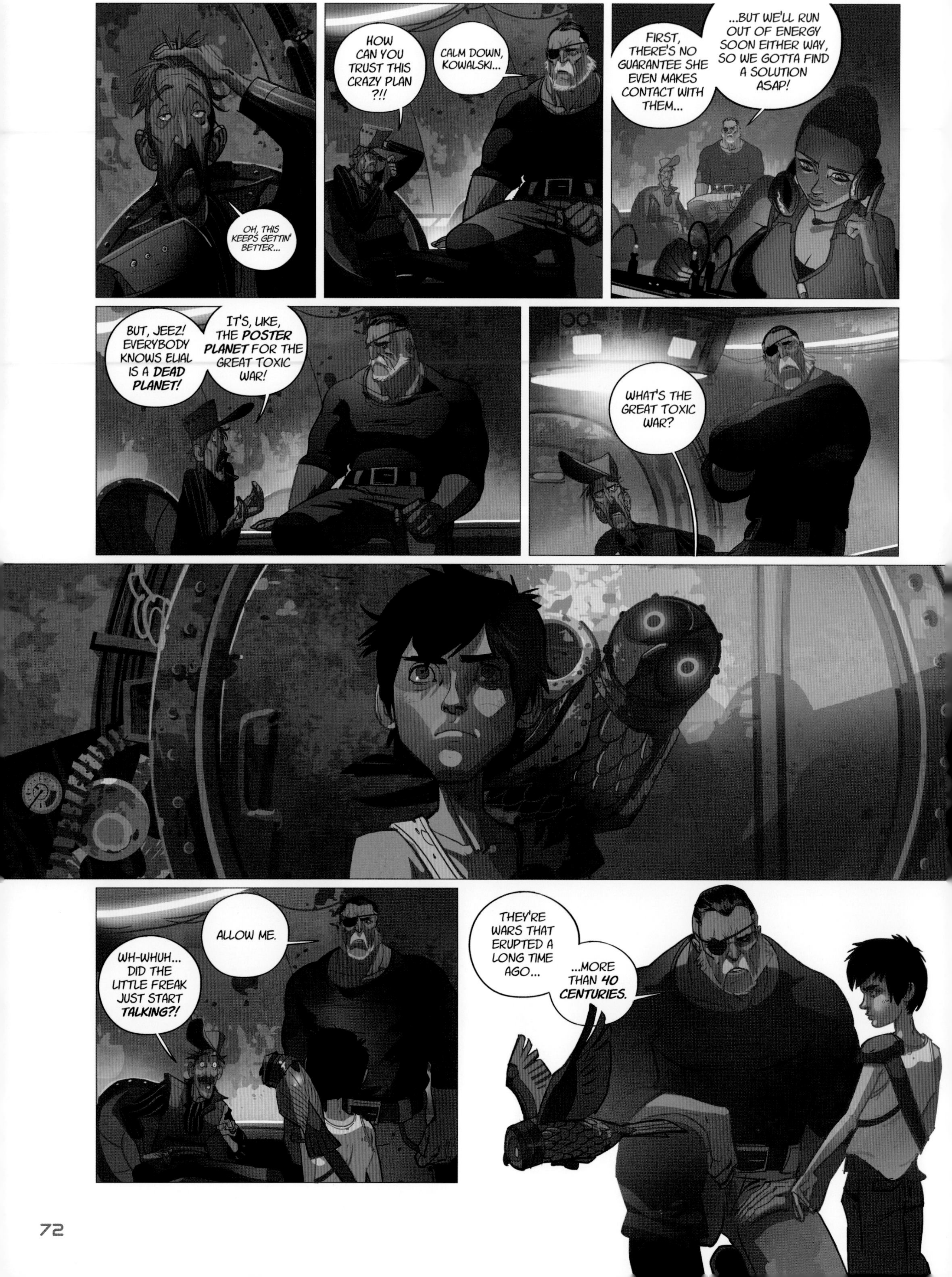
OH, THIS KEEPS GETTIN' BETTER...
HOW CAN YOU TRUST THIS CRAZY PLAN ?!!
CALM DOWN, KOWALSKI...
FIRST, THERE'S NO GUARANTEE SHE EVEN MAKES CONTACT WITH THEM...
...BUT WE'LL RUN OUT OF ENERGY SOON EITHER WAY, SO WE GOTTA FIND A SOLUTION ASAP!
BUT, JEEZ! EVERYBODY KNOWS ELIAL IS A DEAD PLANET!
IT'S, LIKE, THE POSTER PLANET FOR THE GREAT TOXIC WAR!
WHAT'S THE GREAT TOXIC WAR?
ALLOW ME.
WH-WHUH... DID THE LITTLE FREAK JUST START TALKING?!
THEY'RE WARS THAT ERUPTED A LONG TIME AGO...
...MORE THAN 40 CENTURIES.

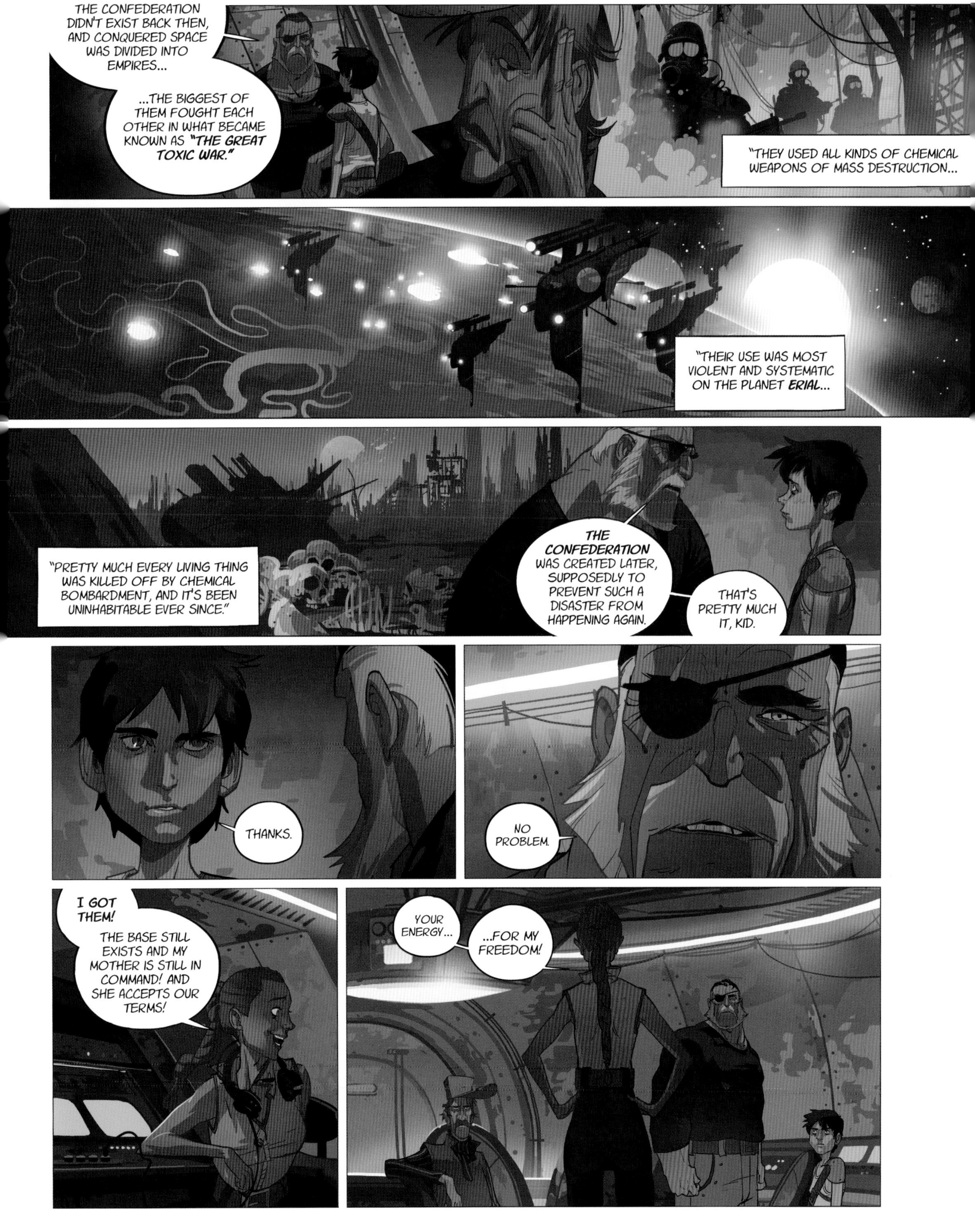

THE CONFEDERATION DIDN'T EXIST BACK THEN, AND CONQUERED SPACE WAS DIVIDED INTO EMPIRES...
...THE BIGGEST OF THEM FOUGHT EACH OTHER IN WHAT BECAME KNOWN AS "THE GREAT TOXIC WAR."
"THEY USED ALL KINDS OF CHEMICAL WEAPONS OF MASS DESTRUCTION...
"THEIR USE WAS MOST VIOLENT AND SYSTEMATIC ON THE PLANET ERIAL...
"PRETTY MUCH EVERY LIVING THING WAS KILLED OFF BY CHEMICAL BOMBARDMENT, AND IT'S BEEN UNINHABITABLE EVER SINCE."
THE CONFEDERATION WAS CREATED LATER, SUPPOSEDLY TO PREVENT SUCH A DISASTER FROM HAPPENING AGAIN.
THAT'S PRETTY MUCH IT, KID.
THANKS.
NO PROBLEM.
I GOT THEM!
THE BASE STILL EXISTS AND MY MOTHER IS STILL IN COMMAND! AND SHE ACCEPTS OUR TERMS!
YOUR ENERGY...
...FOR MY FREEDOM!

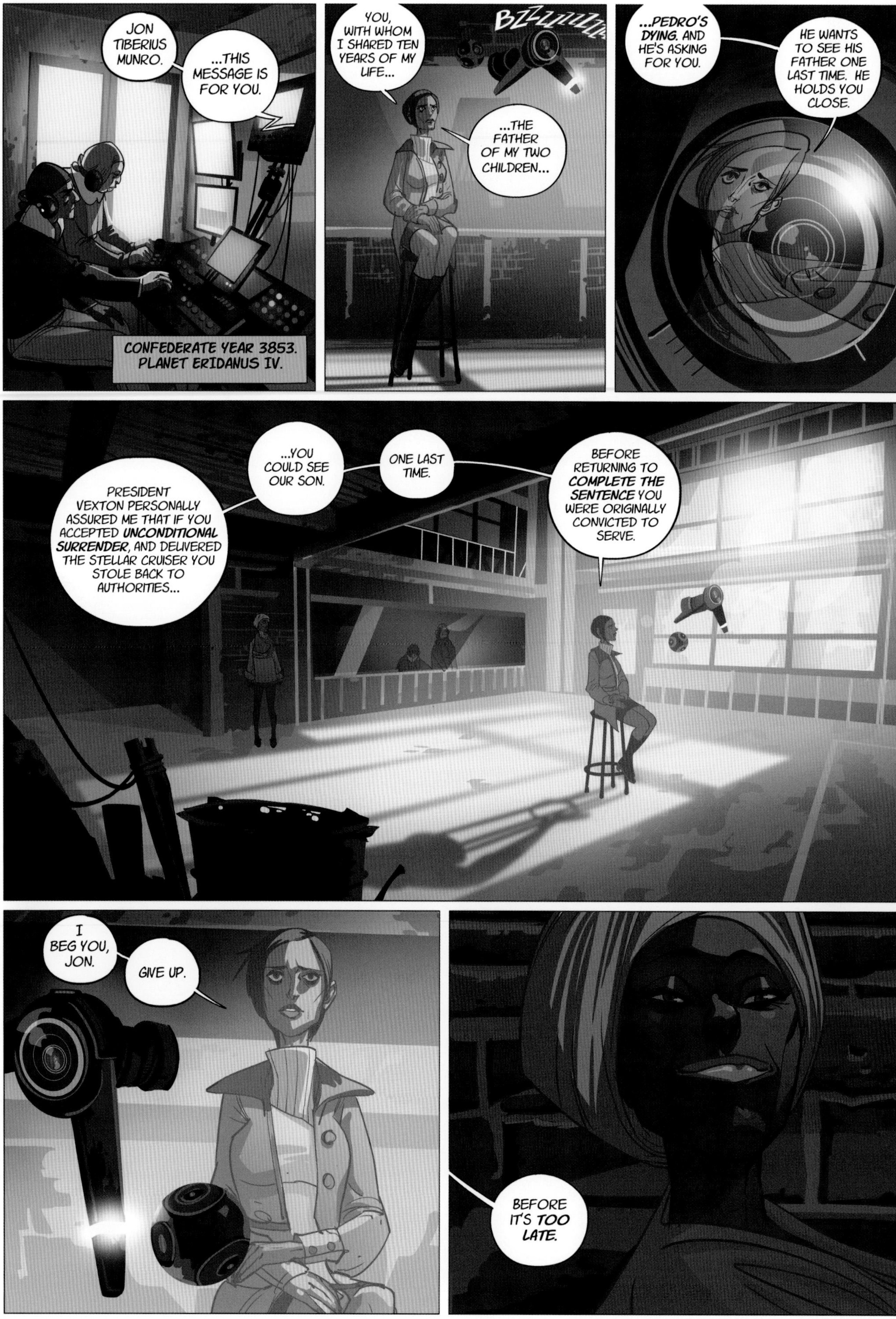
JON TIBERIUS MUNRO.
...THIS MESSAGE IS FOR YOU.
CONFEDERATE YEAR 3853. PLANET ERIDANUS IV.
BZZZZZZZZ
YOU, WITH WHOM I SHARED TEN YEARS OF MY LIFE...
...THE FATHER OF MY TWO CHILDREN...
...PEDRO'S DYING. AND HE'S ASKING FOR YOU.
HE WANTS TO SEE HIS FATHER ONE LAST TIME. HE HOLDS YOU CLOSE.
PRESIDENT VEXTON PERSONALLY ASSURED ME THAT IF YOU ACCEPTED UNCONDITIONAL SURRENDER, AND DELIVERED THE STELLAR CRUISER YOU STOLE BACK TO AUTHORITIES...
...YOU COULD SEE OUR SON.
ONE LAST TIME.
BEFORE RETURNING TO COMPLETE THE SENTENCE YOU WERE ORIGINALLY CONVICTED TO SERVE.
I BEG YOU, JON.
GIVE UP.
BEFORE IT'S TOO LATE.

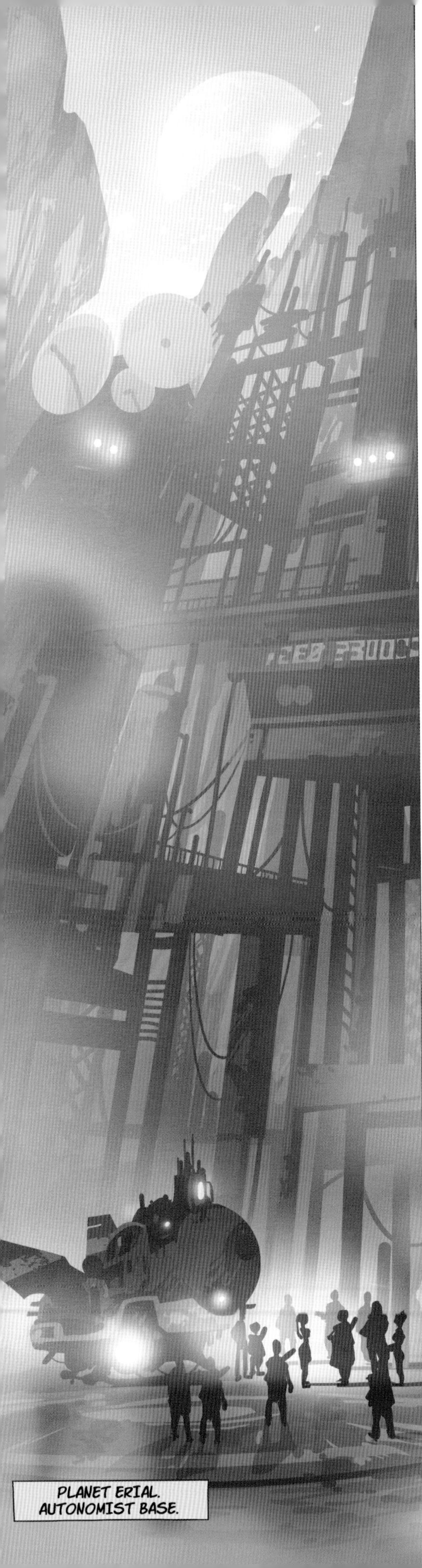
PLANET ERIAL.
AUTONOMIST BASE.

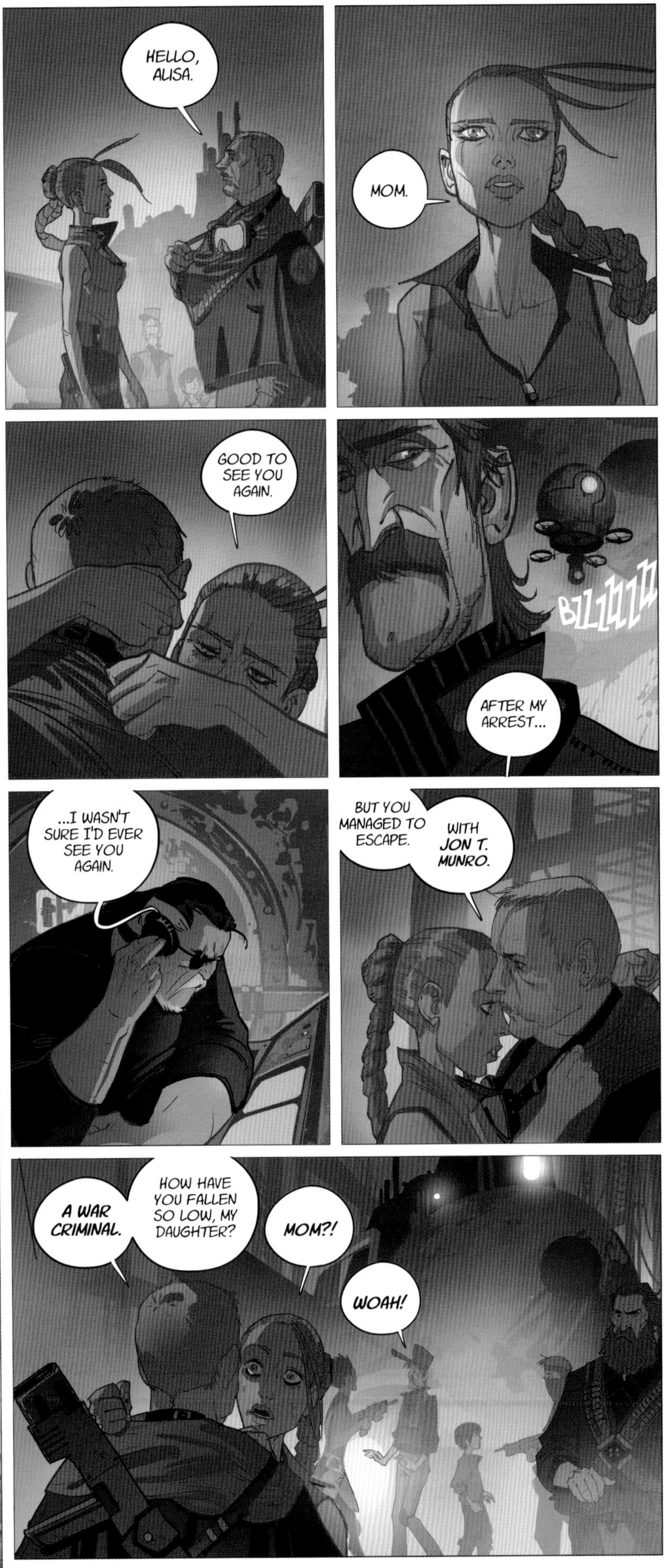
HELLO, ALISA.
MOM.
GOOD TO SEE YOU AGAIN.
BZZZZZZZ
AFTER MY ARREST...
...I WASN'T SURE I'D EVER SEE YOU AGAIN.
BUT YOU MANAGED TO ESCAPE.
WITH JON T. MUNRO.
A WAR CRIMINAL.
HOW HAVE YOU FALLEN SO LOW, MY DAUGHTER?
MOM?!
WOAH!

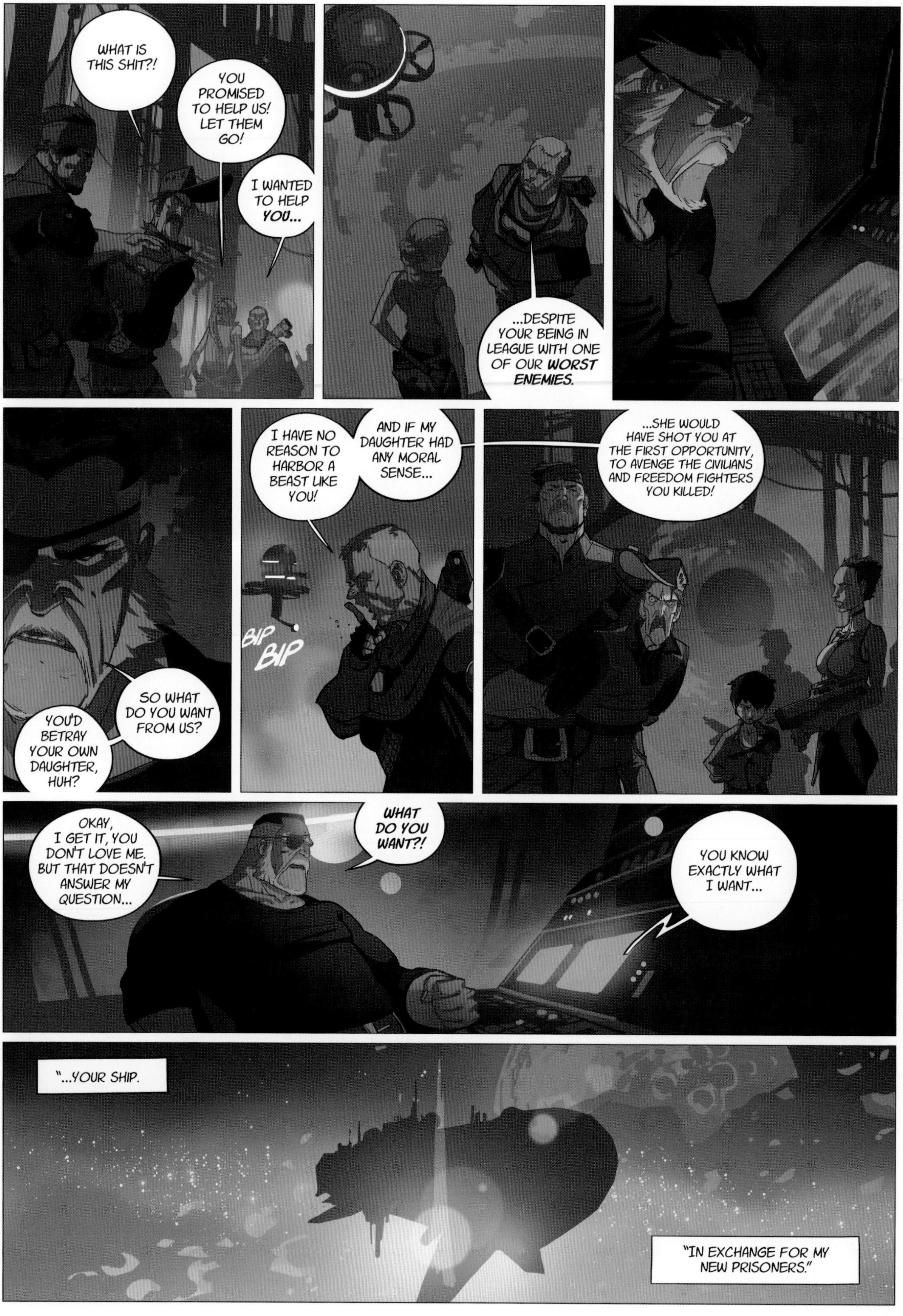
WHAT IS THIS SHIT?!
YOU PROMISED TO HELP US! LET THEM GO!
I WANTED TO HELP YOU...
...DESPITE YOUR BEING IN LEAGUE WITH ONE OF OUR WORST ENEMIES.
SO WHAT DO YOU WANT FROM US?
YOU'D BETRAY YOUR OWN DAUGHTER, HUH?
I HAVE NO REASON TO HARBOR A BEAST LIKE YOU!
BIP BIP
AND IF MY DAUGHTER HAD ANY MORAL SENSE...
...SHE WOULD HAVE SHOT YOU AT THE FIRST OPPORTUNITY, TO AVENGE THE CIVILIANS AND FREEDOM FIGHTERS YOU KILLED!
OKAY, I GET IT, YOU DON'T LOVE ME. BUT THAT DOESN'T ANSWER MY QUESTION...
WHAT DO YOU WANT?!
YOU KNOW EXACTLY WHAT I WANT...
"...YOUR SHIP.
"IN EXCHANGE FOR MY NEW PRISONERS."

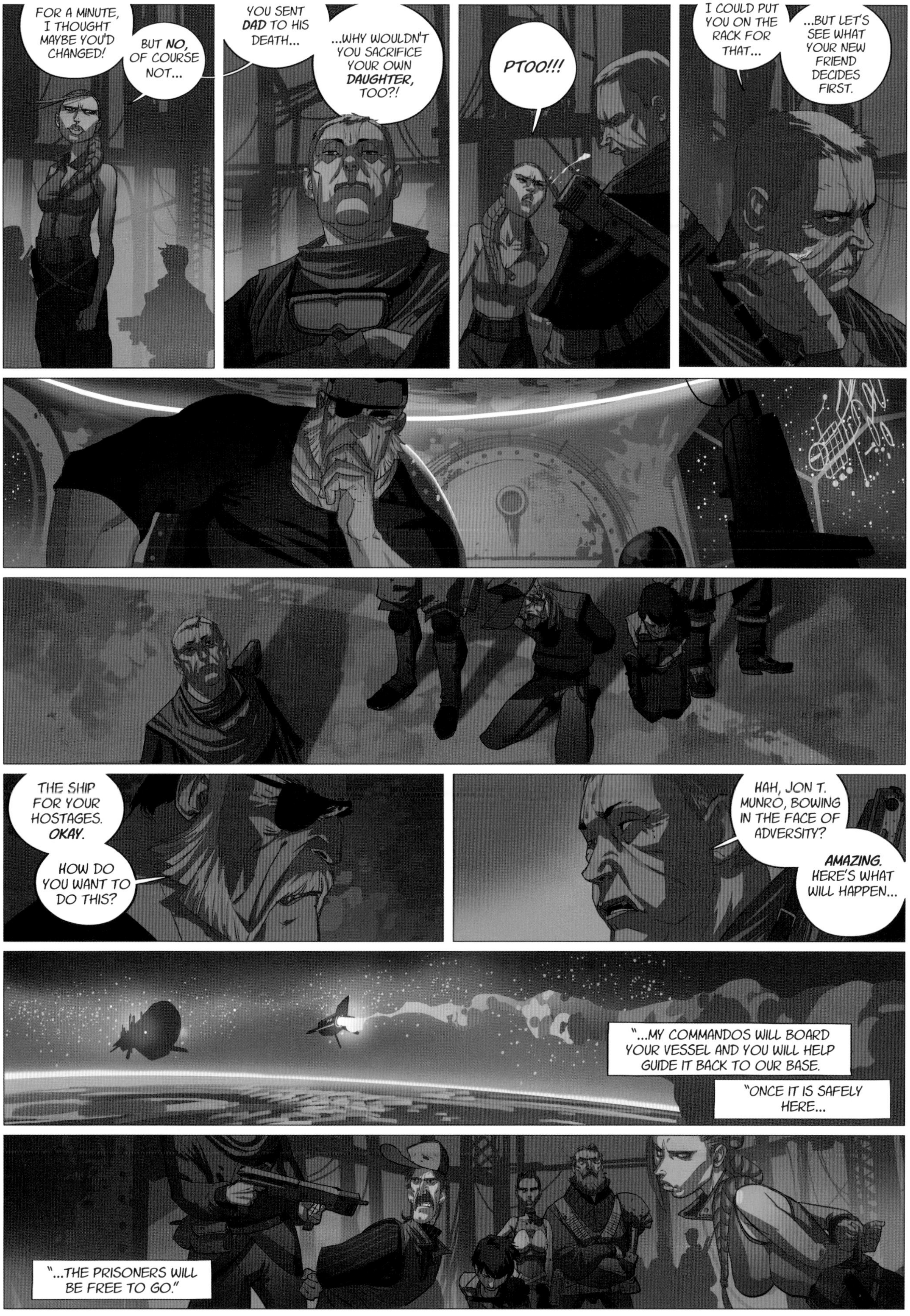
FOR A MINUTE, I THOUGHT MAYBE YOU'D CHANGED!
BUT NO, OF COURSE NOT...
YOU SENT DAD TO HIS DEATH...
...WHY WOULDN'T YOU SACRIFICE YOUR OWN DAUGHTER, TOO?!
PTOO!!!
I COULD PUT YOU ON THE RACK FOR THAT...
...BUT LET'S SEE WHAT YOUR NEW FRIEND DECIDES FIRST.
THE SHIP FOR YOUR HOSTAGES. OKAY.
HOW DO YOU WANT TO DO THIS?
HAH, JON T. MUNRO, BOWING IN THE FACE OF ADVERSITY?
AMAZING. HERE'S WHAT WILL HAPPEN...
"...MY COMMANDOS WILL BOARD YOUR VESSEL AND YOU WILL HELP GUIDE IT BACK TO OUR BASE.
"ONCE IT IS SAFELY HERE...
"...THE PRISONERS WILL BE FREE TO GO."

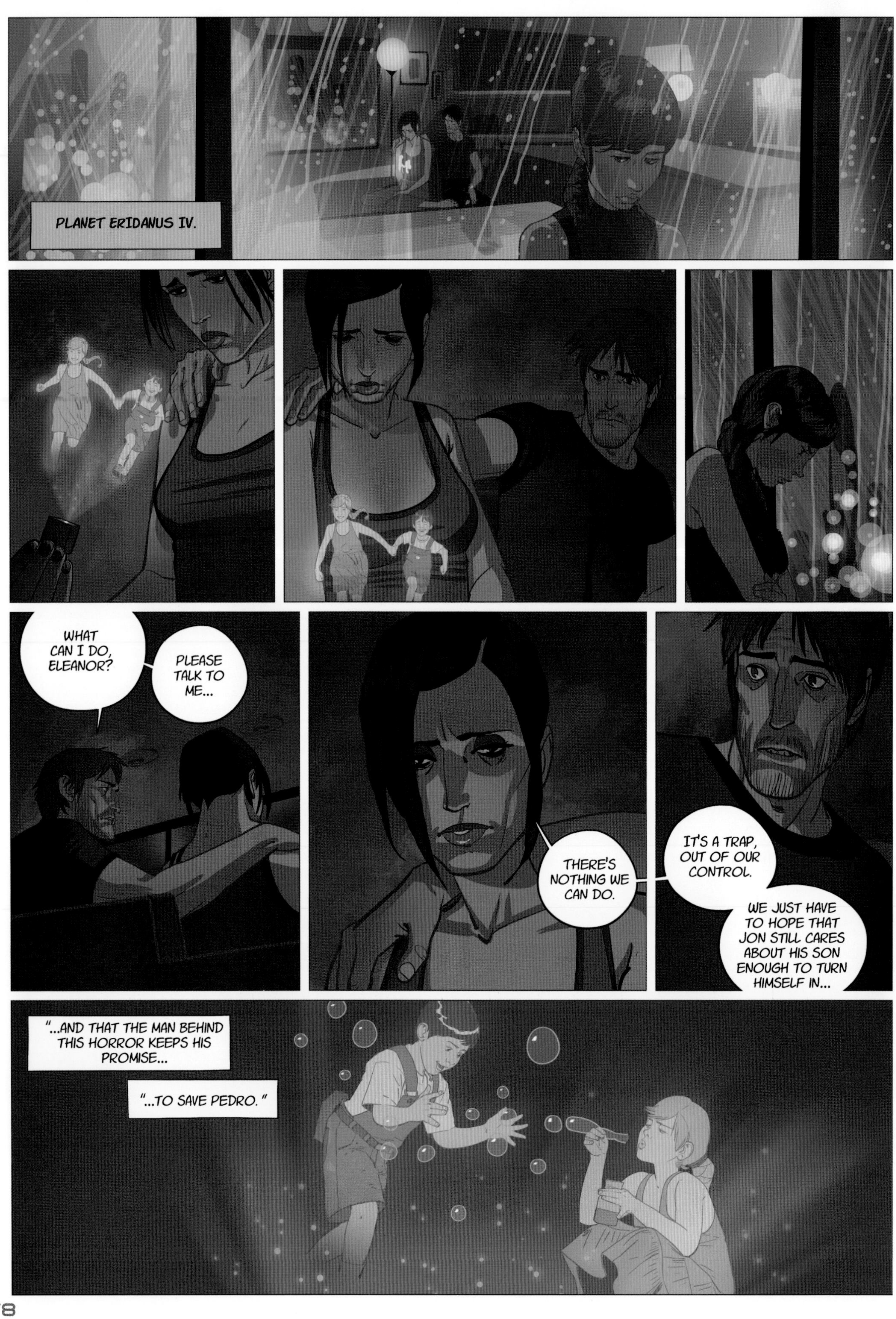
PLANET ERIDANUS IV.
WHAT CAN I DO, ELEANOR?
PLEASE TALK TO ME...
THERE'S NOTHING WE CAN DO.
IT'S A TRAP, OUT OF OUR CONTROL.
WE JUST HAVE TO HOPE THAT JON STILL CARES ABOUT HIS SON ENOUGH TO TURN HIMSELF IN...
"...AND THAT THE MAN BEHIND THIS HORROR KEEPS HIS PROMISE...
"...TO SAVE PEDRO."

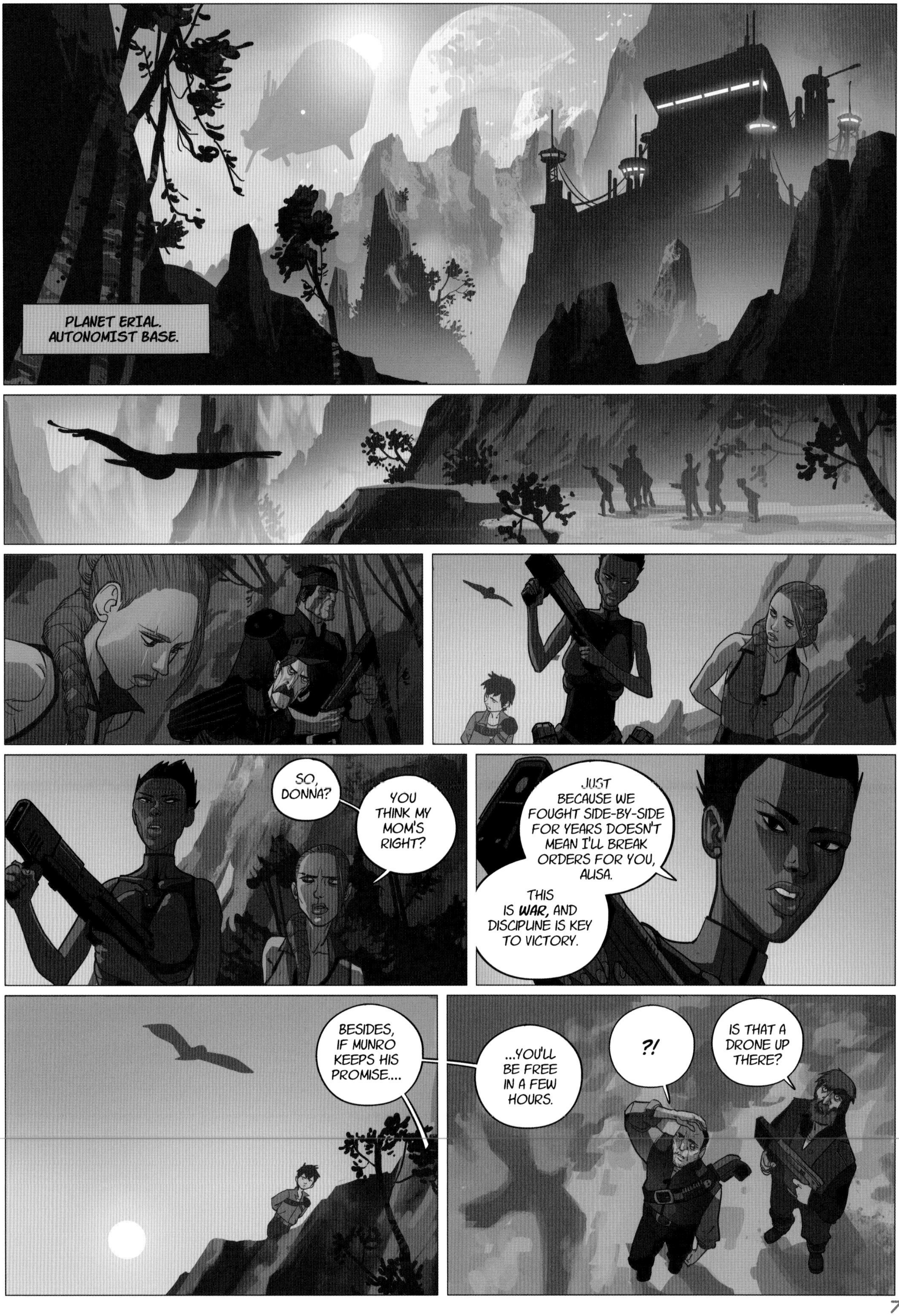
PLANET ERIAL. AUTONOMIST BASE.
SO, DONNA?
YOU THINK MY MOM'S RIGHT?
JUST BECAUSE WE FOUGHT SIDE-BY-SIDE FOR YEARS DOESN'T MEAN I'LL BREAK ORDERS FOR YOU, AUSA.
THIS IS WAR, AND DISCIPLINE IS KEY TO VICTORY.
BESIDES, IF MUNRO KEEPS HIS PROMISE....
...YOU'LL BE FREE IN A FEW HOURS.
?!
IS THAT A DRONE UP THERE?

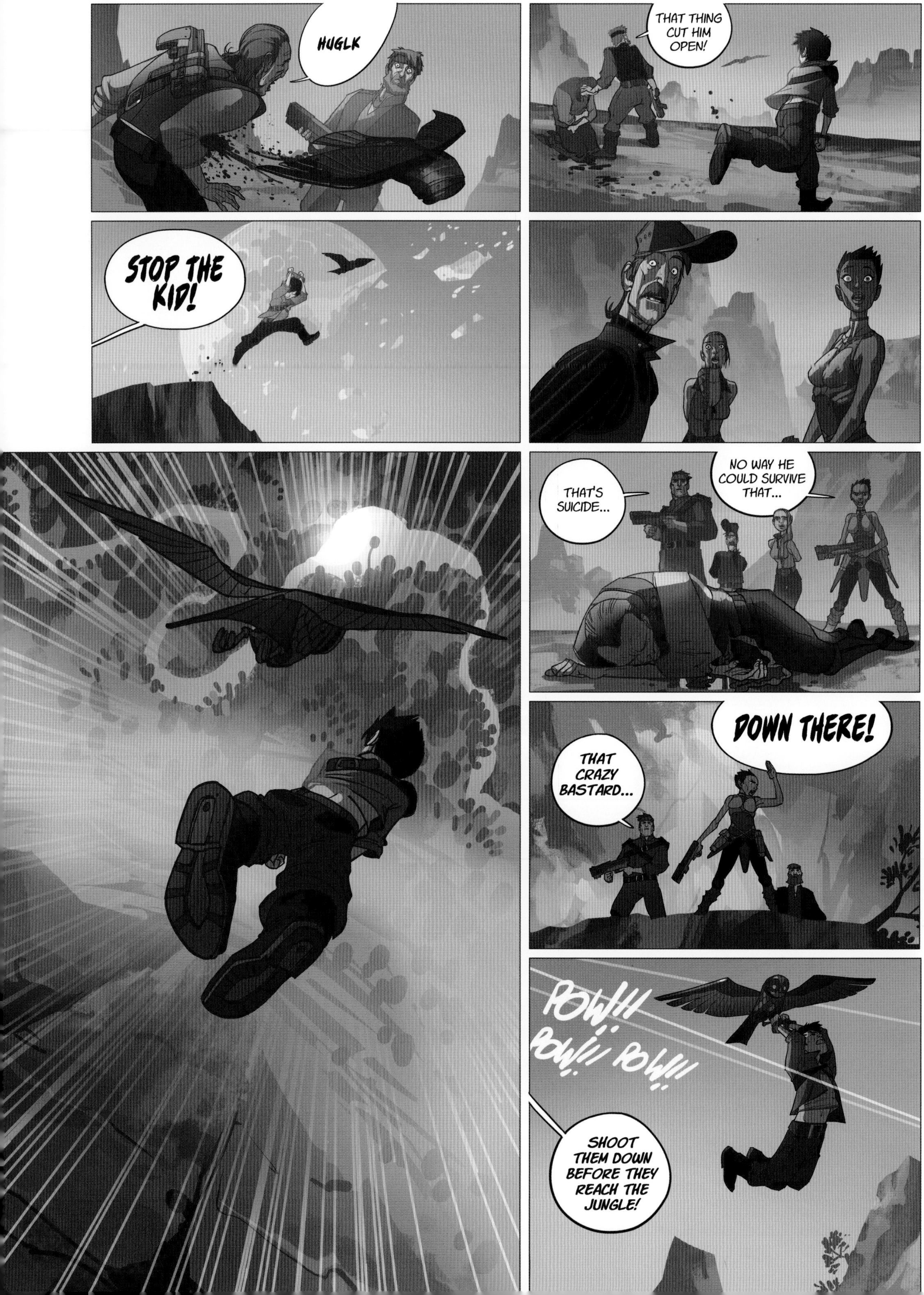
HUGLK
THAT THING CUT HIM OPEN!
STOP THE KID!
THAT'S SUICIDE...
NO WAY HE COULD SURVIVE THAT...
DOWN THERE!
THAT CRAZY BASTARD...
POW!!!
POW!!!
POW!!!
SHOOT THEM DOWN BEFORE THEY REACH THE JUNGLE!

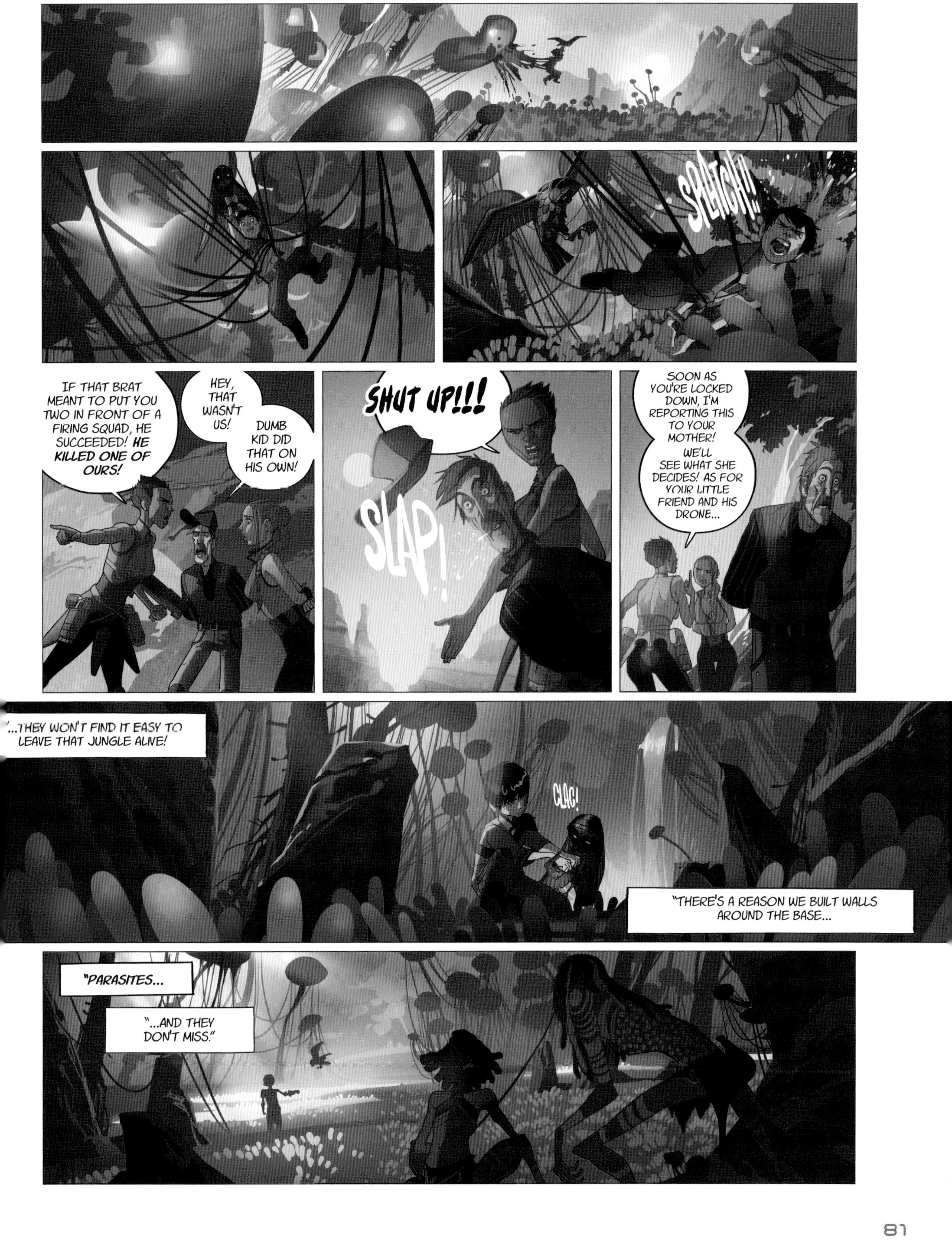
SPLATCH!!
IF THAT BRAT MEANT TO PUT YOU TWO IN FRONT OF A FIRING SQUAD, HE SUCCEEDED! HE KILLED ONE OF OURS!
HEY, THAT WASN'T US!
DUMB KID DID THAT ON HIS OWN!
SHUT UP!!!
SLAP!
SOON AS YOU'RE LOCKED DOWN, I'M REPORTING THIS TO YOUR MOTHER!
WE'LL SEE WHAT SHE DECIDES! AS FOR YOUR LITTLE FRIEND AND HIS DRONE...
"...THEY WON'T FIND IT EASY TO LEAVE THAT JUNGLE ALIVE!
CLAC!
"THERE'S A REASON WE BUILT WALLS AROUND THE BASE...
"PARASITES...
"...AND THEY DON'T MISS."

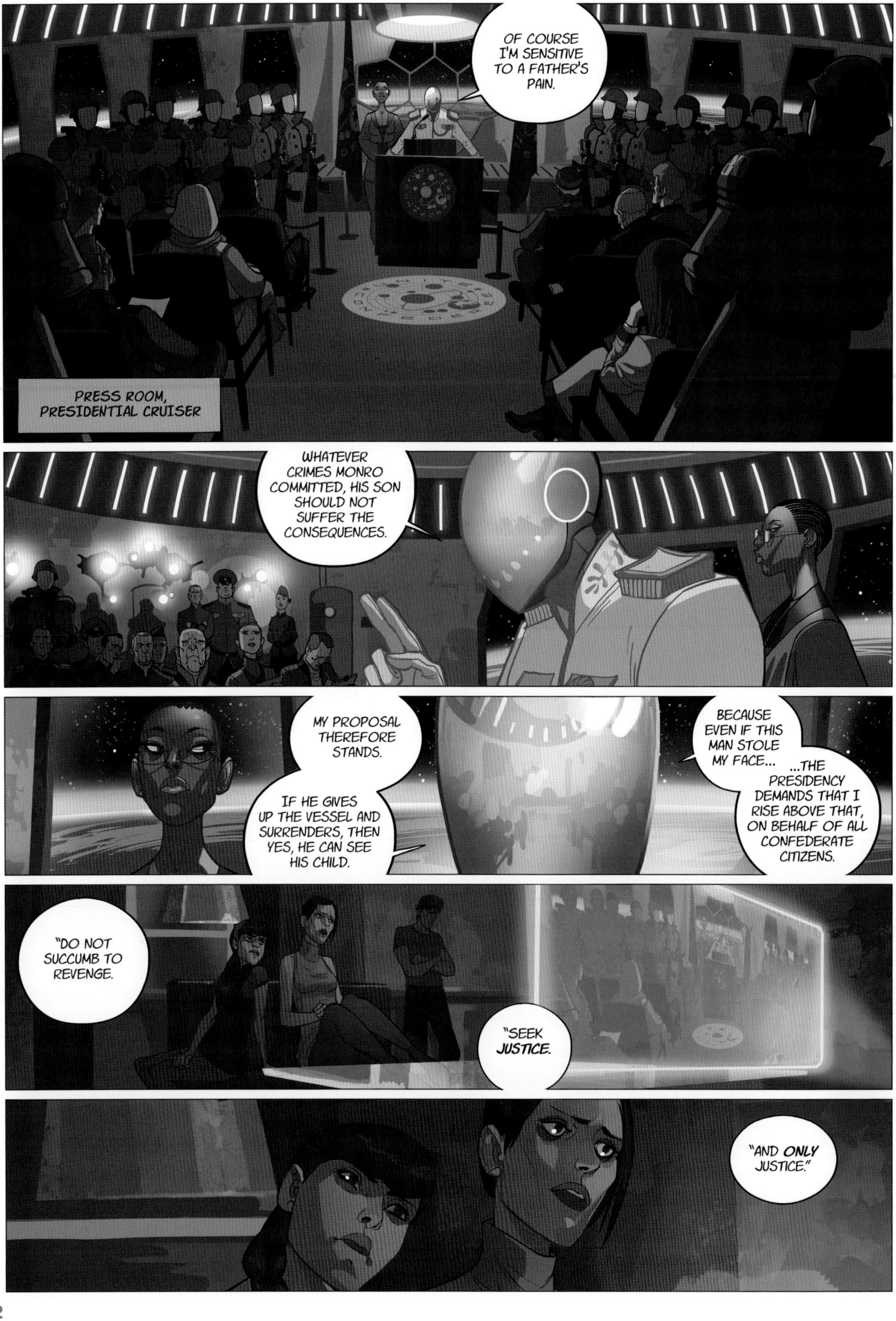
OF COURSE I'M SENSITIVE TO A FATHER'S PAIN.
PRESS ROOM, PRESIDENTIAL CRUISER
WHATEVER CRIMES MONRO COMMITTED, HIS SON SHOULD NOT SUFFER THE CONSEQUENCES.
MY PROPOSAL THEREFORE STANDS.
IF HE GIVES UP THE VESSEL AND SURRENDERS, THEN YES, HE CAN SEE HIS CHILD.
BECAUSE EVEN IF THIS MAN STOLE MY FACE...
...THE PRESIDENCY DEMANDS THAT I RISE ABOVE THAT, ON BEHALF OF ALL CONFEDERATE CITIZENS.
"DO NOT SUCCUMB TO REVENGE.
"SEEK ***JUSTICE.***
"AND ***ONLY*** JUSTICE."

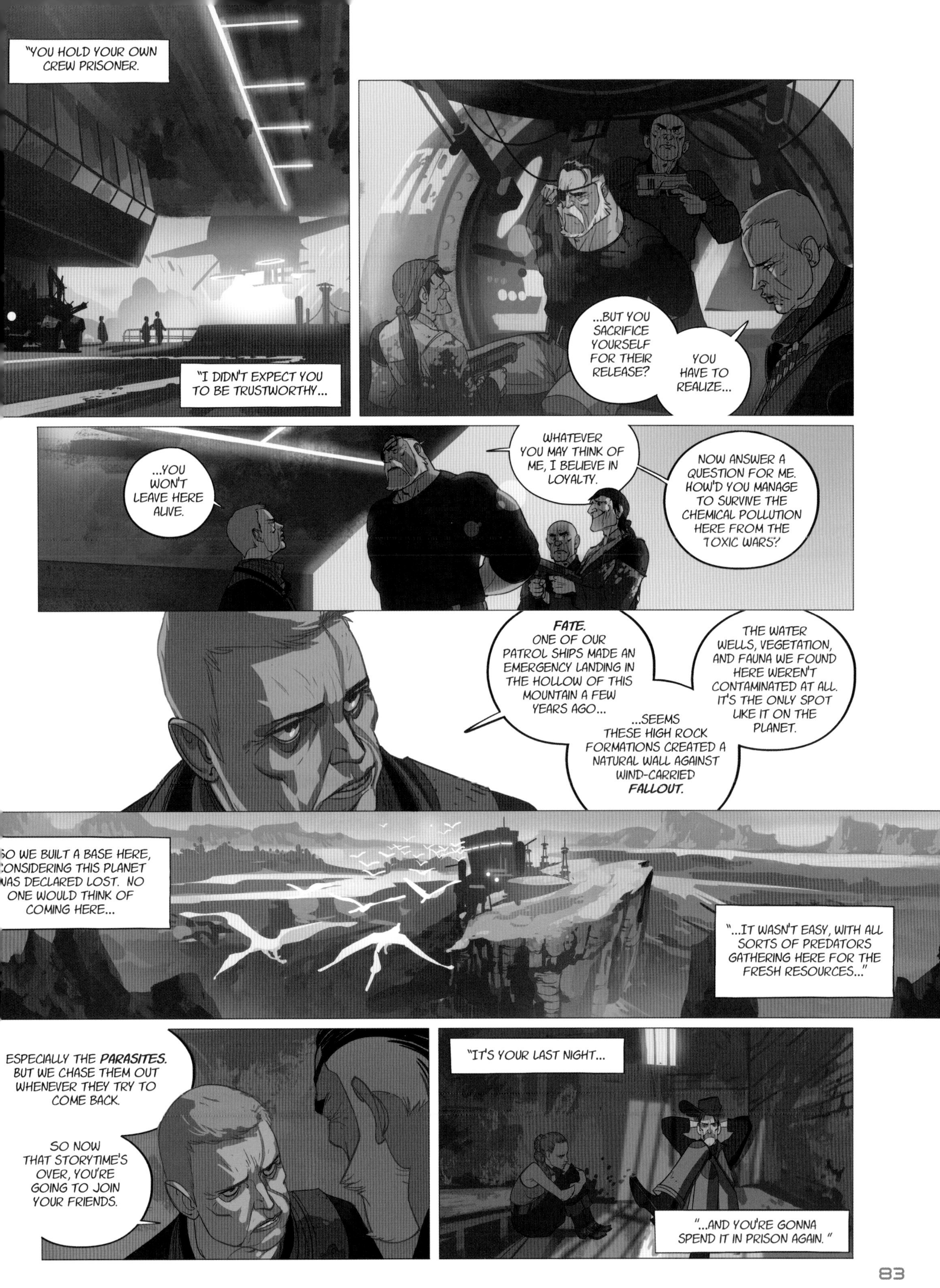
"YOU HOLD YOUR OWN CREW PRISONER.
"I DIDN'T EXPECT YOU TO BE TRUSTWORTHY...
...BUT YOU SACRIFICE YOURSELF FOR THEIR RELEASE?
YOU HAVE TO REALIZE...
...YOU WON'T LEAVE HERE ALIVE.
WHATEVER YOU MAY THINK OF ME, I BELIEVE IN LOYALTY.
NOW ANSWER A QUESTION FOR ME. HOW'D YOU MANAGE TO SURVIVE THE CHEMICAL POLLUTION HERE FROM THE TOXIC WARS?
FATE. ONE OF OUR PATROL SHIPS MADE AN EMERGENCY LANDING IN THE HOLLOW OF THIS MOUNTAIN A FEW YEARS AGO...
...SEEMS THESE HIGH ROCK FORMATIONS CREATED A NATURAL WALL AGAINST WIND-CARRIED FALLOUT.
THE WATER WELLS, VEGETATION, AND FAUNA WE FOUND HERE WEREN'T CONTAMINATED AT ALL. IT'S THE ONLY SPOT LIKE IT ON THE PLANET.
SO WE BUILT A BASE HERE, CONSIDERING THIS PLANET WAS DECLARED LOST. NO ONE WOULD THINK OF COMING HERE...
"...IT WASN'T EASY, WITH ALL SORTS OF PREDATORS GATHERING HERE FOR THE FRESH RESOURCES..."
ESPECIALLY THE PARASITES. BUT WE CHASE THEM OUT WHENEVER THEY TRY TO COME BACK.
SO NOW THAT STORYTIME'S OVER, YOU'RE GOING TO JOIN YOUR FRIENDS.
"IT'S YOUR LAST NIGHT...
"...AND YOU'RE GONNA SPEND IT IN PRISON AGAIN."

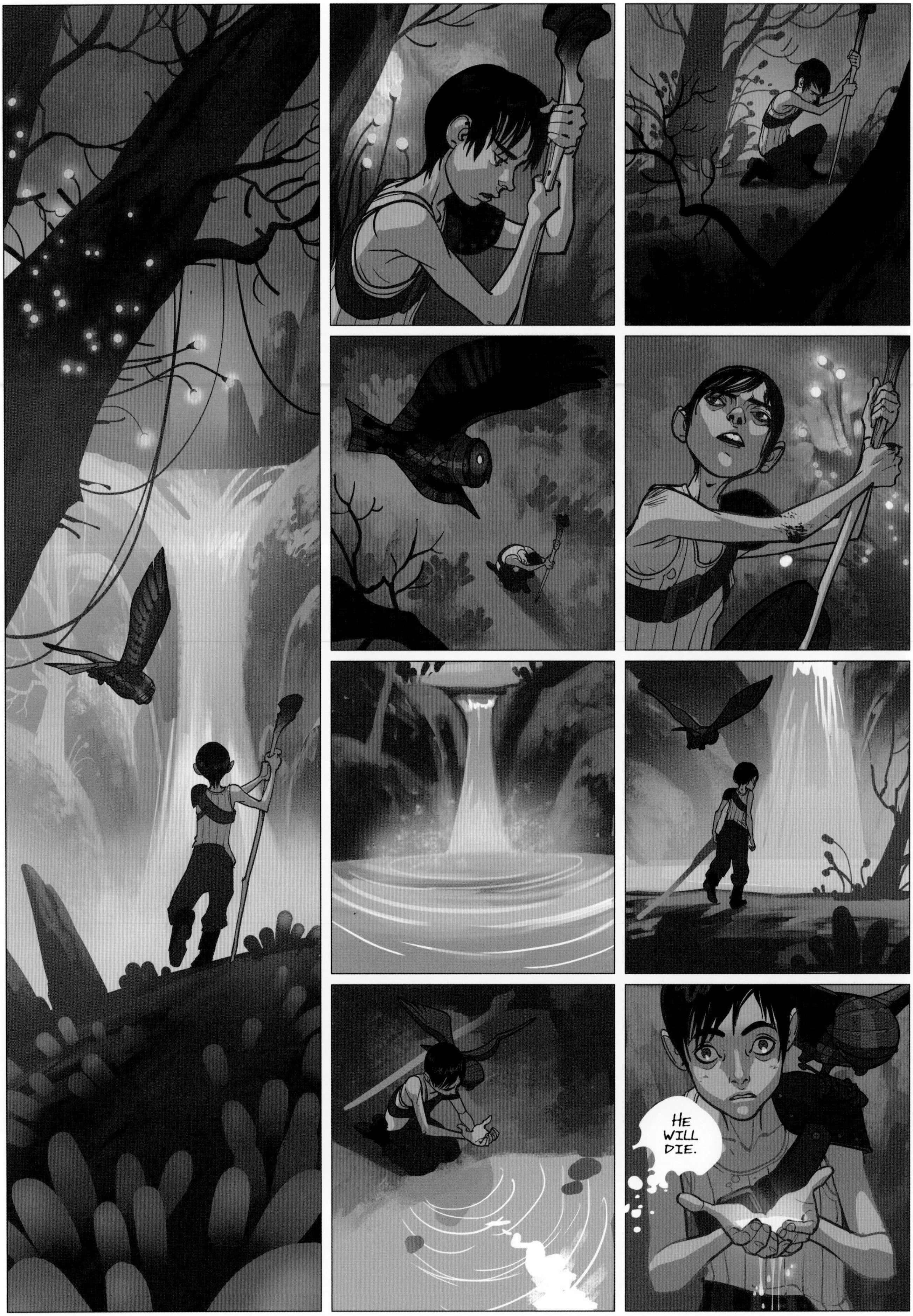
HE WILL DIE.

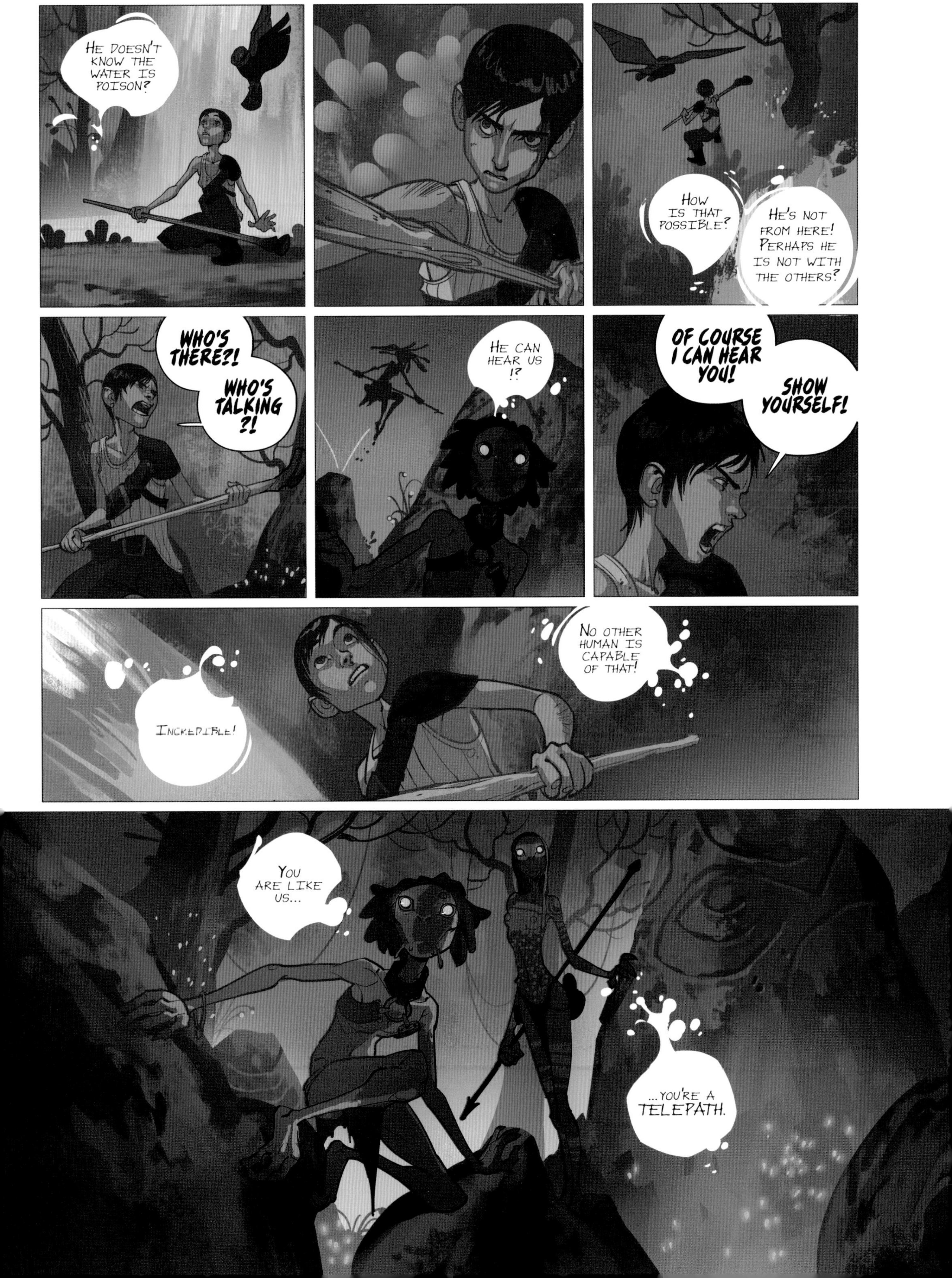
He doesn't know the water is poison?
How is that possible?
He's not from here! Perhaps he is not with the others?
Who's there?!
Who's talking?!
He can hear us !?
Of course I can hear you!
Show yourself!
Incredible!
No other human is capable of that!
You are like us...
...you're a telepath.

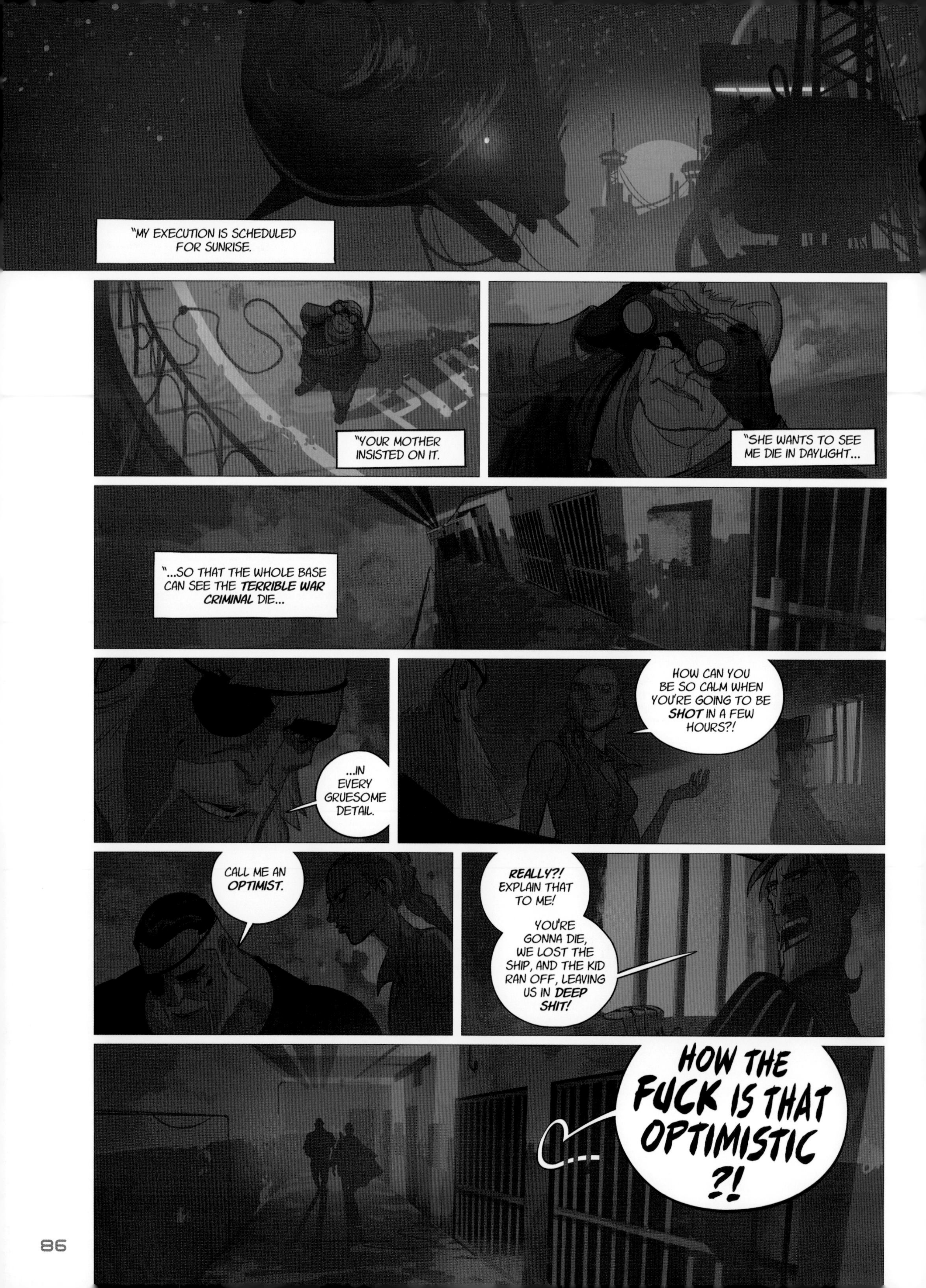
"MY EXECUTION IS SCHEDULED FOR SUNRISE.
"YOUR MOTHER INSISTED ON IT.
"SHE WANTS TO SEE ME DIE IN DAYLIGHT...
"...SO THAT THE WHOLE BASE CAN SEE THE **TERRIBLE WAR CRIMINAL** DIE...
...IN EVERY GRUESOME DETAIL.
HOW CAN YOU BE SO CALM WHEN YOU'RE GOING TO BE **SHOT** IN A FEW HOURS?!
CALL ME AN **OPTIMIST.**
REALLY?! EXPLAIN THAT TO ME!
YOU'RE GONNA DIE, WE LOST THE SHIP, AND THE KID RAN OFF, LEAVING US IN **DEEP SHIT!**
HOW THE FUCK IS THAT OPTIMISTIC ?!

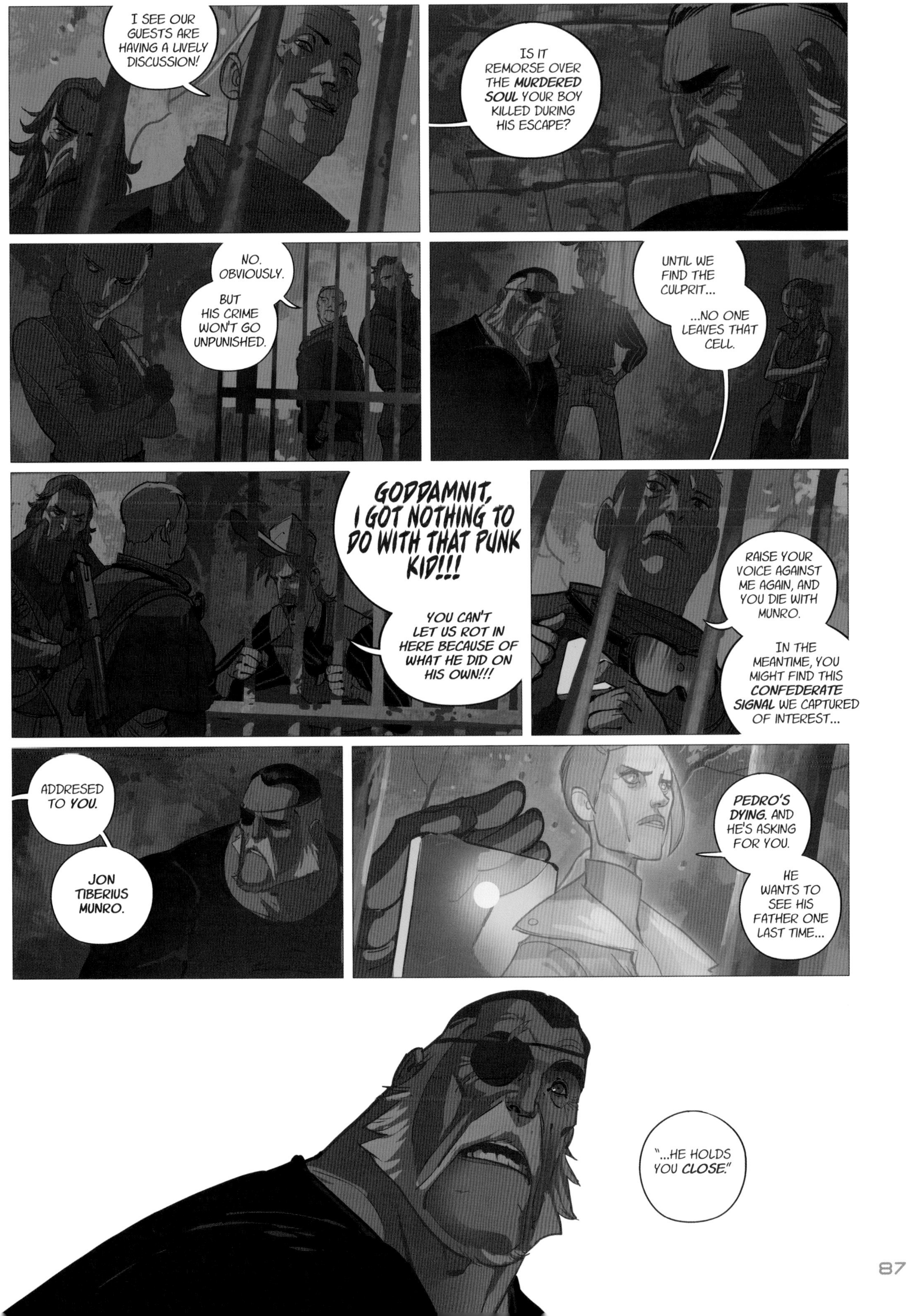

I SEE OUR GUESTS ARE HAVING A LIVELY DISCUSSION!
IS IT REMORSE OVER THE **MURDERED SOUL** YOUR BOY KILLED DURING HIS ESCAPE?
NO. OBVIOUSLY.
BUT HIS CRIME WON'T GO UNPUNISHED.
UNTIL WE FIND THE CULPRIT...
...NO ONE LEAVES THAT CELL.
GODDAMNIT, I GOT NOTHING TO DO WITH THAT PUNK KID!!!
YOU CAN'T LET US ROT IN HERE BECAUSE OF WHAT HE DID ON HIS OWN!!!
RAISE YOUR VOICE AGAINST ME AGAIN, AND YOU DIE WITH MUNRO.
IN THE MEANTIME, YOU MIGHT FIND THIS **CONFEDERATE SIGNAL** WE CAPTURED OF INTEREST...
ADDRESED TO **YOU.**
JON TIBERIUS MUNRO.
PEDRO'S DYING. AND HE'S ASKING FOR YOU.
HE WANTS TO SEE HIS FATHER ONE LAST TIME...
"...HE HOLDS YOU ***CLOSE.***"

OF COURSE WE ARE HUMAN.

OUR ANCESTORS WERE HUMAN, BEFORE THE GREAT WARS.

WHY WOULDN'T WE BE AS WELL?

BUT... YOU'RE SO DIFFERENT FROM US...

I MEAN... YOU...

WE ARE THE DESCENDANTS OF A PEOPLE WHO SURVIVED THE CHEMICAL WARS 4000 YEARS AGO.

THE WASTE OF THAT WAR CAUSED GENERATIONS OF MUTATIONS...

...INCLUDING TELEPATHY.

ABSORBING FOOD AND DRINK THROUGH THE PORES OF OUR SKIN BEING ANOTHER.

WE SURVIVED, ADAPTING TO OUR NEW ENVIRONMENT.

WE LIVED IN THE MOUNTAINS, UNTOUCHED BY THE CONTAMINATION.

BUT THEN THEY ARRIVED. THESE FIGHTERS. UNABLE TO SPEAK WITH US, THEY TOOK US TO BE ANIMALS, A NUISANCE TO HUNT.

THEY CALL US "PARASITES" AND SLAUGHTER US WITHOUT MERCY, FORCING US BACK INTO THE CONTAMINATED AREAS.

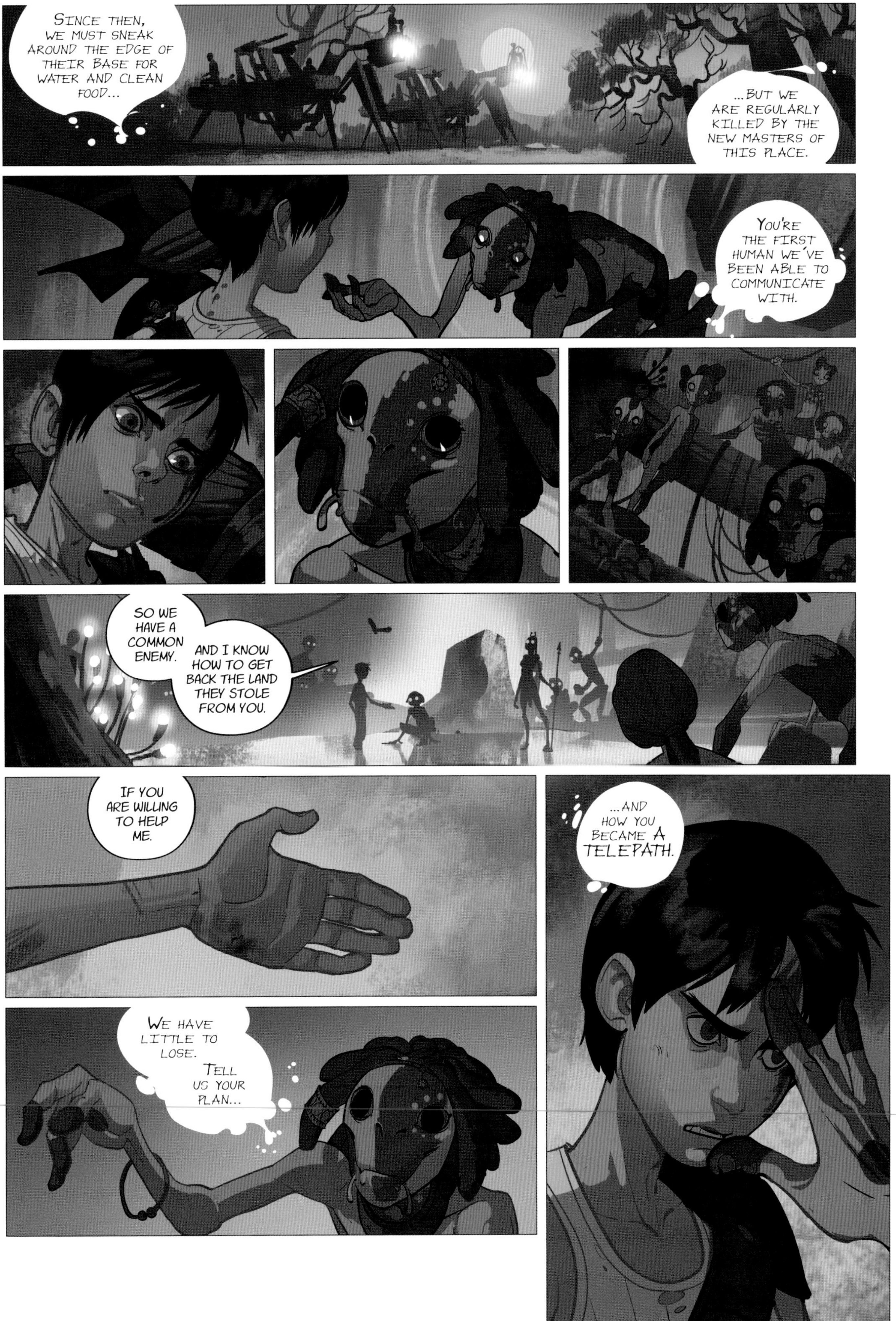

SINCE THEN, WE MUST SNEAK AROUND THE EDGE OF THEIR BASE FOR WATER AND CLEAN FOOD...
...BUT WE ARE REGULARLY KILLED BY THE NEW MASTERS OF THIS PLACE.
YOU'RE THE FIRST HUMAN WE'VE BEEN ABLE TO COMMUNICATE WITH.
SO WE HAVE A COMMON ENEMY.
AND I KNOW HOW TO GET BACK THE LAND THEY STOLE FROM YOU.
IF YOU ARE WILLING TO HELP ME.
WE HAVE LITTLE TO LOSE.
TELL US YOUR PLAN...
...AND HOW YOU BECAME A TELEPATH.

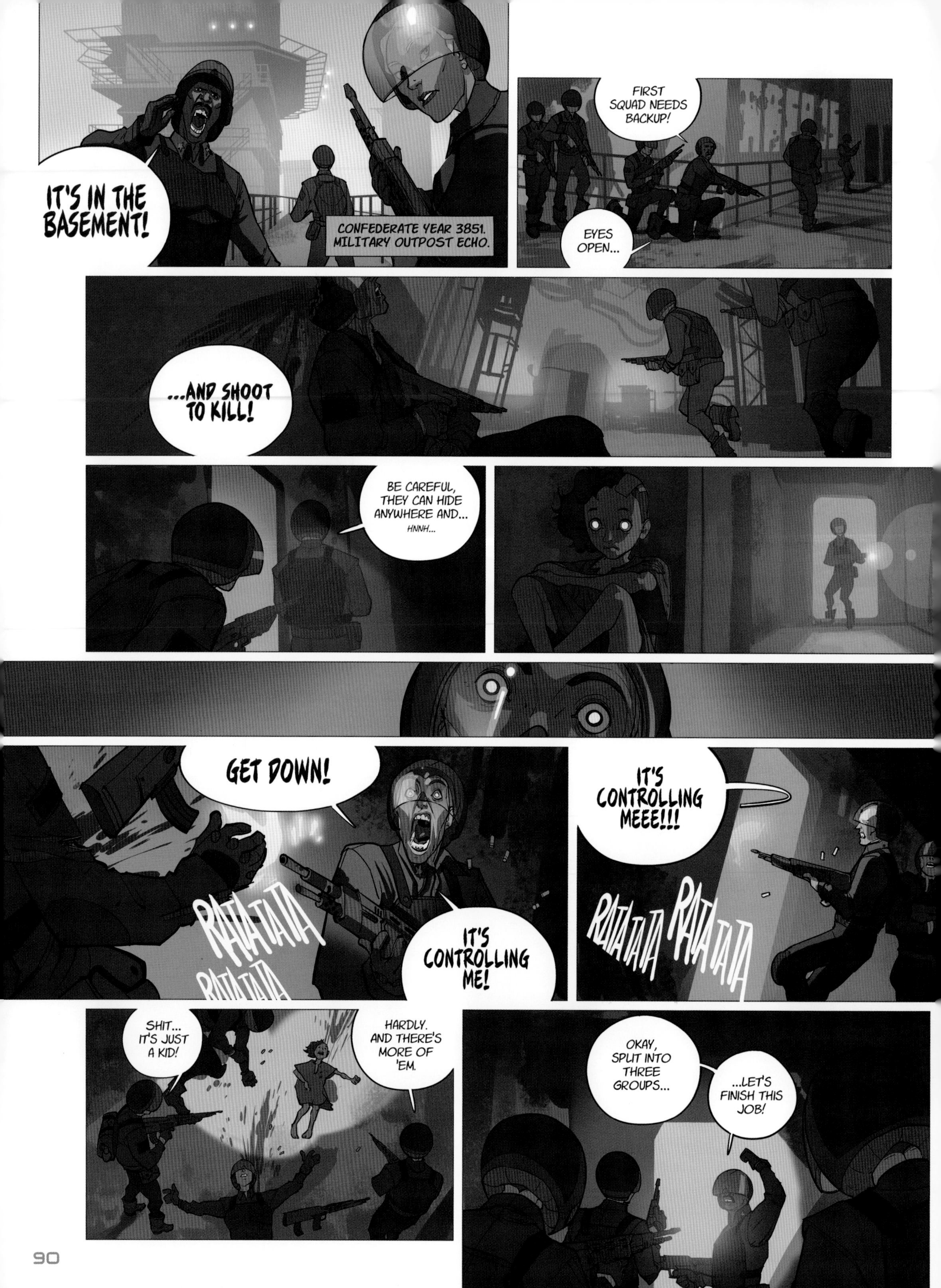
IT'S IN THE BASEMENT!
CONFEDERATE YEAR 3851. MILITARY OUTPOST ECHO.
FIRST SQUAD NEEDS BACKUP!
EYES OPEN...
...AND SHOOT TO KILL!
BE CAREFUL, THEY CAN HIDE ANYWHERE AND...
HNNH...
GET DOWN!
RATATATA
RATATATA
IT'S CONTROLLING ME!
IT'S CONTROLLING MEEE!!!
RATATATA
RATATATA
SHIT... IT'S JUST A KID!
HARDLY. AND THERE'S MORE OF 'EM.
OKAY, SPLIT INTO THREE GROUPS...
...LET'S FINISH THIS JOB!

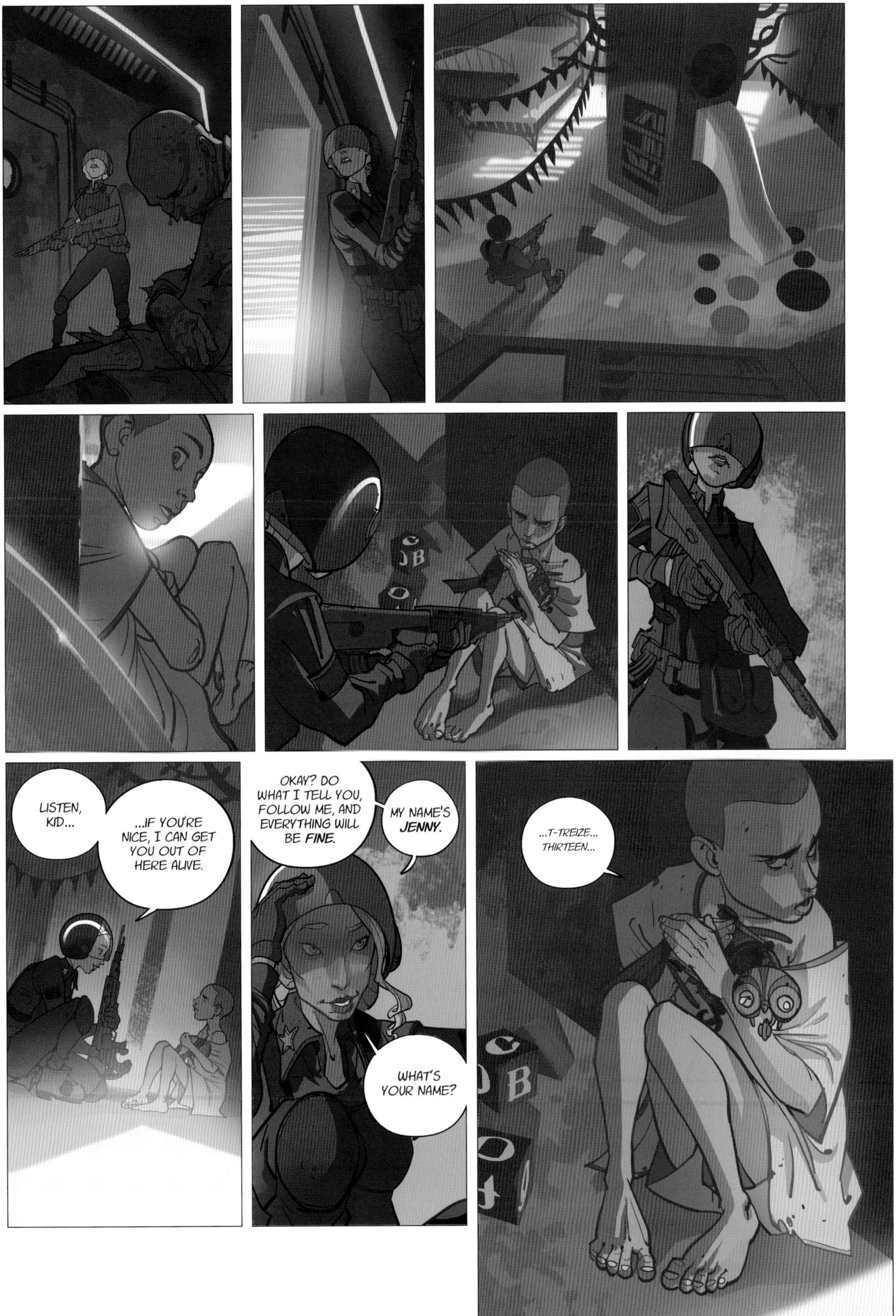
LISTEN, KID...
...IF YOU'RE NICE, I CAN GET YOU OUT OF HERE ALIVE.
OKAY? DO WHAT I TELL YOU, FOLLOW ME, AND EVERYTHING WILL BE **FINE**.
MY NAME'S **JENNY**.
WHAT'S YOUR NAME?
...T-TREIZE... THIRTEEN...

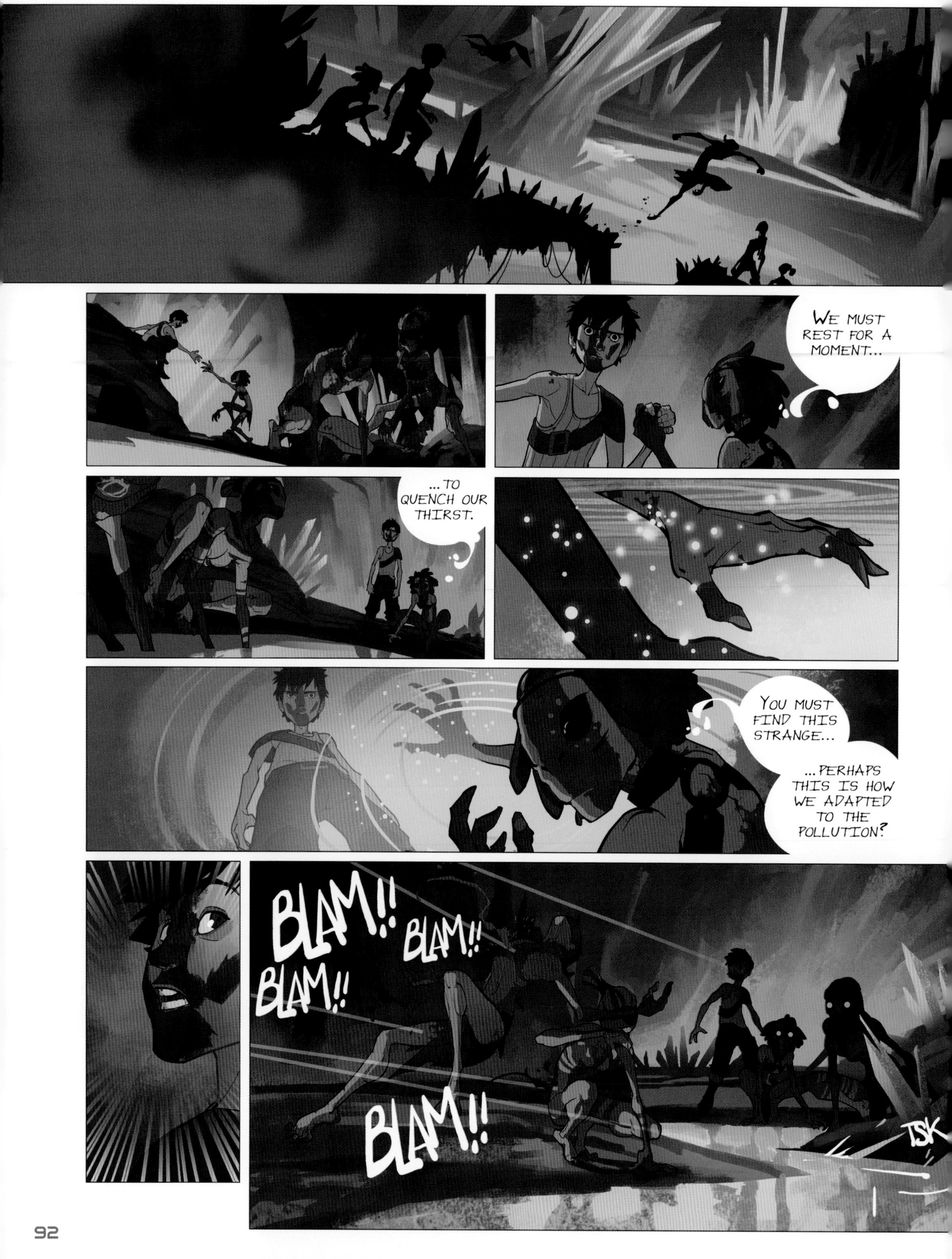
WE MUST REST FOR A MOMENT...
...TO QUENCH OUR THIRST.
YOU MUST FIND THIS STRANGE...
...PERHAPS THIS IS HOW WE ADAPTED TO THE POLLUTION?
BLAM!! BLAM!!
BLAM!!
BLAM!!
TSK

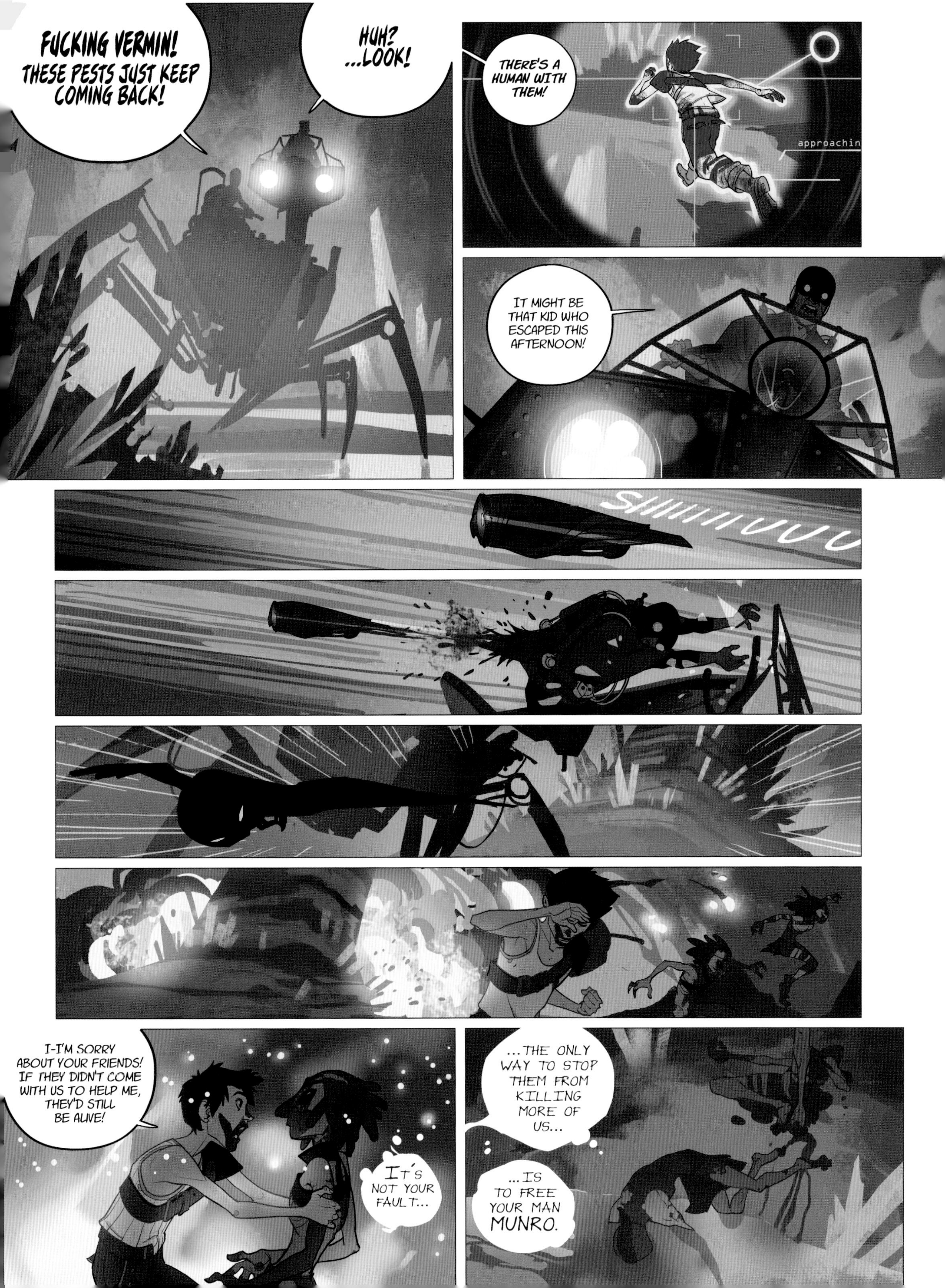
FUCKING VERMIN! THESE PESTS JUST KEEP COMING BACK!
HUH? ...LOOK!
THERE'S A HUMAN WITH THEM!
approachin
IT MIGHT BE THAT KID WHO ESCAPED THIS AFTERNOON!
SHIIIIIUUU
I-I'M SORRY ABOUT YOUR FRIENDS! IF THEY DIDN'T COME WITH US TO HELP ME, THEY'D STILL BE ALIVE!
IT'S NOT YOUR FAULT...
...THE ONLY WAY TO STOP THEM FROM KILLING MORE OF US...
...IS TO FREE YOUR MAN MUNRO.

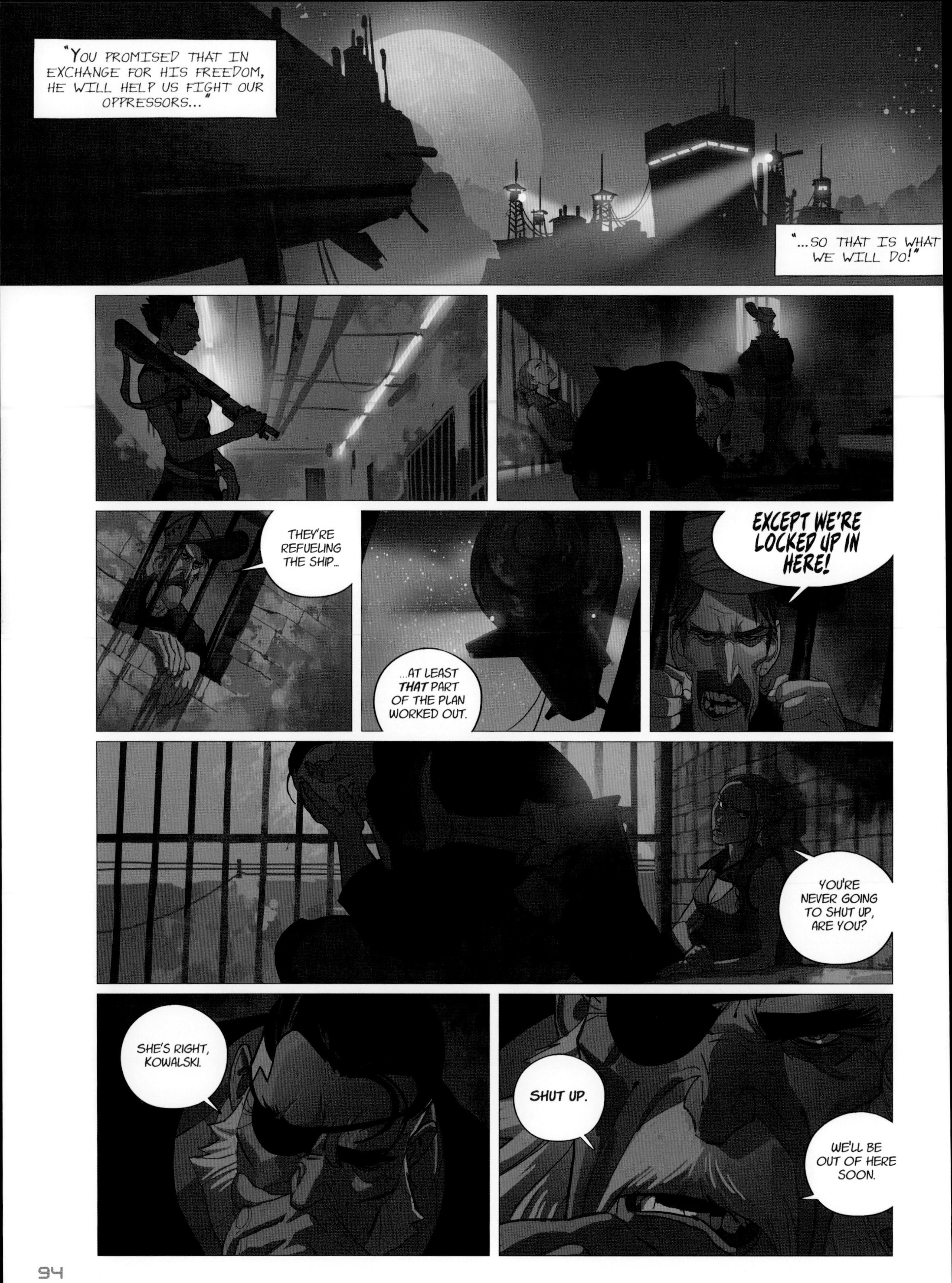
"YOU PROMISED THAT IN EXCHANGE FOR HIS FREEDOM, HE WILL HELP US FIGHT OUR OPPRESSORS..."
"...SO THAT IS WHAT WE WILL DO!"
THEY'RE REFUELING THE SHIP...
...AT LEAST THAT PART OF THE PLAN WORKED OUT.
EXCEPT WE'RE LOCKED UP IN HERE!
YOU'RE NEVER GOING TO SHUT UP, ARE YOU?
SHE'S RIGHT, KOWALSKI.
SHUT UP.
WE'LL BE OUT OF HERE SOON.

"IT WON'T BE EASY, BUT WE'LL GET OUT OF THIS DUMP...

"...AND I'LL GO SEE MY *SON.*"

THERE.

YOU CAN SEE THE BASE.

GOOD, I'LL SEND *OOK...*

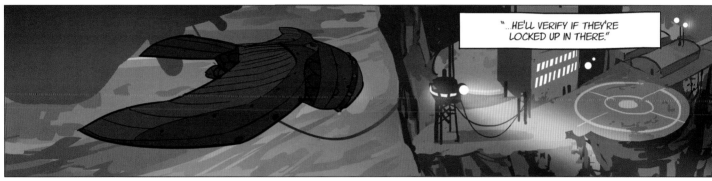

"...HE'LL VERIFY IF THEY'RE LOCKED UP IN THERE."

JUST HOW IS THIS GOING TO BE *OKAY?*

IS THERE SOMETHING YOU'RE NOT TELLING US, MUNRO?

YOU'LL SEE AT DAWN, WHEN THEY COME TO EXECUTE ME.

DO WHAT I SAY AT THAT TIME AND WE'LL BE FINE.

I SEE THEM.

ALIVE. ALL THREE.

CONFEDERATE YEAR 3851.
PLANET HAR-ARATH

IT'S ALL HERE.

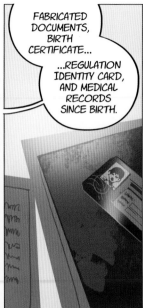

FABRICATED DOCUMENTS, BIRTH CERTIFICATE...

...REGULATION IDENTITY CARD, AND MEDICAL RECORDS SINCE BIRTH.

IT'S ALL FAKE. BUT A PERFECT FAKE. UNDETECTABLE.

I'D EXPECT NO LESS, GLORIA.

YOU'RE THE BEST FORGER IN THE NEAR-SIX SYSTEMS...

...15 YEARS RUNNING NOW!

ACTUALLY, I'M THE ONE WHO'S SURPRISED, JENNY.

YOU LEFT THE MILITARY TO START A FAMILY?

AREN'T YOU AFRAID YOU'LL DIE OF BOREDOM?

DEATH AWAITS ONE WAY OR ANOTHER IN THE CONFEDERATE COMMANDOS!

SO, I DECIDED...

"...MIGHT AS WELL DO SOMETHING OTHER THAN BECOMING A WAR-STAT!"

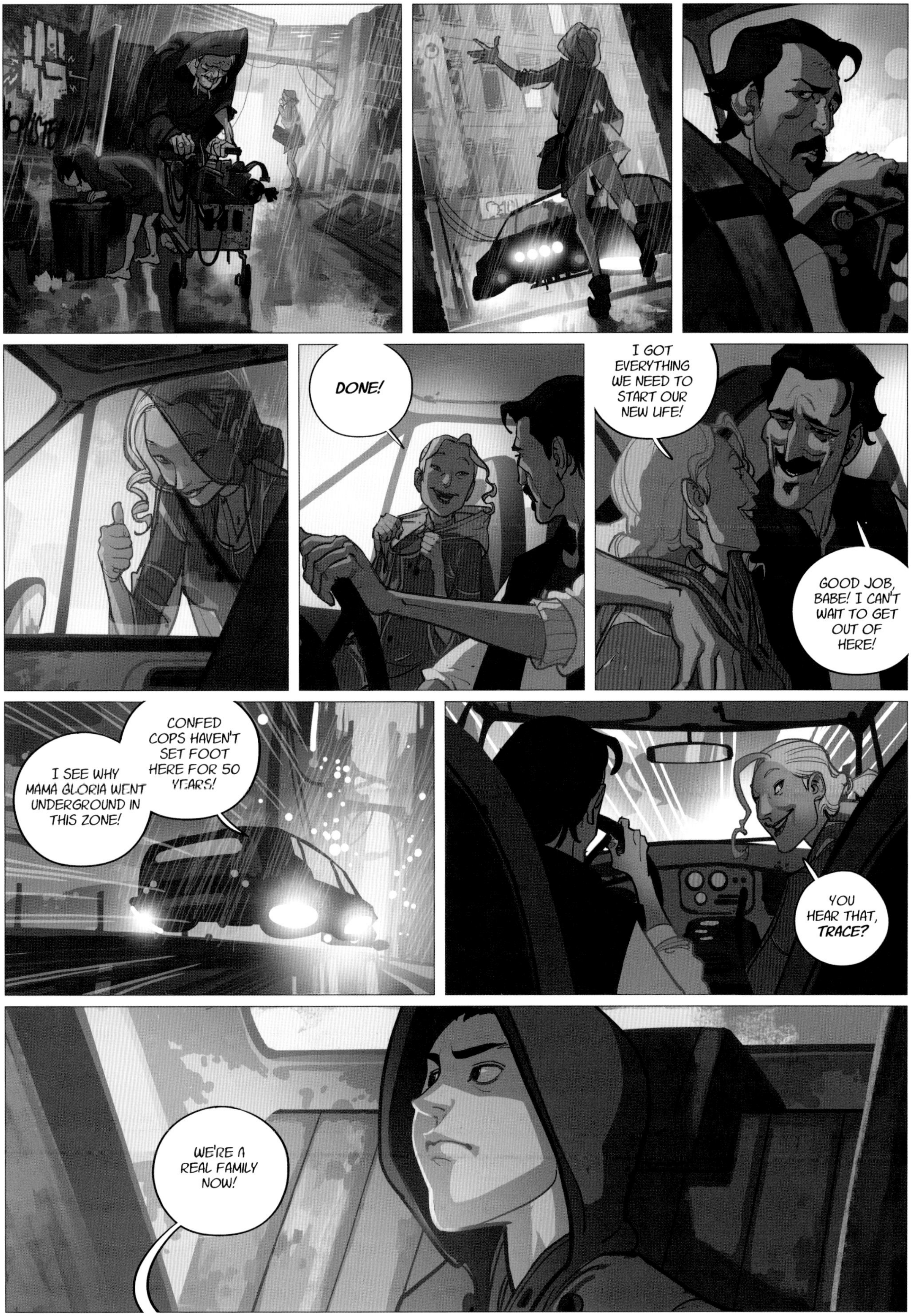
DONE!
I GOT EVERYTHING WE NEED TO START OUR NEW LIFE!
GOOD JOB, BABE! I CAN'T WAIT TO GET OUT OF HERE!
I SEE WHY MAMA GLORIA WENT UNDERGROUND IN THIS ZONE!
CONFED COPS HAVEN'T SET FOOT HERE FOR 50 YEARS!
YOU HEAR THAT, TRACE?
WE'RE A REAL FAMILY NOW!

HERE COMES OOK...

WE TRUST YOU, THIRTEEN, WE HAVE LITTLE CHOICE...

TAP!

...OUR LIVES DEPEND ON YOU AND YOUR DRONE!

JUST TELL US WHAT YOU HAVE PLANNED, DAMNIT!

NO.

YOU'LL SEE IF YOU FOLLOW MY LEAD.

I'LL FOLLOW YOU. AND I'M SORRY ABOUT YOUR SON.

BUT MY MOTHER IS INTRACTABLE. SHE'S A RADICAL. SHE'LL NEVER CHANGE HER MIND.

I WON'T ASK YOU FOR ANYTHING.

I KNOW.

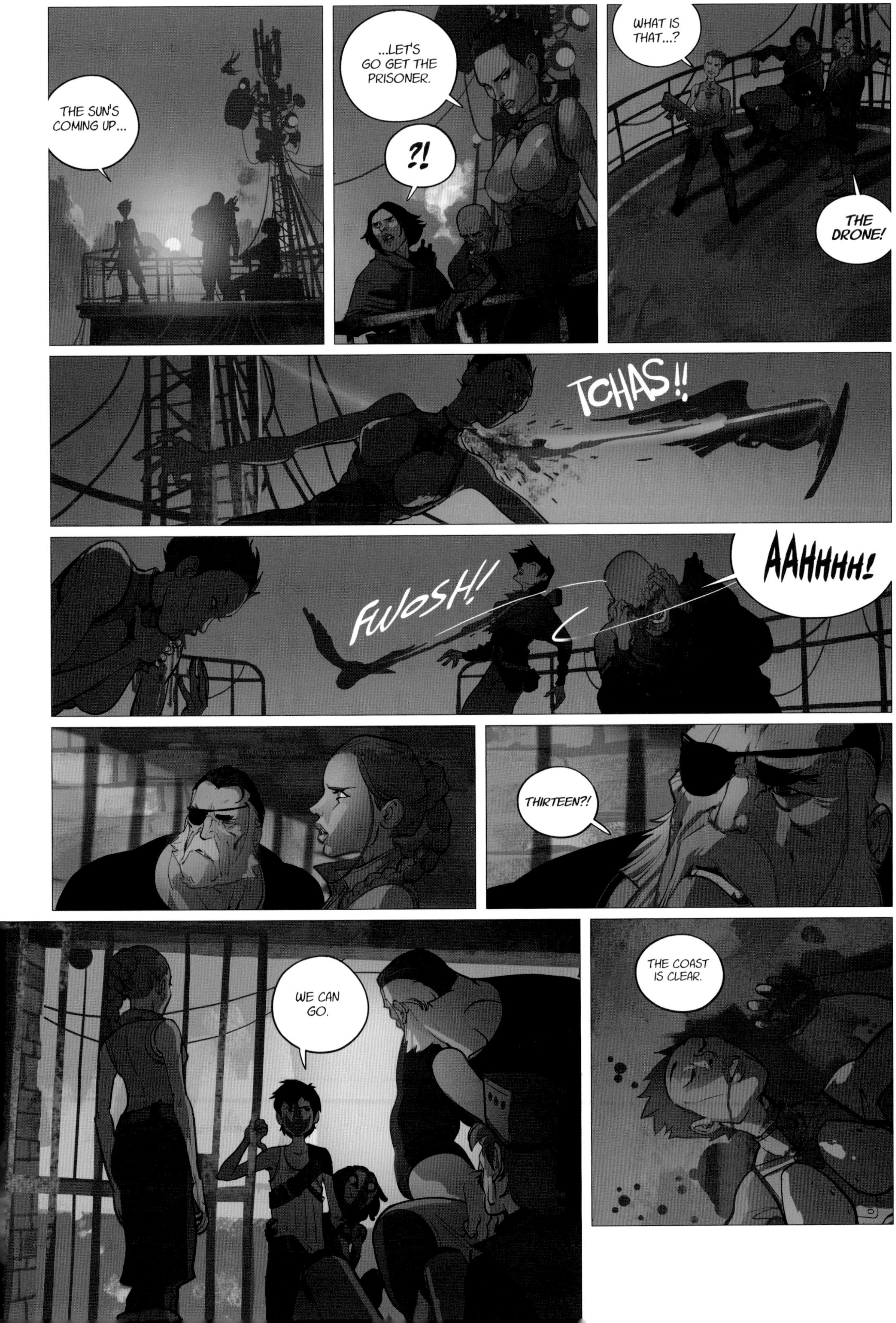
THE SUN'S COMING UP...
...LET'S GO GET THE PRISONER.
?!
WHAT IS THAT...?
THE DRONE!
TCHAS!!
FWOSH!
AAHHHH!
THIRTEEN?!
WE CAN GO.
THE COAST IS CLEAR.

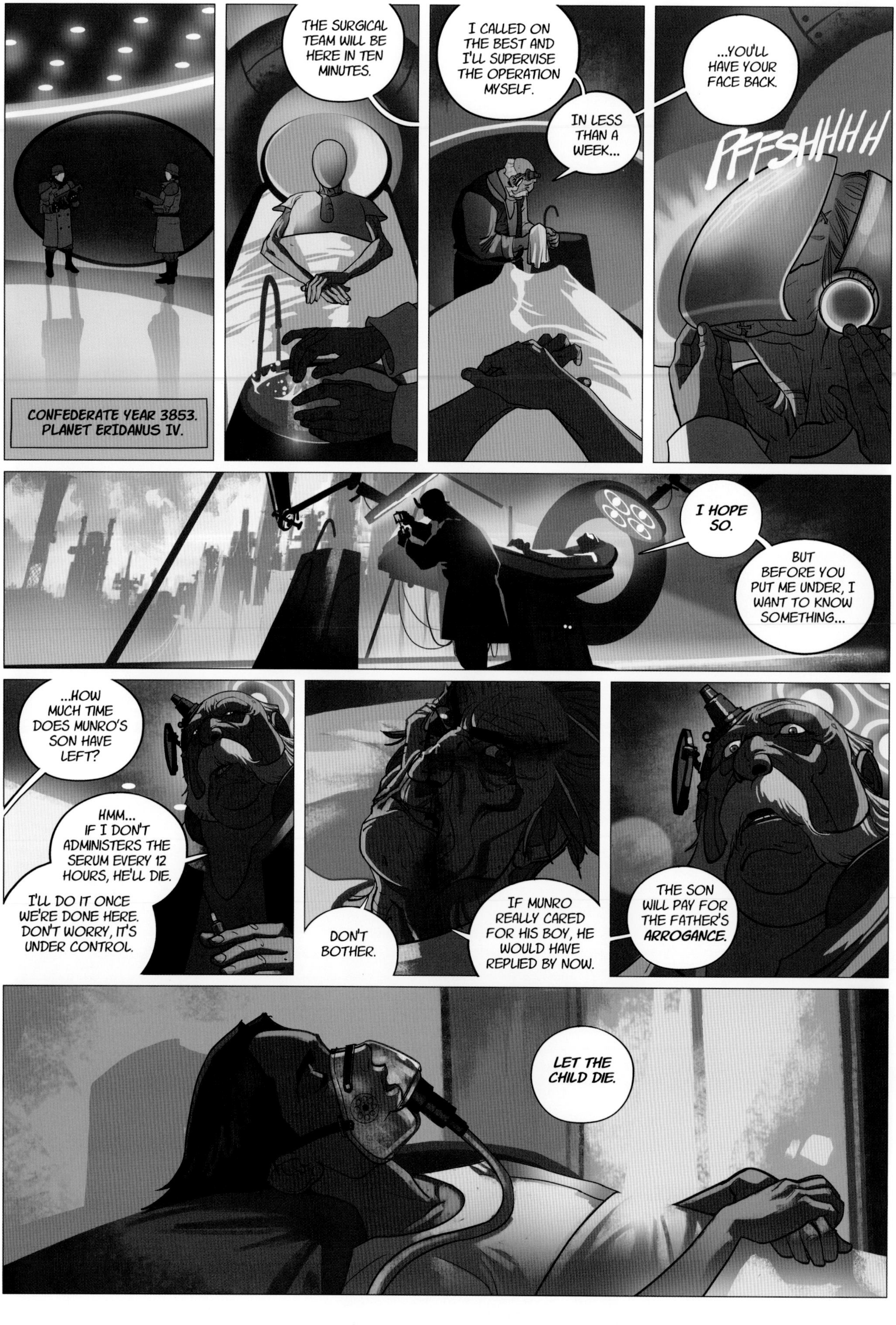
CONFEDERATE YEAR 3853. PLANET ERIDANUS IV.
THE SURGICAL TEAM WILL BE HERE IN TEN MINUTES.
I CALLED ON THE BEST AND I'LL SUPERVISE THE OPERATION MYSELF.
IN LESS THAN A WEEK...
...YOU'LL HAVE YOUR FACE BACK.
PFFSHHHH
I HOPE SO.
BUT BEFORE YOU PUT ME UNDER, I WANT TO KNOW SOMETHING...
...HOW MUCH TIME DOES MUNRO'S SON HAVE LEFT?
HMM... IF I DON'T ADMINISTERS THE SERUM EVERY 12 HOURS, HE'LL DIE.
I'LL DO IT ONCE WE'RE DONE HERE. DON'T WORRY, IT'S UNDER CONTROL.
DON'T BOTHER.
IF MUNRO REALLY CARED FOR HIS BOY, HE WOULD HAVE REPLIED BY NOW.
THE SON WILL PAY FOR THE FATHER'S ARROGANCE.
LET THE CHILD DIE.

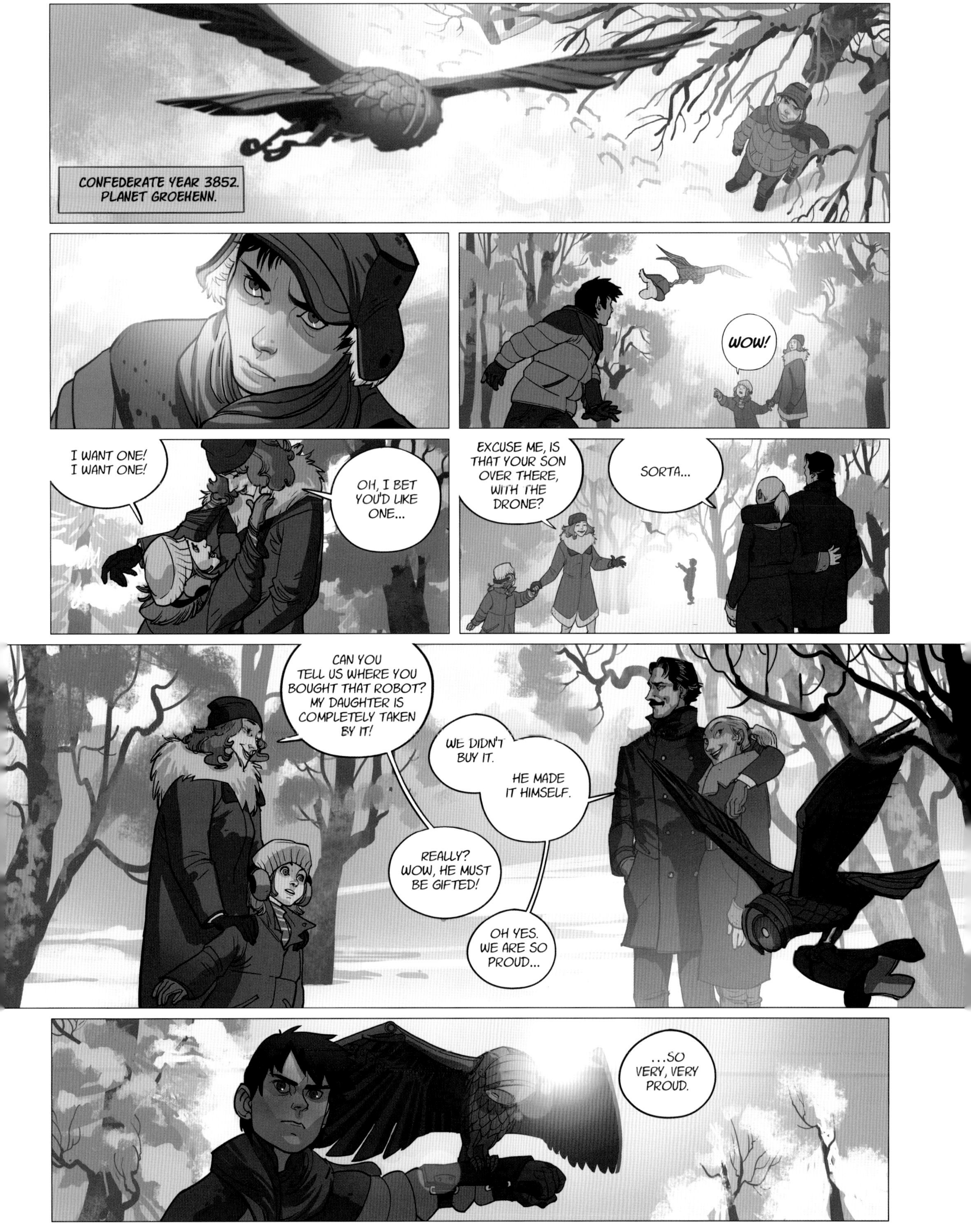

CONFEDERATE YEAR 3852.
PLANET GROEHENN.
WOW!
I WANT ONE! I WANT ONE!
OH, I BET YOU'D LIKE ONE...
EXCUSE ME, IS THAT YOUR SON OVER THERE, WITH THE DRONE?
SORTA...
CAN YOU TELL US WHERE YOU BOUGHT THAT ROBOT? MY DAUGHTER IS COMPLETELY TAKEN BY IT!
WE DIDN'T BUY IT.
HE MADE IT HIMSELF.
REALLY? WOW, HE MUST BE GIFTED!
OH YES. WE ARE SO PROUD...
...SO VERY, VERY PROUD.

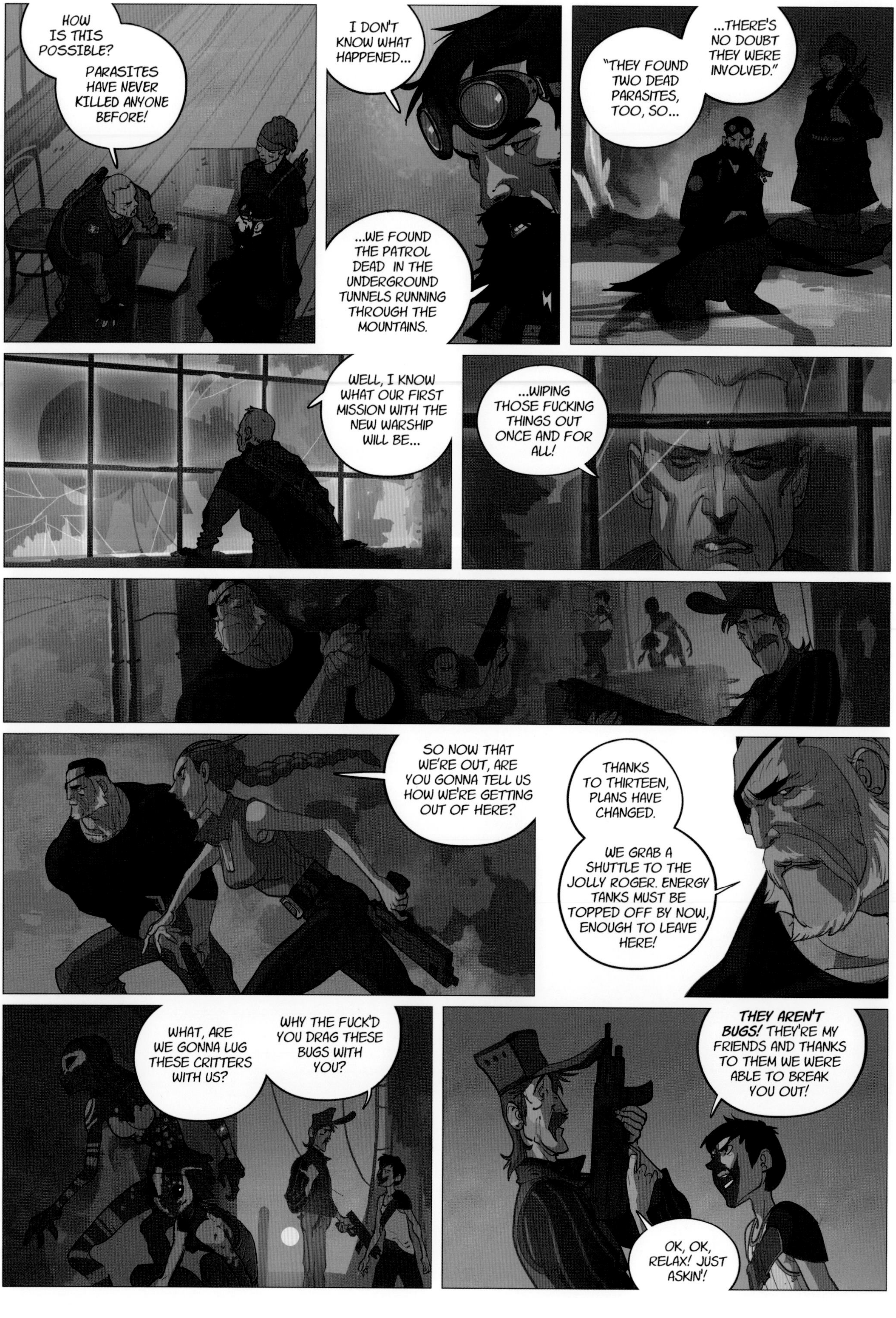
HOW IS THIS POSSIBLE?
PARASITES HAVE NEVER KILLED ANYONE BEFORE!
I DON'T KNOW WHAT HAPPENED...
...WE FOUND THE PATROL DEAD IN THE UNDERGROUND TUNNELS RUNNING THROUGH THE MOUNTAINS.
"THEY FOUND TWO DEAD PARASITES, TOO, SO...
...THERE'S NO DOUBT THEY WERE INVOLVED."
WELL, I KNOW WHAT OUR FIRST MISSION WITH THE NEW WARSHIP WILL BE...
...WIPING THOSE FUCKING THINGS OUT ONCE AND FOR ALL!
SO NOW THAT WE'RE OUT, ARE YOU GONNA TELL US HOW WE'RE GETTING OUT OF HERE?
THANKS TO THIRTEEN, PLANS HAVE CHANGED.
WE GRAB A SHUTTLE TO THE JOLLY ROGER. ENERGY TANKS MUST BE TOPPED OFF BY NOW, ENOUGH TO LEAVE HERE!
WHAT, ARE WE GONNA LUG THESE CRITTERS WITH US?
WHY THE FUCK'D YOU DRAG THESE BUGS WITH YOU?
THEY AREN'T BUGS! THEY'RE MY FRIENDS AND THANKS TO THEM WE WERE ABLE TO BREAK YOU OUT!
OK, OK, RELAX! JUST ASKIN'!

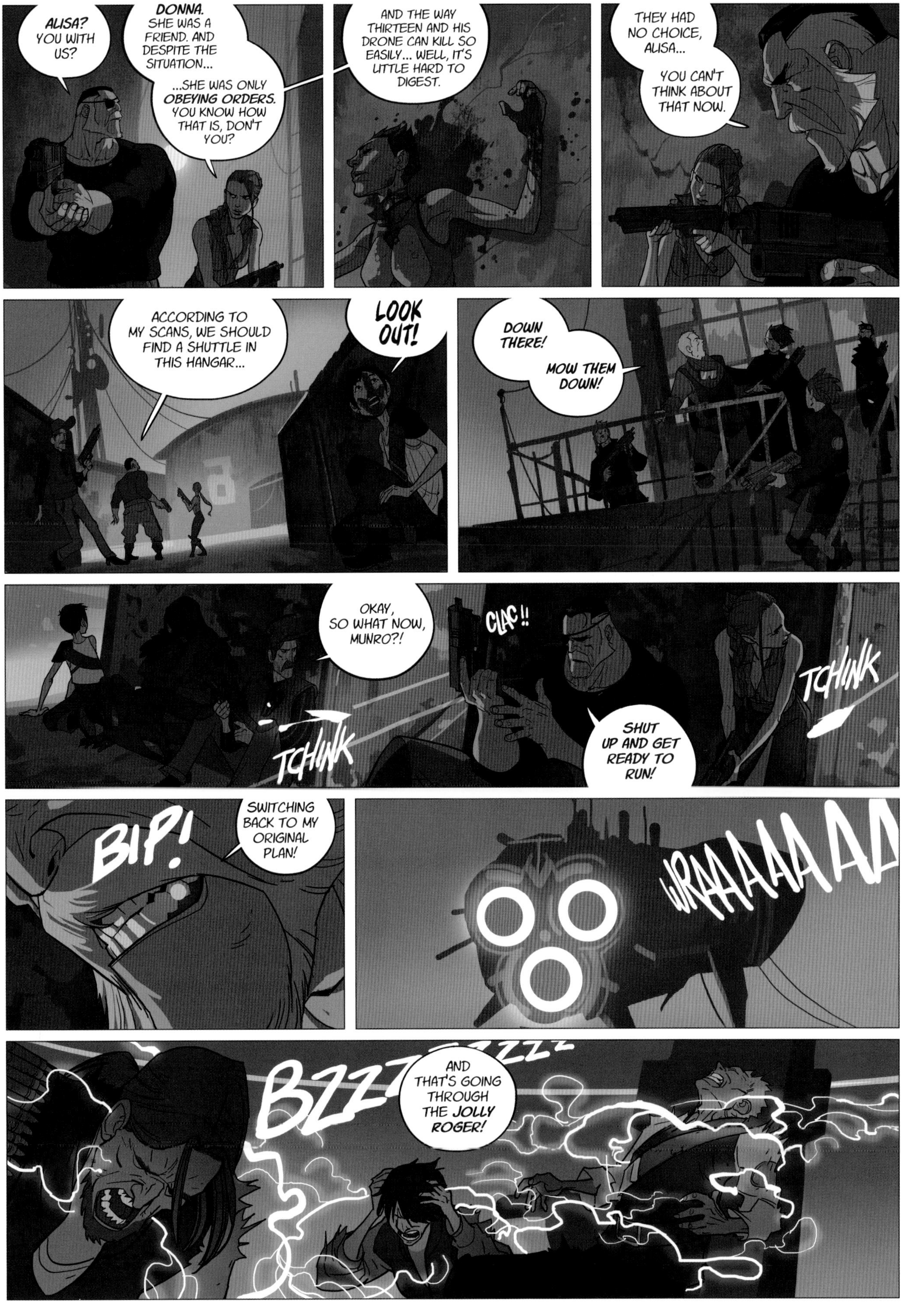

ALISA? YOU WITH US?
DONNA. SHE WAS A FRIEND. AND DESPITE THE SITUATION...
...SHE WAS ONLY OBEYING ORDERS. YOU KNOW HOW THAT IS, DON'T YOU?
AND THE WAY THIRTEEN AND HIS DRONE CAN KILL SO EASILY... WELL, IT'S LITTLE HARD TO DIGEST.
THEY HAD NO CHOICE, ALISA...
YOU CAN'T THINK ABOUT THAT NOW.
ACCORDING TO MY SCANS, WE SHOULD FIND A SHUTTLE IN THIS HANGAR...
LOOK OUT!
DOWN THERE!
MOW THEM DOWN!
OKAY, SO WHAT NOW, MUNRO?!
CLAC!!
TCHINK
SHUT UP AND GET READY TO RUN!
TCHINK
BIP!
SWITCHING BACK TO MY ORIGINAL PLAN!
WRAAAAAAAA
BZZZZZZZZ
AND THAT'S GOING THROUGH THE JOLLY ROGER!

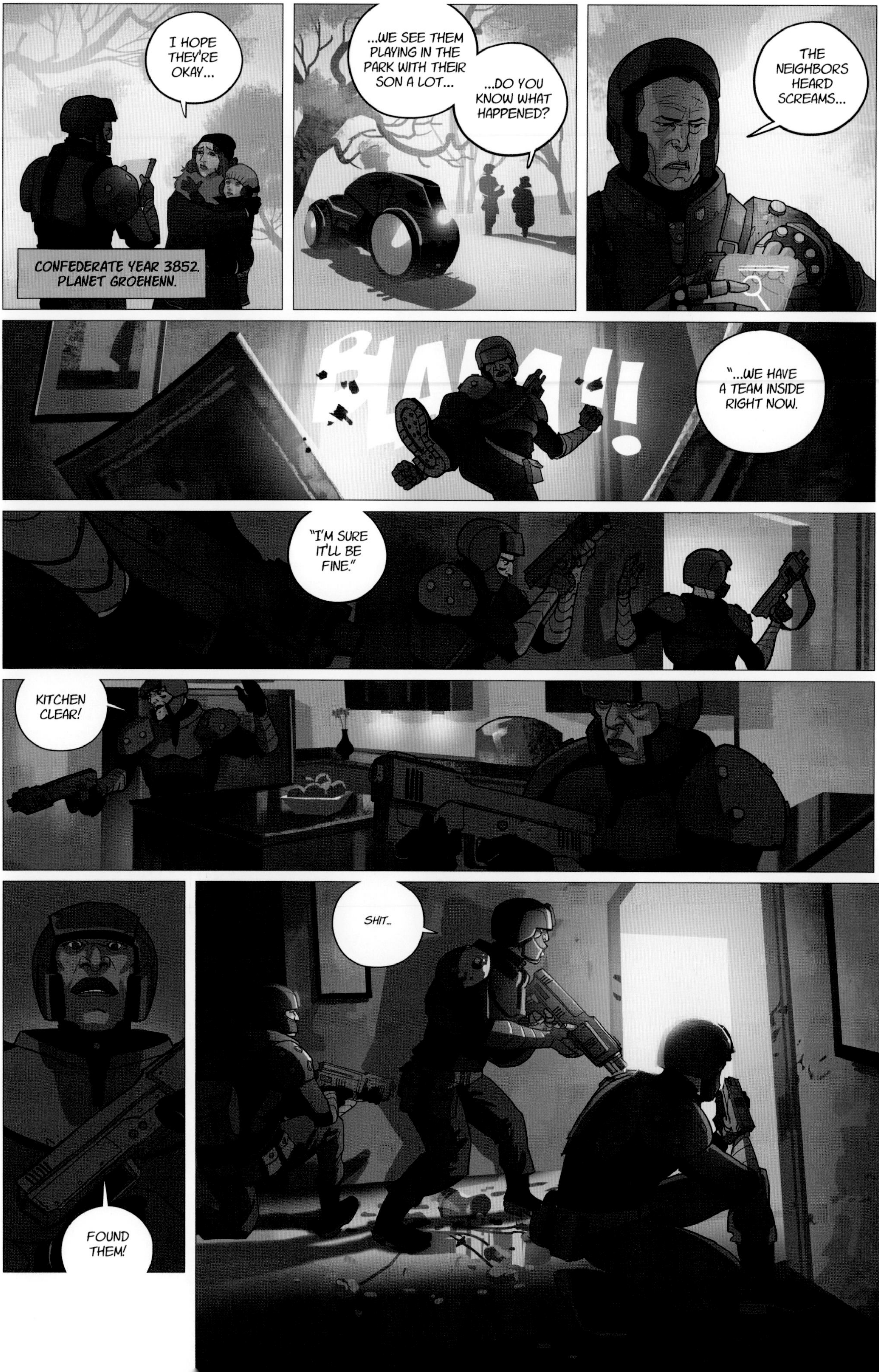
I HOPE THEY'RE OKAY...
CONFEDERATE YEAR 3852. PLANET GROEHENN.
...WE SEE THEM PLAYING IN THE PARK WITH THEIR SON A LOT...
...DO YOU KNOW WHAT HAPPENED?
THE NEIGHBORS HEARD SCREAMS...
BLAM!!
"...WE HAVE A TEAM INSIDE RIGHT NOW.
"I'M SURE IT'LL BE FINE."
KITCHEN CLEAR!
FOUND THEM!
SHIT...

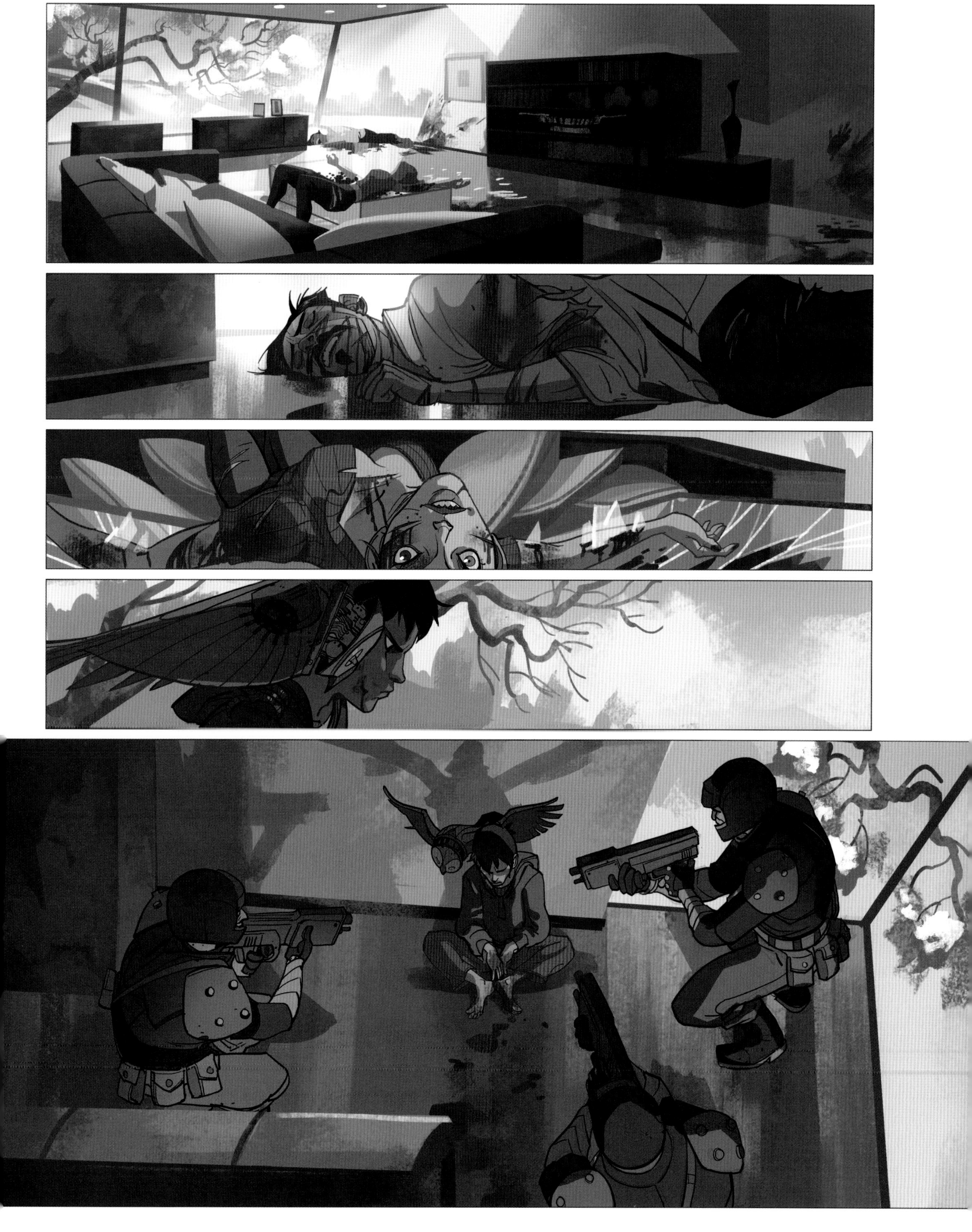

"IT'S CALLED AN *OFFENSIVE PRE-SEQUENCING.*

"AND ONLY OFFICERS AT MY RANK KNOW THE PROCEDURE.

"BEFORE I CAME DOWN, I SCANNED THE BASE AND RECORDED *TARGET DETAILS...*

"DCA TURRETS, GUARD POSTS, ASSAULT VEHICLES... WE'D ANNIHILATE THEIR DEFENSES.

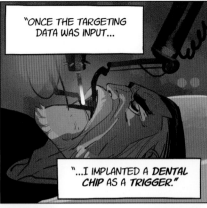

"ONCE THE TARGETING DATA WAS INPUT...

"...I IMPLANTED A *DENTAL CHIP* AS A *TRIGGER.*"

CLAC!

IT ACTIVATES BY GRINDING PRESSURE.

I WAS GONNA TRIGGER IT BEFORE MY EXECUTION, ONCE I KNEW THE JOLLY ROGER HAD BEEN RECHARGED.

BLAM!!

"BUT THEN THIRTEEN CAUGHT US ALL BY SURPRISE..."

I HOPED WE COULD AVOID COMBAT, BUT I WAS WRONG!

BUT HOW'RE YOU CONTROLLING THE SHIP'S GUNS?!

I'M NOT! THEY'RE PRE-PROGRAMMED!

I JUST MARKED THE TARGETS AND SET A *FIRING PATTERN!*

I JUST HOPE I REMEMBER THE SEQUENCE...

BETTER STAY CLOSE!

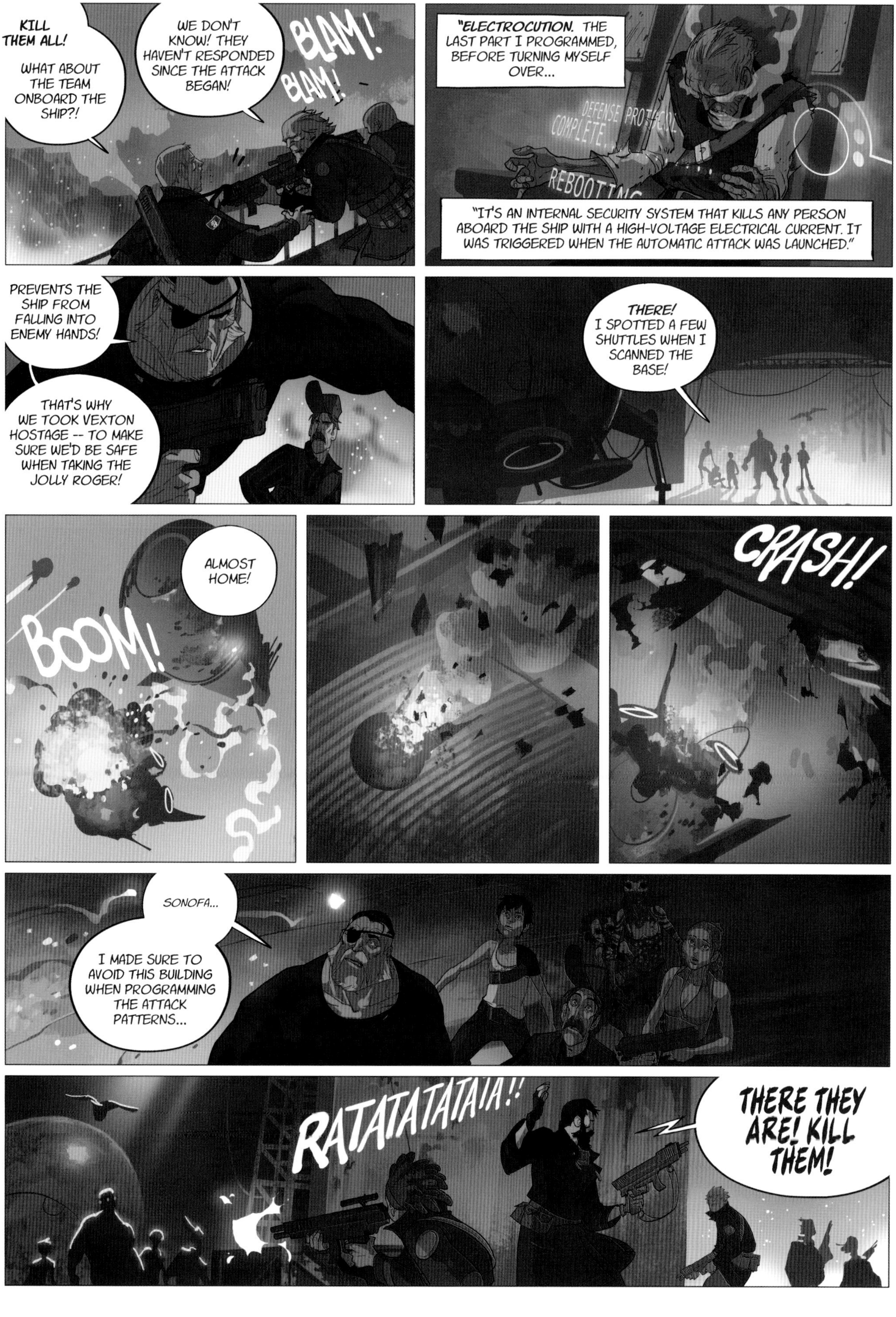
KILL THEM ALL!
WHAT ABOUT THE TEAM ONBOARD THE SHIP?!
WE DON'T KNOW! THEY HAVEN'T RESPONDED SINCE THE ATTACK BEGAN!
BLAM! BLAM!
"ELECTROCUTION. THE LAST PART I PROGRAMMED, BEFORE TURNING MYSELF OVER...
DEFENSE PROTOCOL COMPLETE.
REBOOTING
"IT'S AN INTERNAL SECURITY SYSTEM THAT KILLS ANY PERSON ABOARD THE SHIP WITH A HIGH-VOLTAGE ELECTRICAL CURRENT. IT WAS TRIGGERED WHEN THE AUTOMATIC ATTACK WAS LAUNCHED."
PREVENTS THE SHIP FROM FALLING INTO ENEMY HANDS!
THAT'S WHY WE TOOK VEXTON HOSTAGE -- TO MAKE SURE WE'D BE SAFE WHEN TAKING THE JOLLY ROGER!
THERE! I SPOTTED A FEW SHUTTLES WHEN I SCANNED THE BASE!
ALMOST HOME!
BOOM!
CRASH!
SONOFA...
I MADE SURE TO AVOID THIS BUILDING WHEN PROGRAMMING THE ATTACK PATTERNS...
RATATATATATA!!
THERE THEY ARE! KILL THEM!

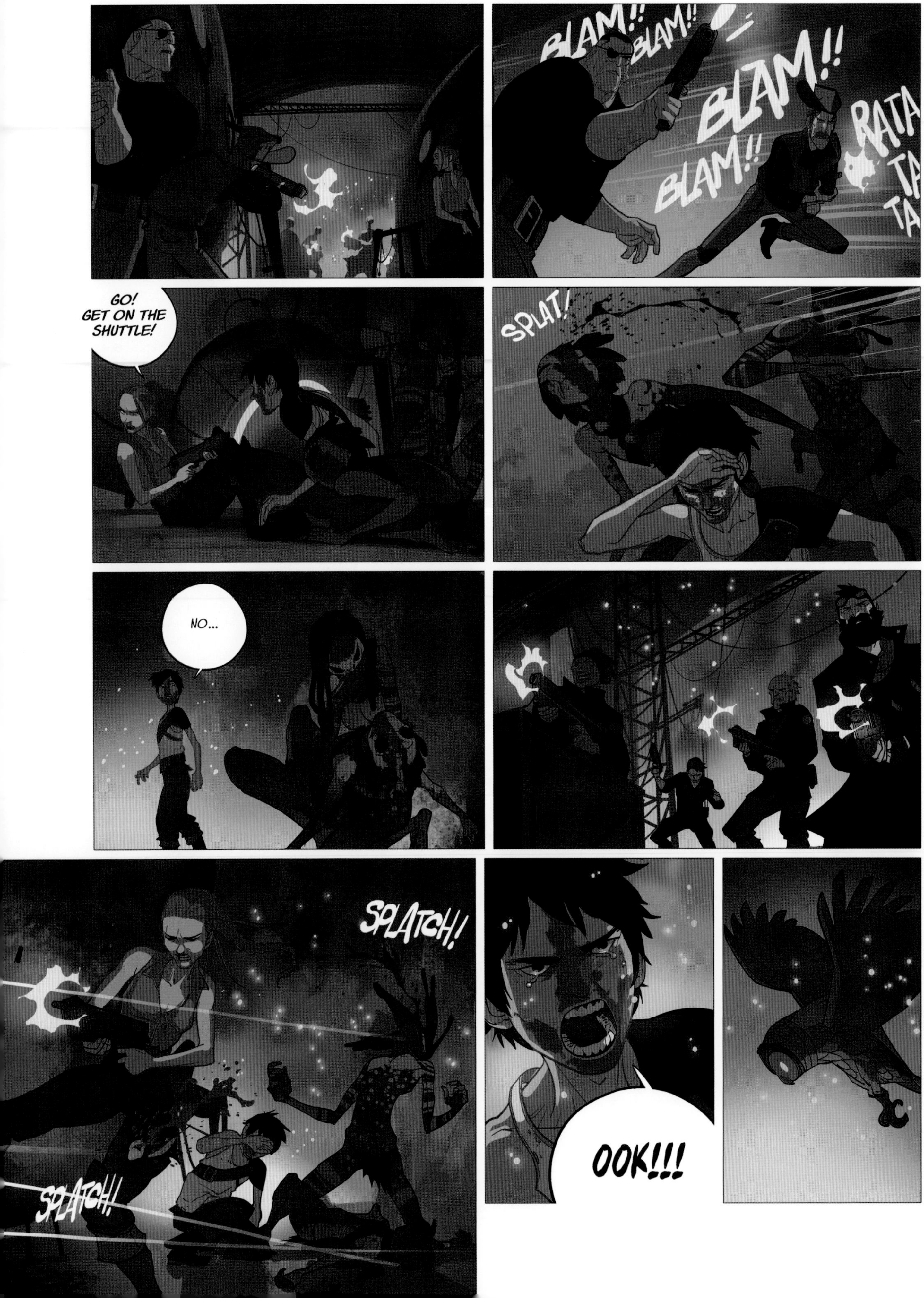
BLAM!!
BLAM!!
BLAM!!
BLAM!!
RATA TA TA
GO! GET ON THE SHUTTLE!
SPLAT!
NO...
SPLATCH!
SPLATCH!
OOK!!!

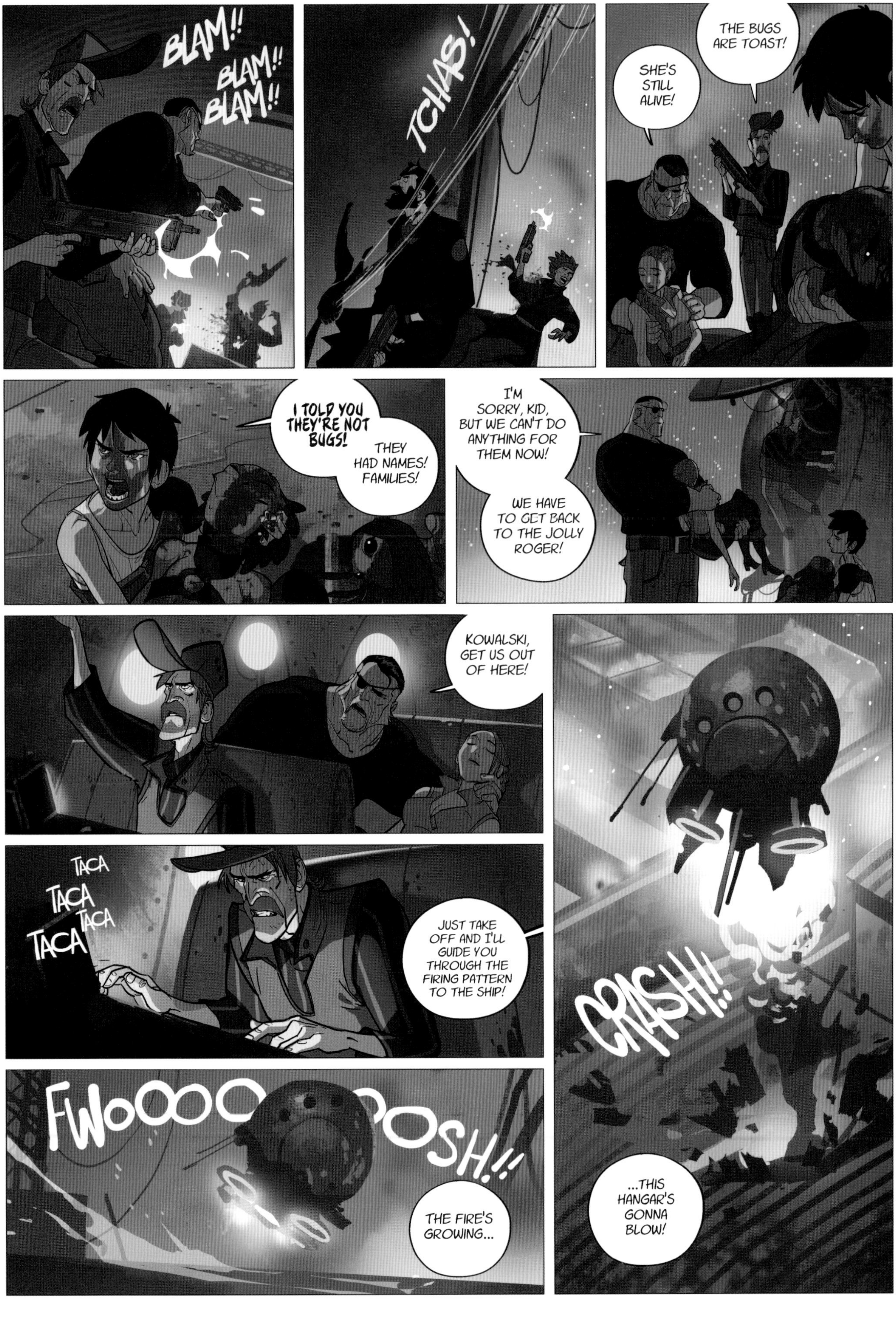
BLAM!!
BLAM!!
BLAM!!
TCHAS!
SHE'S STILL ALIVE!
THE BUGS ARE TOAST!
I TOLD YOU THEY'RE NOT BUGS!
THEY HAD NAMES! FAMILIES!
I'M SORRY, KID, BUT WE CAN'T DO ANYTHING FOR THEM NOW!
WE HAVE TO GET BACK TO THE JOLLY ROGER!
KOWALSKI, GET US OUT OF HERE!
TACA
TACA
TACA
TACA
JUST TAKE OFF AND I'LL GUIDE YOU THROUGH THE FIRING PATTERN TO THE SHIP!
FWOOOOOOOSH!!
THE FIRE'S GROWING...
CRASH!!
...THIS HANGAR'S GONNA BLOW!

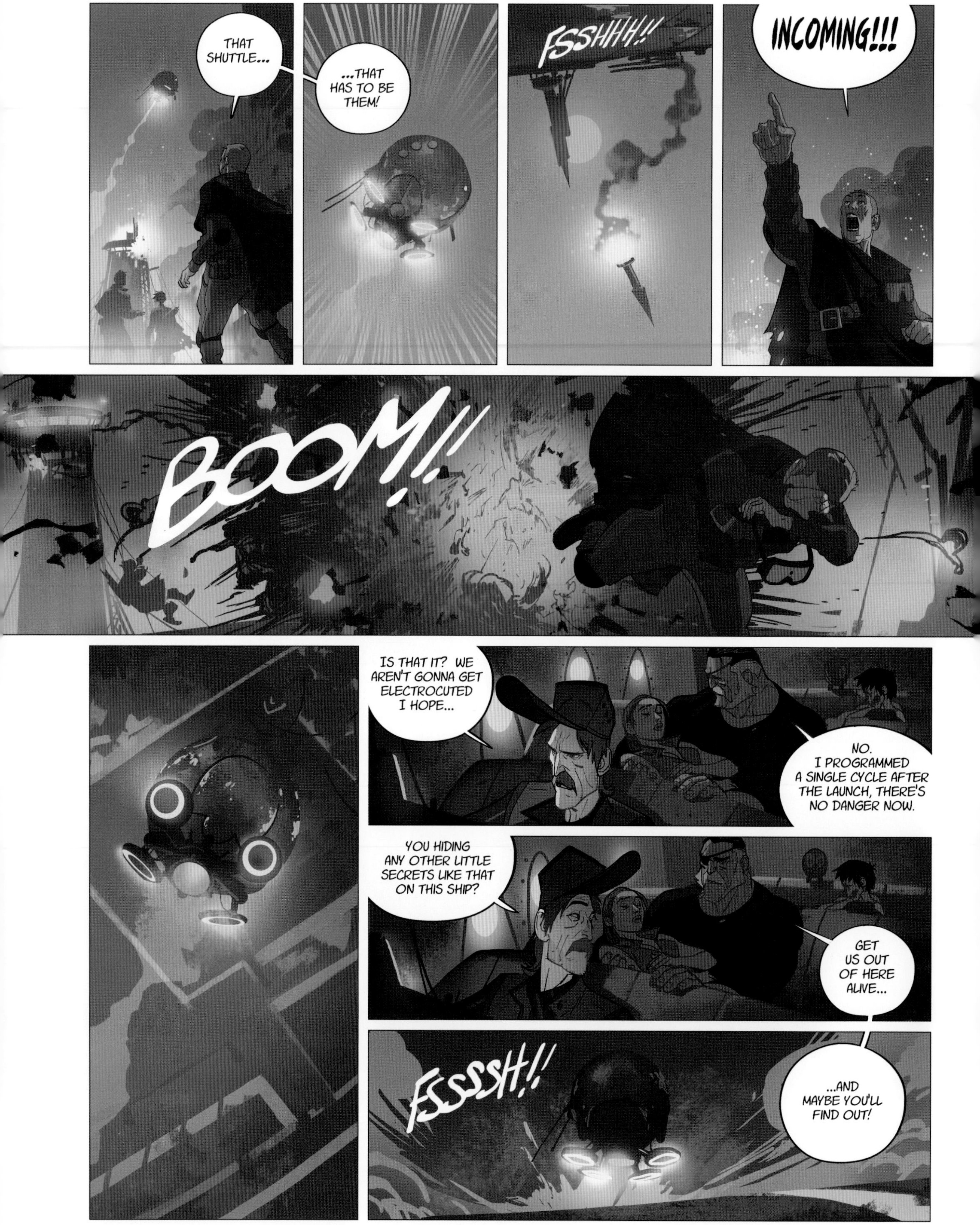
THAT SHUTTLE...
...THAT HAS TO BE THEM!
FSSHHH!!
INCOMING!!!
BOOM!!
IS THAT IT? WE AREN'T GONNA GET ELECTROCUTED I HOPE...
NO. I PROGRAMMED A SINGLE CYCLE AFTER THE LAUNCH, THERE'S NO DANGER NOW.
YOU HIDING ANY OTHER LITTLE SECRETS LIKE THAT ON THIS SHIP?
GET US OUT OF HERE ALIVE...
FSSSSH!!
...AND MAYBE YOU'LL FIND OUT!

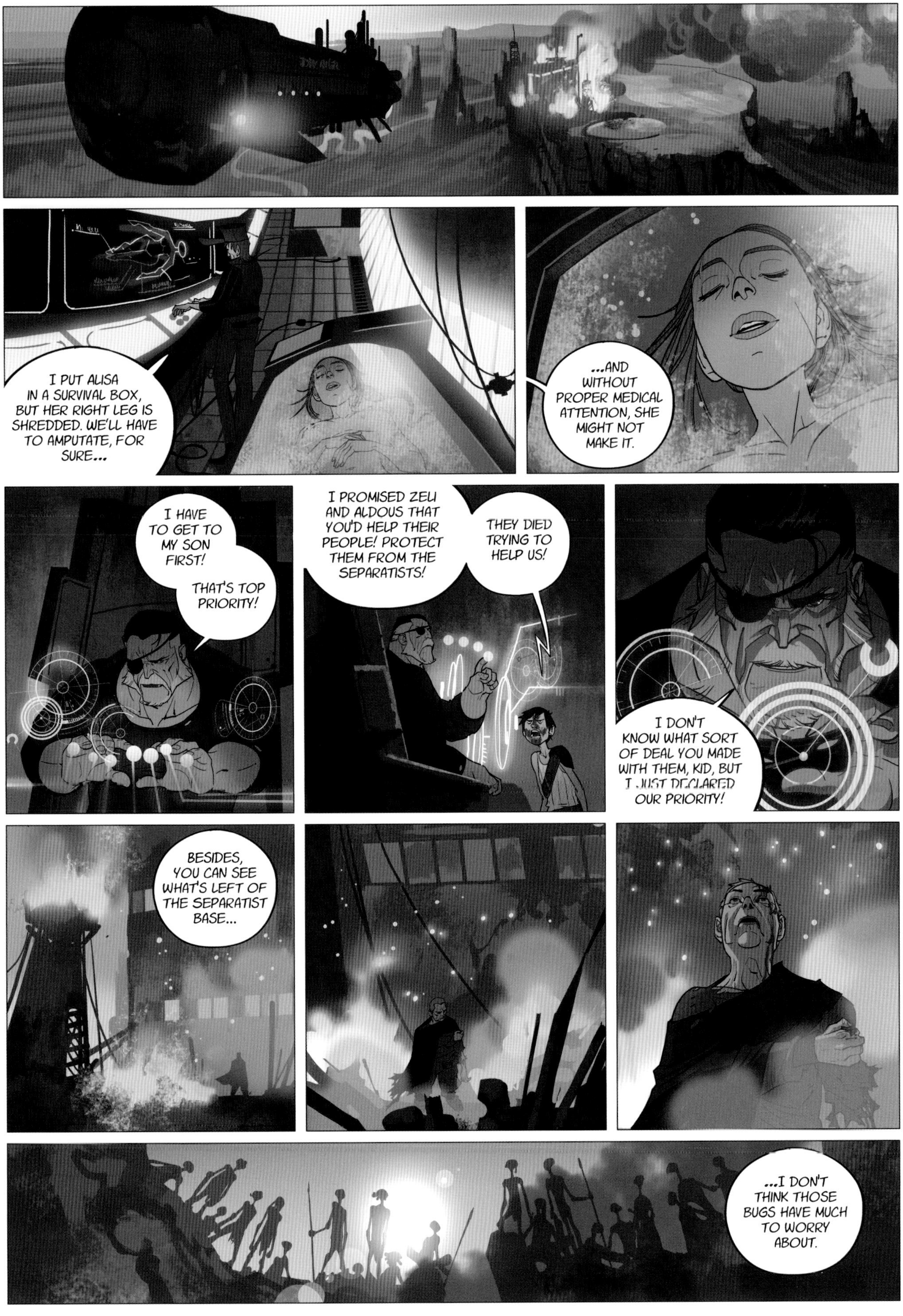

I PUT ALISA IN A SURVIVAL BOX, BUT HER RIGHT LEG IS SHREDDED. WE'LL HAVE TO AMPUTATE, FOR SURE...
...AND WITHOUT PROPER MEDICAL ATTENTION, SHE MIGHT NOT MAKE IT.
I HAVE TO GET TO MY SON FIRST!
THAT'S TOP PRIORITY!
I PROMISED ZEU AND ALDOUS THAT YOU'D HELP THEIR PEOPLE! PROTECT THEM FROM THE SEPARATISTS!
THEY DIED TRYING TO HELP US!
I DON'T KNOW WHAT SORT OF DEAL YOU MADE WITH THEM, KID, BUT I JUST DECLARED OUR PRIORITY!
BESIDES, YOU CAN SEE WHAT'S LEFT OF THE SEPARATIST BASE...
...I DON'T THINK THOSE BUGS HAVE MUCH TO WORRY ABOUT.

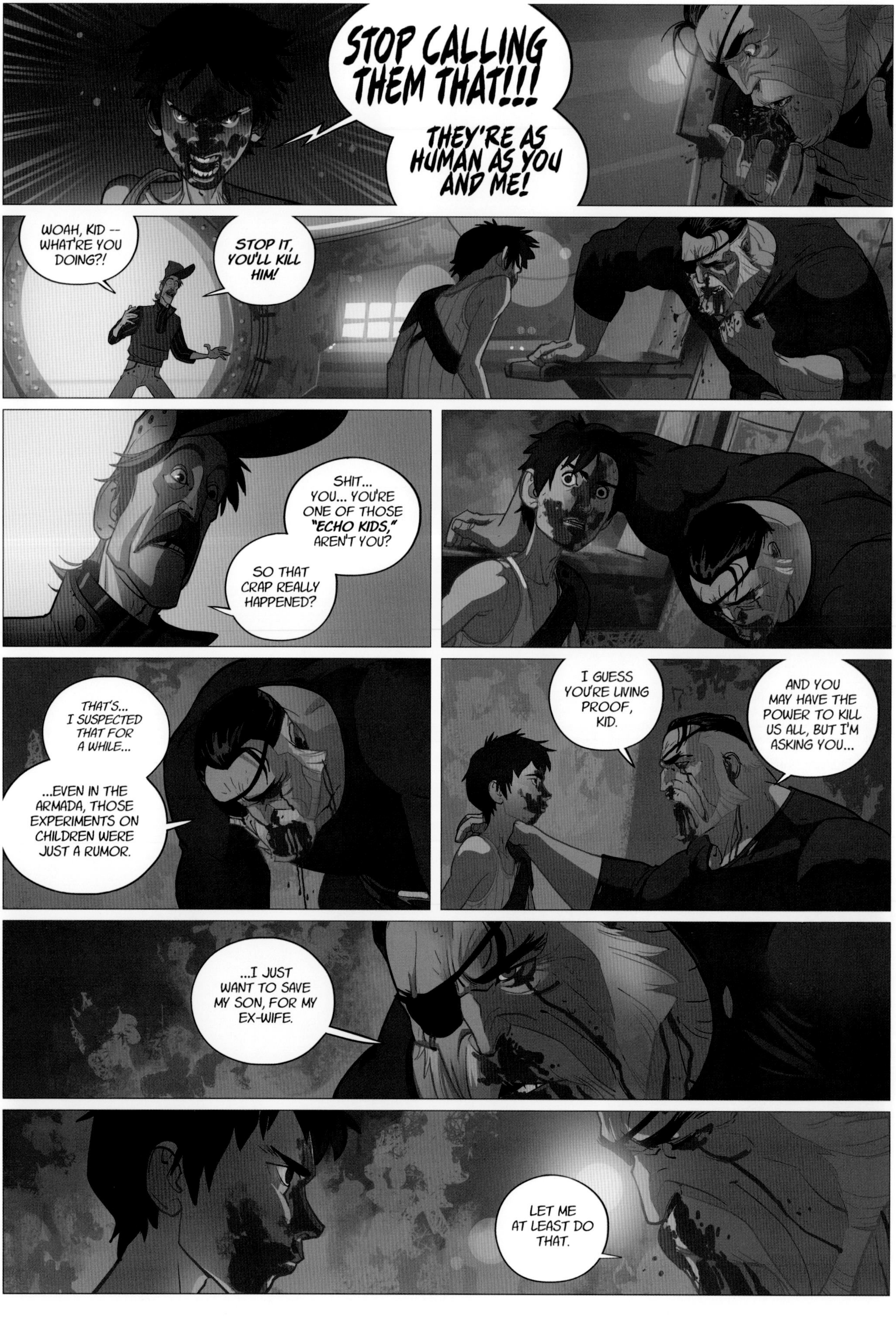
STOP CALLING THEM THAT!!!
THEY'RE AS HUMAN AS YOU AND ME!
WOAH, KID -- WHAT'RE YOU DOING?!
STOP IT, YOU'LL KILL HIM!
SHIT... YOU... YOU'RE ONE OF THOSE "ECHO KIDS," AREN'T YOU?
SO THAT CRAP REALLY HAPPENED?
THAT'S... I SUSPECTED THAT FOR A WHILE...
...EVEN IN THE ARMADA, THOSE EXPERIMENTS ON CHILDREN WERE JUST A RUMOR.
I GUESS YOU'RE LIVING PROOF, KID.
AND YOU MAY HAVE THE POWER TO KILL US ALL, BUT I'M ASKING YOU...
...I JUST WANT TO SAVE MY SON, FOR MY EX-WIFE.
LET ME AT LEAST DO THAT.

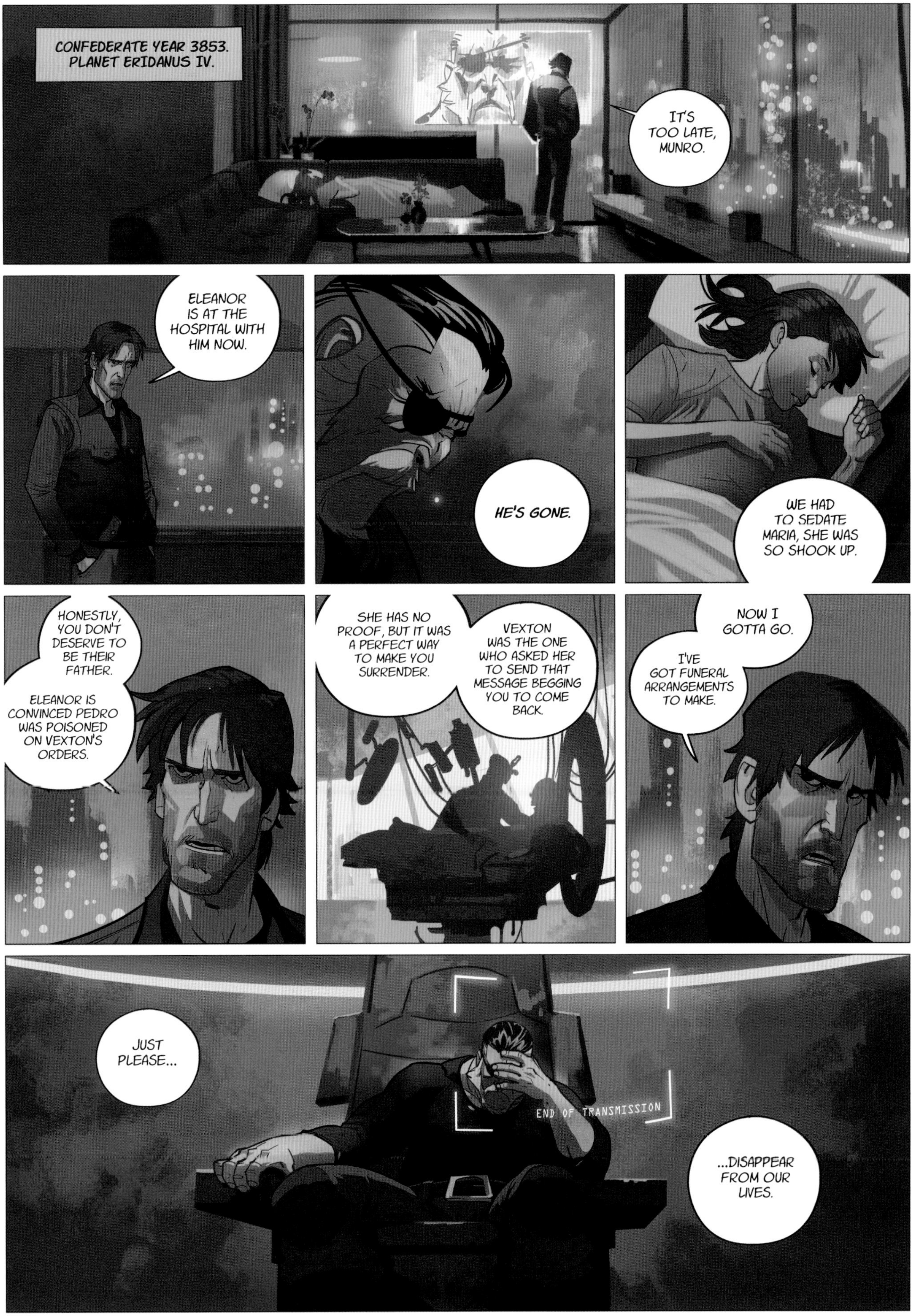
CONFEDERATE YEAR 3853. PLANET ERIDANUS IV.
IT'S TOO LATE, MUNRO.
ELEANOR IS AT THE HOSPITAL WITH HIM NOW.
HE'S GONE.
WE HAD TO SEDATE MARIA, SHE WAS SO SHOOK UP.
HONESTLY, YOU DON'T DESERVE TO BE THEIR FATHER.
ELEANOR IS CONVINCED PEDRO WAS POISONED ON VEXTON'S ORDERS.
SHE HAS NO PROOF, BUT IT WAS A PERFECT WAY TO MAKE YOU SURRENDER.
VEXTON WAS THE ONE WHO ASKED HER TO SEND THAT MESSAGE BEGGING YOU TO COME BACK.
NOW I GOTTA GO.
I'VE GOT FUNERAL ARRANGEMENTS TO MAKE.
JUST PLEASE...
END OF TRANSMISSION
...DISAPPEAR FROM OUR LIVES.

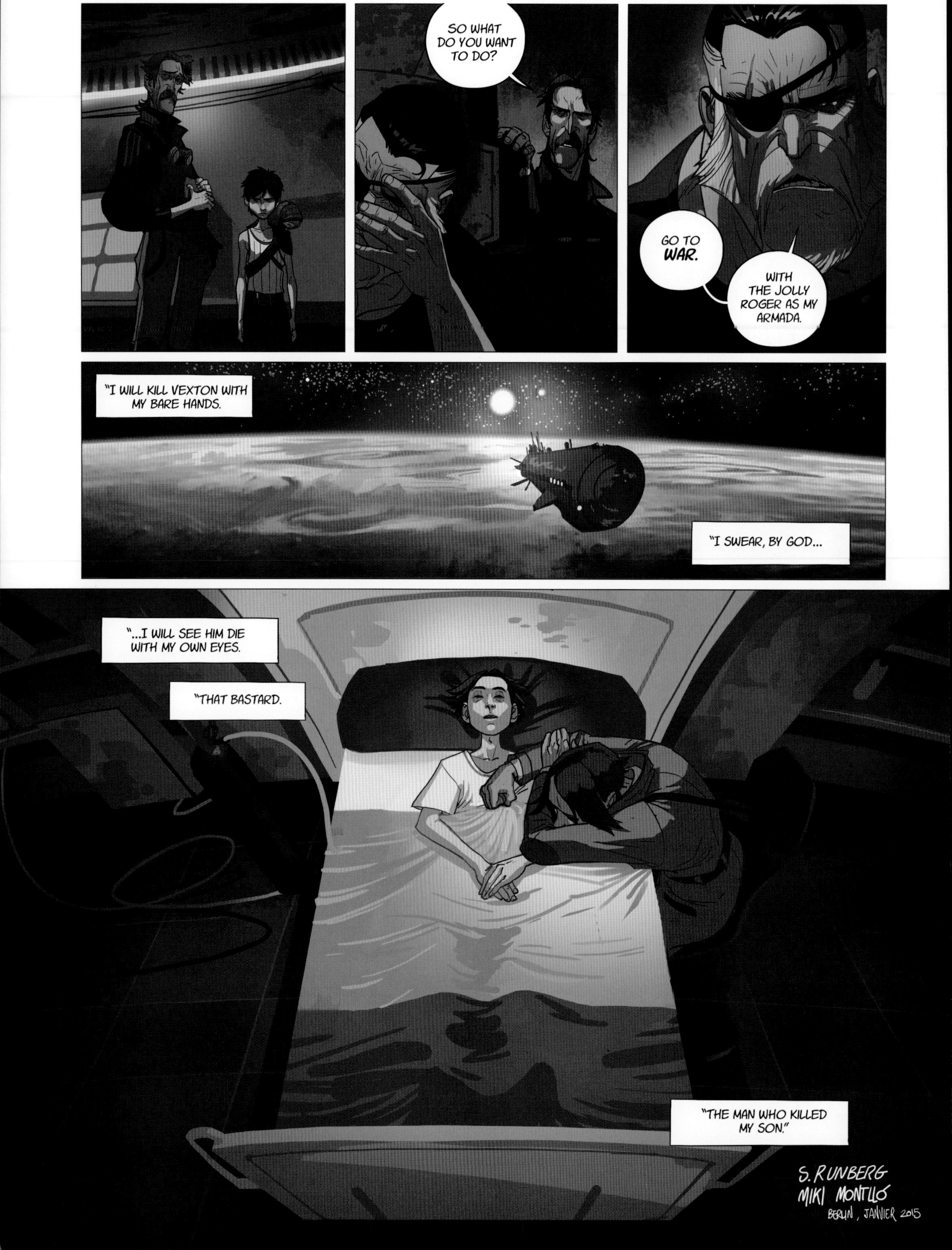
SO WHAT DO YOU WANT TO DO?
GO TO WAR.
WITH THE JOLLY ROGER AS MY ARMADA.
"I WILL KILL VEXTON WITH MY BARE HANDS.
"I SWEAR, BY GOD...
"...I WILL SEE HIM DIE WITH MY OWN EYES.
"THAT BASTARD.
"THE MAN WHO KILLED MY SON."
S. RUNBERG
MIKI MONTLLÓ
BERLIN, JANVIER 2015

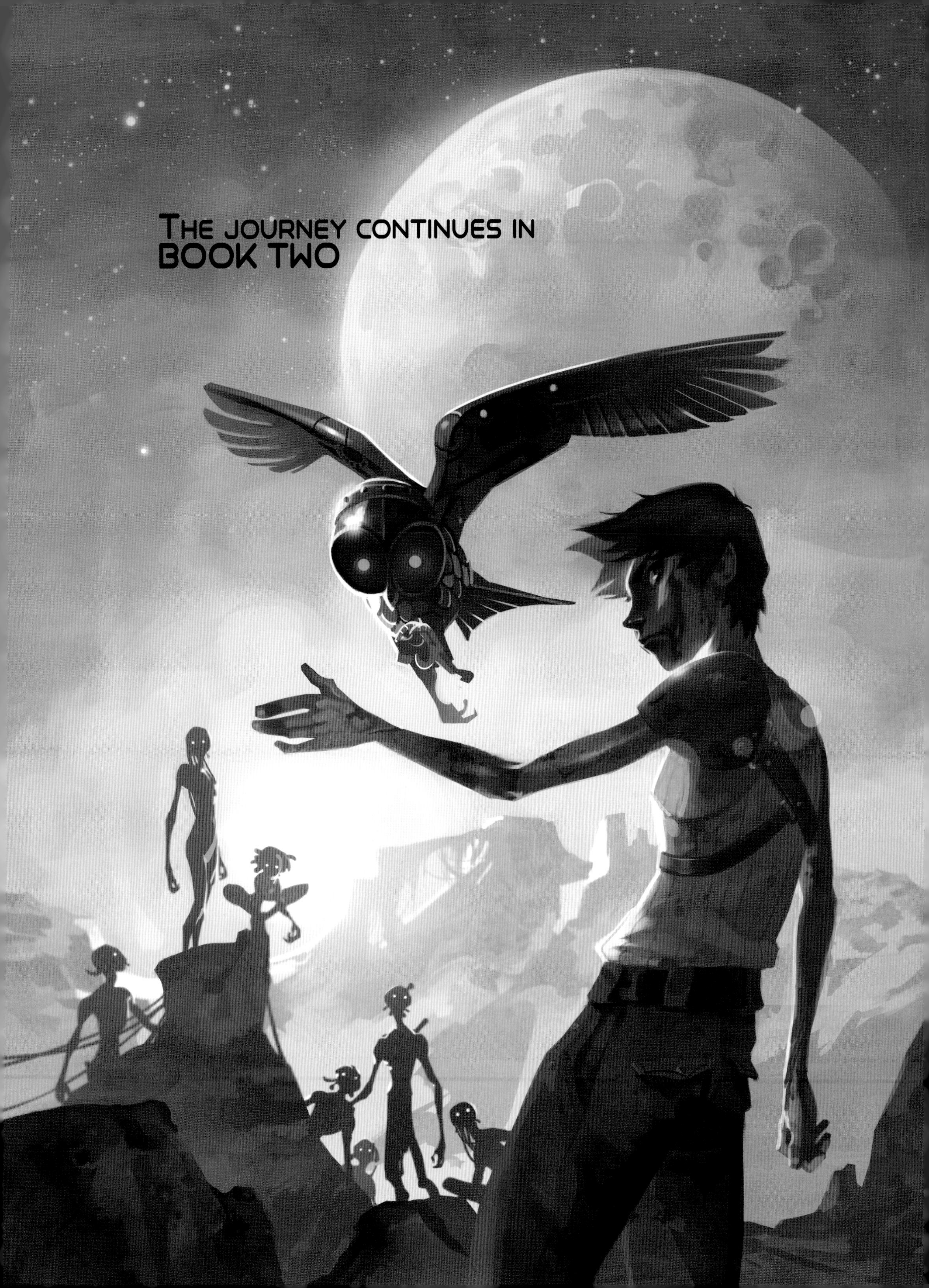
THE JOURNEY CONTINUES IN
BOOK TWO

CONCIEVED FULLY GROWN.

Production on WARSHIP JOLLY ROGER was treated like an animated feature, with rounds of character studies, model sheets, and color boards generated before any panels were drawn. The feature-quality, cell-style presentation is the genius talent of MIKI MONTLLO, who originally conceived the story and concept for WJR before partnering with acclaimed writer SYLVAIN RUNBERG to complete the picture within a fully-fleshed-out universe.

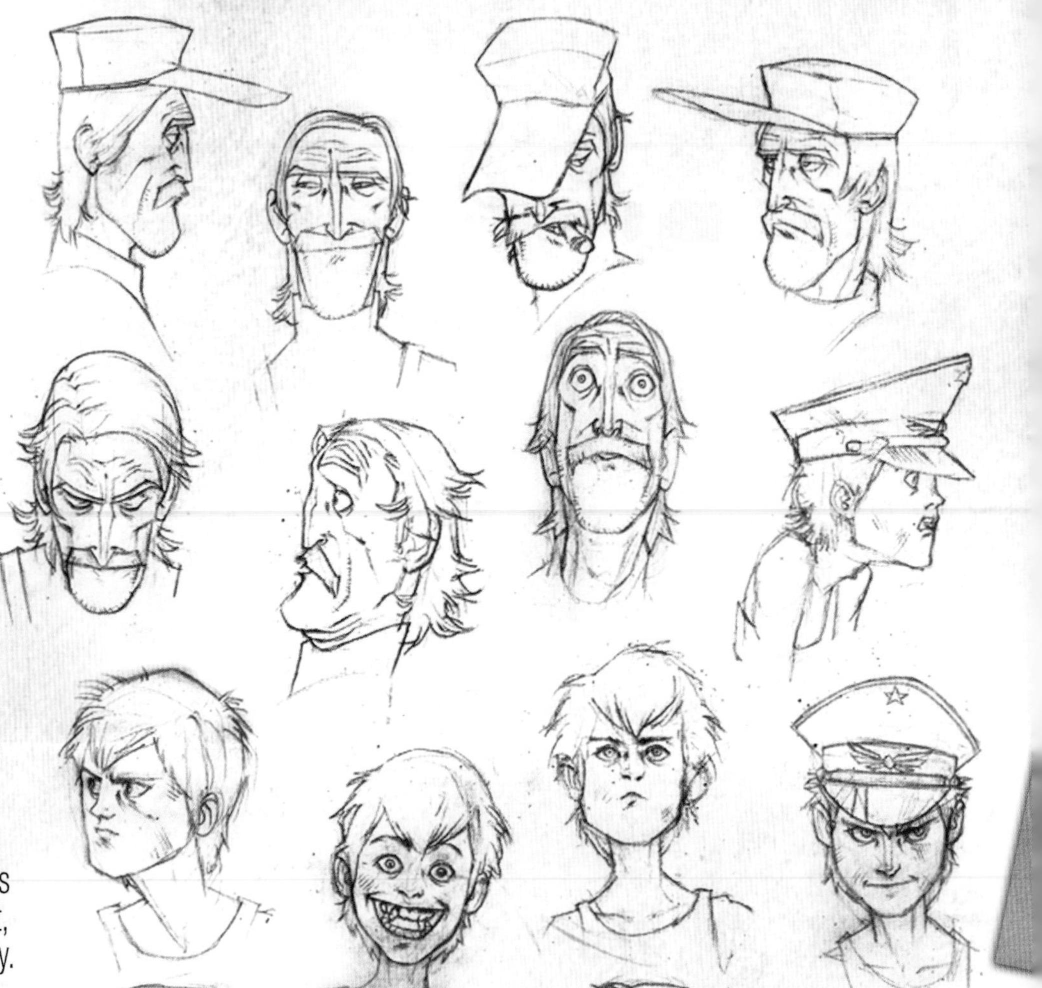

THESE PAGES:
Various character studies and evolution of the cast, between 2011 and today.

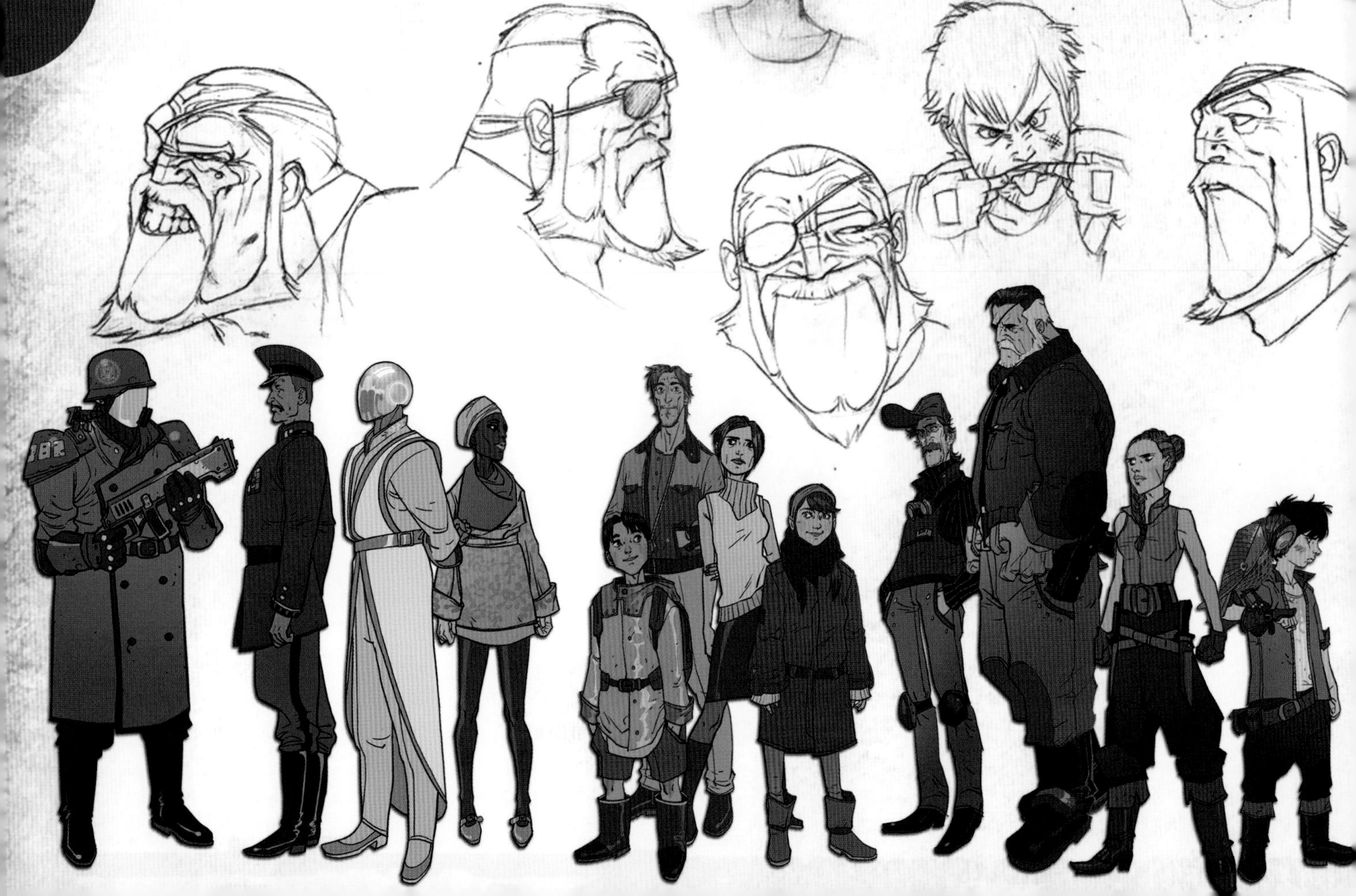

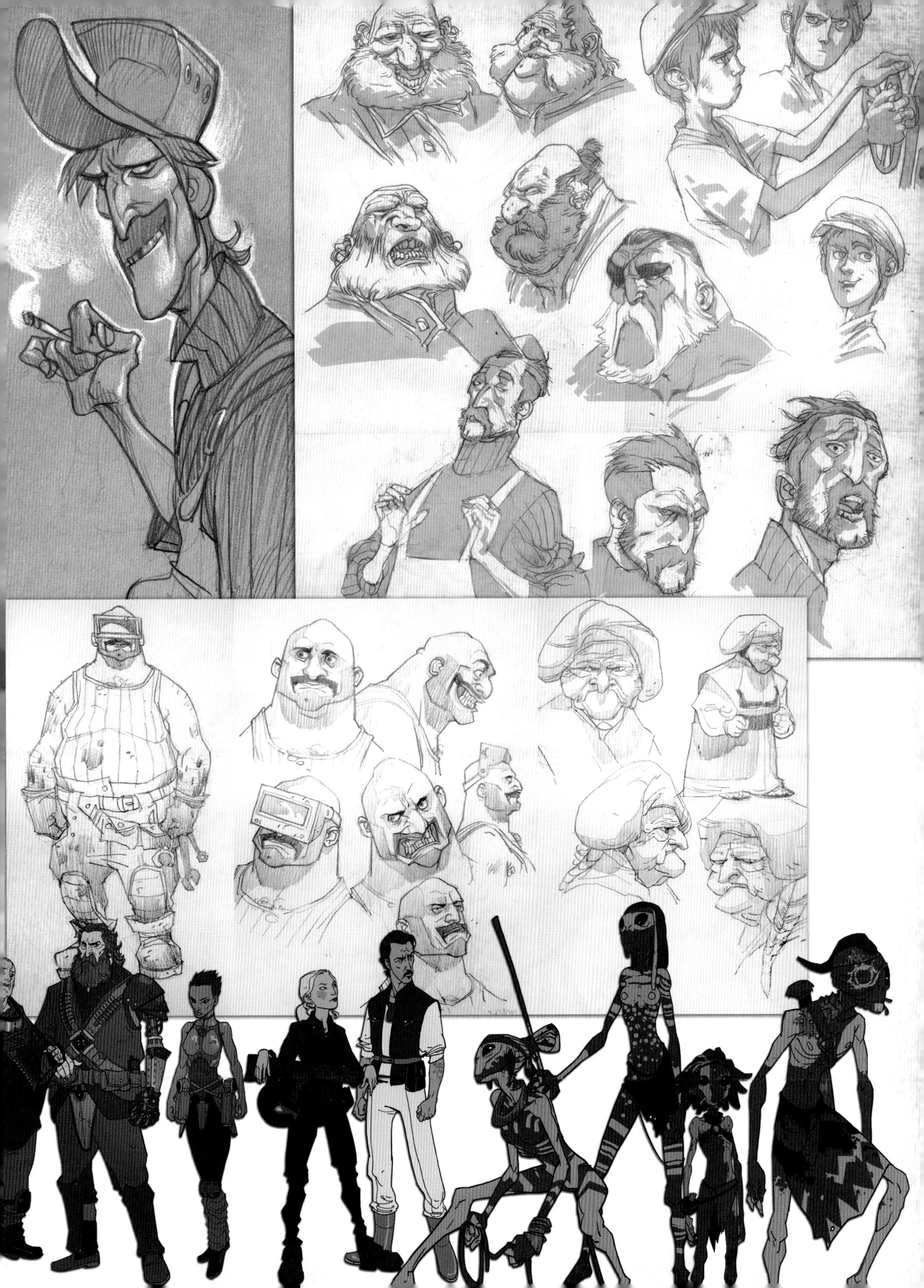

THIS PAGE:
Environment and pallette designs -
Elial Base (top),
Elial jungle (middle), and
Jolly Roger Green Room (bottom).

NEXT PAG
The never-before-se
4-page pitch from Mi
original JOLLY ROG
proposal packa

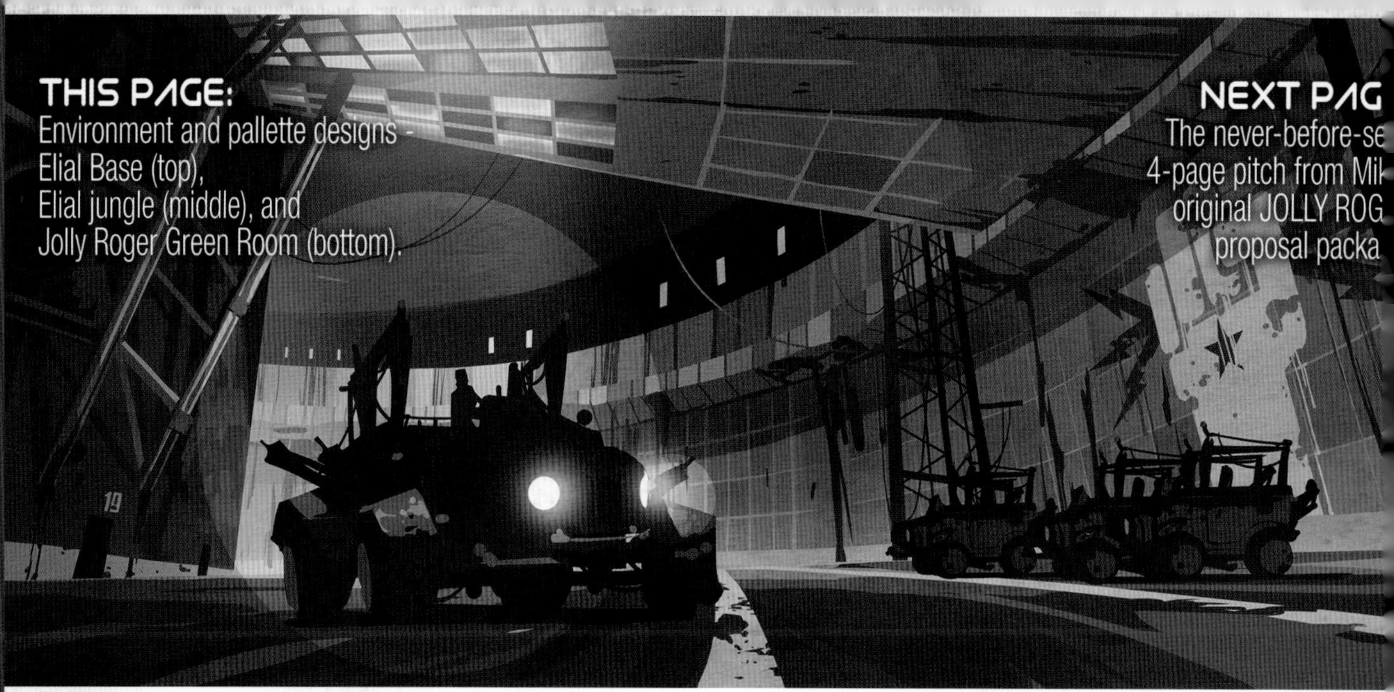
19

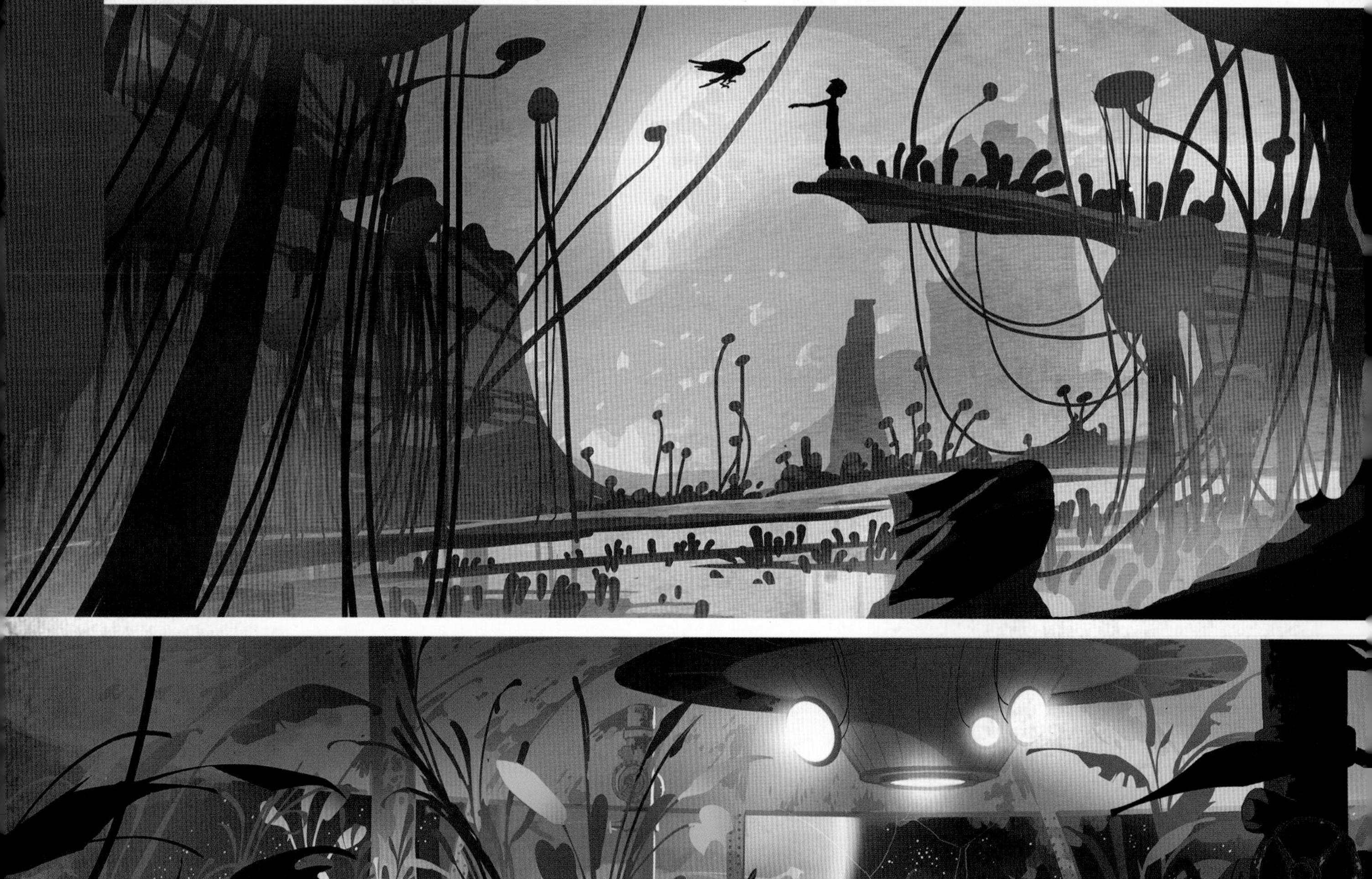

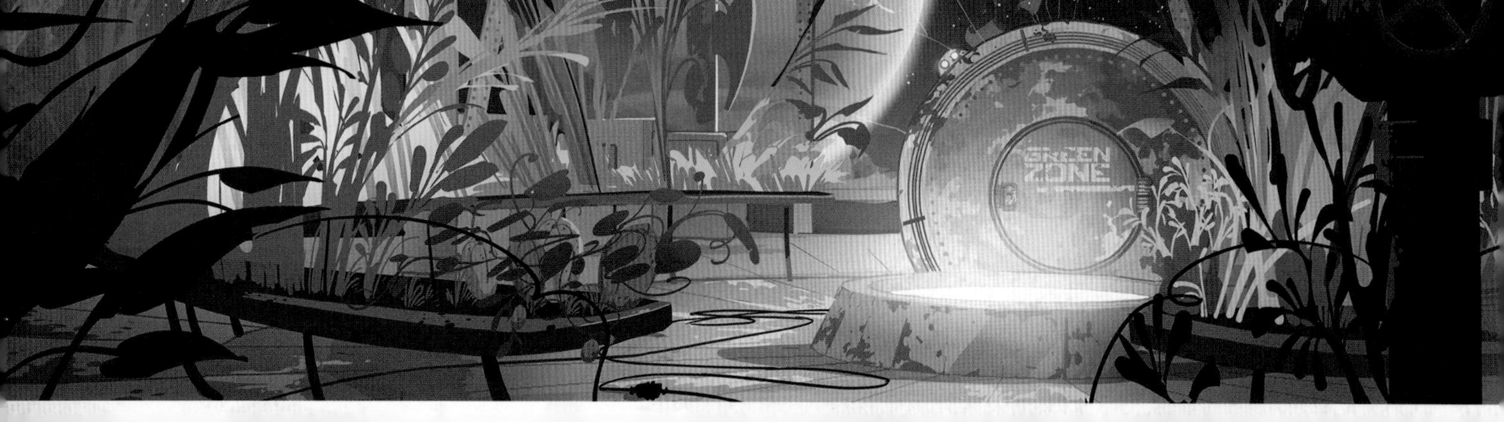
GREEN
ZONE

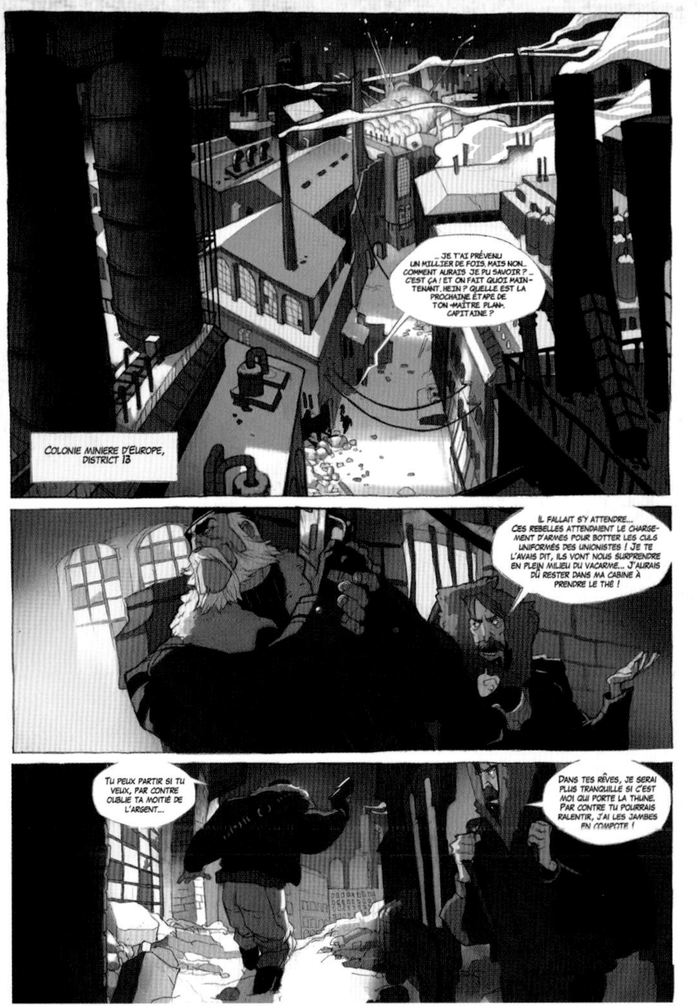
COLONIE MINIERE D'EUROPE, DISTRICT 13
... JE T'AI PRÉVENU UN MILLIER DE FOIS, MAIS NON... COMMENT AURAIS JE PU SAVOIR ? ... C'EST ÇA ! ET ON FAIT QUOI MAINTENANT, HEIN ? QUELLE EST LA PROCHAINE ÉTAPE DE TON «MAÎTRE PLAN», CAPITAINE ?
IL FALLAIT S'Y ATTENDRE... CES REBELLES ATTENDAIENT LE CHARGEMENT D'ARMES POUR BOTTER LES CULS UNIFORMÉS DES UNIONISTES ! JE TE L'AVAIS DIT, ILS VONT NOUS SURPRENDRE EN PLEIN MILIEU DU VACARME... J'AURAIS DÛ RESTER DANS MA CABINE À PRENDRE LE THÉ !
TU PEUX PARTIR SI TU VEUX, PAR CONTRE OUBLIE TA MOITIÉ DE L'ARGENT...
DANS TES RÊVES, JE SERAI PLUS TRANQUILLE SI C'EST MOI QUI PORTE LA THUNE. PAR CONTRE TU POURRAIS RALENTIR, J'AI LES JAMBES EN COMPOTE !

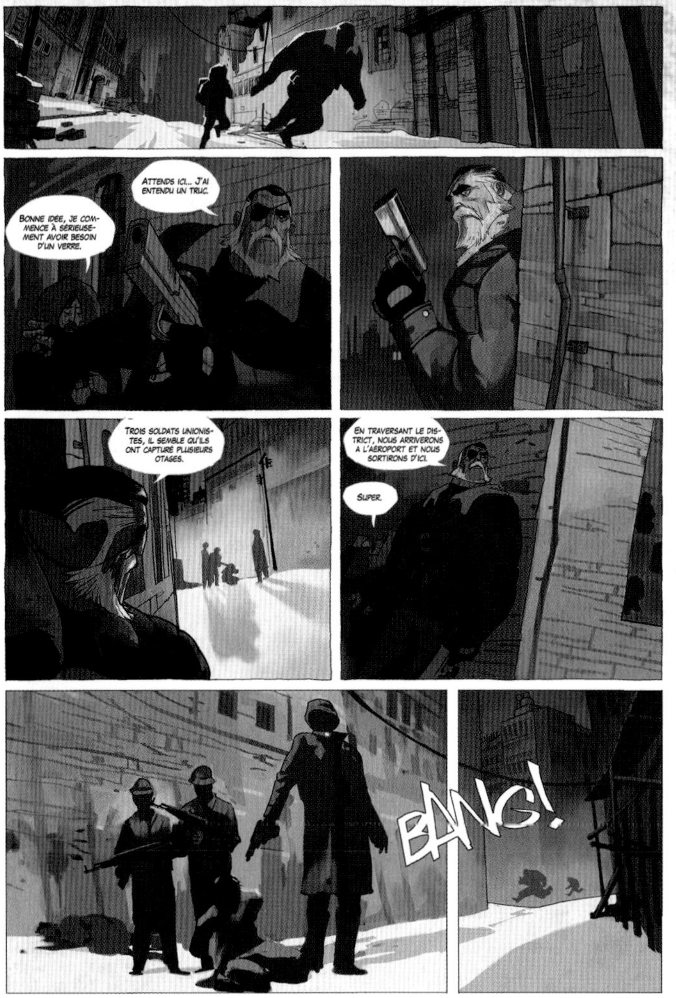
ATTENDS ICI... J'AI ENTENDU UN TRUC.
BONNE IDÉE, JE COMMENCE À SÉRIEUSEMENT AVOIR BESOIN D'UN VERRE.
TROIS SOLDATS UNIONISTES, IL SEMBLE QU'ILS ONT CAPTURÉ PLUSIEURS OTAGES.
EN TRAVERSANT LE DISTRICT, NOUS ARRIVERONS A L'AÉROPORT ET NOUS SORTIRONS D'ICI.
SUPER.
BANG!

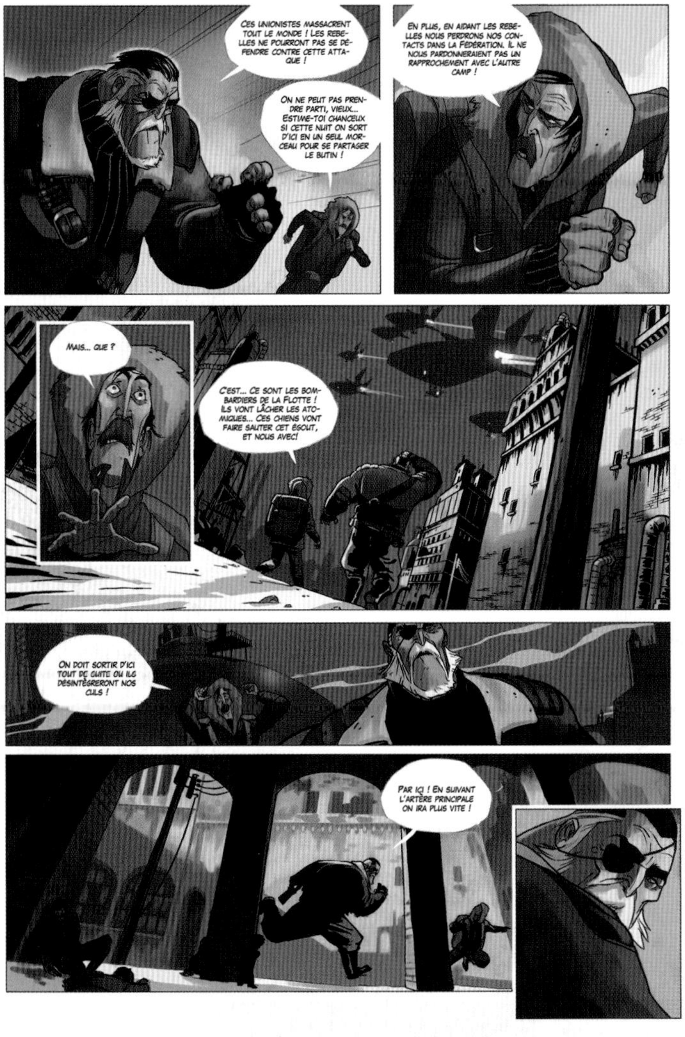
CES UNIONISTES MASSACRENT TOUT LE MONDE ! LES REBELLES NE POURRONT PAS SE DÉFENDRE CONTRE CETTE ATTAQUE !
ON NE PEUT PAS PRENDRE PARTI, VIEUX... ESTIME-TOI CHANCEUX SI CETTE NUIT ON SORT D'ICI EN UN SEUL MORCEAU POUR SE PARTAGER LE BUTIN !
EN PLUS, EN AIDANT LES REBELLES NOUS PERDRONS NOS CONTACTS DANS LA FÉDÉRATION. IL NE NOUS PARDONNERAIENT PAS UN RAPPROCHEMENT AVEC L'AUTRE CAMP !
MAIS... QUE ?
C'EST... CE SONT LES BOMBARDIERS DE LA FLOTTE ! ILS VONT LÂCHER LES ATOMIQUES... CES CHIENS VONT FAIRE SAUTER CET ÉGOUT, ET NOUS AVEC!
ON DOIT SORTIR D'ICI TOUT DE SUITE OU ILS DÉSINTÈGRERONT NOS CULS !
PAR ICI ! EN SUIVANT L'ARTÈRE PRINCIPALE ON IRA PLUS VITE !

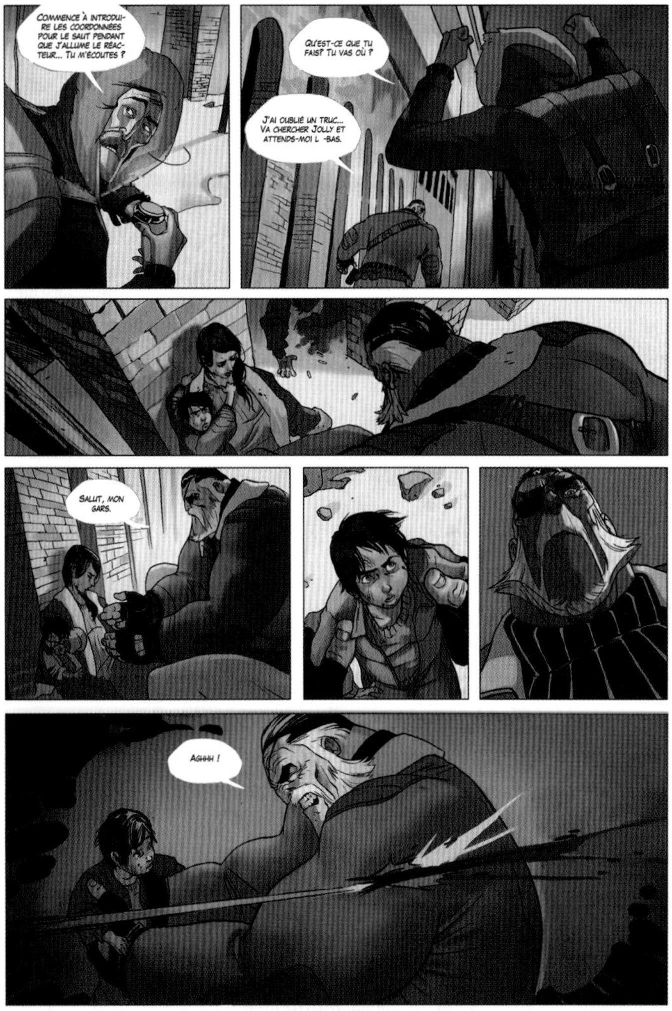
COMMENCE À INTRODUIRE LES COORDONNÉES POUR LE SAUT PENDANT QUE J'ALLUME LE RÉACTEUR... TU M'ÉCOUTES ?
QU'EST-CE QUE TU FAIS? TU VAS OÙ ?
J'AI OUBLIÉ UN TRUC... VA CHERCHER JOLLY ET ATTENDS-MOI L -BAS.
SALUT, MON GARS.
AGHHH !

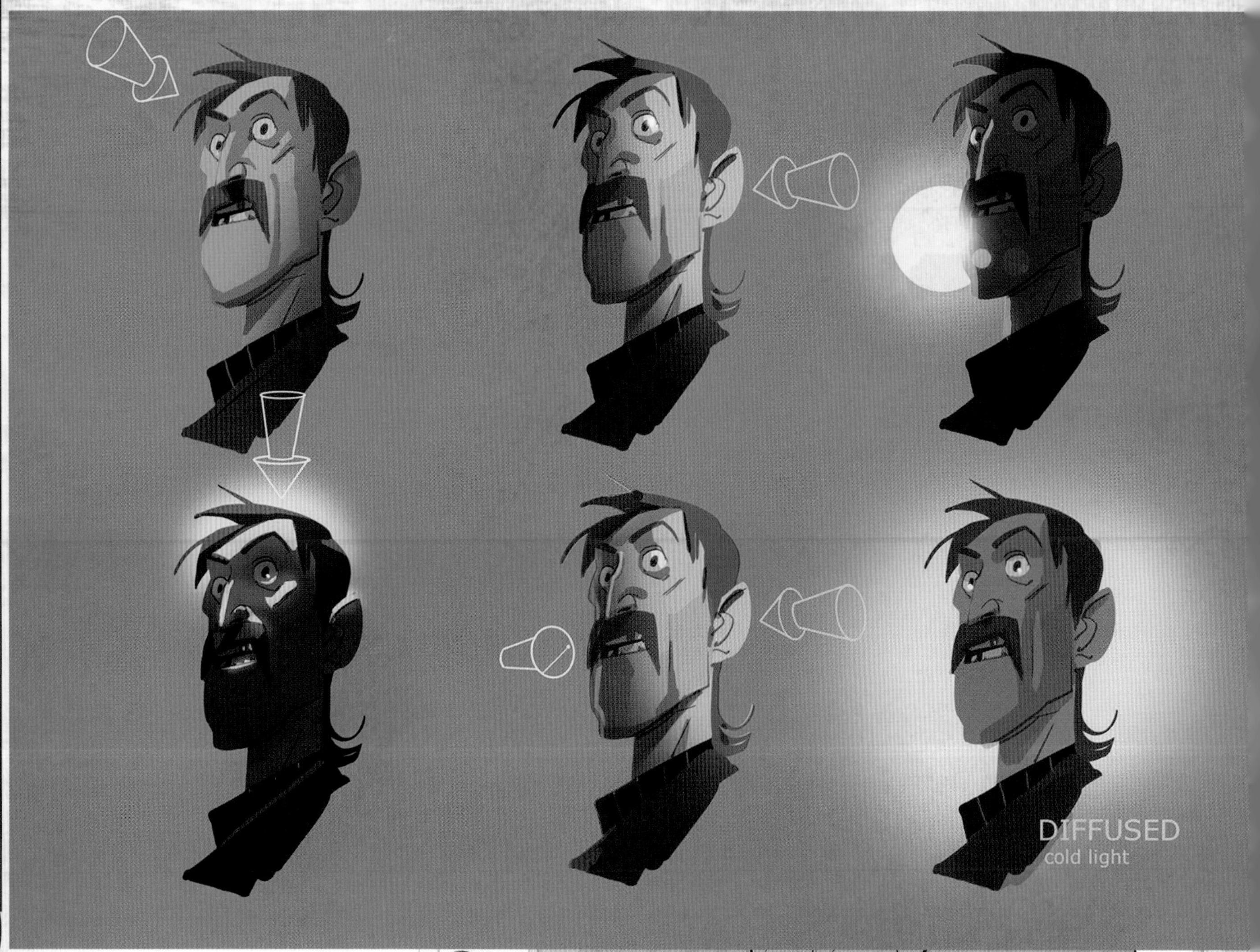
DIFFUSED
cold light

Miki's process involves vivid, cinematic, volumetric lighting. The above image showcases some of the techniques that are applied throughout for dramatic effect.

Below is a step-by-step example of the process from sketch to final rendering.

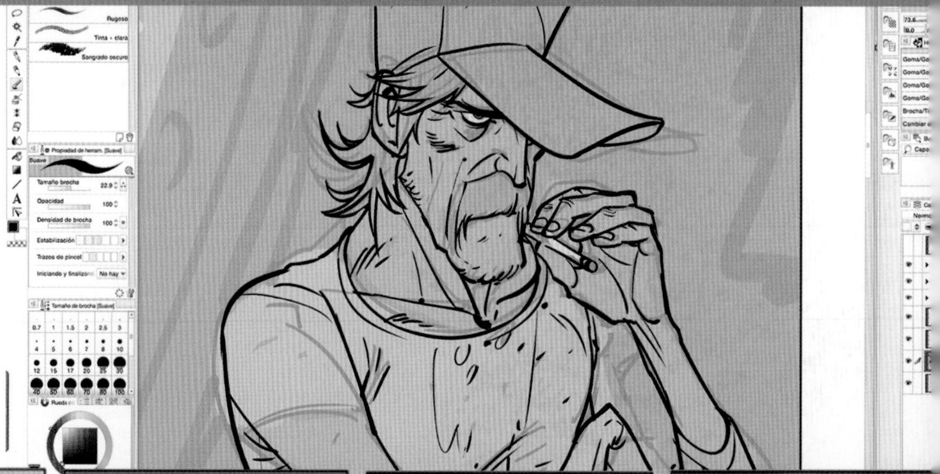
Rugoso
Sangrado oscuro
Tamaño brocha
Opacidad
Densidad de brocha
Estabilización
Trazos de pincel

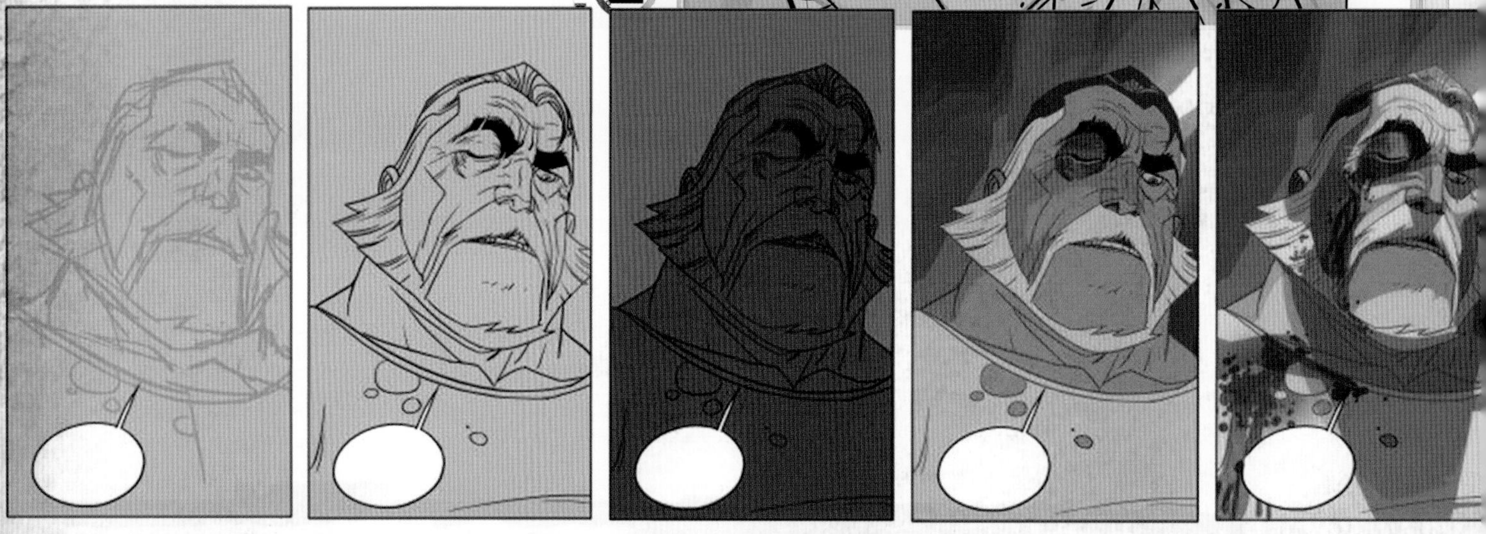

Artist **MIKI MONTLLÓ** was born in Barcelona, Spain, but spent much of his childhood moving from city to city. This may explain his state of constant flux, that may be evident in his constantly evolving style, running the gamut from classic cartoon to academic life drawing. Constantly adapting to new environments, he found a stable universe within his imagination, first inhabited by dinosaurs, giant monkeys, and spaceships, then by Spanish and Franco-Belgian comic characters of the 80s and the 90s, then by American and Japanese superheroes. An enthusiastic fan of science fiction and horror, he has made his attraction to the unusual a characteristic element in his work.

His professional career has also shown a predilection for diversity. After completing his studies at Escola Joso de Cómic in Barcelona, his first major break was on the cult Spanish animated movie "NOCTURNA", which he worked on for over a year. In advertising he has collaborated on projects for brands such as Ikea, Pascual, Evax, Audi, Bimbo, Brugal, Nokia, Vodafone, and Chesterfield, among others. In the video game industry he has collaborated with the Spanish Pendulo Studios and the British Revolution software, creators of the legendary saga BROKEN SWORD. He has also worked on feature films such as the award-winning THE IMPOSSIBLE, by director J. Bayona. But it was in 2011 that he abandoned everything to accomplish his childhood dream of becoming a comic book artist, creating his own project, "WARSHIP JOLLY ROGER," which first attracted the attention of the Belgian publisher Dargaud. He is now finishing the third book of this saga, with the first two books published in French, Spanish, German, and now English.

He combines his professional career with a semi-nomadic lifestyle, splitting his time between Ireland and Germany, collaborating with the Oscar nominated animation studios Cartoon Saloon in Ireland and Laika in the USA. In his down time he teaches for the online art school CGMA.

SYLVAIN RUNBERG was born in Belgium in 1971, and grew up bouncing between the cities of Stockholm, Marseille, and Paris. After graduating with a degree in Plastic Arts and an MA in Political History, he began his literary career working for Humanoides Associes Publishing, handling titles by illustration titans such as Moebius and Enki Bilal.

His first original series, ORBITAL, was released in 2006, quickly spring-boarding a prolific career penning more than 50 original graphic novels published by several of the largest publishers in France, with many of them translated into more than 15 languages. In total, to date, he has sold over 1 million books worldwide.

He is characterized as one of the brightest and most versatile writers in the field by the variety of worlds he has created. Preferring not to be confined to any particular genre, often dipping into his own experiences, personal history, or contemporary reality in order to develop his story ideas, be they space opera, social science fiction, psychological thriller, fantasy, horror, crime, or historical fiction. He has received numerous awards, and has most recently gained widespread acclaim for his adaptation of Stieg Larsson's "MILLENNIUM" trilogy, a 6 volume series noted for is gripping visual presentation by both the European media, with translations published in 13 others countries. He is now working on an official exclusive sequel series to the trilogy, focusing on the continuing story of Lisbeth Salander, for release in 2016